CW01499511

OYSTER SMACK

Oyster Smack

A police detective is called to a desolate island to investigate a suspected murder. He approaches the car parked on the slipway. He peers through the misty glass. Inside, he sees two bodies, a man and a woman. He opens the passenger door. A woman's body falls out. He suddenly realises the bitter truth: the dead woman is his wife.

His long-term associate is put in charge of the investigation. Was it a mutual suicide or is there a third hand involved? Is the wealthy property developer ruthless enough to kill and are the people who work the oyster smacks just innocent fishing folk? Amidst the swirling tidal waters of the Essex coastline, the race is on to fight suspicion and local customs before the case threatens to envelop the whole island.

Also by the writer
Part Free
The System
The Systemski
The System Y2K
The Millennium Murder Case
A Foreign Invasion
Our Noble Friend
Losing It
The Price of Rubies

Copyright © Clive Webster 2008. All rights reserved.
UK bookshops RRP £7.99
Printing and binding by Lulu.com.
Cover illustration: Maldon quayside. C. Webster
This book is sold subject to the condition that it shall not, by way of trade or otherwise, be lent, re-sold, hired out, or otherwise circulated without the author's permission.

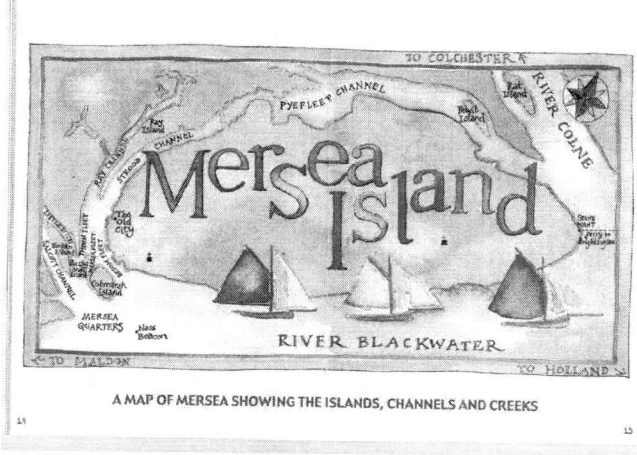

A MAP OF MERSEA SHOWING THE ISLANDS, CHANNELS AND CREEKS

'He was a bold man that first ate an oyster.'

Jonathan Swift

PART ONE

'With me the horrid doubt always arises whether the convictions of man's mind which has been developed from the mind of lower animals, are of value or at all trustworthy.'

Charles Darwin

CHAPTER ONE

When I look back over that period, I struggle to comprehend the immensity of it all. It still seems devastating, powerful and so utterly overwhelming that I have to sit back, breathe deeply and quietly compose myself, so that the nightmares will not reappear. The only thing I can say, categorically, is that the root cause of all this can be attributed to one specific date. That fateful date is etched upon my mind for many reasons; not least the fact that it was, cruelly, the happiest day of my life. It seems like only yesterday…

Friday, 16th October, 1987

It was almost four o'clock in the morning when David Almond peered out through a slither of night between two pieces of curtain. He rubbed his sore eyes and allowed the parted curtain to fall back once more. A few minutes earlier, he'd been sleeping so deeply; dreaming of a Caribbean beach holiday where the sand was eggshell white and the warm incoming tide gently nibbled his toes. He'd been lying with his favourite book in hand and an ice-cold beer by his side and was just about to light up a cigarette: then his wife prodded him.

'Wake up!' she exclaimed, as her finger, pronged with a long nail, dug into his ample side.

'Wake up, David. Listen to it!'

He slowly came round.

The day had barely started, but already he knew it was the beginning of the most eventful day of his life.

His nightmares had ended just recently - almost as abruptly as they had begun - to be replaced by idyllic scenes of peace and serenity. Sometimes it was a desert island; sometimes he was floating on a celestial cloud, once he had been in a harem, sucking on a water bubble pipe, contorted with sensual pleasure as nubile girls writhed around him. He couldn't understand why his dreams had changed, but he wasn't complaining - it meant that he woke up feeling refreshed and invigorated. Today, though, everything was different.

'I've never heard anything like it,' she exclaimed, prodding him again, this time a jabbing motion that became almost mechanical.

'Uh-huh. Okay, I'm awake.'

Susan hadn't been dreaming, nor had she slept - she had much more important things on her mind. Then, to top it all, there had been these angry sounds outside. At twelve fifty-five, she had sent him down to investigate. He had tied his dressing gown to his waist and gone outside to check it out. Now, several hours later it was even stronger.

'Get up!'

He roused himself slowly, blanked out thoughts of a peaceful beach and cocked an ear. He hadn't heard anything like it either. Or seen anything like it. She was right; something very strange was happening…

'Now go out and see for yourself.'

Gingerly, he stepped outside, onto the hard pavement. The door slammed behind him and he felt the full force for the first time, pushing him back, like a great hand. *Damn, no keys.* Head bowed, he struggled across the road. When he reached the other side, he turned to look back. Their Victorian three-bedroom house was still standing but the roof had gaping holes, toothy like a bad set of gums, where slate tiles had once been. Some tiles had crashed down and speared into the garden's sodden lawn, creating a relief like shark-infested waters. The fence had also gone. Many panels had lifted clean out of their moorings and tumbled into their neighbour's garden. Several had pinned themselves against the big apple tree and were now flapping crazily. The dustbin, bloated from a week's refuse, was on its side and rolling along like a barrel, while its innards joyfully cartwheeled down the road.

No, nothing like this, he thought, ever. And the noise: a howling, roaring noise, that receded momentarily and then grew again ever louder and more resonant. He thought it sounded like some fearsome ogre approaching step by inevitable step, thumping his way to catch his prey. Maybe his nightmares were coming back.

His wife wasn't the only one that had heard it. A huddled group of neighbours stood on the street corner, dressed in fluttering dressing gowns wrapped around pyjamas and nightshirts. They gazed upwards, watching events unfurl in the heavens, scarcely believing their ears and eyes. One of them, Mrs Caten, a resident for almost thirty years, stood spellbound, almost paralysed, as the theatre played out above her head. David went up to her and stood by her side.

'What in heaven's name is going on?' he asked.

'Ah, David!' Mrs Caten exclaimed. 'This wasn't forecast was it?'

He had watched the news late last night. He had stayed up, looking after Susan, checking she was okay.

'No, no it wasn't.'

He could see clearly the sky now. Milky clouds, silhouetted against a full moon, skidding across the inky sky as if being tugged on a conveyor belt.

'Well, someone should be made responsible,' she snapped fiercely, 'my wall has just collapsed, the fence is broken and my garden's an absolute mess!'

David tried to remain calm. At least it was dry *and* warm but the movement of air, so rapid and powerful, like a train coming in from the south-west, was making everyone nervous.

''It's like something out of a disaster movie!' Mr Stephens screamed, another long-term resident. His arm stabbed outwards at a clump of maple trees that kow-towed almost horizontally. 'If those trees go,' he continued, 'my bloody house will be destroyed. I'm going to move my car!' he called out. 'It's a sitting target.'

'Me too,' Mrs Caten replied angrily, 'before everything collapses.'

Mr Stephens got in his car, revved it crazily and slammed the car door shut. 'At least something's safe,' he shouted. 'I suggest you all do likewise, unless you want your cars flattened.' The other residents rushed back in doors, fetched their keys and in pyjamas, ran to their cars.

'Be careful.' David advised. 'Just take it slowly.'

They climbed into their cars and drove them well away from the main group of trees, further up the road towards relative safety. As they came back, they heard a loud crack. A thick wayward branch peeled away from its berth and, out of the sky, came tumbling towards them.

'Look out!!' David shouted. He grabbed Mrs Caten and yanked her hard backwards.

'Whaatt!' She stumbled but managed to make vital yards and looked back horrified to see the branch crash within inches of them. It splintered on the roadside and pieces spiralled upwards, propelled by the updraft.

'Good God! That was close,' Mrs Caten gasped. 'Thank you, David. Thank you so much. I never saw it.'

'No problem. Mrs C. Now, I think we should all get back indoors and wait for it to blow over.'

Three hours later, on that memorable Friday, it was almost daybreak. The hurricane-force Southwesterlies still showed no signs of abating and Susan and David had banished all hopes of sleep. They had watched the drama unfurl from the relative safety of the upstairs bedroom. They had heard sirens wail without visible signs of help. Nothing more had come down from their house but there was still much repair work to consider: the blown roof, the broken fence, the limp guttering and the littered garden...and still it was blowing. The timing couldn't have been worse; money was tight right now, they would have to check their insurance policy and see what everyone else was going to do. Then of course, there was the sheer effort of getting everything fixed, what with Susan's condition.

**

From the small sloping window, he looked out of his office. He had made it to work, before most people had set off. By craning his head to peer above the jumble of rooftops he could see a new sky dawning; flakes of creamy white sky filtering uncertainly into the black void. In one hour's time, the whole scale of the damage would be evident. Even now, reports had come in across the county of people injured, roads blocked, houses damaged by falling trees, masonry blown away, people without heating and light and that was before most people had got up and tried to get to work. It had turned into a night like no other.

As he stared across the concrete car park he could see his car, undamaged, parked next to the metal exit gate. There were no other cars around - everyone else had been called out to deal with the storm problems. Of the twenty-five officers normally on duty in Chelmsford Constabulary, PC John Walker and himself were the only ones left in the station. He told the chief, that, today of all days, he couldn't afford to be too far away from the office and the phone. Everyone understood. Many had been in a similar situation. This he stressed was an emergency - well now it was one of two emergencies - but there was really only one that concerned him.

He looked out once more. It would only take a few seconds for him to be away. He took out a cigarette, realised he'd just stubbed one out and put it back in its packet. He would pack up soon, disgusting habit. He began to pace around the office, picking up the file on his desk on the way to the other side of the room, then putting it back on the desk on the way back. He couldn't concentrate on anything. There was too much happening. Today, he was certain, was D-day.

Come on, come on, he muttered irritably to himself, chewing his lip and eyeing his watch as if any moment it might stop working. He sat down again and tried to compose his thoughts. Never before had he needed so much to be in two places at once. He should split himself in half or do that Superman thing of flying round the world backwards to create more time. Maybe he should just go back home, despite all the mayhem. His keys were in his jacket. His jacket was hung up against the door. The door was partly open. The door led into the main corridor. The corridor took him directly to the car park. At most, it was fifty seconds from office to car. All organised.

He'd been going through this procedure now for over two weeks. Every day he'd sit like this, early morning, eyes darting between his car outside and the phone. He'd already had two false alarms, like a cat using up his nine lives. I should be used to it by now, he thought.

Suddenly his phone rang. He jumped to it, nearly wrenching it from its moorings, sending files sliding across the floor.

'Yes...Now? Right, hold on...I'm coming over.'

The switchboard was lit up like a Christmas tree as he raced to the door, before remembering to leave a note. Fifteen minutes later, he was heading westwards on the dual carriageway, lights full on, looking anxiously at his wife by his side. Meanwhile, ten miles away in Jawick Sands, a caravan park was being flattened.

'How do you feel?' he asked.

'Okay,' Susan replied gamely.

'Short, rapid breaths.'

'I know.'

'Want me to drive slower?'

'No.'

'Maybe I should go faster?'

'No.'

'Want some music? How about I put the heater on?'

She shook her head. She tensed and found regular breathing impossible.

He negotiated the car around a sharp turn and then entered a straight piece of road, lined with tall trees. The car picked up speed, exceeding the limit but what the hell.

'What a crazy day! he said. 'I've heard all the schools are shut down for the day.'

'I know.'

'Down on the seafront, hundreds of boats have broken up. Boy, I wouldn't like to be in the insurer's shoes today.'

Susan wasn't sure she wanted to be in her shoes. She just wanted to get it over with.

Suddenly David noticed a large shape lying across the road.

'What the? Crikey!'

He jammed on the brakes hard and the car screeched. 'David!' she shouted, as she let out a stifled scream.

The vehicle slithered and slid until its bonnet ended up within inches of the obstacle.

'Blast! That *really* is dangerous.' He scowled, getting out of the car. The swinging door was caught by the wind and slammed shut. Ahead, a large, spidery branch had come down from an overhanging Chestnut tree. It had fallen right across their path, scattering its debris along the route. He grabbed the main branch with both hands and dragged it onto the pavement. He got back into the car, leant over to give her a kiss and roared off. His wife gripped his arm.

'God, please just get me there in one piece.'

'Right.'

One hour later, he was stooped over his wife, studying her features closely. She lay still on the bed, exhausted, eyes heavy lidded and her long dark hair matted. To David Almond, she looked more beautiful than ever. He traced his fingers across her forehead and wiped away the perspiration.

'I love you.'

She smiled gently. Her thin lips parted slightly to reveal her milky white teeth.

'And I'm so proud of you.'

'I'm proud of me, too.'

'Now there are two of you,' he added. 'Which one is more beautiful?'

She closed her eyes as if overwhelmed with relief. She didn't care. All she wanted to do was rest. For him the answer was obvious. His wife was more beautiful than anything else in the world.

He looked down at the tiny bundle, wrapped in a sheet, gazing out like an old woman with its shrivelled skin and bluish hue. Carefully he picked it up, like he'd been taught and brought it close to his chest. He felt her bird-like weight as he tucked her neatly in the crook of his elbow. Then he stared at this minor miracle, sleeping now and oblivious to the world. Only a few minutes ago she had lain inside the belly of his wife and was now she was out, alive and breathing fresh air, the newest arrival on God's Earth. Maybe in fifteen years time, he thought, she will be just as beautiful.

When the weekend came, he put on his suit and tie, and sat in the front row at the local church. He couldn't help smiling. God is good, he thought, as he opened the hymnbook and sang so lustily that his voice rose clearly above his fellow parishioners and boomed into the courtyard outside. The vicar nodded appreciatively, he had never heard him sing so well. I am blessed, David thought, truly blessed by the Lord. My wife, my child and me, we are all proof that God is indeed love. He looked around at the open and closing mouths and smiled. Mrs Caten was two rows back, she saw him and gave him a little wave that he returned with a thumb's up. Everything was perfect he thought, everything was Heaven on Earth and he praised the Lord.

***

Wednesday, 16th October, 2002.

Outside, the rain lashed down for the third successive day. Detective Inspector Almond looked dispiritedly out of his office. The rain made jagged furrows on the pane, mirroring his morose expression. It clung vainly to the surface before the wind jettisoned it away in a fine spray. Outside, puddles formed and grew, turning the car park into a mini lake. He glanced at the calendar on his desk. October 16th, fifteen years to the day since The Great Storm of 1987. He knew that because it was also fifteen years since the birth of his daughter. Their only child, though no longer a child. She had grown up so quickly in the last few months he hardly recognised her. It sounded a cliché but it was true. Suddenly she was as tall as her mother. She had her mother's long dark hair, her full mouth and those expressive eyes and she carried herself differently now, no longer happy to flop herself down anywhere. However, when she spoke, she spoke in tones that questioned everything. Nothing was right with the world: school, teachers, her parents, her home and the boys that kept ringing her. She may have had the building blocks of her adult life, but nothing seemed to fit.

He had discussed this with Susan many times. It was a phase, it would pass, all girls went through it. He would have thought more about it but, at this juncture, PC Stephen Grayson entered the room. He was just turned twenty-two and had the telltale residual signs of acne that punctuated his otherwise unblemished face; a twinkle of blue eyes and a shock of black hair that varied from wavy to crew-cut to short back and sides, depending on his hairdresser. Grayson was a permanent office fixture. He was Sergeant Alec Grayson's son. His father had never made it to the dizzying heights of non-uniformed ranks and neither would his protégée if he continued like this; perched on the edge of Almond's desk, one leg touching the floor, the other swinging mechanically like a metronome.

'Stop that.'

'What?'

'That.'

The time was now 14:10.

Grayson stopped tapping for a few seconds and looked at his superior. Almond gave him a withering look. Young Grayson was an annoying bugger at the best of times but particularly when he was trying to concentrate. He had already read the same line on this report four times.

'Can't you find something useful to do?'

'I'm trying to do something useful, sir. I'm thinking of something for you to get Cathy.'

'Oh yeah?'

'Well, it's her birthday today, isn't it?'

'Yes, yes it is.'

'The day of the Hurricane,' Grayson noted.

'That's right.'

'Should have called her Gail…Gale.'

'Yes.'

'Or Wendy…Windy.'

'So funny.'

'And you never know what to get her.'

'Correct.'

'What about a blouse?'

'What?'

'A blouse, sir.'

Grayson shifted so that both feet were off the desk. Almond was going to ask him to sit properly on a chair but that was one thing about Grayson - he never observed the rules of protocol.

'No. Girls don't wear blouses anymore…at least I don't think so.'

'Right.'

'Anyway, you should know that, Stephen. You're at least twenty years younger than me.' Grayson looked that…and the rest; fresh-faced and a clean complexion topped with a twirl of boyish curly hair. Almond went back to his report.

'Yeah, but I don't have kids.'

'So?'

'So, I don't know what they think.'

'Neither do I,' Almond confessed. 'It's all changed since my day.'

'Oh, I get it. Unisex.'

Almond hadn't heard that word for years but that was the essence of it.

'Kind of.'

'That should make it easier.'

'Should.'

'Surely there's still a difference.'

'Maybe.'

'Like the way they do up their jackets?'

'Mmm.'

'Though having said that,' Grayson continued, now having moved further along the desk and ominously close to the computer screen, 'I can't say I've noticed. It's all a bit vague really, like bicycles, I suppose.'

Almond lowered the report. 'Bicycles?'

'Yes, sir. Crossbars and all that. These days girls ride boys' bikes.'

'Do they really? Look Stephen, I can see you're trying to be really helpful here but you're giving nepotism a bad name and besides I'm trying to read this flaming report. So can you just stop bouncing around for a few moments and find something useful for you to do?'

'Sure.'

Grayson got off the desk, picked up the desk calendar, and began twiddling with the day and date, moving it forward by several years.

'Only goes up to Year 2020.'

'What?'

'Only another seventeen years before you are going to need a new one, sir.'

That was another thing about Stephen Grayson. He always wanted to pass the time in conversation, he would stop at someone's desk and then just ramble on for ages about just about anything.

'So what other differences are there?' Stephen asked.

'Differences?'

'Yeah. Clothes differences.'

Almond shrugged. 'Crikey, I don't know. Different sizes, different shapes. I suppose there are different styles, colours and textures. Work it out yourself.'

'Designer labels.'

'Exactly.'

'And you don't know the right ones.'

'Correct.'

'Sounds a nightmare, sir. Tell you what, why don't you just give her the money?'

'Yeah, well maybe I'll do that.'

Maybe Almond would, but his daughter had been teasingly insistent: 'Just for once dad, actually buy me something. Go out, shop around and buy something you think I would like…', then she'd really cut off all his escape routes, '…whether it's in fashion or not.'

'How about a T-shirt?' Grayson suggested. 'Maybe a jumper or trousers? Stuff like that.'

Just then, Almond's long time work colleague, John Walker, popped his head round the door. 'How's it going?'

'Up to my neck in this report,' Almond admitted.

'Got a message from Susan. Couldn't get through on your line. Here.'

Almond read the scribbled message. 'Drat,' he muttered, 'she's had to go out on business. Going to be late home. Cathy will be furious.'

'David,' Walker said, 'if you have to pop out, no sweat.'

'Thanks, John.'

Walker disappeared leaving Almond with his protégé.

'Oh, how about a nice piece of jewellery?' Grayson suggested.

'Not a bad idea,' Almond said. 'So that's decided. Now how about you slung your hook and worked on some of that filing?'

Stephen finally got the message and strolled out of Almond's office, along the narrow, tiled corridor, past the notice board to his work place. The time was 14:20. For the next three and a half hours, Stephen was up to his eyes in reports and form filling, calling up the online forms and tapping in the details. It was monkey stuff. Nothing like what he had imagined when he first joined. His eyes grew tired of mug shots and witness statements and pieces of evidence that needed to be catalogued, labelled and bagged. Finally, he got up and went for his coat. As he walked through to Control, the switchboard system was lit up with calls. The operator glanced up, saw Stephen, and made an expansive gesture.

It was now 17:55 precisely.

Stephen rushed back into his room, closed the door and grabbed the ringing phone.

'999 call on line on four. Asked for DI Almond.'

'Got it.'

Stephen scribbled the details on a pad and dashed back into Almond's room.

Almond had some perfume and a birthday card sitting on his desk. 'Better ring my wife,' Almond said as he grabbed his coat. 'Tell her I won't be picking her up, tonight.' He tried the mobile but there was no reply.

At 18:01, the police car was pulling out of the station. Almond was still tugging on his seatbelt as Grayson drove them across the road junction and into the oncoming traffic. They were on their way to investigate the call.

The rain hadn't relented, if anything it was coming down with even more intensity. Rain always brought out the worst in drivers, especially during the evening rush hour. They became impatient and stubborn; they cut corners, literally, as if refusing to acknowledge the dangers. Some of them drove too fast but almost all of them drove too close. As the police car drove along, with the wipers going full tilt, some drivers tried to keep up with them, riding in their slipstream.

'Look at these plonkers, sir,' Stephen said, glancing in the rear mirror. 'They must be driving blind. Shall I pull one of them over?'

'No, one thing at a time.'

'Do you get anything for Cathy?'

'What? Oh, just that perfume. The latest range apparently. I'll have to give her some money.'

'She won't be happy,' Stephen said, shaking his head.

'Look, let's just get there, eh, so how about we step on it?'

Almond glanced at Stephen whose eyes lit up at the prospect. Stephen leaned forward and activated the siren. Soon the squad car was weaving through the heavy traffic like a phantom. The Ford Focus moved swiftly northward along the A12. With his foot pressed down on the accelerator and full headlights straining for clarity through a curtain of rain, Stephen soon lost all his entourage. As he brushed past the traffic, he kept making those arch little comments that annoyed Almond so much: 'Oops', 'sorry', 'coming through', 'excuse me.'

Eventually Almond tapped his charge on the shoulder.

'Look, just behave will you Stephen, and keep it steady. '

'No problemo, sir.'

Stephen then updated Almond more fully: a car had been found on the island. The female caller thought she saw two bodies inside. The caller gave her name as Mrs Dean. Stephen got out a piece of paper and left it flapping against the wheel.

Almond took it and read out the location.

'Know where it is?' Almond asked.

'Approx.'

'So what was Mrs Dean doing?' Almond enquired, his mind already locked into question mode.

'She'd been out walking her dog when she saw this car parked. She went to investigate and found the victims.'

'Did she see anyone about?'

'Not that I'm aware.'

'When did she make the call?'

'Five to six, sir.'

'We got back up?'

'Paramedics are on their way.'

'Anyone else?'

'Johnson should be there in an hour or so.'

'Good.'

Mark Johnson was the Scene of Crimes officer. He had recently joined from the Met and revelled in his job. It was a line of work Almond would have liked, if he'd been younger. There was something intrinsically satisfying about arriving at a SOC, donning a mask, tugging on boots and snapping on latex gloves. It made you special. Finding a place of chaos, you were expected to piece it all back together, as if it never happened. Almost like putting the world to right. All Almond ever did was detection; based on messy signs and mixed signals, that became ever more intractable and opaque as time rolled into the misty uncertainties of the future.

The car took a sharp left off the main dual carriageway. Almond pulled out a map from the glove compartment.

'Why are you going down here?' he asked.

'I know this route like the back of my hand.' Stephen bragged.

Almond didn't doubt it. Stephen knew everything about everything.

'You should have stayed on the A12,' Almond advised, holding the map out, 'right up to Colchester and then headed down on the B1015.'

'Why's that, sir?'

'Less direct, but much quicker.'

'Not really,' Stephen insisted, 'traffic's non-existent down these lanes.'

The road narrowed considerably and traffic concertinaed into a snaking procession. Up ahead, they spotted the source of convergence; a farm tractor.

'Oh yes,' Almond gloated, 'this so-called non-existent traffic of yours. Returning no doubt from a non-existent day in the fields.'

'Don't worry, I'll get pass it.'

Stephen sounded the siren and flashed his lights. The drivers dithered and some vehicles slowed until the procession became almost funereal.

Almond counted eight cars between his and the slow-moving vehicle up ahead. He rang into Centre to update them on their latest arrival time.

'Bloody wankers,' Stephen cursed. 'Why don't they just pull over?'

Pulling over meant going into a ditch the road was so narrow here.

'Just take it steady,' Almond advised.

Stephen had no view of the oncoming traffic. He tried to peer above and around the roofs of the cars in front but eventually returned to his customary hunched position, his body tightening ever more like a coiled spring. The tractor meanwhile trundled on, along the full width of the single lane, spinning off great clods of earth, like sparks from a Catherine Wheel.

'Look at all that poxy mess. Well, I've had enough, sir.' Stephen said flatly.

'Steady.'

Stephen swerved out into the opposite lane, saw a brief glimpse of open road and roared past the vehicles until the road suddenly disappeared and a bend loomed ahead. He applied the brakes sharply and the vehicle's nose came up hard against the tailgate of the tractor, its wide-open blades wavered dangerously close to their bonnet.

'What the flaming heck!' Almond exclaimed. 'Yikes!'

Stephen sat in behind, for a few seconds, shaking his head repeatedly. The driver was now clearly visible.

'Look, he can't even hear us!' Stephen exclaimed, 'he's wearing bleeding mufflers.'

The tractor driver was perched upright on the spring seat, oblivious to the police vehicle; his head encased in bright blue headphones as the agricultural noise largely deafening the siren's wail.

'Shall I book him?'

'No, probably needs them to keep his brains in,' Almond muttered.

The tractor continued snail-like for a few seconds and the road began to straighten, by which time Stephen had had enough. He pulled the vehicle out once more and began to overtake, edging past the tractor's rear wheels. A lorry carrying a load of parsnips loomed in the opposite direction.

'Double shoot!' Almond shouted with an intake of breath.

Stephen put his foot flat against the floor and the rev counter needle soared. The car roared past the tractor, ever closer to the oncoming driver. The driver clearly hadn't expected this; a police car coming out of the rain with siren blaring, on *his* side of the road. The driver braked hard and the large shape shuddered. It arrived at the potential point of collision sufficiently late to allow Grayson to squeeze through the closing gap.

'O-Ouch,' Almond stammered.

'Sorry, thought it best to keep going, sir. Fortune favouring the brave and all that.'

'Nothing brave about that,' Almond shouted. 'More like suicidal.'

'Nah, I had at least four inches.'

In the rear mirror, the lorry had slithered to an ungainly sideways halt. It was now effectively blocking the road for everyone. 'Better alert the traffic police,' Stephen said, as he carried on throttling the gears, pounding up the road.

'Remind me next time to take the wheel,' said an exasperated Almond, '...if there is a next time.'

Stephen ignored him. He was concentrating on the road ahead. They passed through villages like Great Wigborough, Little Wigborough and Peldon in a blur, disregarding the polite signs asking drivers to 'drive carefully through our village.' Stephen continued to gun the car, crunching through the gears and manhandling the wheel until, at 18:23 precisely, the car crossed the small bridge that separated Mersey Island from the mainland.

'Twenty two minutes and ten seconds!' Stephen exclaimed, tapping his watch triumphantly. 'A record from Chelmsford to Mersey. I told you it was a short cut.'

Almond shook his head disapprovingly. 'Okay, boy racer. Now where do we go?'

Immediately ahead was a sign for East Mersey pointing to the road straight ahead while the main route swung right towards West Mersey.

'Right...I think,' Almond said, 'no, straight ahead. Straight ahead!!'

'Okay, keep your hair on.'

Stephen wrenched the wheel and went skidding up the hill into the gathering gloom.

A large flock of birds, with flashes of black and white took off and circled above their heads.

'Wow, guess what they are?' Stephen asked, as he craned his head to watch them

'Lapwings.'

They struck a path out across the salt marshes.

'That's right,' Grayson said, 'also known as Peewits, on account of their call. They tend to stay in flocks and raid the farmers' crops.'

'Look,' said Almond, 'how about we just concentrate on the job in hand, hmm?'

'Sure.'

Mersey was only an island in the loosest sense of the word; only fully divorced for a few hours when the tides embraced the muddy creeks and swirled up the meandering river that sliced diagonally through this barren part of Essex. Population, David Almond reckoned, a thousand or so. Yet, during the summer weekends, the population swelled ten-fold, as large numbers of holidaymakers came down from the towns and the city to stay in the caravan parks and sail at the local yacht clubs. Right now though, this side of the island was deserted; except for a few hardy souls who made their living from farming the rich arable land and harvesting the sea.

Stephen eased off the accelerator and negotiated a series of sharp bends until the road came to an abrupt dead end.

'Great,' said a frustrated Almond, finally. Stephen looked over his shoulder and began reversing hard up the road while Almond grabbed the radio.

'We're at the end of Bowers Lane,' Almond voiced. 'There's no sign, but I know this road. We're looking for Graydon's Creek, can you advise, over.'

There was a brief pause then the voice crackled: 'Top of the road you take a left, then right at the Fisherman's Arms and it's the second turning on the right.'

'Thanks.'

Stephen swivelled the car and, with a shower of grit, spun the car southwards, towards the edge of the island. Soon they reached a wharf. The arc of their headlamps caught the reflected taillights of a vehicle, glowing dimly in the early evening air.

'That it?' Almond asked.

'Sure looks like it.'

'A Peugeot?'

'Yeah, that's what she said,' Stephen murmured. 'Midnight blue, Peugeot 307 Gti, nice car,' he purred, '130 break horsepower, twin cams. Shit hot off the lights.'

Almond ignored him and pointed to the nearby gravel car park. Stephen pulled in, only fifty yards away from the vehicle.

'I guess that's the woman,' Almond said, glancing towards a woman who stood close by, chaperoned by a young police officer in a day-glo jacket. She looked utterly soaked, despite the fact that the officer had gallantly lent her an umbrella. Almond lowered the window and peered across the car park. The officer smiled back grimly.

Almond had a quick scan around. There was a small of group of bystanders standing on the other side of the police officer, their shoulders hunched collectively and their collars turned up, like a flock of birds, protecting themselves against the wind and rain. Probably a big deal for these folks, thought Almond. Locals rarely ventured out at this time of year, they usually stayed behind the clapboard frontages of their fishing cottages that straggled the shoreline, like driftwood. It needed something big to happen: like the oyster carnival, an earthquake, or a bloody crime, to bring so many out into the open.

The Peugeot was parked half way down a slipway, facing outwards across the river creek and the marshland beyond. Almond opened the police car door and felt a keen wind, coming from the North East. It was a colder and more spiteful wind than normal, arrowing in straight from the North Sea. Locals knew all about this wind, they called it Winter's Wind, as it swung around a full 180 degrees away from the prevailing Southwesterlies. It arrived late October and stayed until the New Year bringing with it driving sleet and the first falls of snow. Stephen could hear it whistling though the metal chain links of the masts of boats, harboured in their winter moorings in the boatyard.

'Let's go,' said Almond as he stepped out of the car. He did a quick recce of his own and walked quickly across the gravel, eyes darting to take in the whole scene. The salty tang of air caught his breath. A flock of knot rose up like a swarm of insects, sashayed, zigzagged and then sank back into the marshes as if shot. The female police officer came up to greet him.

'Sir, Officer Parker. I got a call on the radio; I was the nearest car to the scene. Got here ten minutes ago. We've got two bodies inside the vehicle.'

'Cause of death?'

'Gunshot wounds, I think.'

'Think?'

'Pretty certain.'

'Both of them?'

'Think so.'

'Okay, any witnesses?'

'Mrs Dean who made the call.'

'Taken her statement?'

'Yes.'

Mrs Dean stood nearby, in earshot, looking frustrated, as the officers continued to refer to her in third party terms.

Finally, Grayson walked up to her.

'What time did you notice the car, madam?'

She wore a raincoat with a hood up but the rain had plastered strands of hair to her face. She looked visibly shaken and her eyes were staring. She was older than he had first thought.

'Between five and six.'

'Can you be more specific?'

'Oh, I can't remember.'

'Try, madam.'

She screwed up her face, as if trying to improve the power of recall. 'It was probably about five thirty-five.'

'Did you see anyone else around at the time?'

'No.'

'We received your call at five fifty-five. Why didn't you ring immediately?'

'I tried the public phone over there,' she gesticulated airily into the darkness, 'but it didn't work. Then I went back to my house and tried to call there but the lines were down. Always happens when you need them. I was walking to the pub,' she glanced momentarily towards the crowd, 'when I met this woman. She let me use her mobile.'

'What were you doing when you saw the vehicle?'

'I was out with Toby.'

'Toby?'

'My dog, a Labrador.'

'Where's your dog Toby, now?'

'In the house,' she said, hugging the beige raincoat around her. 'He started sniffing around the vehicle so I took him home. It's awful.'

Almond had been walking around the site examining the single route onto the slipway.

'Anyone else see anything?' Almond asked turning to the officer.

'No, just her,' Parker replied.

'Well, get all their names, addresses and statements. Then move these people along will you? Johnson will be here soon to cordon off the area.'

Parker walked up to them and began waving her arms, trying to usher them back towards the main road.

'Islanders,' Almond muttered under his breath as they were corralled into one final huddle. At the best of times, they had an air of dulled sensibilities, but right now, they looked utterly enervated, pounded by the rain, depleted of any kind of life.

'Come on, please!'

Finally, they moved off, hunched like a group of craven parishioners, shuffling their way back to their cottages. All except one woman. She held an umbrella so her face was partially obscured. Behind the protection, she was seething.

'You have us stand out here in the bleedin' rain for ages and you dismiss us like that!'

Almond scowled. Maybe they were late but they'd got there as soon as possible, faster than was legally permissible. She must have thought they spent all day sitting around picking their noses.

'Sorry madam, we were held up,' Grayson said. 'We'll be in touch if we need you.'

She stood defiant, assertive and questioning.

'Sorry madam,' Grayson said, 'I need *everyone* to disperse.'

'Tough,' she replied. Clearly, she wasn't a local.

Grayson looked away, then he gestured to Parker. The police officer put her arm under the woman's and attempted to lead her away. 'Madam.'

'Let me go!' she said, wrenching herself free.

Parker held up her hands in despair. God knows how she would cope with a violent demonstration, Almond thought.

'Madam,' Almond repeated, 'this is crime scene. We have to protect the general public.'

Finally, she backed off.

'Get her statement Parker, and she can go,' Almond shouted.

Almond didn't want anyone getting too close to the scene, not now he feared the worst.

Parker ushered the woman towards a tree. The police officer told her to stand in a spot where they were both shielded from the wind and the rain. As Parker fumbled for her notebook, the woman turned on her 'Why are you asking me questions? What 'ave I done?'

'Nothing Madam. It's all routine.' Parker flicked a few pages and got out her pen. It didn't write so she got out another and began to scribble.

'Okay, madam. Name?'

'Mind yer own business!'

'Name?'

'Mrs Stevens.'

'When did you get here?'

'Dunno.'

'Approximately.'

'Five o'clock, s'pose.'

'What were you doing here?

'I just come across the island to visit a churchyard.'

'So how did you meet Mrs Dean?'

'I saw the old gal wandering around on the pathway. She was in a right two and eight. So I stopped and asked how she was. Anyway, she gives me all this spiel and tells me she thinks she's seen somefink so I let her use me phone.'

'What time was this?'

''Bout ten to six.'

Parker made a couple of notes and finally released the woman.

With the way clear, Almond slowly waved for Grayson to move in. As Grayson approached the vehicle, he heard the distant chug of an engine. He looked up to see a small fishing vessel making its way along the creek out towards the river estuary. The water across the creek was muddy brown and small tufts of spray were being picked up and scattered downstream like confetti. He stepped closer. The tide was swirling up the slipway and then falling back as if defeated. The slime of seaweed had turned the slipway bottle green. He found if he timed it right he could just about walk around the front side of the vehicle without getting his shoes wet. As he passed the bonnet, he slipped on the green gunk and cobbled stones.

'Steady, Stephen' Almond warned, 'we don't want you going in the drink.'

Grayson just managed to keep his balance. 'It's why they call it a slipway, sir.'

'Very good. Let's say we forget the funnies.'

The car stood inert and silent. David Almond held back. He sensed something deep in the pit of his stomach, the weighty presence of some impending doom. He hated this part of the job, the coldness, the inhumanity, the sheer brutality of it all. The last time he had investigated a vehicle murder had been in 1995, down a farm track at Rettendon. The inside of the vehicle had resembled an exploding strawberry milkshake. The three victims had had their faces blown off, just a mess of cheekbone and skin and hollowed eye sockets where they eyes had been. It had taken forensics two days to clear up the upholstery of flesh and blood and another day to get positive ID's. Sawn-off shotguns were a messy business; particularly within the confines of a Range Rover. But this was a Midnight Blue Peugeot, a much nicer class of vehicle.

The wind picked up, sending a chill across his spine. Almond approached the back of the vehicle from the top of the slipway. He held his hands both sides of his head and peered through the rear window. The window was smeared, the view inside murky, distorted and confused but in the front he could make out the rigid outlines of two lifeless bodies. The walnut dashboard and creamy leather upholstery looked intact. He walked around the far side of the vehicle. The driver's window was closed but he felt for the door handle. As he prised open the driver's door, the driver slumped out, his head falling against Almond's thigh. His left eye stared up at him. He had a neat hole in his temple and blood had trickled down his cheek and neck until it blurred into the car fabric. Almond raised his knee and balanced the head before pushing the body back into the car.

The Detective Inspector skirted around the back of the vehicle to the passenger's side. Meanwhile Stephen was busy examining the car, noting the registration number, following the tyre marks etched across the gravel and opening the boot. When he looked up, he noticed his superior wasn't moving, he had just stepped away, staring into space. Almond was peering out across the grey, pitted sea.

'Sir?'

Stephen noticed his colleague's face had turned deathly pale.

'What is it?'

Almond turned away and began to stumble his way across the grassy bank.

Stephen chased him.

'Sir?'

He just heard Almond's cries, 'No, no, Christ no! No!' as the rain came down once more.

Grayson went back to the vehicle. He opened the passenger's door. A handgun lay on the floor, between the two. The smell of dried blood mingled with a smoky aftertaste. Grayson covered his mouth to prevent himself from gagging. A dead female lay with her head on the head rest, her face still perfectly formed, her eyes staring upwards. He slammed the door and walked away, crouching into a small ball. The body was DI Almond's wife.

CHAPTER TWO

Wednesday, 23rd October.

To many watching Detective Inspector John Walker, sitting in the Seafood Café, at the junction of Chelmer and Beckstone Road, they could have been mistaken for thinking he was doodling. He was pouring over a piece of paper, pen in hand while his mug of strong, black coffee got cold. He had that air of childish preoccupation about him as his stubby hands moved excitedly across the paper and that wide-eyed innocence as the image in front opened up before him.

To keener observers, it would have appeared that DI Walker was hard at work and enjoying himself. He was hard at work but he was not enjoying himself. He was making a list of possible reasons why Alan Thomas, a prominent solicitor, would have killed Almond's wife and then ended his own. It was one thing to take another's life but another to take your own. Was it premeditated, was it impulse, or was it an accident? This was always the key part of any investigation - trying to engage the criminal mind. A criminal mind that did not have a great deal of difference from any normal, law-abiding citizen's cranial matter. And, as he knew too well, the mind could be as impenetrably opaque or as bleakly transparent as it chose to be. It was all a question of circumstances.

Circumstances; in other words, the particular situation the criminal happened to be. Circumstances made the action and the action made the crime. This simple casual link was often beyond the whit of others, some of whom were several times more senior than he was. He could paper the walls with the writings of theorists, sociologists, criminal profilers and psychologists who all thought they knew better. Meanwhile Walker stuck to his stick men; crudely drawn figures who could act out his thoughts on a piece of paper right in front of his eyes. Easy really, with arrows for actions and bubbles for thoughts, much less complicated than all those expensive crime profiling models, where you supposedly fed in all the data, set the search parameters and up popped the murderer. Not that it ever did.

A large truck passed outside, the other cup sippers lifted their heads and gazed abstractly out of the window. Walker continued to draw his figures, positioning them half way down the paper and slightly in from the left margin. He wanted to give them lots of space. He drew one man and one woman and had them sitting next to each other, just like the people sitting in the café. Someone was complaining about their order, something about the fried bread not being on the same plate. The waiter who was also the cook and manager lifted the bread and let it slide gently onto the pile of beans and fried sausages. 'There, one nice big pile,' he said and stormed off.

Walker ignored it all and sat back to ponder. Circumstances, the first bolt to unlock before the crime is solved. Circumstances: a senior lawyer and the wife of a police officer are found dead together in a vehicle on a deserted strip of coastline. It was hardly the normal run-of-the mill circumstance he encountered. Most crimes he investigated came within the confines of a house or outside a pub or even down a grubby back street. This one was unusual. His thoughts stalled for a few seconds and then went into overdrive:

Circumstance 1. Mrs Almond and Thomas have been making whoopee for some time. Thomas gets a call, it's Mrs Almond. She wants to talk in private. He suggests Mersey Island - about as private as you can get. They remain quiet during the short car journey. Each is suspicious. They wonder how much they can trust each other. He parks on the slipway. It gives a good view of the island coastline. She tells him it's over. He gets mad, pounds the wheel, venting his rage on an inanimate object. They begin to shout. Then he reaches for the gun. He puts one pellet into her, then realises the sheer awfulness of what he has done. There is no way out, his life will be ruined so he puts the second bullet into his head. A latter-day Romeo and Juliet - but without the romance.

He scrunched up the piece of paper. *Crime passionelle*, in the heart of Essex, on Mersey Island, with a middle-aged couple? Unlikely. The gun just being there, loaded and cocked, ready to be used just in case of such a rebuff? Do me a favour! He stuffed the paper in his pocket and began again, this time with new arrows and bubble thoughts.

Circumstance 2. Mrs Almond's is a regular visitor to Thomas's house - playing away is the only option with a policeman for a hubby. One day she discovers something, maybe some business deal or confidential info about a client (Thomas was the sort of workaholic who would always take work home with him). She questions him. He decides that the wife of a police officer is too dangerous and decides to blow her way. He lures her to some quiet spot. Then, the same situation as before; racked by guilt, blah, blah, blah, he goes and tops himself.

He took the sheet of paper and despatched that to his pocket too. Premeditation was a more likely explanation but unless Thomas was Mr Squeaky-Clean, the very notion of bonking the wife of a police officer was just *asking* for trouble.

Circumstance 3. No romantic entanglements now, it's purely business. They are both in trouble - deep trouble - it's what's brings them together in the first place. Now it stands to tear them apart. No one can help, no one can prevent the inevitable, not even a highly skilled lawyer and the wife of a respected police officer. They decide on the last, most drastic option, the ultimate cop out.

He held this piece of paper up in front of his eyes for closer inspection and meditated at some length. This one didn't mentally collapse in front of him. Sure, a suicide pact wasn't great but it held it's own, fortified perhaps with more than a shred of truth. The scene of crime report and forensics; no sign of a struggle, no contusions on the bodies, no tears in the clothing also reinforced it. The revolver was a Smith and Wesson.38. The serial number had been scratched off. The gun chamber was empty. Only two bullets were needed. The two bullets were lodged into the skulls, one per body. Neat, symmetrical and dead efficient - but then lawyers like Thomas weren't prone to going to needless expense.

The car had been impounded and forensics had gone to work examining hair particles and smears of blood and the contents of the boot. Most of the possessions were work papers of Alan Thomas. A briefcase, two files and three textbooks - he took his work with him. There was also a digital camera, with no photos. Both victims were found to have wallets inside their jacket pockets. Thomas's revealed the usual cluster of credit cards, debit cards, membership cards, loyalty cards and cash. Susan's had no cards, just a couple of passport-sized photos and some scribbled addresses. Thomas had two hundred in notes, Susan Almond, one-fifty - not that they were competing - at least, not anymore. There was cigarette ash in the ashtray and some sweet wrappers, so he did have some vices.

Ballistics said that the first shot was Susan Almond's and the second was Alan Thomas's. Both had their prints on the gun. So how did that work? They both sit there with the gun lying on the dashboard:

'You first,' Alan Thomas says, handing the revolver across to her.

'No, *you* first,' corrects Susan Almond, handing it back. 'Age before beauty, Alan.'

'Ah, that's frightfully decent of you, Susan, but I insist. Ladies first.'

'Oh well, thank you, but no, you do it. I'm frightfully clumsy with firearms. Please make it nice and tidy? I want my daughter to have this dress.'

'Absolutely, my dear. Tally-ho!'

DI Walker had read somewhere, that sixty per cent of solved crimes were solved within the first week. It was a staggering statistic but it fully reinforced his own personal experience. In that first week, information was coming in from all sides: statements, forensics, pathology and ballistics. It was like an adrenalin rush, with emotions riding high, when everything happened in a blur of insight and drama. Carrying it all along were the media, buoyed by public opinion and testing police resources to stretching point. In that first week, criminals made mistakes; sometimes they compounded the error, sometimes they just broke down and confessed, sometimes they repented like they had had an epiphany, and sometimes they did nothing but still broke the surface of suspicion because their alibi crumbled. Then, when the hectic first seven days passed, nothing.

It was now exactly one week since the bodies were found. John Walker had already ploughed through all the files. Some he had gone through several times and, each time he had, he felt that he was only reading the first act in a long-running play. The autopsy had confirmed that both victims had died from gun shot wounds to the head. Her wound had entered the frontal lobe and lodged in her skull. The direction of the bullet was downwards from the right. His bullet had entered through the right temple and stayed there, from the same direction. The bullets extracted were the same size and calibre of the gun. The driver's prints were found all over it. Two spent cartridges lay on the floor. The owner of the car was Alan Thomas. He was a solicitor, a partner in the firm Ridgely, Turner and Fowler based in Chelmsford, the county town. He had been Susan

Almond's work colleague for the last eighteen months. That much had been easy to obtain. The bare facts in act one always were.

The waitress brought over Walker's order. Just then, the door opened and in walked PC Stephen Grayson. He took off his helmet and sat down.

'See you've got the usual sir?'

Walker looked up. He wasn't pleased to see the young man quite so soon. They had arranged to meet up later. 'You're early.'

'I know.'

Walker thought sending Grayson to the Registrar would have taken at least three hours.

'Have you been?'

'Yes.'

'And?'

'Thought I'd come in and have one of their greasy spoons.'

'Did you?'

'Breakfast is the most important meal of the day.'

'Is it?'

'I mean, a fry up can't do much harm once in a while can it?'

Walker made a little harrumph. 'This is the Seafood Café. They specialise in seafood.'

It was a fact that DI John Walker was a true omnivore. It was legendary within the force that here was a man that could eat almost anything at anytime from almost anywhere in the world. In fact, his nickname amongst the elder members of Chelmsford Constabulary was Hoover. He loved food more than anything else, but most importantly of all, he adored seafood. He was as devoted to seafood as a loving man was to his wife. Yet, if he was limited to seafood monogamy then he would happily subsist of a diet of shellfish.

He inhaled the heady broth of clam chowder, momentarily lost in the moment. Then he saw Grayson staring at him. 'What did you find out?'

The foreign chef-cum-waiter arrived. 'I'll have the full English, double portion of bangers, two eggs, two slices of bacon, black pudding, one slice, cup of tea, milk, two sugars, with the meal please and a glass of orange juice.' Walker groaned.

'We don't have juice,' the waiter said.

'Fine, I'll have a coffee.'

'With the tea?'

'Not with the tea, but as well as.'

'I understand. Not in the same cup. '

'No. Want one, sir?'

'No. Now what did you come up with?'

Stephen grabbed the ketchup bottle and steered it in front of him.

'Did you know Essex was the gun capital of England?'

'Yes.'

'Seems that after that Dunblane massacre in 1996, nearly seven thousand guns were handed in by people in the county.'

'I know.'

'It's all on something called the NBIS.'

'Is it.'

'It stands for National Ballistic Intelligence Service.'

'Does it. Any good?'

'Not really, still being developed. Lots of incomplete information. Excuse me.'

Stephen got up and came back with a pot of mustard and some sachets of vinegar. He lined them up in regimented fashion, next to the ketchup as if he was going into war.

'So what have you found out?' Walker asked.

'Not a lot. The murder weapon was a Smith and Wesson .38.'

'I know. And?'

'No record of it.'

'Great.'

'Are you sure?'

'Positive.'

'Who did you speak to?'

'I didn't. I just logged on and went back almost ten years. Nothing.'

'Young man, that's because the files are protected. You need to get proper access. Now go!'

Just then, Stephen Grayson's food arrived.

'Can't I have my breakfast first?'

'Go on then.'

He started to rub his hands and then took the ketchup bottle and squeezed it hard. The sauce flowed viscously over the piled-up sausages, across the strips of streaky bacon and down into the rivulets of fat where it began to glisten. He was now fully occupied. He speared one bulbous sausage and dipped it repeatedly into a greasy fried egg until the yolk bled copiously. DI Walker quickly consumed his soup, got up and left - he had his own horror show to deal with.

Ridgely, Turner and Fowler was a new name to Walker. Like many corporate businesses, they moved silently, unbeknown to the police, operating in their own private world of deals and business lunches - that was until something like this happened. Then they became part of a game, where they only revealed as much as was absolutely necessary to ensure the police would go elsewhere. Walker was used to games, he used to play football for the Sunday side, cricket for the local village team and he ran for the county. Twenty years ago if anyone wanted to give him the run around, he had the aptitude, the stamina *and* the lungs for it. Now he got breathless running a bath.

He did a quick business search and found that the firm had ten offices, in the county and London. Press clippings revealed Alan Thomas in front of their head office, a face amongst the smiling ranks of smartly dressed employees. Thomas won a scholarship to Cambridge, first class honours and was called to the bar eight years ago. A man fully acquainted with the cloistered environments of the Inn's of Court. What made him come down here, wondered Walker, to this commercial backwater? What were the circumstances? Was it the dirt, noise and grime of London? Was it a prick of conscience; appalled by the obscene amounts of money it was possible to earn by playing with words and stretching the credulity of the jurors? Or was it the sense of power; moving from a very average fish in a large pond of excellence to a very large fish in a puddle of mediocrity. Maybe it was none of these, maybe he just wanted to be with Mrs Almond? How long had they known each other? Where did they meet? What made their sexual sparks fly, as fly it must to have risked marriage and the wrath of a high profile copper.

He contacted a friend and colleague, lawyer Jack Richards.

'Jack, wondered if you could fill me in?'

'No problem, John, what do you want to know?'

'What kind of work do Ridgely's do?'

'The solicitors?'

'Yes.'

'Well, up until recently most of their work was traditional, civil and mercantile law. Now it's more topical: cases for unfair dismissals, slander and libel, all that shit, not to mention matrimonial disputes.'

'Business good?'

'John, dealing with other people's messy lives always pays the rent.'

'If the clients are rich.'

'Oh, they are.'

'So what are they up to now?'

'Well, they got involved in providing on-line work.'

'What kind?'

'Offering their services over the internet.'

'Do you know a guy named Alan Thomas?'

'Vaguely. I met him once. Now I know why you're ringing me. I read about it in the papers.'

'Yeah, so you know he was found dead in a car with the wife of a prominent police officer?'

'Yes, I knew David and Susan well. We used to go out, with my wife, the four of us to pubs and clubs, many years ago. Good days they were. Happy Days.'

'What do you think happened?'

'God knows. When I read about it, it just knocked me for six. The whole thing is a tragedy but the detail sounds weird.'

'Weird?'

'Yes, unusual, sort of undignified.'

'Murder is never dignified.'

'Well, seedy then, conduct unbecoming. Not the sort of thing you would expect.'

'What, from a barrister? Don't be so sure. What was he like?'

Richards sighed. 'Pretty much like many of them, jumped-up, a big shot who thought he knew it all.'

'Did he?'

'He wasn't short of grey matter, did the lecture rounds at the local University, wrote papers for the Law Society, that sort of thing. He even spoke at police conferences.'

'What about?

'Criminal law, the rights of suspects.'

'So he was a radical?'

'He'd call himself a liberal.'

'What was his role in Ridgely's?'

'Officially, Head of Product Development but he got involved in most things. He was the guy selected to drive the firm to a brave new world.'

'At least as long as it lasted.'

'That's right.'

'This new world, what did it involve?'

'Oh you know the kind of things: empowerment, hot-desking, first-come first-seated arrangement. No one had their own space, everything was shared: it was a so-called flat hierarchy.'

'Some of the guys here would like to do that.'

'Couldn't say I went along with it, John. It seems that you spend the first part of your career being treated like shit, working your nuts off to get your qualifications, to earn a little respect in your life. Then along comes some fad and pretty soon you're up to your neck in 360 degree reviews and having to kowtow to spotty-faced, brain-dead adolescents who don't have a pot to piss in.'

Walker hadn't invited the tirade. He just wanted the facts. 'And this was all Thomas's brainchild?'

'Not really, you can pick this up on any business course stateside; Harvard, Yale. They all preach that baloney.'

'Did he tread on people's toes?'

'Sure.'

'How was that?'

'Everyone was supposed to tap into this so-called virtual law centre, where a team of solicitors and legal exec's would provide advice to anyone who dialled-up. No introductory meetings, no face-to-face contact, no fee. The theory was that you'd get advice flowing across cyberspace, through time zones and political barriers.'

'So, how do they make money?'

'Thomas was an idealist, particularly with other peoples' money. He didn't care if it didn't make money. He convinced everyone that as soon as the client needed to solve something thorny, like a trade dispute or they wanted redress or something in writing, like a contract or a codicil, the clock would kick in.'

'But it didn't work.'

'No, people just went elsewhere for casework. It was an inglorious failure. Cost the company hundreds of thousands. No brand loyalty, you see?'

'How did the firm react?'

'They weren't impressed. Rumour was he was on the way out when this happened.'

'And Thomas?'

'The guy was a barrister - he was bound to blame someone else! But personally, I think he took it pretty badly. No one wants that kind of stigma on your career card. It was his first real failure.'

'Jack, is there anything else you can tell me about Thomas?'

'Like what?'

'The usual: habits, sexual orientation, addictions.'

'He was a bit of a loner, never socialised.' He paused. 'It's all a terrible shame. Susan was a lovely woman.'

'I know.'

'It must have come as a real shock to David.'

'Yeah, he's taken it pretty bad. Anyway, keep in touch.'

'Well, give him my regards, bye.'

John Walker heard the phone click and sighed. He didn't need reminding that he needed to speak to David Almond. They had been colleagues for years. He kept putting it off, hoping that somehow it would become easier with time but the longer he left it the worse it got. The phone rang. A local journalist wanted to know what progress had been made. She was sent packing with a cold 'no comment' and the phone number of the press officer. It wouldn't stop the press from hounding him but it sure made him feel better to send someone packing.

Walker got up from his desk and looked at the photo. The cadet recruitment photo all those years back. David Almond and he had passed with merit. They were smiling in the glare of the summer day, in their smart ties and uniforms, tall and proud, like they were ready to take on anything. Now David Almond was on compassionate leave - and going through his own personal hell.

He blotted it out and went back to Thomas. A visionary, academically gifted, that was the man on the outside, at least earlier in his career, an evangelist, ready to stand up and spread the word according to Philip Thomas. Yet, maybe this recent shift in emphasis was a sign, a signal that he wanted to withdraw: move away from the daily practices of meetings to anonymity, hiding behind electronic mailboxes and chat rooms. Something had started to make Thomas insecure, something that would send him off the rails. And somewhere, thought Walker, behind that astute business brain and the daily preoccupations of a successful businessman, were dark, brooding thoughts, and the sinister circumstances that caused him to take a gun and end it all.

Next day, on a damp, squally morning, John Walker walked up the worn steps and past grainy, yellow stone columns that flanked the portal of Ridgely House. He pushed open the large swing doors. They swished pleasingly on their axis. He walked purposefully across the shiny black marble floor, his shoes clacking noisily. Above, the mezzanine, and people moving about in a purposeful manner, and in the atrium, large, green potted palms and a series of corridors that radiated outwards like bicycle spokes.

The building had once been the home of the town's wealthiest man, Victorian landowner Richard Pinkerton. He had designed the elaborate architraves and porticos, the stone statues adorning the frontage and the formal garden with its south-facing wall, now a mass of clinging ivy and trailing wisteria. When he died without inheritance, the building became a library, then the local museum and when that too foundered, due to lack of funds, it became the home of Ridgely, Turner and Fowler.

It had stayed with Ridgely's for nearly fifteen years now, almost a landmark for people visiting the town. Ridgely's employed over three hundred people, at least that's what their promotional brochure said and they were regularly featured in the local newspapers as a model local company. For three years they had been voted 'best local employer' and now they had to deal with death, inquiries and an ill-educated policeman.

Businesses and the law never mixed - until they needed each other. Now, he needed them. Preliminary enquires amongst their work associates revealed that the relationship between the two victims had been businesslike and cordial. Nothing more, or at least that's what one interviewee had said, as if pre-empting further questions. Others said similar things, almost the same words as if they had been briefed beforehand. Walker didn't like stereotyped replies even if his questions were equally stereotyped. It spelled collusion.

He walked across to the reception desk and flashed his ID. The receptionist looked up, produced an instant smile and gave instructions on how to navigate the labyrinth. 'Just follow the signs,' she added when she realised he would get hopelessly lost. He took the first corridor and then came back, the receptionist eying him out of the corner of one eye. He set off again plunging once more into the busy and lively working environment. From what he'd read, business appeared to be booming, taking on new staff and winning lots of work - which made Walker wonder even more why one of its leading lights would want to go and top himself?

The first person Walker saw was Gabrielle Simons. She was the corporate partner - whatever that meant. She had worked with both victims for the last two years and apparently knew them personally. She had lived in Chelmsford all her life. Walker figured she was about his age, maybe a year younger. They may even have been to school together, sitting their exams and wondering what career paths to take. Now she was walking into a very large office and probably earned five times his salary.

He had called her out of one of her oh-so important meetings. It gave him a tiny pinprick of pleasure, sometimes it was good to pull rank on people that would normally never pass the time of day with you.

She smiled briefly and then ushered him into her office.

'Please,' she said pointing to a leather chair. He sunk into its deep contours and looked around. The office was a standard mixture of office décor: ash desk, metal filing cabinets, a computer with a dizzying screensaver. The walls were tastefully brightened with limited edition Cloué prints. She settled into her seat, comfortable in a dark brown trouser suit and sensible flat shoes. As she flicked her mid-length brunette hair behind her ears, he noticed there were no photos of loved ones.

She began moving a stack of important looking files to one side of the desk. It was, surmised Walker, what they excelled at - shifting paper *and* responsibility.

'Looks like you're busy.'

'I have to be in court in two hours,' she stated, 'so please be quick.'

In this kind of place, files meant work and work meant money. Lawyers had their own method of alchemy. It started with a pile of base metal papers that began to transmute as soon as a lawyer looked at them. Each review added to their value until they finally arrived at the court, groaning under the weight of solicitors' fees. By the time they came to the attention of some hapless police officer, they were worth their weight in gold.

'I'll try.'

'So Mr Walker,' she began, 'I understand you want to talk about the tragic death of two members of our firm?'

'Just a few areas I'd like to tie up…and it's Detective Inspector Walker.'

She nodded. 'I'm sorry. Detective Inspector, do you know that I have already given a statement?'

'Yes.'

'Then is there anything else to say?'

'I understand you were a close friend.'

'Yes, they were acquaintances of mine. Look, I'm going to call one of my partner's in.'

'Ms Simons. That really won't be necessary.'

'I'll be the judge of that.'

Walker harrumphed. 'I only want to ask a few questions about the victims.'

'Very well but any deviation and I'll call a halt to the proceedings.'

'Fine. So, how acquainted were you with them?''

'We had a good working relationship. Susan was my bridge partner. Alan was one of our most high-profile people.'

'I understand that Alan Thomas was making some big changes within the firm.'

'Technology wise, yes. We were in the dark ages before he came.'

'And it all went wrong.'

'Not at all. It wasn't all plain sailing but we have become much more efficient.'

'Apparently he was on the way out.'

'My, you have been busy.'

'He must have been unpopular.'

'Not at all.'

'Did either of them have any enemies?'

'Not that I was aware of, they were well respected. In professional firms there are always differences of opinion.'

'Quite so. Life wouldn't be normal without the odd tiff would it?'

Gabrielle Simons frowned.

'Did either of them ever express any concerns about their safety?'

'No, not to me.'

'Did they ever strike you as being the type of people that might want to end their lives?'

'Absolutely not, but it's only my opinion.'

'Sure, and did anyone else in the firm know they were lovers?'

Their eyes met fleetingly, a confusion of professional aloofness and distain.

'What people get up to in their spare time is their business…but yes, I knew.'

'It was common knowledge?'

'No, but some of us knew that their relationship was not merely professional.'

'How's that?'

'Sometimes they left the office holding hands.'

How sweet, Walker thought. He couldn't remember the last time he'd held hands with someone.

'In public?'

'Not as such, but as you can see,' she said spinning around on her chair, 'the car park is visible from here.'

'Did you see them leave on the day of the murder?' Walker asked.

'No, I didn't. I had to leave early. My child was poorly.' So she did have a family and somewhere probably a heart.

'Is there any CCTV of the car park?'

'No, it was Alan's intention to install one. The cars get vandalised sometimes - kids from the local estate seem to think that solicitors are fair game. Anyway, we never got round to it, it became a cost issue.'

He'd heard the 'cost issue' excuse trotted out on numerous occasions by his boss but never by a lawyer. 'Did anyone see them leave?'

'I've already asked, inspector. My secretary saw them leave at two thirty-five.'

'She's sure about that.'

'Absolutely. She's very reliable.'

'Name?'

'Penny Adams.'

'So she was probably the last person to see them alive?'

'Yes, if you put it like that.'

'I'll have to speak to her.'

'Sure. I'll ask her to meet you in one of our seminar rooms.'

'Thank you,' Walker said. 'Did Susan Almond ever confide in you about their relationship?'

'No, she didn't.'

'You said in your statement that Susan, Mrs Almond, was working on something called the Biggs case.'

'Did I?'

'Yes. Can you tell me a little about it?'

Gabrielle Simons looked harshly at the police officer.

'Inspector, you know the rules.'

'I know that two members of your firm have been found dead and I know that I have to explore all avenues.'

'Not all. Only those you have legal access to.' Walker waited for her to continue. He was expecting something pious and wasn't disappointed. 'Naturally we will comply with your enquiries,' she made a little cough, 'provided they don't raise issues that might implicate anyone in this firm or breach the firm's ethical guidelines on client confidentiality.'

'Naturally.'

'Otherwise,' she continued, moving to the offensive, 'you'll find yourself up against a very high wall that will only lead to a dead end.'

'Look, Ms Simons,' Walker said quietly, 'we could get a court order, we could argue it's in the public interest or we could just prosecute you for withholding vital evidence.' He was even imagining himself kicking the wall down.

'Please don't lecture me on the law, inspector.'

Walker backed off. He knew that solicitors knew the law far better than he did.

'I wouldn't dream of lecturing anyone on anything. I'm just after the facts.'

'We all are.'

'When does the Biggs case come to court?'

'Two weeks time. Although I can see it being put back.'

'What are they contesting?'

'It's a property deal.'

'How much?'

'Eighty million pounds.'

Walker stifled his attempt at a whistle.

'Chicken feed, these days, inspector.'

Ms Simons must keep expensive chickens, Walker thought. 'How long has the case been going on?' he asked.

'Oh, it's been on our books for at least the last two years.'

'Do you think you'll win?'

'We wouldn't have taken up this case if we didn't think we'd win.'

'How much does your firm stand to gain?'

'It's a no-win no-fee arrangement.'

'So you have a vested interest in winning?'

'You could say that,' Simons said testily, clearly annoyed at any implication of impropriety. 'But that's the law these days. Naturally we receive a retainer but most of our work is performance-driven.'

She was performance-driven, Walker thought. He gauged that this was not the sort of face for picking an argument with. It had an icy edge to it, one unlikely to melt as long as he remained in the room.

'Just a few more questions?'

'Quickly.'

'Can you show me their workplaces?

'Yes, but they've had all their personal items removed.'

'Computer files?'

'Archived.'

'A list of cases they worked on in the last six months?'

'I think we could get their timesheets.'

'Appointment diaries?'

'Again, electronic. Contact archives.'

She began moving her papers again, another few pounds on the clock.

'Thank you, Ms Simons. We'll be in touch.'

She didn't get up or look up but heard the welcoming click as he closed the door behind him.

DI Walker made his way slowly along the corridor. It all seemed so respectable; shiny shoes, new suits, clipped vowels - cleaner than a hospital - but that didn't make it healthy. He figured that Ridgely, Turner and Fowler got involved in just about anything to do with disputes, personal or business. Walker didn't profess to understand the finer points of the legal profession but he figured they must be like one big retribution tribunal, a clearing house to deal with relationships that had broken down irrevocably. The poor victims would walk in through their doors and bleat about how bad their oppressors were. All the firm had to do was ride in, beat the shit out of their opponents with writs and lawsuits and mete out their own form of punishment. Not exactly subtle but then these solicitors weren't much different from him; they got most of their kicks from stitching up their enemies - the only difference being that they were paid handsomely for their efforts.

Walker followed the signs to the seminar room. Simons's secretary was sitting, nervous as a kitten, taking the time out to chew her nails to the quick. 'Ms Adams?'

'Yes.'

'I'd like to ask a few questions concerning the deaths of Alan Thomas and Susan Almond. Don't worry, it's just a formality.'

'Right. Could you give me five minutes, please?'

He was going to ask her to take her fingers out of her mouth but left it. She was already close to break down.

He backed off and stood outside. Time dragged on endlessly. People in suits and good complexions walked up and down the stairs, along the corridors. Sometimes phones rang in distant rooms and mobiles bleeped. Offices were habitually dull places, Walker concluded, more so than cemeteries and shoe shops. Throughout the organisation, everyone was sifting pieces of paper from one place to the next.

Oh, everyone kidded along that life was great in an office; warm, cosy, lots of networking, intrigue and gossip but really, everyone dreamed of being somewhere else. He figured that most people would prefer to be on holiday first, doing hobbies second, being at home third. Only, Gabrielle Simons; divorcee (to be confirmed), living with single kid, zero social life, really wanted to be sitting in an office.

'At last, Simons's secretary beckoned him in.

'I understand you saw them leaving the car park on the day of their death?' Walker asked.

'Yes.'

'What time was this?'

'Two thirty-five. I know it was then because that's when I leave. I have to pick up my child.'

'Did anything appear unusual?'

'Like what?'

'Did they appear rushed, was he forcing her into the car, were they carrying anything?'

'No, they walked quickly out of the office. It was raining. They had their coats on and they got into his car.'

'Can we go and look?' Walker asked.

'Yes, of course.'

She led him out of the room, along the corridor to her office. She sat at her desk. The window was to her side but it gave a clear view of the staff car park.

'Where were they parked?' Walker asked.

She pointed directly in front of her.

'Who got in first?' Walker continued.

'I think she did.'

'Did he open the door for her?'

She hesitated 'I couldn't see very well. It was raining, the window was smudged.'

'Try to remember.'

'No, I think he just unlocked it remotely. That's right because the indicator flashed. I saw that clearly. Then he walked round to the driver's side.'

'Did you see anyone else hanging around?'

'I don't think so.'

'Were there any unusual cars in the car park?'

'There were lots of cars in the car park, I wouldn't know if they were employees or visitors.' She got out a tatty tissue and began wiping her eyes. 'Sorry.'

'Not at all,' Walker said. 'Just one more question. When they drove off, did they leave quickly?'

'No, I wasn't really looking but I think the car just drove out normally.'

'Thank you very much. That's all. I'll let you get on.'

She was still dabbing her eyes. 'Here.' He gave her his handkerchief, the one he always took as a spare. He really was all heart. Then he got up, paced quickly along the corridor and headed towards reception.

Typical, he thought, a key witness and all she does is blubber. Not a good sign if she was going to have to stand up in court. He saw a sign pointing towards exit. He kept on going. He got to the end of the corridor and then looked up. The exit sign was pointing left. There was another sign. It was pointing downwards, indicating another route.

The sign read: *Archives*.

One quick glance, then he made the descent. The steps were steeper than he'd imagined and winding too. There were no carpets here or handrails to guide him down the staircase and presumably no entrance to a sumptuous, chandelier-laden ballroom. There were not even twinkling fairy lights to steer his path, just a faint shadow coming from basement below. As he descended the steps, he heard a low, monotonic droning noise in the background. It got progressively louder, like an approaching vehicle. When he finally reached the bottom, the suffocating heat caught his breath.

People made jokes about basements and this one was no different. It felt like entering another world: The Land that Time Forgot. How could anyone actually work here? *Did* anyone actually work down here?

Hierarchy was a well-established fact of life at Ridgely, Turner and Fowler. At the very apex of things sat the Scribes, people like Simons and Thomas who went out to see clients and obtained all the legal work. Below them were the Hacks, people like Susan Almond who got the information and managed the case work. Below them were the Scribblers, a band of people who produced affidavits, contracts and legal agreements. Reporting to them were the Word Crunchers who typed up all the agreements. Then came the Grunters who checked and called over the agreements, until they were word perfect. Way below these groups were the Serfs, people like Simons's secretary whose job was to serve, and some way below them were the Office Gonads. Joined since birth, Office Gonads were unable to operate as separate units and walked around like Siamese twins. They were responsible for such challenging office tasks as shifting office furniture, moving doubled parked cars from the staff car park, shifting rubbish and delivering the internal mail.

Walker had gone below that stratum and was now entering the very base of the firm's food chain: *the archives*. He stepped across the concrete floor. It opened out into a large expansive room that disappeared into the hazy distance. One ripped chair was lying propped up against the wall, while the rest of the floor was covered in piles of files, rising up from the bare concrete floor like columns of stalagmites. To one side was a large metal door leading no doubt to the main archive area where all the files should have been. On the other side were enormous silvery metal pipes that emerged from a metal housing and snaked their way up the walls before disappearing through the roof. This was clearly the source of the noise and the heat.

Through the weighty oppressiveness, he noticed a counter on the far side. Behind it sat a man: *Archive Man*. He was hunched; head down, tapping at his keyboard, looking slightly dwarfed by the surroundings. Walker went up to the counter.

'Excuse me?'

The man looked up. He was gaunt, thin as a butcher's pencil but he was neatly attired in a crisp white shirt secured with a royal blue tie. He was also clean-shaven and looked almost like an executive, except that he was working in a basement. Walker began to speak and the man's head moved back slightly, as if startled.

'Sorry, I didn't mean to surprise you.'

The man was now staring right at Walker. The fixed expression seemed to stay for an age. *Hey, hello. Is anyone in there?* Then he blinked.

'That's okay,' he said, his voice reed-thin. 'It's just we're not open, officially.'

'Oh.'

'Anyway, what's the problem?' he asked flatly, as if problem was the most familiar word in his language.

'There's no problem,' Walker said. 'It's just we've been playing phone tag and I thought I'd come down and sort it out. It's about those files?'

The man just looked blankly at him. 'Do you have a pink?'

'Sorry?'

'A requisition slip.'

'No I don't. Gabrielle Simons just instructed me to come and collect them.'

The name had some effect. He blinked again. She was obviously a big cheese.

'I'm sorry, sir. Not without a pink.'

'She sent me down here specifically. It's important. You know the Biggs case?'

'I know of it.' Another blink.

'Colour?'

Walker hesitated. 'Sorry?'

'The colour of the file.'

'Look, I'm in a dreadful hurry. It was a beige file.'

'No beige files down here.'

Walker made a little laugh. 'Not so easy when you're colour blind is it?'

The man looked at Walker again, almost peering into his eyes as if looking for evidence.

'No, it isn't. I'm sorry.'

'Look, Ms Simons said it was urgent. The case goes to court any day now.'

'Sorry, sir. What department did you say you were in?'

'Didn't. Corporate. Look, how about you give her a ring? Check it out?'

The man frowned.

'She's there right now,' Walker said, 'waiting for your call.'

It was clearly circumventing the rules.

'Ext 3456.'

At last, *Archive Man* clicked into action. 'Wait there,' he said as he disappeared into a cubby hole office. He turned his back and Walker observed him picking up the receiver.

Walker didn't have much time. He lifted up the counter flap, crept past the cubicle towards the archive area.

The door was ajar. He pushed it gently and it swung open. Spread out before him were rows of metal stacks. He counted five either side of the central walkway - ten sets of stacks in all. Each stack had at least three sets of six tiers of shelves and five rows. That meant ninety slots or bins, as he thought they were called, in each stack. Maths was never a strong subject but even he knew that nine hundred files in each stack meant he didn't have a hope in hell of finding what he wanted.

He began pacing up the aisle, his eyes racing along the rows of endless files. All this paper, all this money, he thought. He really shouldn't be here, it was the sort of ridiculous thing that a younger version might have got up to but not a senior officer - he'd retired. The metal stacks had to be almost nine feet high, rearing up in front of him like stalks in a cane field, or maybe haystacks. To find the proverbial needle would take him at least a week and he had no idea of the indexing code or whether files would be here at all. They could have all been sitting in Gabrielle Simons's office along with all the other papers - her airport-sized room could hold anything. He reached the end of the row and found himself enveloped in a peaty darkness. All he heard was the soporific whirr of the boiler.

In the gloom, he could just make out the numbers and letters scribbled down the spine of the files. It seemed to be an alphanumeric code. Some of the files started with an eight and others with a nine. As he walked further, the numbering suddenly began with zero ones and zero twos.

'Oh, it's been on our books for at least the last two years.'

Walker stopped and went back through some of the codes. Then it hit him. The first two digits were the year, probably when the case first came in. He moved away from the stacks and began following the route of the numbers.

Walker hurried along the sets of rows; there was no time to dawdle. At last, he found the year. Then he realised that the next letter must indicate the month. From several thousand, the list of files was shrinking by the second. He began pulling some of them from their slots. He nervously flicked through their contents. Pieces of paper dropped out and he stuffed them back. Not logical, he realised, *think man, think*! He hurriedly placed them back and stepped away.

Meanwhile, one floor higher, Gabrielle Simon's was speaking to reception. . 'Penny, it's Gabrielle. A Mr Walker has just left my office. He's heading your way. Please make sure he leaves the premises.' At this precise moment, *Archive Man* was trying to get through.

John Walker's eyes were slowly acclimatising to the meagre light. Looking up to the highest shelf, he noticed that all the files had letters as the last few characters. It could mean anything but suddenly he spotted three files, all neatly placed together, not so dusty. Each one had the code 'OOS' crudely written. 'OOS?' What calendar had nineteen months in it? It was hopeless. Then he looked again. The S could have been a G. Filing clerks, often scrawled their inscriptions, as if they alone needed to read the information. That's why they worked in the basement. It had to be July.

Walker spotted a ladder ten yards away but he didn't have time. He didn't want ladders moving all by themselves - he just wanted a file to disappear unaccountably. He stood onto his toes and reached up. His fingers were touching the files. He could feel their rough exterior. With one final stretch, his fingertips clasped the files and down they came, scattering across the floor like a tickertape and spilling under the stacks. He began crawling on his knees, sweeping his hands along the floor, his face turning purple. He managed to Hoover up every document and stuff them back in their files. It took only the briefest of glances.

The documents had Gabrielle Simons name all over them. She was the lead partner in charge. The very first item on file was a letter written in 2000 and signed by an official acting on behalf of someone called Joe Biggs. Quickly, he gathered up the papers.

Then he heard the metal door clank shut.

CHAPTER THREE

Thursday, 24th October.

John Walker stopped in his tracks. His exit route had suddenly been removed. No wind could have caused the door to close, let alone the gentle draft caused by the whirring boilers. Maybe it was on a spring mechanism but most likely, it was *Archive Man* asserting his territorial rights. He tucked the files under his arm and raced along the walkway towards the door. The door handle turned but nothing happened. He tried again. Nothing. Damn!

To be locked in anywhere was embarrassing but to be locked in someone's security area with no authorisation and not even the flimsiest explanation was beyond the pale. He wondered what the hell anyone would say, but it didn't bear thinking about - he knew what they would say. The only way to get some benefit from this self-inflicted mess was to make his exit as unseen as possible.

The source of artificial light had effectively been extinguished. All he had was a slither of creamy white from a tiny, metal-grilled window that was situated in the top corner of the room. Shadows occasionally flashed across so he assumed it was people walking past, on the pavement above. If only he could lever himself up with the ladder and bang on the window...he soon realised it was crazy - when he clambered up the ladder and rattled the metal grille nothing moved. It was stuck fast. All he could see was a flurry of people's feet. The heating must have had a shaft but when he tried to follow the trail of pipes and cables he only found a tiny vent with yet another grille.

He didn't have much time. Sooner or later, someone, or maybe a whole gang of corporate cronies, would come stomping through the aisles looking for him, like *he* was the criminal.

He was beginning to get desperate, he was even tempted to ring HQ and ask for back-up. That would only make matters worse. Then, as he peered through the gloom, he saw something. The room went further back than he had first imagined. There was an archway at the far end. He ran towards it and when he crossed the threshold, he stepped onto a stone floor. It was a tiny anteroom, and almost immediately, he banged his head on the low ceiling. He put his hand to his head, but mercifully, there was no blood. Then he realised he had entered an old cellar, part of the original building constricted by Pinkerton in the early nineteenth century. There were no files here, no racks of storage just a stone floor, thick concrete walls and an old oak door with rusting metal hinges. He was about to investigate further, when he heard a distinct clack followed by footsteps and vague murmurs. A man and a woman. The door was open again and people were coming to investigate.

A light flickered and suddenly the whole archive area was flooded with illumination. He drew himself further back into the shadows of the tiny cellar, like a modern day Dracula. Suddenly he noticed a large brass key lying on the floor. He picked it up and worked it feverishly into the lock. After several attempts it finally turned. Yet still the door refused to move. The voices were clearly audible now, a grunt probably *Archive Man,* a couple of Office Gonads and a shrill woman's voice that had to be a Scribe. At least four - quite a welcoming committee.

'An 02G file, you say?' the Scribe asked. 'So he didn't give his name and you don't know where he went?'

'Uh, he just seemed to disappear, like,' replied *Archive Man.* 'I couldn't get through on the phone so I closed the door and decided to go and see you personally.'

'Think he's in this room?' she asked.

'Dunno.'

'Hmm. What's down here?'

The footsteps came closer. There were two metal bolts running across the door. Calling on all his physical reserves, he grabbed hold of the bolts and drew them across. Now his attention was fully on the door. He tried the door once more, there seemed to be some lateral movement.

Maybe there was another lock, *on the outside.*

He put his shoulder into it, the one he hadn't used so effectively for many a year. He barged the door full on. It moved and, with a second shove, it gave way grudgingly with a disturbing creak. It hadn't been locked at all, just jammed, the wooden door probably warped through years of suffering the tropical heat of the basement.

'Hear that?'

The footsteps of Office Gonads quickened but Walker was already racing up stone spiral steps, and through a glass door that lead into a corridor. He suddenly found himself in familiar territory, walking past Gabrielle Simons's door and a few seconds later he was back in the foyer. He slowed down, breathing heavily and walked rapidly towards the exit doors and the street beyond.

He felt the eyes of the whole company bearing down on him. He kept walking. One man crossed his path, two young professional Hacks stood and stared and the Serf behind the desk locked her gaze onto him. A uniformed security guard was loitering by the door. He was big and wide. As he saw Walker approach, he stepped surprisingly deftly to one side and Walker was out, onto the busy street and dissolving into a sea of people.

Walker got to the street corner. He could hear his breath pound, he could swear a bead of sweat was forming across his forehead and there was that telltale trace of a headache coming on from the bang on the head. All in all, a terribly unprofessional feeling. He wasn't as fit as he thought he was or maybe he was just getting past it. He didn't wait to hear the barking noise of the security guard or the looks of astonishment on the faces of the Office Gonads as their heads swivelled this way and that. By then, he was too far away.

No doubt, his boss would soon be receiving a stiff letter of complaint couched in lots of legal jargon. Yet, despite all this, Walker didn't care. In fact, he felt an inescapable sense of pleasure; buoyed up by the notion that he'd put one over these fancy office types *and* had the files. That sense alone helped to assuage any sense of guilt or remorse. And, of course the whole episode had a familiar ring to it, repeated over the years; police push for evidence, suspect stalls - attempts to fob off police - police try another route, suspect blocks that too, then police take another course. Eventually they find the thing they were originally looking for. The police weren't fools - even if the public thought they were.

Of course, in those early days, it had been much easier. No internal affairs committees or whistle blowers to come chasing their tails, it was more of a game then. They were an act; himself and whoever they teamed him up with, working and supporting each other; sometimes Clarke, usually David Almond. One watched the door while the other deposited the stuff: sometimes a quarter of ganga dropped in the water closet, sometimes a shooter stuffed down the back of the sofa, sometimes an incriminating photo slid into a drawer. Compared to fabricating evidence, misappropriating a lawyer's file was a mere bagatelle. And in this case, he wasn't *adding* evidence he was simply *removing* it. Moving things; away from, rather than towards, the suspect. He afforded himself a moment of levity. Sometimes, things had a habit of going around 180 degrees.

He put the files in the boot of his car and got in. He flicked the ignition switch and as the engine came abruptly to life, he pointed the car towards Chelmsford HQ.

Within a few minutes of his return, PC Stephen Grayson was in his room. This time he had found a chair to sit on.

'Sir, look what I've got here,' he said, smirking. Grayson unrolled a large poster. 'It's our new mission statement. It's going to be on all our notepaper, in the stations and get this, on the side of the cars.'

'Walker read it out aloud: 'Taking a lead in making Essex safer'.

'Naff, eh?' Grayson observed.

'It's anodyne.'

'What?'

'You went to college.' Walker retorted.

'Yeah, but they never taught anodyne.'

'Maybe that's because your course was anodyne.'

'Maybe. So what does it mean?'

'Go look it up.'

'How about taking a lead. What does *that* mean?'

'It means, Grayson, that we no longer barge in, we pussyfoot around, like prima ballet dancers.'

'Banging up the bad. That would have been better.' Grayson suggested.

For once, Walker was inclined to agree with him. Somewhat alliterative but pithy and there was no doubt that policing had gone soft while the criminals had got smarter. He could have railed on about twenty-first century policing techniques for ages but he just wanted this case closed.

'Oh, by the way,' Grayson added, 'we've got a witness rang in. He swears he saw the two star-crossed lovers walking along the shore, just a few minutes before their death.'

Walker sat up immediately. It was a week since the death and no one had come forward.

'Really?'

Grayson nodded.

'An islander?' Walker asked.

'Think so.'

'Okay, bring him in, and while you're out there, keep your eyes peeled. See if SOC missed anything. Johnson isn't always on the ball.'

Grayson put on his jacket and stepped out. Walker got up to close the door. He carefully levered out the files from his plastic bag. Then he replaced it with official police covers and put the package back in his safe. He would go through them later, in his own time.

Grayson headed back to Mersey Island. He took the same route but this time, without his boss and unruly tractors, he made it even quicker, shaving one minute-ten off his personal best. It wasn't raining either and a gentle fluid light cascaded across the mudflats and spread out to the meadows, where a few indolent cows grazed. He always noticed the light out here. Crystalline, a prism of blues, greys and pinks and the sky spreading itself from one horizon to the next, like a protective shield.

In fact, the sky was more impressive than the land, which stood vacant and sparse, yielding itself to the Essex clay-based soil and oily mudflats. Ten minutes later, Grayson was in the thick of it; crouched on his hands and knees poring over the rough ground, looking for clues.

He could see there were new indentations. Someone had visited the scene recently. It wasn't that hard to identify the type of tyre - cross-ply radial, retreads - but it was well nigh impossible to identify the type of vehicle. All he guessed was that it was a car. The marks went from the slipway, all the way back to the car park. It could have been police officers but he doubted it. It could have been visitors but very few people came out this way at this time of year. So, he concluded, there was a high likelihood that it was of one of the press folks sniffing out a story or one of those sicko's who loved to visit a murder scene. The only thing it showed for sure was that the tide hadn't come this far for several days. As he got up off his knees, he spotted a boat passing the creek just like it had the day of the murder.

'Hello!' he shouted, 'or should I say, Ahoy!'

The man in the craft just waved and turned back into the wheelhouse.

'Excuse me, can I have a word. Police!'

The man put his hand up in recognition and eased off the throttle. The noise of the engine subsided and the boat began to bob in the brown swirling waters.

'Police you said?' the fisherman shouted back.

'That's it. Police! I'd like to talk?'

The man cupped his hands around his mouth. 'Kind of busy right now! Just going to collect my nets!'

'Won't be long, sir. Would you mind pulling in?'

The man pulled a long face. 'How and where exactly do you suggest?'

Grayson looked around. The tide was too low.

'Well, where are you going?'

'To the layings. Be two or three hours. Be back on the incoming tide round 3.15, then back to the sheds for a cup of tea and a ciggie.'

'Where are the sheds?'

'Pyefleet channel!' called out the man. 'You can't miss them!'

Grayson waved the fisherman on. He needed to track down the witness, anyway. The call had been made from a public phone box that was working now. Grayson spent a futile couple of hours driving around the island asking if anyone knew the man. Curtains flapped, doorbells stayed unanswered and pedestrians shuffled past him as if he had the plague. The name must have been wrong, thought Grayson. Nothing unusual there - most people liked to give false names - but the voice had suggested an elderly man with a strong local dialect so he kept looking. It probably narrowed the potential candidates down to a couple of hundred.

By mid-afternoon, Stephen Grayson had exhausted all possibilities. He was disillusioned and found himself sitting on the sea wall, dangling his tired legs. If the mountain won't come to Mohamed, he mumbled to no one in particular. He picked up the latest NYPD detective novel and joined it at chapter 2.

Protagonists and police procedurals were infinitely more glamorous and exciting in a book.

He looked up when he heard the low drone of an engine. Ten minutes later, the 22-foot smack eased into shore. The skipper cut the engine and coasted the last few yards. His crewmen leapt off and dragged the boat ashore.

'Ah, the policeman!' he exclaimed, as he came up the shore.

'That's right, sir.'

'Give me five ticks.'

He removed his salty-stained baseball cap and thrust it into his pocket. Then he unclipped his overalls, pulled out a tin of tobacco, and began rolling his own. He inhaled deeply, sucking in his cheeks until his jaw went hollow. Then he pulled out a thread of tobacco from between his lips and turned to the police officer.

'Now, what can I do you for?'

'Good catch?'

'Average.' The man said abruptly.

'What do you fish for, Mr…?'

'Hookey.'

'Hookey?'

'It's my nickname.'

'Full name.'

'Mister George Chalmers.'

'Right. Mister Chalmers.'

'Oysters, that's what we do here. More like farming though these days.'

'Any good?'

'Best oysters in the country.'

'Been doing it long?'

Mr Chalmers made a wheezy little laugh to himself. 'Laddie, oysters have been eaten here since Roman times. My family have been in the business for nearly two hundred years. What about you, how long you been a policeman?'

Stephen straightened his shoulders.

'Two generations. I've been in it for three years.'

'So, long enough to know when someone needs a hand. Here.'

The fisherman held up a crate from the deck and thrust it in Grayson's hands. It was full to the brim of silvery, grey-green shells that scraped and clacked together like castanets.

'A good haul?' Grayson asked.

'I've had better.'

'What do you want me to do?'

'Just take them into the sheds. There's a good fellow.'

Grayson grabbed hold of two crates and lifted them up. Then he noticed all the grit and mud slime was oozing down over his clean trousers. Chalmers began to roar with laughter.

'One at a time and let them drain. Don't they teach you common sense at college anymore?'

'Not about oysters, no.' Stephen put back one of the crates and staggered across the shingle to the entrance. He looked back quizzically.

'That's it. In there. There! Alice won't bite.'

Stephen saw a large woman standing at the back of the shed dressed in a sack apron and holding a long hose.

'Just plonk them down there,' she said.

Stephen walked away and heard the swish of a high-pressure hose go to work.

There were four more buckets, six crates and several trays to take through before he had done the work. Meanwhile, Chalmers had parked himself on the seawall cradling a cup of tea in his large stubby hands.

'Thanks, laddie. We have to get them cleaned and stored as soon as we land. One of those bloody EU regulations. You can put the rest over there,' he said, pointing to a penned area of muddy shoreline.

Stephen staggered out again to the boat. He was handed a shard and began scraping the remaining oysters off the deck. Then he was sent clambering over pits, laying out the remaining oysters.

'That's it, officer, put them in the pits!' cried out Chalmers. 'They'll get washed by the rising tide. We'll sort them later!'

Ten minutes later, Stephen had emptied all the buckets. He came back puffing hard with bright red cheeks.

'Out of steam are we? Fit young laddie like yourself - should be a doddle.'

'Not my kind of physical work really,' Stephen said, panting breathlessly, 'I'm more of an athlete.'

'Well you're certainly not a weightlifter,' Chalmers joked as he drew on the small cigarette that drooped between his lips. 'Sit here,' he said, patting the seawall. Stephen obliged. 'This, my friend, is the best part of the day this, tea and a fag and the work done for another day.'

Stephen could at last pause to admire the stillness. There was no sound across the whole island, except for the gentle lap of water rubbing itself against land.

The fisherman put his arm out, so that it pointed across the water. 'Beautiful, isn't it? See how the low sun catches the water? The water turns into thousands of tiny, diamond necklaces.'

'More like pearl necklaces,' corrected Stephen. 'Oysters, geddit?'

Chalmers pulled a sour expression and drew on his cigarette again. 'You don't get pearls with these oysters. You're a few thousand miles off course.' He flicked the dog end into the mud and drained the contents of his tea. 'So what brings you to this neck of the woods, in case I can't guess?'

'It's about the deaths here, seven days ago.'

'Ah, that,' he said grumpily. 'Rum business. Shocking state of affairs. It's such a peaceful place. Now it's put our festival into jeopardy. Mayor is thinking of calling it off.' He stopped momentarily to scratch his head. 'Anyway,' he said finally, 'we're still better off than the two in the car, that's for sure.'

'So you've heard about it?'

'Nothing but,' the fisherman moaned. 'Been in the radio, in the papers, even on the telly. The phone hasn't stopped ringing with people asking if the festival is happening this year. I says, I haven't got a clue, I says, ask all those flaming dignitaries. They get paid to do that sort of thing. Me, I just get on with me fishing.'

'You do the same route every day?'

'In season, October 'til April, come rain or shine.'

'I wondered if you saw anything between two-thirty and five-thirty?'

'Tuesday, weren't it?'

'That's right.'

He put his cup down on the wall and gazed across the water.

'Foul weather if I remember. Visibility poor, lashing it down, easterly force five. Perfect.'

'Why's that?'

'Because when it blows, it stirs up all the sediment. Brings all the oysters to the surface, you see, so you can pluck them like ripe cherries.'

'When was high tide, Mr Chalmers?'

Chalmers stroked his bristly chin. It made a noise like sandpaper. 'Now you're asking. Anytime between five and six. Big one, it was. I was probably going past the creek around one o'clock. Can't say I saw anything then.'

'You didn't see a Midnight Blue Peugeot 2000 on the slipway at Graydon's creek?'

'Would that be black?'

'I guess so, from a distance.'

'No. A car like that would have stood out but I was busy at that stage.'

'Doing what?'

'Putting the spats, broods and half wares back in the beds, clearing out the starfish and crabs.'

'I see.'

'That's where the farming comes in. You can't take it all and you have to tend to what you've got. So you see, I'm not really watching the slipway. Sorry.'

'Any other boats do that run?' Grayson asked.

'Only Pookie.'

'Pookie?'

'My cousin. Jim.'

'Jim Pookie?'

'No, that's his nickname. It's Jim Chalmers.'

'Anyone else?'

'There's only us two left now.'

'Think this Pookie may have seen something?'

'I'll ask, if you like.'

Just then, the woman came out of the sheds, wiping her hands on a towel.

'Alice,' Chalmers said, 'this gentleman is a police officer. He wants to know if we'd seen anything?'

'Oh yeah? What did you tell him?'

'Not much to say really. Terrible state of affairs.'

She came up to him, giving him a quick glance before walking past and sitting on the wall.

'I was in Colchester all day, going round the restaurants, trying to get them to buy our produce. You can check if you like. Bloody hard work. You'd think I was selling the plague. I didn't get back till gone eight o'clock.'

'Thank you,' Grayson said.

'Mind you,' she added, in a lower voice, 'I said to George once, I said, this would be an ideal place for a murder.'

'Why's that?'

'Deserted, lots of places to hide a body. Folk's round here like to keep to themselves.'

'You think they'd refuse to say, if they saw anything?'

She shrugged her shoulders. 'Maybe. Maybe not. People round here really don't like strangers. They'll take your money of course, but they prefer if you weren't here at all. They can't wait for the visitors to leave. They think it's *their* island. Very territorial, you see?'

Her husband nodded.

'Sorry, we can't be of more assistance,' Mrs Chalmers said, finally.

Grayson got up to go 'That's okay, madam,' he said, with an air of resignation.

Chalmers gestured to his wife who went into the shed. She came out carrying a foil tray, wrapped in cling film. 'Here,' she said. 'Take them to your fellow police officers. Bet none of them has ever had anything like it. Say it's compliments of the Chalmers of Mersey.'

'Why, thank you very much,' said Grayson dutifully, as he walked towards the squad car. He didn't like shellfish, but he knew someone who did. Just then, he stopped and turned around. 'One more question. Do you know a Mr Burns?'

'Burns? Never heard of him.'

'Oh well, never mind.' Grayson rested the oysters carefully on the car roof. Then he opened the car door. 'Thanks for the oysters.'

'Baines?' Chalmers shouted out. 'I know a Baines.'

Grayson closed the door and walked back towards him. 'Old fellow.'

'That's him. Bainesy.'

'You know him?'

'Know him?' Chalmers said, his eyes going northwards. 'Course I do! Everyone knows Bainesy. Lives just over there!' Chalmers pointed to a small shack with a corrugated roof, situated on a patch of scrubland, overlooking the sea. A puff of smoke was trailing from a piece of tin piping, poking out of the roof.

'In that?'

'During the summer and autumn. He combs the beach. Might still catch him before he goes away for the winter to stay with his sister in a caravan.'

'Thanks.'

Grayson placed the tray of oysters on the back seat and locked the vehicle. Then he walked quickly, down the sandy track, towards the smoking shack.

Two hours later, Walker was squeezed into the tiny kitchen area of Chelmsford police station, along with some cadets working the microwave with takeaway gunk. He pushed his way through and rubbed his eyes with disbelief. In front of him, lay a feast, glistening and silvery, like a treasure chest. As he approached the tray of shimmering oysters, he could scarcely conceal his glee.

'*Ostera Edulis*! Grayson, you have delivered.'

'Whatever, thought you might be impressed.'

'Impressed? These are some of the finest oysters in the land!'

Everyone knew that Walker could happily drive thirty miles in his car, wait on the quayside for five hours and pester the local fisherman to sell some of their catch. It wasn't quite clear what Walker offered, but it wasn't money. Rumours circulated that stolen goods came into the hands of fishermen, just a few days after a heist, but nobody could prove a thing.

Ping! went the microwave as another curry came off the production line, seized on by a young cadet. 'S'cuse me, sir,' she said, grabbing it and plating up. 'Coming through, curry in a hurry.'

From the humble winkle to the majestic lobster, and every mollusc and crustacean in between, John Walker was addicted to shellfish. His deep freezer was always full, overflowing with North Atlantic prawns, New Zealand mussels, clams from Hawaii, spider crabs from Japan and Scottish crayfish. He ate shellfish everyday and once he was believed to have eaten fried, garlic prawns for breakfast, seared, hand-dived scallops for lunch and boiled, local cockles for tea. Suggestions that he polished the day off with a plate of rubbery whelks and consumed them in bed were not discounted. In fact, though he was teased and tormented mercilessly by his peers, none of it concerned him for he had developed his own carapace.

Another curry rolled off the production line but Walker blanked it out. He simply stood in raptures, facing the apex of his culinary desires. For while he regarded all seafood as regal, it was the oyster that remained the true prince of the sea. He drew his fingers lingeringly across their gnarly silvery shells. The encrusted calcium carbonate felt brittle yet was razor sharp with an edge that could cut fingers to shreds. It could even, mused Walker to himself, be used as a murder weapon.

To many, including their predators, shellfish looked intimidating yet to Walker that was part of the attraction. They deceived, they fooled their opponents, they hid themselves behind a rock-like carapace. Yet, to appreciate fully their worth, it was necessary to delve deeper, go behind the surface. He took his own special knife and levered it into its side. He partially lifted away the case, revealing the tiny creature, with its adductor muscles exerting a vice-like grip. Then he prised open the shell fully and held it aloft as the dove-grey treasure pulsed within its opalescent bed.

'The moment before ecstasy,' he announced, to the small group of cadets who were still waiting for their microwave fodder, 'is to be treasured as longingly as possible.' Then he picked it up slowly by the narrow end of its shell, lifted it to his lips and opened his gaping mouth. He held it suspended above his mouth while his audience looked on. Finally, he poured the mollusc and liquor and swallowed with a great gulp. 'Quite simply,' he said, 'nectar and ambrosia, all in one.'

'That is so gross,' one of the cadets said, wincing.

Walker placed the empty shell back on the tray and looked disdainfully at the cadets. He then proceeded to eat seven more, each one more closely savoured that the one before. To Walker, oyster eating defied the Law of Diminishing Returns.

'Go, Hoover, go!' they shouted.

'One for the road,' Walker said, as they clapped and another one went down.

He then offered the tray to cadets.

'You've got to be joking,' one said.

'They've like snot,' said another.

Soon the kitchen was empty, leaving Walker feeling slightly euphoric and confused. 'Peasants,' he muttered coldly as he put the rest away.

He headed for the interview room. An old man, with a white grizzled beard and a scruffy grey overcoat was slouching in the interviewee's chair. His gnarled hands were clasped around a mug of steaming tea as if they were clamped to it.

'That's the way I like it,' the old man said, smacking his lips. 'Hot, sweet and strong, just like the women in my life.' Walker's mood darkened once more. He couldn't imagine a woman going within fifty feet of this repellent man. 'Mr Baines,' Walker asked stonily, 'why did you say that your name was Burns?'

'Baines.'

'Yes, but you said Burns.'

'Cloth ears - must have misheard.'

'You told one of my officers that you saw a man and a woman on the day of the killings.'

'That's right.'

'Why has it taken you a week to come forward?'

Baines sniffed and wiped the tip of his nose with his mucky sleeve.

'Only have chips once a week.'

'Sorry, you've lost me.'

'I saw it in the chippie, wrapped up in a newspaper.'

'Go on.'

'I normally go to the chippie on a Tuesday, this week I went in on the Wednesday.'

'Watching our figure are we?' Walker asked.

'Maybe; so anyway, it was on the front page. Then I remembered seeing them, strolling along, arm in arm. Not a care in the world.'

Grayson appeared with a file, which he opened and left in front of Walker.

'And you say you got a good look at them?' Grayson prompted.

The man put the tea down and leaned forward. Walker caught a strong whiff of salty odour and recoiled back as far as his chair would allow him.

'Sure.'

'Can you describe them?' Walker asked.

'He was about five-eleven. She was shorter, say five-six maybe.'

'You say she was five-six?' Grayson repeated.

'Yeah. About.'

Mrs Almond had been no more than five-four. Walker read. Thomas was six-two. That made them almost ten inches apart. Any normal person would have observed the marked difference in height. 'Mr Baines, are you sure about these heights?'

Baines picked up his mug again and slurped. Then he shrugged his shoulders, pouting his lips, in Gallic fashion.

'Hmm. Could have been taller or shorter. It was hard to tell.'

'Why's that?' Walker asked.

'Because they were walking on the scarp.'

'Go on.' Walker said

'It was raining,' Baines said. 'They both had long coats so I couldn't make out their builds too well but she looked well upholstered,' he added with a wink, 'if you know what I mean?'

There was something else Walker remembered. Both were wearing jackets when they were found in the car although their coats were on the back seat.

'Mr Baines. Did you actually see these people?'

The old man looked circumspectly into his mug of tea.

Walker got up and circled around Baines. 'Get me a coffee,' he said to Grayson.

He waited until his coffee arrived and then placed the plastic cup on the table. Then he beckoned Grayson to leave the room.

'Mr Baines, did you actually see these people?'

As he raised his head, his face creased into a scowl.

'Of course I did. Not only that, I saw someone else.'

'Oh, and who was that?'

'Hanse Cronje.'

Walker stopped momentarily. His hearing wasn't so great these days.

'Who?'

'I was on me bicycle and this silver Ford Mondeo pulls out in front of me. Well, driving it was Hanse Cronje.'

'The cricketer?'

'Yes.'

Walker had heard stories of ghosts and apparitions being seen by the islanders. Some swore that on a certain day each year legions of Romans could be seen walking across the mudflats in their clanking armour. St Stephen's church was supposedly inhabited by a benign spirit of a young woman. However, this was a new one on him.

'The ex-South African cricket captain? The one who died in a helicopter crash?'

'That's the fellow. Dunno about a crash. He was wearing a moustache but I figured it was fake on account of him not wanting to be recognised.'

'But *you* did, Mr Baines.'

'Ah, but I have an eye for that kind of thing.'

Walker sighed. 'I'm sure you do. And where, may I ask, were the rest of the team: Jonty Rhodes, Jacques Kallis?'

That's what threw me at first. He was on his own.'

'So he didn't have Shaun Pollock sitting in the back seat?'

'No.'

'Mr Baines,' Walker said, wearily, 'do you follow cricket?'

'Love it. Used to go and see Essex every week. Tracks a bit flat and we've always lacked a decent seam bowler ever since-.'

Walker looked briefly away from the interviewee. Then, he pushed his hand forward so that the coffee went shooting over Baines.

'Bloody hell!'

'Oh, sorry sir.'

'That's bloody hot, that is. Scold me it will.'

'I do beg your pardon.' Walker replied.

'Blimey, you're a right clumsy oaf, you are!'

'Well, here's a word of advice, Mr Baines,' Walker said, leaning over and tapping him sharply on the shoulder. 'Stick to watching cricket, hmm? Just go and sit quietly in the stand and watch the game.'

Baines head nodded mechanically.

'That way you won't be fucking us around. Now one more of these publicity stunts Mr Baines and I'll book you for wasting police time. Got that?'

Baines was already brushing off the spilt coffee and shuffling towards the door, which he found open.

'Well, that's bleeding gratitude for you,' he muttered.

'Oh, we're grateful all right. Here take this,' and Walker lunged out with his large boot narrowly missing the old man's receding rump.

Walker found Stephen Grayson by the coffee machine.

'How'd it go, sir?'

'Grayson, a word in your shell. Next time you have a material witness check him out first will you?'

'No good?'

'He claims he saw the two victims. But get this, he also saw Hanse Cronje, disgraced and late ex-South African cricket captain sitting behind the wheel of a Ford Mondeo.'

'Yeah, he did seem a bit odd.'

'Odd? He lives at the bottom of a cracker barrel. He is several raisons over a standard fruitcake. Now in future, young man, think before you act. Decide if you really want to waste half an hour of my valuable time because the more of my time is wasted, the more you have to make up for it. Got it?'

'No problemo.'

'That means that you're going to go down and check through the gun register again.'

'Again?'

'Again. Meanwhile,' added a tired Walker, 'we're going to run through the facts one more time.'

'Okay.'

Two minutes later, they were both in Walker's office. Grayson perched on the edge of the desk until Walker sent him to get a chair.

'Thomas and Mrs Almond were found dead in Thomas's car,' Stephen began mechanically.

Walker nodded dutifully. He'd had heard it all before, but it still needed to be repeated. Sometimes things just didn't make sense first time round.

'They both died from gunshot wounds to the head,' continued Grayson. 'Certified time of death between three and four. Thomas's prints were found on the gun.'

'And Mrs Almond's.'

'So she handed him the gun. He shot her and then he shot himself.'

'Why would he do that?' Walker enquired.

'Seems they had a thing going at work. Apparently it was common knowledge.'

'Do we know for sure that they were having an affair?' Walker asked.

'You spoke to Gabrielle Simons,' Grayson noted, 'and I spoke to several of their work colleagues. They either suspected it or knew directly.'

'Aren't lawyers supposed to be good at covering up the truth?'

'Yes, but Thomas's secretary said it had been going on for years.'

'So Grayson, do you think they had an argument?'

'Maybe.'

'And he decided he wanted to shut her up. Permanently.'

'Yeah.'

'Then why would she hand him the gun?'

Grayson shrugged.

'Why would he want to kill himself?' Walker added.

'Maybe it was a suicide pact.'

Walker's eyebrows arched momentarily. 'Look,' Walker said. 'these two were middle-aged solicitors in the middle of a long term affair, not star-crossed lovers.'

Stephen stayed silent. He couldn't ever imagine Walker in a relationship.

'It's not frigging Romeo and Juliet, Grayson. It's two hard-nosed lawyers,' Walker said angrily. 'This is all about a legal case that went seriously wrong, nothing more, nothing less. So can we agree on that?'

Grayson nodded. It was best not to argue. John Walker could be a surly individual at the best of times, even at Christmas, when he always missed the office party by pretending to be ill. He was, what was known in the force as a maverick, which meant being an uncommunicative sod and doing whatever the hell he wanted. Now he appeared to be in his element; cut off from the outside world, ploughing his own mud-caked furrow.

Walker looked intensely at Grayson. He knew that behind that unlined face was someone who just didn't understand. Walker didn't do disgruntlement because he *wanted* to; he did it because the world was a violent, unpredictable place and if his colleague's loved one had her brains blown out for no apparent reason, then Walker had every right to feel damned aggrieved.

Grayson tried to change the subject.

'How's David taking all this?'

'Badly. We've had welfare officers going in every day but he just chases them off. Seems he doesn't want to see anyone, just stays indoors with his daughter.'

'Has anyone else spoken to him?'

'Oh, the social workers have tried…'

'No,' Grayson interrupted, 'I mean, anyone from our side of things.'

Walker pursed his lips. 'You mean me?'

'Only to offer support.' Grayson said defensively.

'Not sure on that one. It's early days.'

'Did he know his wife was having an affair?' Grayson asked.

Walker paused, 'No, I suppose not.'

'But you don't know for sure?'

'No, I don't. Look, I'm in charge of this case. If I don't think it's time, then it isn't time. Now, is there anything else?'

Grayson's pained expression was almost pleading. 'No. Maybe some flowers?'

Walker dismissed him. He was getting a little over zealous here. All these young cops were the same, thought Walker, trying to push too hard. Police work was about patience, waiting for the opportunity. Then it was about moving as quickly as possible, before the thing blew up in your face.

Grayson couldn't learn that from a college, he had to gain that knowledge through experience. Yet, Grayson had been right about one thing, Walker knew David Almond better than most. Fifteen years, in fact. That meant he stood a better chance of getting at the truth. Truth had never been at a premium when they worked together, it was more about getting their stories right and covering for each other. Yet, Almond had dug him out of a hole so many times, he at least deserved a visit. Walker knew it wasn't the right time for questioning - it was never the right time for questioning - but, as he stepped into his vehicle and pointed it in the direction, there was no other way.

David Almond lived on a new estate on the fringes of what was left of the Essex countryside. Walker ignored the neat gravel driveways and tended lawns until he reached the house. He took a deep breath and rapped on the door. No response. He leaned back to see the front room window curtain twitch. He waited and wondered if he should knock again or go. After all, it was only three days since the burial. He had seen him at the thanksgiving service and had exchanged a few words afterwards but they were barely adequate. He noticed that David Almond had gripped the hand of his fifteen-year-old daughter throughout the service as if scared that he would lose her too. He was turning on his heels when a muffled noise came from the other side of the door.

'What do you want?'

'David, is that you?'

'What do you want?'

'It's John. I want to talk to you…and I've brought some flowers.'

'Leave them on the doorstep, will you. Thanks.'

'David, please. Open the door, mate.'

Walker really didn't want to push it. The least he could do was take a hint from his friend.

He had reached the end of the path when the latch clattered open and the door swung inwards to reveal Almond standing in his pyjamas.

'Better come in.' Almond called out.

Walker walked quickly over the threshold.

'Jeez, you look rough.'

David Almond was standing motionless with a three-day growth across his chin. His silvery hair stood out like branches of an ash tree.

'What do you want?'

'Just a quick word. I'm not going to stay long.'

'Good.'

'Just wanted to see how you were.' Walker could see all too clearly. Almond's eyes were puffy and reddened, his whole face crumpled like a paper bag. The craggy face had always been a point of conversation in the station, lived in, some said - more like a house full of squatters, thought Walker.

'I'm feeling awful if the truth be known,' Almond said with a scowl, 'go through.'

Walker went through the hall and a young girl ran past him. He only caught a glimpse of her and then heard her feet thumping hard up the carpeted stairs and across the landing.

'Cathy?'

'She doesn't want to see anyone.'

Walker found his way into the lounge and laid the flowers on the table. Then he sat down on the settee. Almond disappeared into the kitchen. Walker heard a door close upstairs. Then Almond walked in, looked around as if he had lost something and went out again. Walker tapped his fingers on the armrest and sighed. This is bloody pointless, he thought. At last, he got up and trailed Almond into the kitchen.

'Look, I'm sorry. It must have been a terrible shock. We haven't spoken since…'

Almond was standing with his back to him, facing the kitchen sink.

'How long do we go back?'

Silence.

'Fifteen years. That's how long. Remember the first day I arrived? The day before the hurricane? You were the first guy I met. You sat me down, got me a coffee and asked me some questions.'

David Almond stood motionless. He would never forget that time. It was the happiest time of his life.

'You gave me some advice. Do you remember what that was?'

Almond's back was hunched and bony. His shoulders and arms moved slightly. There was a sloshing of water and Walker realised that Almond was doing the washing up.

'You told me that if I was taking this job for the money or for career advancement or for some perverse kind of enjoyment I should get out immediately. You said there was only one reason for doing this job and that was out of duty.'

'That was then,' mumbled Almond.

'Yes, it was a long time ago,' admitted Walker, 'and at the time I thought it was all crap. I was dead bolshie, I don't mind admitting that. It seemed that duty was to the establishment and private property and keeping the rest of us in our place. But duty doesn't stop there. It's duty to the community, our families, to ourselves. It's part of everything we do. It's what keeps us going. We all know how awful it gets,' Almond went on, 'Christ, many days I've wondered why I am I doing this job and I sit down in front of a mirror and I look at myself hard. And every time I do, I know it's something deep inside me that keeps me going. Call it a sense of responsibility, a case of unfinished business or duty but I know it doesn't go away. I know it burns just as fiercely inside you as me, I've seen it.'

Almond began shaking his head. 'Not any more, not any more.'

Walker stepped up to Almond and rested his hand lightly on his shoulder. 'You've been through hell. Bloody hell. It must have been the most devastating experience of your life but I do know something else. You'll going to pull through it, mate, don't you worry about that.'

Walker waited for a reaction, but there was only silence.

'I remember when Cathy was born,' he continued. 'We went off to Lasers to wet the baby's head. I was invited to the christening and got off with one of your cousins. Remember? It was a happy time. I actually felt part of your family.'

Almond's head lifted slightly but no words came out.

'Young Cathy is like family to me,' Walker owned up, 'but I'm worried. How is she?'

'Not good,' Almond said flatly. 'She doesn't want to talk to anyone.'

'Do you think she'd see me?'

Finally, David Almond turned to face his companion. 'Not a chance. Look, Cathy and I are going to see this out together. Let's just leave it at that.'

'Sure. Tell me, how are you coping?'

'Oh. Close friends and relatives come around and offer their services. My sister-in-law Carol visits sometimes, preparing meals and keeping the house tidy. She took all Susan's clothes out of the wardrobes and drawers and bundled them into a sack which she handed over to the local charity shop. I couldn't do it myself, just couldn't do it. Now, if you please...'

'Okay, I understand. All the guys down at the station send their regards. We're all truly sorry. Anytime you need some help, just call.'

'I don't need to, you'll be back.'

'Why's that?'

Almond stared at his ex colleague and his eyes opened wide. 'Because the husband is always the prime suspect when his wife dies. Isn't that right, John?'

Walker backed away without replying and stepped quietly down the hallway. He paused only to notice a framed photo of Almond's wife, Susan, lying face up on the table. A thin hairline crack had zigzagged its way across the glass frame.

Friday, 25th October.

The following morning, John Walker was back with his model. Not a six-foot blonde or an Airfix kit of an Avro Bomber but his model of the killing. Into the model came the vital ingredient to any case solving: intuition. It helped glue the whole shaky edifice together. His first leap of intuition was that the murderer was likely to be a first offender, someone squeaky-clean like Thomas - that much he was sure. The action that precipitated the crime, or criminal intent, was always, to Walker's way of thinking, much greyer than the psychologists made out. It was he felt, not so much about one's upbringing or one's immediate environment; it was more a shift in personal circumstances. It was something natural but so intensely disturbing and insoluble that it sent the hapless perpetrator spinning over the edge. It was to Walker's eyes, the Martini Effect, happening anytime, anywhere.

The Martini Effect was so profound and so pervasive that it brought the person face-to-face with his own destiny and the dastardly crime. Maybe that's why he turned the gun on himself - he didn't like what he saw. Yet what kind of motive would create this effect? He turned the page of his scribbling and began writing big broad headings: envy, lust, greed, something akin to the seven deadly sins. It might have appeared a somewhat naïve list of motives considering the so-called complexities of modern day behaviour, yet it often proved surprisingly accurate. People didn't change; it was everything around them that did.

The interview with Baines had set the ball rolling, one fabrication followed by another untruth, a series of observational errors and then a barefaced lie. He was the only one who claimed to have seen anything, the two lovers hand in hand, strolling along, not the behaviour one would expect minutes before a double suicide. Or was it one final macabre dance, one last lingering moment of tenderness before the curtain came down on their lives forever? Then he had seen a Mondeo - he was quite specific about that - occupied by cricketers, not English but South Africans. Not visitors from the grassy meadows of Middle Essex but all the way from the lush Veldt of Southern Africa. If he did see something, it was so wrapped up in untruths it would never pass a legal examiner. Yet maybe there was another, someone out there who saw something but did not realise the significance, someone not fully in contact with those on the island, someone slightly detached.

Down one side of the paper he wrote the clues. It wasn't a very impressive list but it included the car, the murder weapon and the fact that the two persons were suspected lovers. It also included the fact that they were work colleagues, even working together on the same case - the one involving a wealthy property developer called Biggs. Walker also had the file stashed away in the boot of his car. He would come to that later. Walker completed the matrix by matching motives and clues together. He used his famous ranking system: one, most probable; two, a likely; three, a possibility and so on. Then he wrote a number weighting each co-ordinate based on fifteen years experience; lust and lovers got a one (it always did), work and jealousy got a two (depending on their proximity and potency) and so on.

He drained his coffee. People were passing by his window, on their way to the shops. Some of them were probably thinking about the time, others about their shopping requirements, maybe one person was thinking how much they hated someone else. Maybe last night they had been dumped, humiliated, or maybe they had had to put up with a mouthful of abuse or a flail of fists. Maybe they had decided over a period of time, that this person was becoming intensely repellent to them. Perhaps, now they were looking at ways of ridding themselves of this person. He paid his bill. Maybes, suppositions, theories - even his idea of intuition - were great on paper but ultimately had to be placed side by side with the facts. Things always went downhill from then on.

Walker drove the short route to the surgery. He left the radio and tape player off and began to fill his mind with possibilities. Two lovers work in a solicitors on a high profile case. They sign a suicide pact. They drive to a lonely spot on an island and blow their brains out. The Pathologist reported that Mrs Almond had a history of hypertension and a clinical history of palpitations. Traces of cipramil were found in the blood, an anti-depressant. No alcohol or other types of drugs were found. They went to their deaths stone cold sober.

So what was so bad about their lives? Something so rotten that they thought they'd be better off dead?

Walker got to speak to Susan Almond's GP just after her surgery had closed. She had already had the pathologist contact her and was well prepared.

'I've already told him everything,' she said implacably.

'Well I'd appreciate it if you repeated it to me.'

A client's confidentiality no longer applied once the patient was deceased so he could ask away. Fortunately, she was forthcoming and even produced the medical records for him to examine. The doctor's handwriting was no less intelligible than a Chief Superintendent's so he asked for a translation.

'How long had she been receiving treatment?' Walker enquired.

'Several weeks.'

'So what did you prescribe?'

'Initially tricyclics…anti-depressants.'

'Initially?'

'Yes, they take time to take react and can have side effects.'

'Like?'

'Dry mouth, constipation, hormonal upsets.'

'Anything else?'

'A loss of sex drive.'

'So you changed it?'

'Yes, we began to use a faster-acting drug.'

'Which one?'

'Lithium. We used Prozac.'

'So you gave her Prozac?'

'Yes.'

'Sorry, I'm an amateur here. I thought Prozac was dangerous.'

'Only for patients with a history of acute agitation or suicidal tendencies.'

'And Mrs Almond didn't have those?'

'No.'

'What does Prozac actually do?'

'It's used to treat bipolar depression. It works by increasing the serotonin in the brain's synapses. Low levels of serotonin are associated with depression.'

'So you're saying she was clinically depressed.'

'That's correct.'

'So what's the background to Mrs Almond's depression?'

'Oh, I think it's been going on for a long time. It started almost fifteen years ago.'

'Fifteen years?'

'Depression is often triggered by an event. In her case it was just after the birth of her daughter. Clinical depression takes place when the victim is unable to recover from a setback in a reasonable time.'

'I'd say fifteen years was long enough.'

'Sometimes depression is often part of a cycle of disadvantage: unhappy childhood, abuse, loss of esteem.'

'What did she do about it?'

'Oh, she tried various therapeutic remedies: gestalt, group therapy, cognitive behavioural therapy. I suspect they may have had a minor effect on her but none of these would have actually cured her.'

'So you think it's incurable?'

'Often yes. It is likely that her illness affected her child too, who will have experienced the depression first hand.'

Walker thought of Cathy. She must have had a tough time of it, and now she was going through even more pain.

'So, doctor, how does clinical depression manifest itself, apart from going round and topping people?'

The doctor frowned. 'It's usually quite mundane actually: loss of appetite, tiredness, inability to concentrate and make decisions. That kind of thing.'

'And these drugs, do they work?'

'Only in a small proportion of people will people be permanently cured, most others muddle by and accept it.'

'Like Van Gogh and Rembrandt?'

'Possibly.'

Walker rose from his chair, held out a hand and removed it quickly.

'Well, thank you, doctor. I'll be in touch if we need anything more.'

She sighed audibly, 'no doubt you will, inspector, no doubt you will.'

CHAPTER FOUR

Saturday, 26th October.

Cathy was fifteen years old. She was studying for ten GCSE's. They were getting in the way of her social life. At least they had been until her mum's death. It was only a month ago that she been having terrible rows with her mother. It had gone on and on: what time she had to be in by, who she could see, what clothes she could wear, how much TV she could watch, how long she could spend on the phone - everyday a new dispute, new lines of a battleground drawn. Now it had suddenly stopped; now she wasn't having any rows at all - or studying or having a social life.

Some of her friends liked to hang around the nearby park. They would get some drink from the local off-licence and stock up on fags and drugs. Then they would go for it; out of sight of the prying eyes of their parents and people in authority. Grown-ups called it binge drinking but it was just about having a good time. Smoking dope and popping pills was a blast and no different from the behaviour of their parents, judging by the old newsreels of pop festivals.

Next day in school, they would all boast about how 'awesome' and 'mega' it was. She would have liked to have socialised with them. Somehow, it was always the best-looking, most adventurous boys and girls that went to the park, people like Jo and Roz and Andy. They were the hardcore party animals. But she couldn't join them, not with her being the daughter of a police officer - she owed at least some allegiance to her father. Many of the so-called friends taunted her, saying she had a pig for a father but she ignored it all and went her own way, which wasn't anyway in particular, just not the same places as her classmates.

As soon as she woke each morning, she turned over to pick up the photo lying on the bedside table. Each night she turned it down, and each morning she turned it up. It was a little ritual, like a connection, a thread of a relationship no longer alive. She didn't know why this photo, of all of them, was so significant but she figured it must be because it was of her mum at fifteen. She was dressed in a long floral dress, she wore her auburn hair long and she was laughing as she sat on the grass in front of a family picnic in the New Forest. It was a heartfelt, joyous laugh, so infectious and sparkling it cheered her up instantly.

She hoped that she had inherited her mum's looks and her brains too. Right now, with her mock GCSE's looming, she wasn't so sure. She couldn't be bothered with breakfast right now, she just made a coffee and went straight back to her room. There she lay, on the bed, staring at the ceiling, surrounded by all the posters of hunks on beaches. She wasn't sure she knew her mother anymore. She couldn't imagine her having an affair; she couldn't imagine her going to another man when she already had a husband. Sure, some of her friends' parents had split up but they had had rows, fights, and trial separations. How had it happened? Did this other man lure her to a deserted place, force her to comply with his wishes or did she act compliantly, knowing all along what she was doing?

Everyday, when she had come home from school, she had heard her mother telling her about work and how exciting it was. She had mentioned Alan Thomas. Her dad had looked up but had never said a word. She had said how important it was to give young adults a decent start in life. She had said that what she was doing would make it better for the next generation. It felt like she had been on a mission. Was it all lies? Was it a cover for deceit and adultery? Did she put her lover before her husband and daughter or was it just a bit of fun, what Grandma referred to as a bit of slap and tickle? She told Cathy the facts of life when she was eleven and said that it was always up to her to make decisions and follow her head, not her heart. So what was this behaviour, something from the heart or the head? Carol would never know now, she would never be able to ask. All the motherly advice had been cruelly extinguished and all she had left were doubts and a keen, gnawing sense of abandonment that made her sick in the pit of her stomach.

She turned once more to the photo. Her smiling face, her flouncy dress, her innocence. It was the only framed photo left in the house. She had broken the other by throwing it against the wall. It seemed a natural reaction when her dad had told her that he had found her body on a rain swept island with another man. If her mother could be killed then so could something as transitory as a photo of her. At that moment, she had wanted to destroy all recent images of her mother. There were too many lies behind them. Only this photo, as a fifteen-year-old, made Cathy really feel close to her mother, only made her feel that she was from her mother's womb and one and the same.

How would her mother have reacted to this news if she had been in the same situation? How would she, as a slightly toothy, long-legged girl, have dealt with the loss of her own mother? It was true that her own mother, Grandma Birch was still very much alive, but one night, all those years ago, it hadn't seemed possible. She and grandpa had been on a cruise ship touring the Canary Islands when the ship capsized in atrocious storms off the coast of Tenerife. There was no news for two days; it seemed that there was no hope until a message came through to say that they had been picked up by a fishing boat and were exhausted and suffering from hypothermia but were still very much alive.

Some mornings, Cathy woke up and thought her mum was still alive. She had been on the brink of going to rush into her bedroom when she suddenly realised that it was a dream, and that her living morning was in fact a nightmare. That realisation of loss was something that kept coming back; like a knife or dagger repeatedly being inserted, just to make sure. It caught her every time and made her so depressed that she couldn't see why she would want to carry on. Somehow, there didn't seem to be any different between the mental and physical pain, it was all one, covering her everyday, like a shroud.

Sunday, 27th October.

At 3.30 p.m, DI John Walker was sitting on an old oak garden seat. The seat was situated on a patch of grass leading down to a stream that opened into the village pond. The wind had blown itself out and the clouds had passed to reveal a pleasing blue tinge of sky. Mallards padded around him, inquisitive and expectant of food. One waddled to the edge and took off for a paddle across the still waters. A grey heron stood by the side of the pond, the long angular legs of a frog dangling from its yellow bill. It kept dabbing it into the water as if basting it before attempting to swallow it whole. Finally, it jerked back its neck and the frog slithered down its throat.

Walker raised his pint of Ridleys and sipped quietly. He looked up to see a well-built, dark-haired barmaid bringing a plate of seafood salad piled high with potted brown shrimps and freshly baked bread to the next table. He smiled gently and she returned the compliment. He ordered one for himself. On any normal occasion, the situation would have relaxing, satisfying, but this was part of a working weekend, and there was absolutely nothing in his thoughts that offered a trace of serenity.

He removed the papers from his bag. The case file was worryingly thin. Mrs Almond had not been a woman who put herself about. She didn't appear to possess any credit cards, or subscribe to any groups or societies. Her work was her life, a compulsive worker who got in early and left late. Sometimes she worked weekends and never took her full holiday entitlement. It looked like she was trying to catch up, as if the ten years bringing up her daughter had to be clawed back somehow. David Almond and Susan probably passed each other on the stairs as one was coming in while the other was going out. What was the point of being married, he wondered, if you barely saw one another? And then there was the suspected affair, which must have made the atmosphere tense with deceit every time they all sat together round the kitchen dining table. God, marriage could be a living hell.

She was known to be a hard taskmaster, competitive but she always led from the front. There was no doubt that her zeal and devotion to duty had won her friends amongst the senior partners but where had it got her? Walker got the impression that she was still trying to prove herself right up to the day of her death. Maybe insecurity lurked at every corner or maybe there were factions within the firm remaining to be convinced. Could that be jealousy? The fact that she had teamed up with Thomas was perhaps inevitable. They worked together, had common interests, or at least one, work. With a powerful ally such as Thomas, a fast track to the partnership seemed assured. Then they went to Mersey Island and never came back.

He cast an eye over a photo of Mrs Almond. There was a forced smile, hair in a brown bob, a face not unpleasant but not exactly kindly either. He didn't see her as a scheming, manipulative woman; she could have made it to the top on her own, given time. Thomas just provided a leg up if that was the right phase to use. She had grown distant from her husband, moved on, as they euphemistically liked to call it, moved apart more like, apart from her husband, her marriage and her daughter.

As the barmaid brought over the meal, he found his smile had been exhausted. 'Down there please.' He said, ungraciously.

He piled the shrimps on the plate and spread them across a large slice of crusty brown bread. Then he sank his teeth into them and for a moment, his mouth tingled. It was hungry work, tracking down killers. Much of his investigative efforts were carried out before, during or after a hearty meal as if the nutritious effect of the wholesome shellfish food actually nourished his mind. He ordered another pint. Beer helped too - or so he'd heard - it loosened the senses and helped to speculate possibilities without the constraints of probabilities. He began throwing some crumbs in the general direction of the ducks when the phone piped its shrill tones.

'Walker.'

It was Stephen Grayson.

'Yes, it's the complete list.'

'Five stock issues of Smith and Wesson .38 over the last five months,' repeated Walker.

'Correct.'

Five issues was just about right. S & W's weren't very popular with the station. They were called 'girlie guns' They were also expensive and American. Most officers preferred a semi-automatic. However, sometimes they were issued as 'top-ups' when a suspect was armed and police had to force an entry. In the early days, officers would also issue them for some off-duty target practice or just as likely to stitch up a suspect but of course, that never happened now.

'How many returns?' Walker asked.

'Four.'

'Who did the guns go to?'

'I've got a list here.'

'Read it out, will you?'

There was a pronounced pause.

'Grayson?'

'Er, no problemo,' Grayson said in his *faux-naif* accent.

'Give me the names.'

'Jones, Clarke, Jones, Phillips and…'

'I'm waiting.'

'DI Almond.' Grayson said, slowly.

'When was this?'

'October, 11th.'

'Five days before the killing,' Walker noted, just in case Grayson hadn't checked. 'When was it returned?'

Another pause.

'When was it returned?'

'Sir, it's still open.'

Walker switched the phone off, closed the lid and slid it into his jacket. Thankfully, Grayson had done his job - even if he had moaned about working on a Sunday. It was the first time DI Walker had worked with PC Grayson. Worked that is, on a case. He'd shared a beer with him and attended general training courses together but this was different. He didn't know if Grayson was the right man at all. After all, he had been Almond's stooge, a flunkey who jumped to attention and would have gone through flaming hoops if DI Almond had told him to.

This was a decent case involving two bodies, a high profile police officer and an island community not used to finding dead bodies on their doorstep. Solving it would involve discretion, thorough and painstaking attention to detail and the ability to problem solve. Notwithstanding an aptitude for thinking laterally or as his superiors referred to it, 'thinking outside the box'.

He polished off his seafood salad in one mouthful and then ordered another pint. Slowly, he began removing the other files from his case - the ones he had obtained himself. He had looked at them repeatedly in the last two days, like a stash of illicit cargo. He had flicked through the papers, checked the information and made sure he had it right in his mind. He removed the police folder and began to unwrap them from their original buff folders, tied in a bow with pink ribbon. The pink made them seem innocent, frivolous, playful even, yet that was lawyers all over; presenting a thin veneer of light heartedness to hide their dark and grisly secrets.

The two files were headed up 'Biggs & Co - Mersey Island', and 'Biggs & Co - Sundry matters '. Mersey Island went back several years and contained a painstaking account of the trials and tribulations involved in planning consent. There were reports, surveys, letters, copies of articles and accounts estimated total costs. Throughout the acrimonious project were Ridgely's bills, ten thousand here, another fifteen there, all neatly itemised and supported by time and cost summaries, yet incredibly expensive for glorified paper shuffling. In the last couple of months, these bills had been increasingly regularly suggesting that Biggs had upped the stakes and was getting desperate. In fact, the last bill showed a monthly account due of over forty-thousand pounds. Once more, Walker realised he was in the wrong job.

Most of the correspondence was technical; discussing the proposals and changing them to accommodate the concerns of others: boundaries, rights of way, wildlife, soil contamination, infrastructure, water tables, flooding, noise and road safety were just some of the issues. Every time one matter was dealt with, three more appeared, fuelled no doubt by media and activist types. One of the more innovative proposals suggested building an apartment complex on the shore with pontoons connecting houses built on stilts, as they did in Amazonia and the Mekong Delta. The only difference being that Biggs was expecting people to shell out a cool quarter of a million each for a bunch of coastal shacks.

Apart from the bills and some old letters from the practice headed up Baines, Ridgely, Turner and Fowler there was very little written documentation supporting the relationship between Ridgely's and Biggs's, except one letter. It was dated the first week of October, two weeks before the bodies were found. It was a letter signed by Alan Thomas. John Walker knew it off-by-heart.

Dear Mr Biggs,

In view of the deteriorating situation regarding our business relationship, I have to advise you most strongly that we are seriously considering our position. Many of the issues you have brought to my attention and my colleague Ms Almond have been discussed before ad nauseum and we have always striven to give you the best of our professional advice in a polite, speedy and efficient manner. However, if we experience any further behaviour from you that undermines our position and leads to distress amongst our esteemed members of staff then we will not hesitate to take appropriate action.

Yours faithfully,

Alan Thomas

It wasn't a statement of guilt, it wasn't even admissible evidence, in view of the fact that he had stolen it from a firm of lawyers, but it was a clue. Not the smoking gun type of clue but the slightest thread of a strand that if fully unravelled might just lead to the reason why Biggs might have wanted to kill them or why they might have taken their own lives. He particularly liked 'behaviour that leads to distress' it suggested verbal abuse, harassment but it could also have meant acting unprofessionally, avoiding payment, playing one firm of lawyers against another or simply being an asshole. It was classic lawyerspeak. Walker knew that disagreements and disputes happened all the time but multiplied sixty million times and it could become a life-threatening situation. If Almond and Thomas had bungled, then their lives would have been made hell by someone like Biggs, who just did not tolerate failure.

He turned to the other file; the one marked 'Sundry Matters'.

He always associated sundry with laundry as if it was all the stuff pushed into one place that needed cleaning. It was where all the messy, grubby, smelly things ended up; just the place, in fact, to find motives for dirty deeds. Maybe the association wasn't so far off whack. At the back of the file, Walker found some standing data on the client: age, education, qualifications (none except for an OND in building construction), interests (philately, horse racing), relationships (he had been never married but he had once had a relationship with a man and was described as bisexual) and wealth (based on the Rich List, he was ranked number 436 in the UK and most of it was invested in property and land stretching from Mersey Island to Jersey Island). Throughout, there was nothing to suggest a criminal background, which tallied with Walker's own check on police records.

There were photos of Biggs at school, at work and at play, rarely smiling, never caught unawares, a steely gaze as if he were posing for a sculptor, even in his school uniform of blue cap, blazer and shorts. Where had this air of seriousness arisen? Parents dead. Mother a loving housewife, father a builder. Only child. At the age of eight, he had a paper round, by nine, he was helping out on a vegetable stall in Mile End and doing car cleaning jobs. At twelve, he was selling car accessories like go-faster stripes, tip-up seats and in-car radio systems. At fourteen, he was buying up scrap cars and customising them for others who lived in his council block. One year later, he bought four greyhounds and won two thousand pounds in one night at Haringey racetrack. By the time he was sixteen, he had left school, hitchhiked across Europe, travelled through Iran, Pakistan and Afghanistan disguised as a journalist and then spent two years in Poona, India with the Orange People. When he returned, he discovered his parents had died in an accident.

It didn't stop there. He enrolled at the local technical college to study business. He dropped out three months later. One day, walking past a house renovation, he stopped to talk to the builders. They told him they had gone private. They would be making thirty grand on this one house. Not bad, for four months work. From then on, Joe Biggs became obsessed with property.

When he was just turned twenty-one he began renting out property. He met a stunning young woman and let her move in with him. She completely took his attention for six months. For the first and only time in his life, he let his heart rule. They went into business together. He later discovered she was using information to buy flats for another organisation. He dropped her immediately. That was the last time he had a relationship with a woman.

Five years later, he began dating young men, mostly English but also a Swede, called Thomas from Gothenburg, Eastern Europeans, an American from the Deep South named Jake, a Thai taxi driver and an African witch doctor from Mali. Ten years later, all his relationships fizzled out, leaving Mr Biggs, a man of his own persuasion. At least, that's what the file said.

Slowly, Walker's scepticism with the information he had in front of him was beginning to evaporate. Everything in the file was indexed, cross-referenced and given provenance by providing detailed source references including dates of interviews and photos. It was inclusive; no gaps, everything neatly placed in chronological order, as if it were Biggs's own personal diary. Walker was left in no doubt that Ridgely's were as ruthless and thorough as their client, obtaining each and every morsel of information as part of a package; back-up in the event of the client-lawyer relationship going awry. And it had. Which left one immovable object against the irresistible tide of Biggs - a clash of Titans. With both sides so dogmatic and entrenched, something was bound to snap.

Walker closed the file and ordered another pint. This Biggs character didn't fit into his nice identikit. He was an enigma: rich but unhappy, a man of the world but unsophisticated, part of the establishment but isolated, eligible but single, envied by many but hated by more. Such contradictions could lead to confusion, dislocation and a brooding sense of resentment. Yet, was his ruthless streak capable of making him so determined that nothing would stand in his way, least of all a couple of lawyers? In short, could it lead to murder?

Walker had met hundreds of self-made men like Biggs; operating in a similar world of consultants, graduates, old school ties, fighting that indefinable stench of privilege. They too ran their businesses as a crusade to show the rest of society that they were just as good, if not better. They saw themselves as self-styled St George's puncturing egos, lancing pomposity and spearing the self-inflated opinions of the ruling classes. But so what? They didn't go round taking folks who got in their way to a remote spot and blasting them full of lead, so why the hell should Biggs?

The late lunch, the phone call to Grayson and the reviewing of stolen files were just three reasons why John Walker was sitting in a pub. The fourth reason he was sitting in a pub garden on a late Sunday afternoon was because he needed some Dutch courage - lots of it. He hadn't done this for ages, not houses anyway. He had already consumed five pints of Ridleys bitter in the last two hours and was feeling slightly woozy. Dutch courage wasn't all it was cracked up to be.

The final reason he was sitting in a pub garden in the middle of autumn, was that he was overlooking a view of a house. Not just any house, but Alan Thomas's. The pub garden was the only way of seeing it without actually going down the winding, leafy road. He could see that the curtains were closed. Dusk was settling in. There were no lights on.

He took the empty plate to the bar, stashed his files in the car and shoved a pair of bolt cutters inside his jacket. Then he headed down the road on foot. He stopped to empty his bladder by the roadside and inadvertently splashed his boots. Shaking himself down, he kept walking until he reached a metal gate where a sign announced: Private Road. Locals referred to it more tellingly as 'Millionaires Row'. Every few yards were speed humps and a speed restriction of 5 mph and, if anyone doubted its exclusivity, another sign stated that the inhabitants employed their own private security firm.

Most houses in the road were mock, built during that period in the sixties when everyone wanted to 'make a statement'. There were statements of half-timbered, mock Tudor dwellings, ersatz Georgian stucco ornamentation, and faux Regency. Some had plundered architectural styles further afield: Tuscan villas, German Schloss's and Spanish-style haciendas complete with adobe walls and paddocks for their horses. Another had built a futuristic home, with cube-like rooms fronted with enormous circular windows and assembled beneath glass sloping roofs. It all felt vulgar to Walker's puritanical tastes, but he couldn't help making a low, admiring whistle when he reached 15, Melstone Court, Thomas's residence.

Here was a large rambling Victorian residence with the ashen limbs of wisteria and honeysuckle trailing across the walls and framing the leaded windows and entrance porch. The dusty walls and peeling ochre paint glowed faintly in the failing sunlight. Walker glanced at his watch, four-thirty, on a Sunday, a quiet time, he thought. He unhinged the front gate and walked up the curved gravel driveway, peering left and right across the broad sweep of lawns and cultivated beds and towering conifers. He noticed that the flowerbeds had been cleared, dug over and raked methodically, only the herbaceous borders remained untouched. He made his way briskly along the block-paved pathway until the owner's house came fully into view.

At this stage, John Walker should have felt his inside pocket and located his search warrant. That would have enabled him to conduct a thorough and official search. But search warrants took time. There was endless paperwork to complete and signatures to obtain. Normally, someone else got their first: a relative worried that there might be incriminating evidence or a greedy in-law getting first go at the family silver. He had even experienced thieves ransacking a place while a search warrant lay on his senior's desk, awaiting action. No, search warrants were for losers.

Suddenly a familiar noise: loud, resonant and excitable. It made Walker stop in his tracks. It came from the other side of the house, from behind the metal side gate. He wasn't an expert but he surmised it emanated from a deep, cavernous canine mouth, like a Great Dane or a Bullmastiff - certainly nothing as commonplace as a Rottweiler. He moved forward cautiously. The bark became even more agitated and then stopped abruptly. Had his handler intervened? Walker kept walking towards the gate, almost goading the dog into action. The noise turned into a low menacing growl and Walker could sense its wild-eyed look, with its gnarling incisors engaged in a slavering mouth - definitely not a poodle. As he finally reached the side gate, he heard the scraping sounds of paws and saw the outward bow of the gate as it buckled against the beastly force.

There were no cars in the driveway and the triple-garage doors were closed - Sunday afternoon indolence. No one appeared - maybe the neighbours were used to the sound of guard dogs. The dog was between Walker and the back garden. A rear entry would be much favoured but dogs didn't obey the laws of nature. They attacked humans for no apparent reason, not for food, not for survival, not even for revenge. Dogs defied human odds, they ignored the size and strength of their opponent, and they even ignored their desire for self-preservation. Dogs didn't even conform to any kind of human ethical code that Walker knew; they simply attacked people because they were there. There were in short, inhuman.

Walker stayed rooted to the spot. He felt his legs trembling and his heart pounding - his bodily presence all too visible to a beast that could smell the slightest whiff of fear. Somehow, he needed to get inside.

He walked around to the front door and rapped hard. No reply. He stepped back and looked up. A red box alarm protruded from under the eves and a wire ran across the snowcemed wall and down one side. Just underneath was the CCTV camera, pointing down at the door, its red light winking knowingly. It whirred into activity and moved mechanically outwards to take in fully his standing position. He was tempted to raise a smile but that would have been pushing it. The lens opened and he could sense the operator at the other end, almost peering through the screen. On one side of the wall was a large bay window. One of the curtains fluttered momentarily in a fleeting breeze. That's absent-minded, thought Walker, leaving a window open but then no sane individual would contemplate shinning up a twenty foot rusting drainpipe and then traversing across bare wall before attempting to perch on a one inch crumbling window ledge in full glare of the security camera.

Walker ignored the notion that he might be crazy and, in the time it took for the eye of the camera to rotate 180°s, he hauled himself up to the porch. Then he levered himself across, snatching branches of clinging vine like a poor man's Tarzan and then crazily, the electric wire. Finally balancing on the ledge, he slid his hand through the window gap and lifted the latch from the inside. He pushed in and, moving aside ornaments and various knick-knacks, landed nimbly on the bedroom floor.

He could feel all his nerves steady. He was inside the house. He could take his time. Then something strange happened. As he cast a fleeting glance to where he had just been, as if to elicit some sense of self-satisfaction, like a golfer playing back a shout in his mind, he suddenly saw two men walking away from the house. He only got a glance of one balding head and the shoulders of another man before they both disappeared from view down the private road. He thought of following them, but they could have been anyone, so he closed the window and moved into the centre of the room.

Next to him was a dresser and a large four-poster bed. The bed was empty but made. Around the bed were clothes and photos. He was just about to open the drawers when an ear-piercing screech rent the air. It drowned the noise of the dog and briefly threw him. Instinctively he took a pillow and covered his ears. Then he leapt across the room as quickly as he could. The loud electronic rasp heckled his progress but he leaned out of the window and, with his pair of bolt clippers, he snapped the CCTV wire once and for all.

He didn't have much time, he didn't have *any* time. The guard would be on-site in minutes and thumping his clumsy way up the winding staircase to arrest him. One swift look around and Walker got his bearings: either side were two more bedrooms with en-suite shower, toilet and gold-plated bidet. Yuck! At the far end, a games room including mini-gym and slate-based snooker table - that must have taken some lifting. Finally, to the left, overlooking a back garden, with allotment and obligatory shed, was the study...always the study.

The room had that unmistakeable musty tang of seasoned oak, thickened by the cloying taste of dust; millions of motes, elevated by the sudden draft. The room was square but along the length of one side ran a large library that gave the room a narrow and claustrophobic feel. In the massed ranks of reading material Walker noticed how neatly ordered they were and filed with almost military precision. X before Y and after W. His finger ran a passage along their spines, collecting a film of dust and jettisoning more. He thought he heard the door click downstairs. There was not a moment to lose.

He rushed to the desk drawer. It was locked. He stood back. It looked secure but not impregnable - not against brute force. He crunched the wooden drawer hard with his heel as brawn overcame brain. The panel splintered, yielding a thin slither of space, space enough for Walker's bony hand to enter. He rolled up his sleeve and pushed his hand inside. There were papery objects, writing implements and items of stationery. His trembling fingers fluttered over documents and books. What to take, what to leave? Walker felt a prickle of fear. The steps were echoing across the marble hallway downstairs. He decided to take everything he could, yanking them out from their resting place and stuffing them deep into the pockets of his overcoat.

Walker turned and made towards the door. Beyond the door, he could hear a shuffling noise and the sounds of a man whispering. At least two, he thought. The same two? Possibly, or maybe two more? This was getting to be a popular place. The only exit route was the garden. He pushed open the window and stepped out onto the roof. The garden spun dizzily below. His feet and hands scraped along the loose clay tiles, trying to gain purchase. His backside provided a broader platform and he bum slid his way to the edge of the roof before grabbing the drainpipe with both hands. He found himself dangling over the edge. He was hanging helplessly, as the ground swayed over twenty feet below. He felt frozen to the spot. Then he heard the screech of metal scraping. The piping was coming away from its rusty moorings.

This is it, he thought, prepare for broken bones. But the pipes simply buckled and bended and lowered him, almost theatrically, like a descending high wire artiste, until he was inches from the ground. Momentarily he stopped to scan the horizon. Garages and outhouses blocked his view on either side. At the back, rearing up, was the safety of the rear fence.

Then he heard it, scuttling round from the side and into his path - a Giant Schnauzer. Peppery, mange-ridden coat, whiskered muzzle and a gaping mouth - not a dog to befriend. Its feet almost gave way as it righted its taut body. Walker could see its wild eyes now, glinting with excitement. Then it attacked, like a cat; agile, quick with its powerful head surging towards him. Walker turned and ran towards the fence, bursting into a sprint. He could feel its stale breath and sense its jowls snapping wildly behind him. Then with one final effort, he launched himself against the fence and hurled himself over into the open road beyond and safety.

CHAPTER FIVE

Walker took the remainder of the weekend off. He had a headache, his clothes were ruined and he had a bulging case of booty to plough through. It wasn't the greatest haul of his career - he had had much better when he worked in Special Branch (those guys really knew how to vacuum up a house - another reason he'd been called Hoover) but he was satisfied. David Almond would also have been pleased; in fact he didn't think it beyond the realms of fantasy that one of those voices might have been David himself, visiting the home of his dead wife's paramour. Strange how they often thought along same lines: the end justifies the means being a common refrain.

Walker's time with Almond was part of a halcyon time when policemen were respected and even feared. Yes, they stretched their areas of authority to the limits or 'worked outside the box' but it was always part of a plan and very rarely affected innocent people. Nowadays, the force always split up pairs; it created cliques and stifled interaction. Pairs were to be resisted. Now it was all about being part of a team: black, white, brown, male, female, short, fat, tall, disabled, yes, they even had a one armed WPC (it provided a nice symmetrical balance when facing one-armed bandits) mothers, over-fifties and weedy graduates (who were lousy at their job but wrote nice reports). Teams had to have multi-dimensional skills and so everyone became part of this team ethic (He knew what sort of person he'd want in a raid on a gang of thugs). Teams invariably under-performed, members got lazy and accepted each other's faults but that was okay, because it was all a team effort. Of course, it was all horse shit. Walker knew it, his bosses knew it and so did the poor saps put in the firing line, but the force had to do something, or be seen to do something. Catching criminals was no longer the main thrust of the work, it was about prevention, rehabilitation, being part of a team and 'engaging' with the community. Now he had to work with PC Grayson in a team that had done nothing but tread water for the best part of two years.

Monday, 28th October.

The dusty dial of the clock on the uniformly grey wall indicated 7:45 a.m., ridiculously early for some, but not for John Walker at Chelmsford

Constabulary. He had already been in one hour, on account of being unable to sleep. The workloads were getting crazy; having shifted from taxing, to onerous and now plain ridiculous. The only way to deal with it was to get all paperwork completed before anyone arrived, especially if you didn't want anyone to see what you were doing. One report was giving him problems. He had only read through it once but it had effectively ruined his day. It incorporated the comments of Chief Superintendent Jones, the force's very own Perfect Storm.

It was a summary of the last case, a stake out of some drug dealers and that led to arrests and several prosecutions. Not a literary masterpiece but accurate, timely and to the point. He thought he'd done a good job but in one paragraph Jones had drawn a red crayon across the text and added 'what about the big picture?' That was rich, thought Walker, coming from someone like Jones. Here was a man so petty and small-minded he wouldn't recognise his own mother if she jumped up and bit his arse. He could initiate clear desk policies throughout the whole of Essex Constabulary but he couldn't do anything about rocketing juvenile crime. Such hypocrisy would have made Walker furious if the man hadn't added as a final contemptuous comment on page eight of the report that there were 'too many split infinitives'.

Jones was the boss and Walker was an employee: fact one. Walker was there to serve and Jones was there to serve it up: fact two. Jones could say and do just what the hell he wanted: fact three. Yet, despite all this power and supremacy, that wasn't enough. He had to try and humiliate one of his senior officers by talking about split infinities. Well, if they were so split, thought John Walker, then why the fuck didn't he just join them up?

Walker threw the report across the desk and stormed along the passage. He went past the staff room and was surprised to see Grayson in so early.

'What the hell are you doing here?'

'Couldn't sleep. Got a lot of things to do today,' Grayson said, putting down a greasy burger.

'Glad to hear it,' Walker said, 'what the…?'

'It's a jumbo breakfast burger,' Grayson said.

Walker plonked himself next to Grayson and leaned uncomfortably towards him. Grayson began licking his fingers of sesame seeds. Then he belched, wiped his nose with the back of his hand, keeled onto one buttock and finally blew off.

Walker turned away in disgust. 'Grayson!'

'Whaatt?' Grayson replied, smirking like a schoolboy.

'You know what.'

'I don't.'

'Your chronic flatulence, that's what.'

'It wasn't me,' Grayson pleaded.

Walker winced. Sometimes Grayson was capable of the most pathetic and infantile responses. 'Don't try and kid me.'

Through a mouthful of food Grayson spluttered, 'David Almond always said, 'better out than in.'

'Not in your case, Grayson.'

'He also said it was important to express yourself.'

'That's the biggest crock of shit I've ever heard.'

Grayson picked up the remaining piece of burger and crammed his mouth with greasy meat and bread.

'You know something, Grayson?'

'What?'

'I don't bloody care what he said. Now, swallow that processed garbage, wipe your mouth properly with a handkerchief and tell me all about Alan Thomas.'

'Clean as a whistle,' Grayson said at last, finally working his teeth free of gunk.

'Interesting…so what's this?'

Walker opened his pocket and spilled his catch onto the table. The bullet cartridges rolled along the table and then clanked onto the floor.

Grayson looked dumbfounded. 'So he did have a gun? Where did you get these?'

'Never you mind.'

'Look sir, I checked the car. Honest.'

'The house?'

'I just did a routine check to make sure it was secure.'

'So why didn't you use your search warrant?'

'Haven't got it yet, sir.'

'Could have warned me about the dog.'

'What? You? That big softy?'

'Hmm.'

'I gave it a big, fat juicy bone from the butchers,' Grayson said. 'Like a pussycat he was. Sorry sir, about the bullets.'

'Relax and listen hard. If you're going to be part of my team, you need to be thorough. None of this, yeah I've done it, bullshit. Thorough means that when you get a search warrant you check everything from the bottom of the owner's laundry basket to the back of the water closet.'

'No problemo.'

Walker began picking up the bullets and putting them back in his jacket. 'Oh well, now I'm going to destroy this little discovery because, even if they were from a Smith and Wesson, everyone, from Thomas's second cousin once removed to the estate agents will have crawled over his house now that he's dead.'

'Sorry.'

'Stop saying sorry.'

'Right.'

Walker peered across Grayson's desk and saw some unopened mail.

'Don't you open your mail?'

'Yes.'

Walker picked out a large A4 envelope and held it limply aloft. 'What about this one?'

'Not yet.'

Walker tore open the envelope. 'Aha!' exclaimed Walker. 'The famous search warrant. The one you haven't got! It's postmarked five days ago, posted first class. Look, I'm no Sherlock Holmes, but even Mrs Hudson would know that this has been on your desk for three days.'

Grayson sighed. 'I've been busy with all these computer searches.'

'Yes of course, Grayson; busy, busy, busy. We don't want to try doing two things at once do we? Might get confused. Hmm? Now, I know it's Monday morning but as soon as young Goldilocks gets here, you can both renew your friendship with that lovely canine.' Walker said, slapping the warrant around Grayson's face. 'Oh and use the front door, the drainpipe's a bit iffy.'

Two hours later, Grayson headed out of the office clutching the warrant – the one that was pointless anyway, because no one was going to ask for it. He stormed down the corridor. God, Walker could be a smug bastard. He never told anyone what he was thinking, yet he expected his underlings to explain everything. No wonder the Super didn't rate him. At least with David Almond, you knew where you stood. He could share a joke and horse around but when it had got serious, Almond had always delivered. That's what made him a good cop. Everyone thought so, even the chief. David Almond was dependable, generous and helpful; this bloke was just a miserable son-of-a-bitch.

'Come on. We've got a conduct a search.' Grayson said, as Officer Parker was just about to take her coat off. 'Pronto.'

'Now?'

'Yes, now.'

'Can't I even grab a coffee?'

'Okay, I'll see you downstairs.'

'My, we're dynamic today,' she said as she clambered into the passenger seat and the car pulled away.

'Monday's are always busy,' was all Grayson said as he drove the squad car towards Alan Thomas's three-bedroomed detached house on the outskirts of town.

'So this Alan Thomas. What about the CRO?' Parker asked.

'You're familiar with this, are you?' Grayson challenged.

'Not really, just thought I'd ask,' she said.

'Actually, he's clean, no record at all.'

'Think Thomas killed Susan Almond?' Parker asked.

'Maybe, maybe not.'

'I do.'

Grayson drove the car into the private road and parked outside the house.

'Come on,' he said, 'let's go to work. Grayson pacified the dog with more food and pushed open the front door.

'We have to be thorough,' he said in the hallway, 'that means we're looking for anything and everything that might tell us more than we already know. Got that?'

Parker made a mock salute.

Grayson outranked Officer Amy Parker so he sent her to all parts of the house on the top floor while he snooped around in the study. They found nothing. Parker went in every room, every storage cupboard, every drawer and handled every article of clothing and daily object. Nothing questionable, not even valentine cards or love letters. Nothing to connect him to Susan Almond or indict him for murder.

'What do we have?' he asked Parker as the red-faced cadet reappeared after twenty minutes.

'Nothing,' replied Parker. 'No diary list of call girls or sauna houses. No incriminating piles of pornographic material, no dubious images on his PC. No trapdoor leading to a chamber of torture replete with leather thongs, whips and rubber bondage trousers. Nothing.'

'You sound disappointed?' Grayson suggested.

'Of course I'm disappointed,' she said, 'a dash of kinky sex always adds a *frisson* to any murder enquiry.'

Stephen Grayson would have been happy with any type of sex. Maybe she wasn't quite as innocent as he thought. At first, he had taken her for an old-fashioned softy, inclined to curl up her long legs at night on the sofa and fantasise about the dashing Count Vronsky of her dreams. Now, he was changing his views by the minute.

Parker had been with the Force for only six months. Before that, she had been working on the cruise liners. It wasn't all moonlit nights, boxes of praline chocolates waiting in the cabin, red roses draped across the bed. It was people being sick, long, hard working hours, never being able to relax fully. Not that she ever regretted it; she improved her Spanish and German, sailed through Panama, Suez and even went to the Galapagos, met hundreds of funny, sad, interesting people, got new found confidence, improved her dancing and acting skills (even if the ship's entertainment was only slightly superior to Clacton Hippodrome on a Monday night) and learnt to deal with bolshie people.

Firm but reasonable, that was her manner. Firm; like shouting and using self defence if the male passengers got out of hand (and most of them did at one point in time) and reasonable; treating everyone with honest scepticism until they proved they were for real; (half the single people on board adopted an alias). People skills became her strongest suit and when she later returned to the

UK (it could have been anywhere - she had loads of offers to go and live with people from as far away as Orange County, California and the swamplands of Georgia to a studio on West side New York), looking for work proved to be a breeze. Now she had ended up with Stevie Wonder for company.

'Did you check the garden? *Inside* the shed?' Grayson asked.

'No.'

'Off you go,' Grayson said insistently and Parker disappeared in a huff.

Fifteen minutes later, Grayson had finished going through all the papers. It was all academic stuff, couched in legal jargon, work-related and deathly boring. Alan Thomas really had been dull as ditchwater. Grayson called out to Parker. No reply. Again, this time much louder. He stepped along the hallway, through a deserted kitchen.

'Amy?'

Silence.

He pushed open the door into the conservatory. Light flooded in. He could see the garden and a pathway snaking away through the overgrown lawn but no sign of outside movement. The door was unlocked and he walked down the cobbled path towards the shed. 'Amy!' Still no response. Corrosive doubts began to seep into his mind. Why did he let her go off like that, without checking first? What if the house wasn't deserted at all? Walker had warned him about uninvited guests. What if Alan Thomas had set a fiendish trap, one last deathly secret? God! He had pulled rank too readily. The first time he had had someone junior in rank and he had abused his position. She was just a kid! 'Amy!' The shed door was closed. He tried to peer through the glass but all the windows were covered in grime. He tugged at the door. It wobbled. He tugged once more and it came away. There was an ominous creak. Inside, the shed was black as pitch, cold and musty and there was a tang of earthy manure. He went deeper in, groping his way into the darkness.

'Waaaggghhh!'

'Jesus!'

A ghastly face came towards him out of the musty gloom. He turned and clattered his way out, knocking over a mess of pointy rakes, spades and plastic flowerpots. He clutched the door frantically and spun himself out before lurching onto the grass. He lay prostrate, catching his breath when he heard a familiar voice: 'Only me.'

Parker came out, holding a Mexican death mask in one hand. 'What do you think?' she laughed. 'Isn't it great? Found it in the shed. Think it makes me look like a terrorist?'

'More like a tourist.'

'Hah! Got me in one!' Then she began dancing round the garden with it.

'Cut that out!' Grayson said, as he clambered up, annoyed and relived in equal measures.

'Whooo! Stephen Grayson, you are never going to escape! You are going to die in this garden! There is a curse! Whooo!'

'Put it down, you stupid tart,' Grayson insisted.

Parker removed the mask and followed Grayson further down the garden, sidling up to him. A half-empty wheelbarrow lay tilted on the stony path, waiting for its final delivery to the refuse heap. A compost bag had been ripped open waiting to mulch the ground surrounding the roses. 'Good fun, isn't it, going into someone's house?'

'Dunno, it's just a job,' Grayson replied, trying to recover his composure.

'Job? Phwwoar! Tell me another job where you can break into a stranger's place and do what you like, say what you like and take what you like?'

'On a cruise liner.'

'Okay, apart from that.'

'Granted we are given a licence to act within broad responsibilities,' Grayson said slowly, 'but haven't you learnt anything from this experience?'

'Learnt? What, that you're easy to spook?'

'To do with Thomas.'

Parker struggled with the question. 'I suppose,' she replied, tapping her lips with the tips of her fingers, 'I've learnt that he isn't just a stiff with blood and bits of flesh hanging off him.'

'True.'

'He lived alone, a workaholic.'

'Correct.'

'Staid, middle-class parents, deceased, a few boring old fart college chums and the neighbours who, behind their genteel exteriors, probably bonked each other's brains out after a couple of G&T's.'

'Ahem. Anything else, Parker?'

'He spent half his time trying to make money and the rest of it indulging himself on expensive fripperies like Georgian furniture and chintzy foreign porcelain.'

'So you don't appreciate the Sheraton and Meissen?'

'Complete pants but I'd settle for the Hopper originals,' she added, referring to some bleak American cityscapes.

'Okay, so what do you think of him?' Grayson asked.

'He was a jerk.'

'Yes, but what was he like?'

'Spent all his time whacking off while ignoring the basic principle of life.'

'Which is?'

'To enjoy yourself!' she exclaimed.

'Yeah, like we all can.'

'Everyone has their own choice, Stevie Wonder, oh, and I've also noticed this…' she dragged him by the arm to another part of the garden, '…See?'

Grayson popped his head into the greenhouse. Many of the garden plants had been brought under glass, all neatly laid out, labelled and dated, all protected against the winter.'

'What does that mean?' Grayson asked.

'You're the expert. You tell me.'

Grayson scowled. 'It means he liked to keep everything neat and well-ordered. Not the sort of behaviour of one planning to die or kill someone else.'

'Exactly, Alan Thomas was so stiffly conventional, his arse creaked.' Parker announced.

'Don't think you're entering into the spirit of this, Parker.'

'Call me Amy.'

'Amy, it's like you're not taking this seriously.'

'He obviously did it.'

'DI Almond always warned me not to take everything at face value.'

'Did he? Including women?'

'Especially women.'

'So, do *you* think he killed her?' Parker asked.

'Not for me to say. A life can change very quickly,' Grayson added earnestly. 'All it takes is something or someone to flick a switch and a perfectly sensible, orderly person turns into a killer.'

'Yeah right,' Parker replied, 'just by putting on this mask. Whooo!'

They made their way out of the front door and closed it behind them. The one thing Grayson and Parker hadn't noticed, and couldn't have, was that two men had slipped away from the house while they were on their way back to Thomas's house. The two men had earlier blundered around in the darkened rooms looking for clues. Then when Walker had arrived, they had panicked and left until they spotted the police officer disappearing over a fence. Once Walker had left, they had gone straight to the master bedroom and found what they were looking for. Then they had flown the coop just as Grayson and Parker had arrived.

Grayson and Parker rolled back wearily into the office around midday. Grayson went into Walker's office. There was an empty desk and papers scattered all over. Doesn't practice what he preaches, Grayson muttered. Seems it's okay for him to go off and not tell anybody. He returned to his desk and began writing up his notes, while Parker went off for her afternoon training session.

Tuesday, 29th October.

Next morning, a cool, breezy Tuesday, Stephen Grayson still couldn't find Walker. But he, like everyone else, knew where he was. Tuesday was fish day which meant Walker would be at his local fishmonger. It was the big day of the week when the largest catches arrived. Many came up from Cornwall or were flown down overnight from Peterhead. Walker always concocted some pretence of investigating petty thefts in the high street but that excuse had been going on for months. In fact, the only thing Walker ever caught was the sight of a collection of freshly-caught shellfish glistening in their ice trays.

Walker strode into the shop entrance, wallet primed at the ready.

Ah, Mr Walker!' the fishmonger said. 'How are we today, sir?'

'Capital.'

'Excellent.'

Walker joined the queue of shoppers, tapping his feet, as the fishmonger worked the punters, shouting out prices and best offers.

'Sea bass, three for a pound! Fresh Brancaster mussels, only two pounds a pound! Come on ladies and gents, how about a nice monkfish?'

Grayson crept up behind him.

'Sir, sir?

Walker turned around.

'Grayson?'

'Thought I'd find you here.'

'What the hell do you want?'

'Just wanted to update you on the search.'

'Here? Now? I'm busy investigating some shop thefts.'

'Incognito, are we?'

'No Grayson, just keeping my eyes peeled.'

'I just thought I'd strike while the iron was hot, as it were.'

Walker tutted to himself but he was more concerned with his quarry. He was nearly at the front of the queue.

'Look at all this,' Walker said waving his hands around, 'The wonders of the deep, laid bare. See, their shells move? I like to think they are talking secretly to each other, quietly planning how to make their escape.'

Grayson said nothing.

'What stories they could tell, hmm? A life at the bottom of the sea! How long do you think you could stay alive?'

Grayson shrugged his shoulders.

'Your lungs would collapse before you had even gone fifty metres into their world. They however, can survive quite happily in ours. They have gills and lungs, you see, truly adaptable.' Grayson stood quietly beside his colleague and watched as he pulled out his wallet and began to trade.

'I always feel slightly guilty,' Walker confessed, 'seeing the aristocrats of the sea laid out like this. It demeans them.' He beckoned towards the fishmonger.

'Frank!'

'Yes, Mr Walker. What's it to be today?'

'I'll have those two lobsters please, and a dozen oysters, oh, and half a dozen scallops and while I'm here, I'll have two dozen clams. Are those fresh?'

'Caught yesterday off the pier,' the fishmonger said assuredly to his best customer.

'Then I'll have a pound of mussels.'

'They need a home,' Walker whispered to Grayson, as if talking to a wife about orphan children. 'I can keep them alive longer in my aquarium. Even in the bottom of my fridge is better than lying on a slab, being gawked at by humans. Now, what is it you wanted to say?'

Grayson told him that that the search of Alan Thomas's house had literally been a dead end.

'Don't worry Grayson,' Walker said, receiving the shellfish and cradling them in his arms, 'something's bound to come to light, it always does.'

Walker retreated to his car. He placed the shellfish in the back seat and headed back to the station. He needed to get his head back to the case. With each passing day, he was re-evaluating his views of Almond. He thought he had known Almond well. Surely, the countless stakeouts and hours spent in interview rooms and mulling over crime scenes had to count for something? Yet what was he really like? And what would it feel like to be married with a child and find another lover dipping in his candle? What would it do to a man's mind? Pissed off is how he'd feel, annoyed as hell, but where would he take it from there?

Most people would discuss it - or more likely have an almighty row, something involving verbal insults, pieces of kitchenware, perhaps, like crockery. Then...then you crossed the line, into violence; with a few slaps, scratching and maybe the odd bunched fist. Either that or you stepped back, into despair, remorse or just exhaustion. It could go either way, violence or silence, depending on so many things. Did you step back or step forward? The human condition, that's what it came down to; so what was Almond's condition like when he found out? How did he react - utter force or helpless melancholy?

John Walker had only ever seen Almond act violently once, and it was a long time ago. Some youth had lurched up to them, while they were waiting for the lights to change, asked for some directions and then been sick over their car. He'd never forgotten Almond's face that moment; incandescent, quivering with pure undiluted rage. He'd got out the car, grabbed hold of the youth, thrown him to the ground and then kicked the shit out of him for almost a minute until Walker had pulled him away. Even then, he was still lashing, out, arms and legs seeking to connect with the crumpled body. Not the sort of behaviour expected of a self-confessed Christian.

Walker never found out what happened to the kid - he detected a very slight movement as they pulled away - but one thing was sure, the kid would never puke over a police car again. Walker never told anyone and never discussed it with Almond. It was one of those things that cops did; they watched each other's backs. Walker told Almond to get in quick, before anyone stopped them. He never forgot Almond's face; bright crimson with sweat pouring off forehead, spittle falling from his mouth and eyes that blazed with fury.

Wednesday, 30th October

Getting in early to DI Walker meant avoiding the coffee run and all the greeting paraphernalia that went with the 9-5ers. The only person he had to greet was the cleaner who never spoke anyway, at least not in English. It also meant that he found a space in the car park, had the toilets to himself and could put his feet up on the desk, like he owned the place. In fact, the only disadvantage was that he got to see the horrors before anyone else.

Not this time the facile comments of his superior but horrors like the latest corporate DVD that someone had kindly plonked on his desk without giving a name. The voice-over was nasally insistent, female, with a transatlantic accent shredding through tinny music.

'You know how committed we are to community policing,' she stated smugly, as the camera panned out to a team of police officers that had the correct mix of gender, race, religion, height and sexual orientation. 'Our mission statement specifically highlights this as a key objective. Using the latest, effective call-handling technologies and utilising the best alignment of force structures we intend to solve local community safety problems and make people feel safer.' The shot cut away to a park scene where children played and parents talked to smiling police officers.

DI Walker reached for the metaphorical sick bag. He had heard it all before. Sure some of the words may have been different and there was an added emphasis on technology but it all added up to the same old message - it will get better. Well, it couldn't get much worse. No further on in the murder case, several of the best officers snapped up by private security companies, a raging headache and all this bull about how things will improve.

The young police officer came in just as the DVD was giving its last message. It even made him pleased to see Grayson.

'Ah what a shame, you've missed it!' Walker said, as the drive ejected the disk with a whirr.

'Anything I need to know?'

'Not unless you're three years old. Here take it.' He tossed it across the room, like a Frisbee. Grayson caught it one handed. 'Never dropped one playing for my local team,' Grayson said. 'Known as bucket hands, I was.' He removed his coat and sat down.

'Were you indeed. Sure it wasn't bucket head?'

'No. Definitely hands. Anyway, what's happening?'

'Not enough. You're early again.'

'Just trying to be conscientious. How's David taking it?' he asked.

'Badly, I went to see him last Thursday.' Walker replied.

'Think he knew about his wife and Thomas?'

'I don't know.' Walker eyes were raised in disbelief when he said it. A detective of twenty years not spotting his wife carrying on behind his back for the last three years seemed improbable. 'What do *you* think, Grayson?'

'Maybe he didn't know, maybe he refused to accept it. Not even police officers spend every minute of the day checking up on their loved ones.'

'That's right.' Walker said.

'He's probably thinking right now; why the hell did I do twenty years service? All for nothing.'

Walker nodded. He had similar thoughts about his own career.

'Here we are putting him in the frame, like he's a common criminal.'

'Okay, okay, calm down.' Walker said warningly. 'He hasn't been arrested yet, we're just exploring all the options.'

Grayson took a deep breath and raised his hands despairingly.

'Sorry, I just think we're giving him a hard time, that's all, when what we should be doing is supporting him.'

Walker beckoned Grayson to get up and follow him to the interview room.

'Grayson,' he murmured when they were both seated, 'this information we've got about David. Let's keep it between ourselves, shall we?'

'Sure.'

'I mean, he could have taken that gun out for a host of reasons and we don't even know that it was the same one as the murder weapon. At the moment, it's all circumstantial and anyway, I'm sure he had an alibi.'

'Sure.'

'So, you headed out to Mersey Island with him. Was he with you all day?'

'Yeah, I mean he was around the station.'

'Good, so he's in the clear.'

Grayson began to move disconcertingly. If he had been an interviewee, Walker would have twigged straight away. As it was a colleague, he was only marginally interested.

'All the time?'

'Oh, well he said he had to go shopping,' Grayson recalled, 'but that wouldn't have taken long.'

'I remember now,' Walker said. 'Five, ten minutes?'

'Uh-huh, might have been a bit more. He wasn't sure what to buy. It was his Cathy's birthday. Fifteen, she was.'

'So, I think we can assume that he's okay. Maybe check the CCTV, just in case, eh?' Walker gave a false smile and Stephen swallowed hard.

At the far end of the corridor, plastered with scare-mongering posters and printed memos exhorting the staff to strive for great efficiencies, was the glass-fronted office of CS Jones. Inside, there were no posters, domestic photos, or fancy executive toys, just untidy piles of papers, a telephone and a computer. The Clean Desk policy applied to others, not to him. In the past, Jones would spend at least two hours a day meeting councillors, media and assorted bigwigs, addressing his officers and getting involved in criminal cases whenever it suited him. In short, he had had control over his own destiny.

Now, he spent these two hours staring into his computer screen, peering into a virtual world of criminal databases, images of crime scenes, CCTV screenshots and neatly laid-out electronic reports. When he had some time, he devoted it to the endless stream of ubiquitous emails that found their way into his mailbox. He'd tried to write to his superiors complaining how police detection had gone from leg work to finger work using a silly electronic mouse but his case had been ignored. Soon, he concluded, every officer would become chained to their desks while criminals went about their criminal activities somehow managing to circumvent all electronic surveillance techniques.

He was told that his department needed computers to deal with the additional paperwork but all computers did was create more paperwork and so the notion had completely the opposite effect. Worst of all, he no longer knew the names of all the officers - so many had left or been forced out to be replaced by media-savvy graduates and techno-types who hadn't even heard of the Crays and Harry Roberts.

Almond had recently resigned which left John Walker and himself as the only two members of the original force of the 1980's. Even an old stager like Walker was someone he rarely saw eye-to-eye with.

At 5.25 p.m. he got up from his desk, picked up the file and walked out of his office. He was a burly man with a thatch of unruly grey hair and a suit to match. As he strode purposefully along the corridor, he noticed that there was a disturbing air of quietness; completely the opposite of the mad, noisy, yelling station he had joined all those years ago. Had everyone gone home already? At the end of the corridor, he rapped on the staff room door and walked in. Two men were seated opposite one another at the interview table. They both looked up and one of them got up to leave. Jones temporarily blocked Grayson's exit before moving to one side.

'Okay, you can go. It's DI Walker I want to speak to.'

'Something for your diary, John,' he said, without looking at his charge. 'Chelmsford Crown Court, 12th November at 2.30. The coroner has called an inquest.'

'Bloody hell,' Walker cursed, 'that's less than two weeks away. Too early.'

'Is it? They've got forensics, pathology, ballistics, scene of crimes report, witness statements. What more do they want? Get-well greetings cards?'

Walker shrugged his shoulders.

'So why are we shrugging our shoulders?' Jones asked.

'Because, we're still going through the evidence.'

'Well they seem to think it's a formality.'

'So why have an inquest?'

'To assuage public concerns. The world will be a happier place if Thomas killed her and then shot himself. Anything wrong with that?'

'Motive?' Walker asked.

'He was receiving payments from Biggs to get the development approved. Almond's wife discovered it and threatened to go public but before she could, he lured her out to the island. He knew he'd be discovered so he topped himself.'

'Thomas was a bright guy. So why not just do away with her so that he wouldn't be discovered?'

'I guess, clever clogs, he wasn't a pro in these matters. Anyway, it'll be popular. Means we don't have another killer going around scaring people shitless and then clogging up the prisons at the taxpayer's expense. So do you have any other suspects?'

'No.'

'So what is your problem, Walker?'

'I just like things to be neat and tidy.'

'Well, there's a first time for everything.'

'Thanks. Why not give me a week?'

'No way.'

'Four days.'

'I can't afford the staff.'

'Three.'

Two, maximum,' Jones said sternly. 'Obviously if we charge someone the inquest is postponed but we can't ask for an adjournment unless we have something concrete. Do you have something concrete?'

'Not really but-'

'Two days,' Jones repeated.

'I think I might have something.'

'Do you want to share it with me?' Jones asked.

'Not at this stage.'

'So, it's two days'

'By the way, old Harry Deacon will want to get this one out of the way as soon as possible.'

'Why's that?' Jones asked.

'He always takes a golfing holiday at this time of year.'

'Did I say it was Harry?'

'No, you didn't.'

'Did I say it was a man?'

'No, I just...'

'Someone by the name of Simons,' Jones said and he began leafing through the papers until he fished out a letter. 'Here it is! Blah, blah, blah... and the presiding officer will be Gabrielle Simons, H.M. Coroner of Essex. I presume, John, that since it is Gabrielle with two 'ee's' it is the feminine form and not the masculine, archangel variety. Good luck.'

Jones had already turned and was leaving the room. He didn't see Walker's face collapse

Walker slumped back into his chair. It wasn't unusual for the coroner to work for a firm of solicitors but it was unusual for the person to have worked for the same firm as the two victims. The term conflict of interest rang like a peel of bells but presumably, Jones knew this already and was unconcerned - working for the same organisation as the victims might actually lead to a more thorough investigation. What Jones didn't know, however, was the extent of this conflict. Walker did, because he had visited her office and the basement and stolen some of her most confidential legal files.

He was left with two options. Firstly, press for a replacement and face delays and the risk of legal action from Simons for perverting the course of justice. That would be a one-way ticket to oblivion. Secondly, move Heaven and Earth in the next couple of days to produce some compelling evidence. The latter was marginally preferable but infinitely more difficult. Yet, when he considered that, after fifteen years in the force, his career was very probably on borrowed time, it didn't seem like such a bad choice. It would mean cutting corners, bending the rules, taking liberties and, it would mean being utterly ruthless; yet none of those things fazed DI Walker as he stepped out into the chilly night air.

CHAPTER SIX

Thursday, 31st October.

On a frosty morning, with a hearty breakfast inside them both, Walker and Grayson drove out of town. They passed green and yellow fields of rapeseed. It was a familiar sight in these parts - only this time they were covered in a crusty layer of hoarfrost. Nearly all farmers grew rapeseed - it was the easiest way of getting money from the EU. Grayson had heard somewhere that it played havoc with the bees' navigation system - another pollutant to add to a deadly cocktail of pesticides, insecticides, fertilisers and crop sprays. Yet, with food scares and concerns over GM crops, yellow blooms of rape were seen as the lesser of evils.

They had just passed Tiptree, where Grayson had stopped to buy some fruit conserve, and were heading up the 'B' roads towards Colchester. Grayson had the heater on max, blasting out hot air. It was his favourite part of Essex, where he could rove his eye across the horizon and barely see a house or car. Not for much longer, though. Up ahead, flags fluttered, proudly proclaiming the name of the prospective builder as if they had something to celebrate for bricking over arable land. Soon it would all be paved over for housing estates, shops and a petrol station. These were the only things that ever got built, these days, Grayson cursed. Then the crime would move in. Whatever happened, he wondered, to new schools and hospitals and churches and pubs and…

'Seen the latest targets?' Walker asked, drawing Grayson out of his meditations.

'No.'

'This you won't believe,' Walker said, as he fumbled with a piece of paper and held it out in front of him. 'Our Lord and Master has put it up in the Common Room. I copied it.' He began to read off a list of scribbled numbers.

'Increase primary detection by 10% for *all* categories. Reduce car theft by 15%, Reduce burglaries by 8%. Increase drug arrests by 9%. Reduce road fatalities by 15%. Increase successful court prosecutions by 12%.'

'Can I have a look, please?'

'No, Grayson, you're driving.'

'All with the same number of police?' Grayson asked.

'Well of course,' answered Walker, 'they don't want to make it simple for us.' Walker then spotted something else. 'No, I tell a lie. It appears we get 15 new police officers through the Home Secretary's Crime Fighting Fund.'

'Hallelujah.'

'Oh, more good news. The targets aim for an increase in civilians and support staff.'

'They'll be helpful in a terrorist attack.'

'The downside is that we have to reduce special constables.'

'Sounds like dumbing down,' Grayson observed.

'Any dumber and we'll be taking lessons in sign language.' Walker said, turning over the paper irritably. 'Then they plan to save £3.6m through increased office efficiency.'

'Well I'm not going to use both sides of the toilet paper.'

Walker resisted a smile. 'It's all going to be saved by computers apparently. Now where have I heard that before?'

'How about we just fly in Batman, sir, then we can all go home.'

'Hold on!' Walker suddenly exclaimed. 'What the hell was that?'

Stephen slammed on the brake pedal and found himself seized by the belt as it cut into his shoulder and chest. The car lurched to a halt and he quickly reversed. Walking along the central reservation of the dual carriageway was a figure. She was stumbling along the uneven ground. Her hair was long and straggly and she had her head down but he recognised her immediately. It was Cathy Almond.

Grayson wound down the window and shouted across.

'Cathy! Cathy!!'

She ignored him and kept on walking, her breath making ghostly patterns. He got out, ran across the road, and caught up with her.

'Cathy! It's me, Stephen.'

She continued to walk her own determined way, head down, one foot defiantly in front of the next. He touched her lightly across the shoulder and she stopped and swivelled around. Then she gave him one of the coldest stares he had ever seen before continuing along her way. The noise of the traffic drowned her voice but that expression, that icy daggers-drawn look, suggested Grayson was the last person she wanted to see.

Finally, he ran around in front of her and stood blocking her passage. She tensed and still with her head lowered, tried to bulldoze past.

'Look, Cathy. Stop. Please, let me just…'

She raised her hand. He thought at first she was going to strike him but she was just moving her hair away from her face.

'It's no use. I just want to be left alone.'

'Sure, but come off this reservation. It's freezing cold. Come back to the car and we'll talk.'

She paused, looked down at her muddied shoes, and promptly fell into his arms.

A few minutes later, she was sitting in the back of the police car, her cheeks bright red, eyeing Walker suspiciously.

Grayson made a gesture and Walker got out and went for a walk and a smoke.

'Cathy. I'm real sorry. It must be very hard for you. I know you loved your mother.'

'She looked up and glared at Grayson.

'I hate her. I hate her.'

'No, you don't.'

'Yes I do, I really do.'

Tears were beginning to well up.

'Uncle Stephen, mum went off with someone else and then got herself killed.'

She began to cry and the tears rolled down her cheeks.

Grayson got into the back seat and put his arm around her. He didn't know what to say to her, where to take her, what the future might bring so instead he just sat there and let her cry in his arms. He beckoned for Walker to get back in and the three set off with the heater taking the chill off them all. Walker kept quiet but he knew where he was going. Soon, he drew the car towards the curb.

Walker opened the rear door and ushered her out. They were only a few yards from Almond's house. He didn't actually tell her to go back indoors, but he hoped she would. Also, the last person he wanted to see right now was David Almond. As she walked slowly along the path and up the driveway, he watched her fumble with the key and open the front door slowly, like it was a cell door.

Then she disappeared into the house. The house of someone who once had been his long-term associate and life long friend but was now a key suspect in a murder case.

As the car eased off Walker turned to Grayson. 'You know what to do, don't you?'

'Sure.'

'Get out of that uniform first. Here's the number. Do it tonight.'

'Thanks.'

PC Grayson tidied his hair and clipped on his tie. In his profession, clipped ties were highly recommended if one wished to avoid being strangled by one's own clothing. Only Walker wore a proper tie with a fetching tiepin. Clipped ties could do fearful things to one's image - especially if a girlfriend, drawing him towards her, grabbed hold of it, only for the tie to come away in her hand. What else, he wondered did she think might come away in her hand? Not that there was much chance of that at the moment - not the way he'd been behaving.

He hadn't exactly been firing on all cylinders in that department. Working policeman's hours didn't help and he didn't think the uniform did much these days. In fact, Grayson wasn't feeling too great about his gender. He hadn't felt good about it since he scored the winning goal for the school in the football final some seven years ago. The whole assembly had cheered him next day and he had become unbelievably popular with all the girls. Since then, things had gone consistently downhill. But that was just excuses. The reality was that he wasn't very good at chatting up women.

Veni, Vedi, Vici was his motto, well, two thirds of it was. Girls like Clara: a college friend whom he'd lost track of recently: Betsy, the large breasted beauty who served him in the local corner store; exotic Flavia, his hairdresser, she of a thousand expressions and a body so lithe and lissom that she flowed from one place to the next and Davinia, a class above him, whom he met at a dinner party in Chelsea and actually asked for his phone number. Finally, there was the big boned, blond lassie called Sara with her gung-ho personality, tremendously long legs and an ass to die for.

He gave himself one final look in the mirror. He thought he looked pretty good, as if he was going out for a date. But this wasn't just any old date, this was a date with a very special girl - the only girl he truly cared about.

He took the keys from the kitchen unit, locked up the back door and left the flat by the front door. Then he stepped into his Escort and drove the five miles to his rendezvous. The café was busy, full of locals taking a break from shopping or hanging out with their friends. He was led to a window table by a waitress wearing expensive trainers, tight black trousers and a T-shirt. He squeezed into the narrow space.

As she leant across him to clear the table, he couldn't help noticing her chest. Women didn't have to draw attention to their figures (he always obliged) but this one was different to most other women's chests, it had writing on it. So, he had to read it.

'Farmer's Café' it proclaimed in green lettering. Stretched underneath was the motif, a bale of hay and a pitchfork. She picked up the crumbs, like the eponymous daughter; peachy, freckled face, tousled hair. She then smoothed down the tablecloth and, with an impudent smile, as if she had just had a roll in the farm's very own haystack asked: 'What can I get you?'

It was a foreign accent. Italian, Serbian, Albanian? These days he didn't have a clue where they came from.

'Just waiting for someone.'

'Sorry, you have to order something.'

'I will, when she arrives.'

'No problemo.'

The waitress went away, buzzing around the other tables, like a bumblebee sampling all the flowers' honey. Stephen Grayson straightened his tie. He used to rate girls with marks out of ten but he had grown out of that. Then he moved to a 5-star rating system but he had ditched that too, as being puerile. Ten minutes passed, he began tapping his leg against the leg of the spare chair opposite him, trying to get a rhythm going. He gave the waitress a six, for old time's sake. Then for completeness, he gave her three stars.

Twenty minutes later, his date arrived. Her head was slightly bowed, almost apologetically, but not because she was late. She quickly got her radar working and flounced herself down onto the seat in front of him. She swatted her shoulder bag against the table.

'Hello.' He said.

She made a little harrumph and looked around.

'Coffee?' he asked.

'Why not,' she said, glancing briefly at him. Then she went back to her own preoccupations. She slowly peeled off her coat, one thin arm appearing, her chest and then the other arm. Underneath she wore a white blouse beneath a dark blue sweater. He wondered if it was the same blouse that he had suggested buying her. She wore a loose charm bracelet that jangled.

'That's nice,' he remarked.

She held it out, under Grayson's nose, so that the inscription was visible.

'What does it say?'

'It says: 'Friendship is the golden thread that ties our hearts together''.

She pulled her arm away quickly.

'It's a rough translation from an ancient piece of Chinese text,' she added.

'Do you believe it?' he asked.

'Course I don't. The only think that matters is yourself and surviving.'

'Well, maybe we can be friends,' Grayson suggested. 'Wouldn't do any harm to prove the Chinese right.'

She shrugged her shoulders.

'Nice blouse. Did dad buy it for you?'

'No, I've had it for eons.'

'But I bet he got you something nice for your birthday?'

'Not really, just perfume.'

'A special one?'

'You can get it anywhere.'

Grayson smoothed out the tablecloth once more. 'Look, thanks for coming,' he said at last.

'Whatever.'

She got out her mobile and held it out like a crucifix. Then she began tapping mechanically. He beckoned the waitress, ordered coffees and asked for the menu. He handed it straight to Cathy.

'I hear the ice cream's good here.'

'Fine,' she said without even looking at the menu, 'I'll have the chocolate fudge sundae.'

It was reassuring to know she still trusted him in some matters. She went back to her mobile. *Tap, tap.*

Grayson tried a smile, one not reciprocated. Then he cleared his throat.

'Cathy, I'm glad you turned up. I've been worried.'

She stopped tapping and her face crinkled into a frown, a frown that would one day be a wrinkle but that was a long time ahead.

'Why?'

'Well, because...' He searched for words. Kids at her age always wanted answers to awkward questions. He didn't want to do her a disservice.

'You haven't been to school. We picked you up walking on the central reservation. That's dangerous.'

'I don't want to talk about this morning.'

'Where were you going?'

'I dunno. Just walking.'

'And I want to help.'

She shook her head vigorously.

'You can't. No one can.'

'Of course we can. We all want to help. Me, your friends, your father.'

'He doesn't talk to me,' she said with an air of resignation.

'Of course he does.'

'No he doesn't. He just sits around and prays, but that doesn't change anything, does it?'

Grayson shrugged his shoulders. 'It may do, it certainly doesn't do any harm. Think he's praying for you?'

'Search me.'

'Maybe he's praying for your mother?'

'Why would he do that?'

The sundaes arrived, vanilla ice cream piled high with cherries, chocolate sauce topping and a bright parasol. Grayson smiled at the waitress. 'Enjoy.' she said.

He was going to explain to the waitress that the girl was just a friend but she had gone.

'Maybe, he's trying to put the world to right,' he said to Cathy.

'It's not working.'

'Cathy, did your mother ever speak about a man called Alan Thomas?'

She tensed immediately.

'Did she?'

'A few times,' Cathy said quietly, 'She said he was a very nice man.'

Grayson waited a few seconds. She had gone deathly pale.

'Did your dad ever mention him?'

'No.' This time barely audible.

'Did you know your mother was having a relationship with him?'

Cathy pursed her quivering lips. She began shaking her head, back and forth, with increasingly violence.

'No, No! No!!!' She shouted as her fragile voice suddenly shrieked across the café. Everyone turned to Grayson's table by the window and the source of the noise.

The proprietor came across before Grayson had a chance.

'Sir, this young lady, is she okay?'

Grayson put his hand up. 'She's okay. I'm sorry. Please.' He reached for his badge.

'Madam, are you alright?'

Cathy looked genuinely embarrassed and managed a very deliberate nod.

'I'll have to warn you sir,' said the proprietor pompously, 'that any other disturbance and I'll have to ask you both to leave.'

'Yeah, we're sorry but we're okay, aren't we Cathy?'

She made another effort at nodding.

Grayson sighed heavily and concentrated on his chocolate sundae. He took his spoon into the centre of the glass and mixed it up until all the colours merged into a goo.

'Eew,' Cathy exclaimed.

'Race you.'

He attacked the sundae from all sides. She took delicate mouthfuls, not daring to disrupt the pretty layers. He finished off by sticking his index finger into the glass and wiping around the edges until he had enough to put in his mouth.

'Sorry, manners of a pig. Excuse me.'

She pulled a face. 'That is so yuk.'

'Hey,' Grayson said, 'bet you can't wait until you're grown-up like me?'

'I bet I can.'

'Bet you can't.'

'Do you eat like that at work?'

'Of course not. Worse.'

'My dad always said that you were just a big overgrown kid.'

'Thanks. I take that as a compliment. Better than being a big overgrown adult.'

Cathy shook her head and finally finished her sundae. Grayson delved into his pocket and produced a small package.

'Here, take this.'

She looked up at him and pouted.

'What is it?'

'Open it and you'll find out.'

'I don't want it.'

'Please.'

'Is it a present?'

'Open it.'

She loosened the ribbon and slowly pulled away the wrapping paper. Inside was a leather case. She lifted the lid and peered inside. It was a sapphire brooch inlaid with diamonds.

'Good God!'

'It was my mother's. I want you to have it.'

'No, I can't.'

'Yes you can.'

'Really?'

'Yes. It's yours.'

'Thanks, Uncle Stephen.'

He liked the way she called him uncle, even if he was only her half uncle. She lowered the lid and slid it into her bag.

'Aren't you going to put it on?'

He hadn't expected her to be effusive but he thought all girls loved jewellery.

'No. It wouldn't look right, not in here.'

'Go on,' Grayson urged, 'it will look fantastic.'

'Later,' she said, and then as an afterthought, 'but it is lovely.'

'Don't mention it. I know I'm late but it's your birthday present.'

She leaned forward as if she was going to kiss him but she pulled away and pushed her hair back instead.

Grayson took Cathy's frail hand in hers. It felt cold and unloved.

'Precious, I know how this is eating you up. I know you want to bury yourself and not have to face the world outside, but let me tell you, it's all part of life.'

She narrowed her eyes and creased her forehead before turning on him.

'God, what do you know? When did you last lose your mum?'

He'd lost his mum five years ago, and he thought about her every day but that wasn't relevant right now.

'Sweetheart, just try and take one step at a time. It's going to take weeks, months maybe and during this period, it will seem like the longest time of your life, like setting off down a long, dark tunnel. But as you watch that tiny speck of light grow in front of your very eyes, you will feel your own strength and spirit slowly return.'

'I feel dead inside.'

'No, you don't. You feel deadened, but that's different. It's like being numb. Slowly, you'll get back some feeling.'

She shook her head. He kept talking to her, hoping that somehow his words would get through the barrier she had put around herself. She looked nervous, pinch-faced and scarily white. He could sense a wave of uncertainty borne out in every tentative gesture she made. But she *had* agreed to meet him and the fact that she sat there, her body almost frozen to the chair suggested that it was as good a place as any for her to be right now.

He spoke to her for almost an hour, telling her of all his hopes and fears, speaking as much for himself as for her benefit. He told her about his games of football, how he deliberately tried to score an own goal when he thought his skipper was going out with his girlfriend. He told her about his cross-country runs, that made him feel more alive than anything did, and he talked about the dumb-ass game where he would sit in the back of a cinema with a friend and try and throw peanuts at the other cinemagoers. If they hit someone who turned around, they had to follow them all the way home just to see where they lived. It was a good game. She seemed to appreciate that. He didn't think he'd ever spoken like this before, not in a monologue, with one listener. The words came tumbling out, wrapped in emotions and weighing heavily in the air. They drank two more coffees, ate another ice cream delight and watched as a stream of other customers came and went. Eventually he looked at his watch and sighed.

'Time to go. Swap mobile numbers?' he asked.

'Why?'

'Because we're friends. Call me when you want to talk. No point telling anyone else, okay?'

'Okay.'

He got up and fetched her coat and held it out for her. She slipped into it and wrapped it tightly around her, like a protection blanket. He realised that from now on, there was nothing more he could say. From now on, it was all down to her. As they made their way out of the café, they barely noticed a young man and woman sitting at a table in the corner.

The couple didn't look up. They were both leaning forward, with their eyes and eyes locked together - the plates of cottage pie and beans gone cold and their mugs of tea barely touched. Vying for space at their table were papers, photos and dog-eared articles, all released from the confines of the young man's briefcase. Both diners picked up and examined the evidence, then they placed them back again and continued the conversation. They talked rapidly, barely listening to each other's views until they expounded their own. At times in the conversation, the words rose above their table across to the other diners but then just as quickly subsided into words barely perceptible to the most attuned ear.

The issue that caused most debate was how to proceed. They had diametrically opposed opinions but this was tempered by the fact they both had the same goal. Moreover, they knew that they depended on each other. In just a few days, all their work would come to fruition and the world would see things as they truly were.

CHAPTER SEVEN

The Queen Anne mansion sat squarely in one hundred acres of prime woodland. It remained hidden from the winding country track by a large electrocuted wire fence and a copse of cypress trees. Fallow deer roamed free across the owner's demesne - at least until such time as he decided to take one out by blasting it with his elephant gun. The east wing contained three reception rooms, two dining rooms, a library, two lounges, a drawing room, a gunroom and an Edwardian study. At the far corner of the study, beside a bay window overlooking the ornamental lake and formal gardens, sat one of the largest landowners in the county.

Joe Biggs was a property speculator and the controlling shareholder in Biggs Consolidated, an offshore holding company. He came to prominence in the late 1980's, when all the UK's manufacturing capabilities had gone East. He spotted a gap in the marketplace and used Biggs Consolidated as a vehicle to buy up abandoned industrial estates. Biggs's strategy was simple; wait until the firm was just about to go into receivership, then make a cash offer. It gave most harassed businessmen an escape route, a way to save face and if the firms' played ball, Biggs would see that they showed a small residual profit for their efforts.

It all came down to two words, self contradictory but to an expert speaking volumes. Vacant possession. Vacant *and* possession. They acted like a wake-up call to Mr Biggs. They symbolised the first faltering steps towards progress, ringing loud and true in his aural senses until he saw it all before him: ease of access, absence of tenants or third parties, a vacuum of ownership and finally, a *business opportunity*.

A vacant warehouse or dilapidated factory floor was like a blank canvas to a property artist like Boggs. It was all and everything he needed. And, once the wake-up call sounded, the tolling bell of a planning application followed. All it required was a brief, standard, three paragraph letter, outlining the proposal to replace the old, dilapidated warehouse with what were euphemistically referred to as 'town houses'.

From Angel Lane around Stratford, up through Bethnal Green and Bow as far as Shoreditch, he went to work. Nothing fancy: terraced house, flats, apartments, studios, maisonettes, anything that was needed by locals. Streets and roads were transformed into buildings more recognisable to the public as undersized dwellings or 'shoe boxes.' It was the decade of rising land values and speculators couldn't lose while first time buyers got what they wanted, cheap, affordable housing.

By the time he was twenty-five, he already owned ten properties. By the time he was twenty-eight he had trebled that number. His property fingers stretched westwards, into Essex, where purchase prices were lower. In the next three years, he quadrupled his properties again so that by the day of his thirtieth birthday, he was a multi-millionaire. Everything flowed from there.

To Joe Biggs, it wasn't that difficult, all he was doing was fulfilling a basic need. People wanted new houses and he would supply them. Oh, some people complained, people *always* complained. They moaned about over-development and a loss of community spirit, whatever that was, but those that really mattered: the shopkeepers, the supermarkets, the town councillors, they all wanted it. It was a simple enough circular argument: Housing meant growth. Growth meant prosperity; prosperity meant more jobs, more jobs meant more people and more people meant more housing.

Biggs had realised, at an early stage, that acquiring prime brown-belt land, with roads and transport already in place, was always going to be a safe bet. In the early years, he had little difficulty convincing councillors that it was time for a change. Sales went through in a matter of days, planning permission took mere weeks and he could have the factory buildings, offices and depots bulldozed within a month. Then it was simply up to his army of surveyors, building contractors and interior designers. Oh, Happy Days!

A few vacant possessions a year for five years and he was in clover. This, Mr Biggs referred to as his bread and butter work; the daily machinations of a business that Mr Biggs had built up from scratch. It was his baby, and his alone. Neither his parents, not his grandparents had ever had the faintest inkling about markets and the rudiments of capitalism. They had all worked for employers or the state or expected handouts whenever things got tough. He did it all alone, off his own bat.

Joe Biggs knew that, even without his grander schemes, he could retirement tomorrow if he wanted to. He could live the life of leisure, away from the daily frustrations and spend more time on his yacht in the Caribbean, eating drinking and being merry. But that could all wait, he had bigger fish to fry.

He sat down in his stonewashed jeans and a cotton shirt with button down collar. He never wore a suit, except for business meetings. He liked to dress casual, it gave him a sense of freedom. Somehow, the folds of fat were held in check by his shirt but still rolled over the top of his collar and bulged out from his waist where a moleskin belt strained at the pressure. He hadn't worn this shirt for ages. Breathlessly, he undid the top fly button of his jeans and went to work.

Joe Biggs began to move the pen across the headed notepaper. He penned one simple paragraph and then finished it off with his hurried signature. He lay back and put his hand around his leathery neck. His thoughts darkened. Fat lot of good these letters did now. How times had changed. Now it was applications, surveys, environmental assessments, heath and safety, EU regulations, all red tape, all to keep some petty bureaucrat in a job.

He placed the letter in the envelope and put it in his Georgian silver out-tray. As he sat back, his balding head touched the headrest. He cupped the baldness of his dome in the palm of his hand. It fitted perfectly, the way some island contours mirrored their neighbouring coastline. Maybe the hand and the head had once been attached, he thought whimsically, part of the same physiology. No ridiculous, he realised, he hadn't always been bald. Yet at the rate his hair was receding, his barren head would soon spread across the span of one hand.

He listened to the last few mournful bars of Saint Saen's Samson and Delilah. Then he puffed on the last dying embers of his Havana cigar. The charcoal-grey smoke curled across the room, through which, his personal secretary, Saunders entered, like a phantom. 'Good evening, sir,' he said, sonorously, carrying the customary glass of vintage port on a silver tray.

'Evening, Saunders,' Biggs answered. 'Put it down there, will you?' He didn't know why he said it because Saunders always placed the crystal glass on the small trestle table, circa seventeen sixty-five. He had been doing it for the last ten years and wasn't going to change now. No one else would do it either, Saunders was the only other person allowed into Biggs's inner sanctum.

'Oh, and take this letter will you?' Biggs said, handing him the silver tray, which matched perfectly the colour of his retainer's hair. 'Recorded delivery. Don't want it going into the wrong hands, do we?'

'No, sir.'

'That will be all, Saunders. You can go now.'

'Very good, sir.' Saunders disappeared as silently as he had arrived.

Biggs took the glass and, through the smoky haze, gazed out across the mahogany table in front of him. Sprawled across it was his pride and joy. Twelve feet by eight feet, it was a three dimensional fibreglass scale-model of the county. The model had been built two years ago and had been improved continually. It now faithfully represented all the typographical and land features. Areas painted in shades of browns and greens were dissected by a myriad of curls of silver foil used to denote rivers and streams. Hills, woodland and other natural features were represented in various shades of green. Also highlighted were points of interest including churches, libraries, post offices and public houses. Fifteen red flags were pinned into various places. These denoted land owned by Mr Biggs. Twelve other pins indicated potential sites. Beside the model was a box of spare red flags that he was hoping to bring into action. At night, he could flick a switch and the whole area became illuminated in glowing mauve, amber and green.

He rose from his chair, all five-foot-five of him, and walked slowly around the table, circumnavigating the scale model of his business empire. He felt proud and ennobled but curiously unsatisfied. He had never got the public recognition he had hoped for; no, that he *deserved*. No words of praise, no press cordiality, no long-term business associates, no awards, not even a few letters after his name to embellish his letterhead. Everything he had done had been based on his efforts alone.

As his eyes scanned across the terrain, his mood became gloomy once more. They had alighted on Mersey Island. There were no flags here, it was simply a block of agricultural and marshland, but it had a red line round it. There was only one reason he had drawn a red line round it: it would be an ideal site to build on.

He lifted up the fibreglass section and moved it away from the main model. It was detachable, like any good island should be. Mersey Island sat between two estuaries; the mouth of the Colne and the curling tongue of the Blackwater. It stood like an aging sentinel, guarding nothing except what it could not control. It laid claim to being the most easterly island in the UK and was also famous because it was claimed once to have had a Tsunami.

At 9.18 a.m. on April 22, 1884, the most damaging earthquake ever to hit Britain, measuring 6.9 on the Richter scale, created a vicious tidal wave that swept down from the Wash and ripped through the eastern seaboard. It lifted up all the fishing smacks and smashed them against the seawall, like matchwood, depositing silt several miles inland. More than a thousand buildings were damaged, people were made homeless and crops ruined. The *Essex County Standard* reported: "The ground and the houses were lifted up, shaken two or three times in a manner that made the stoutest heart quake." One eye witness on Mersey Island described how it split and opened up as ''the very jaws of hell.'' Now it was known for more peaceful visitations, a large population of migratory wildfowl that feasted on the rich mudflats and stubble across the autumnal farmlands.

These historical facts had been unknown to Joe Biggs when he had laid claim to one of the richest prizes of all; a three thousand acre site on the eastern tip of the island overlooking the Colne estuary. The area, Biggs considered, was a pimple on the backside of Essex, a backwater of festering, swampy marshland and silted creeks. Within this maze of quagmire lived dull, dim-witted islanders like the oyster fishermen, who had ramshackle houses and farmed oysters for generations because they knew nothing better. They should have been only too happy, Biggs argued, to sell up and go and live in some nice apartment complex in southern Spain.

Yet so far, all he had encountered was suspicion and distrust. He'd lost count of the number of people who had come out against his business methods, demonstrated and tried to attack him in the local papers. Yet, those same people had offered nothing in its place. All they had wanted was to continue their lives without change, without changing the status quo, without moving forward. He, at least, had offered something; promising new, living and vibrant communities out of industrial sackcloth and ashes. Now the conservationists, historians, naturalists and cub reporters had intervened and distorted everything. The area was no longer termed barren it had become 'unique', it was no longer a wasteland it was 'a sanctuary' and worst of all for Biggs, it was no longer an opportunity it had become 'a cause celebre'.

There were some plastic figures on his fibreglass model. They were in the area designated with a red line. He moved them across until they were out of it. Funny, he thought, how it was never the people who actually lived in a place that held sway. It was always the others, outside the line, with no vested interest who piled in; people like Joe Hart, a young journalist working for the *Essex Times* and Alison Holmes who thought ducks and geese had greater needs than people.

Since these activists had arrived, they had commandeered local public opinion and silenced the silent majority - so much for democracy. Once, news of the building proposal had been leaked to the newspapers, his dream had begun to recede by the minute, like the outgoing tides.

Even without his efforts, this little part of rural East Essex would become congested, over populated, clogged up with traffic. Someone else would fill the void. Schools would become overcrowded and utilities would find it difficult to cope. That was also the way things worked: one minute boom, the next bust. Growth then stagnation. There was an elegant symmetry that Biggs admired. Almost like the seasons; winter, summer; spring, autumn, counter balancing one another over the course of a year, so that everything could right itself.

He took a tiny plastic bag with '$' and placed it next to the tiny figures. It was always a case of right people, right timing and right amount. Of course, it wasn't possible to wave cash around anymore but cars and houses were as good as anything. But in the last few days he had heard nothing. His solicitors were just as guilty of foot dragging as the original owner. It had gone beyond the pale. Now, he wanted action.

He went through a labyrinth of recorded voice options. Eventually a live voice was heard.

'Get me Gabrielle Simons.' He demanded.

It was nearly eight o'clock in the evening but to a lawyer, sitting in their office, it only meant they were busy.

A woman's voice came on the line.

'Gabrielle Simons, corporate lawyer.'

'My name's Biggs,' he said gruffly. 'Bit late, been meaning to talk to you.'

Her voice was wavering, slightly nervous. 'Yes Mr Biggs, I've been meaning to talk to you too.'

'I want to know what's going on?'

'I was going to write to you. We have some issues to deal with.'

'You're telling me.'

'I'm not sure what you are referring to, but I'm talking about the couple that were found dead in a car on Mersey Island a few days ago.'

Biggs stayed silent for a few seconds. A squirm of guilt wriggled inside him like a maggot on a line. Then he said in a sour voice: 'I heard.'

'They were our employees,' she said. 'We are going to have to drop this case.'

'They were incompetent anyway,' he growled. 'They didn't file quickly enough. I've lost millions.'

Gabrielle Simons paused, searching for the right words. 'Mr Biggs. I'm still looking into all the ins and outs. As you can imagine, it's not a good time.'

'I'll sue,' he persisted.

'I don't think that would help matters, do you? Do you really think you would do any better elsewhere?'

'Don't be so goddamn sure, Ms Simons. There are people queuing up to work for me on this project.'

'I don't think so.'

'Oh, why's that?'

'You obviously haven't been well informed. The police are refusing to allow any surveyors onto the land. Everything has ground to a halt.'

Joe Biggs slammed down the phone and began tapping his pen furiously. The arrogance of the woman, he fumed, trying to suggest that she knew more than he did. He would soon show her his influence. He slammed the door shut and went back to the phone. He could still wheel and deal with the best of them. He punched out the number but the doorbell interrupted him. Visitors? *At this time?*

He put the phone down and cocked an ear. Saunders spoke in that inimitable low drone, as if the world collapsing would not cause him to raise his voice. The words were muffled but full of import. Then he heard the sound of footsteps.

'There's a Detective Inspector Walker for you, sir. From the local constabulary.'

Biggs showed no sign of alarm. 'That's what I call service, Saunders. Saved me a phone call.'

Biggs shuffled out into the hallway. The two thickset men eyed each other like a couple of Sumo wrestlers.

'Inspector?'

'Mr Biggs.'

They avoided the formality of handshakes and Biggs ushered the man through.

'Must be psychic, eh?' Biggs ventured.

'Pardon, sir?'

'Never mind. We can talk in the drawing room. Walker found himself in an oak-panelled illuminated room full of Persian carpets, Greek vases, a large mahogany *escritoire* and, gazing from all sides, a menagerie of stuffed animals and birds.

'Drink?'

Walker shook his head but his eyes were roving round the room.

'Oh, you've noticed the relatives,' Biggs said. 'Don't worry. They were all here when I moved in. Used to belong to some crusty old barrister. I think he had a penchant for taxidermy. Find it all a bit stuffy, if you appreciate the pun.'

Walker watched as the small, portly man moved surprisingly deftly behind the desk. Biggs lifted up one of his tattoo-scared arms and drew the palm of his hand across his receding forehead, flattening non-existent hair.

'Please, sit down.'

Walker obliged.

'It's a rum business, property development, inspector. One day you think you're doing good for the community, the next day you're demonised. Bit like the police, I suppose. Then you hear that there's a murder inquiry and you can't do anything until they say so. So I said to myself, John Walker, he's in charge of the investigation, he'll be able to cut through all the red tape.'

'Mr Biggs. I've come because I wanted to talk to you about the deaths of Susan Almond and Alan Thomas. Their bodies were found on the sixteenth of October on Mersey Island. Did you know them?'

'Of course, I did. Why do you want to know?'

'Routine enquiries.'

'How routine?'

'It's a preliminary investigation.'

'Am I being charged?'

'Of course not. We just need information.'

Biggs sat down, placed his meaty hands neatly in front of him and breathed deeply. 'Okay, information. Look, I knew of them, shall we say, but I never actually met them. Perhaps I spoke to Susan on the phone a couple of times and Alan Thomas too. As I'm sure you know, they worked for Ridgely, Turner and Fowler who represent me in various business investments. I heard of their death in the papers and a few minutes ago, I stopped dealing with the firm altogether. Need to think of my reputation.'

'Quite so, Mr Biggs. Did you know they were going to Mersey Island?'

'On the sixteenth?'

'Yes.'

'No.'

'You have business interests on the island?'

'Yes.'

'So, they might have gone there on your behalf, to check out the lay of the land.'

'Might have done, but they didn't, at least not at my request. I've got surveyors who do that sort of thing, at least they did until your brigade cordoned off the area.'

Walker ignored the comment. 'Why do you think they went to Mersey?'

'I haven't got the faintest idea, inspector. People do lots of things at their own behest but if I was working on a major lucrative project then I would certainly make sure I knew where it was going to be sited.'

'Have you been on the island?' Walker asked.

'No, no I haven't?'

'Isn't that unusual?'

'Mr Walker, I'm a busy man. I have others that do that sort of work.'

'Are you a demanding person, Mr Biggs?'

Biggs looked at him, unblinking. 'No more than anyone else. I pay people well so I expect results.'

'Where were you between four and six in the evening of 23rd October?'

'Here probably. Now, look, I don't like the way this is heading.'

'All routine stuff,' stated Walker. 'Can anyone verify that, sir?'

'Probably not. Look, I'm going to call my lawyer.'

'Gabrielle Simons?' posited Walker, expecting a reaction and getting none.

'She's not my personal lawyer,' Biggs replied. 'Anyway, as I said, I don't deal with them any longer as from today. They are history.'

'Bit like your stuffed friends.'

'Not funny, inspector. Can we stick to the script?'

'Sure. Was your butler around on that day?'

'Saunders? No, he had the day off. I normally work at home early evening, it's quiet and I can concentrate so no, I don't have an alibi.'

'Just one more question. Do you possess any firearms, sir.'

'Yes, I do, I have a room chock full of them, but I don't go around shooting people, if that's what you're inferring. I shoot the odd game and yes, I would use it if I had to defend myself. Anything else?'

'That's all, Mr Biggs, I'll see myself out.' Walker got up and headed out the door. 'Wait a minute! Biggs shouted. 'When can my surveyors get back to work?'

'We'll be in touch, sir. Don't worry on that score.'

Walker trudged across the gravel driveway, kicking tiny stones as he went. Biggs had only muddied the waters. He was as enigmatic as the stuffed birds and just as forthcoming. Walker sensed that Biggs had deliberately played along with him as if it were a game. Throughout the whole conversation he had sat impassively, eyes straight ahead, balding head tilted back slightly in a manner of mild disbelief with hands clasped neatly in front like a choir boy. No hesitation, no nervous twitch let alone a telltale squirm. He was completely in control. He probably even knew what Walker had been thinking. *Thinking he didn't know who the hell did it.*

Walker climbed into the car and flicked the ignition. As he looked back, he saw the round head of Biggs peering out of the window. Joe Biggs. He could definitely have done it, Walker thought. He had no alibi, he had a motive and he had the opportunity. Yet he betrayed nothing. He was either innocent or utterly ruthless. Either way, he needed watching.

From the bay window, Biggs watched as the policeman climbed into his car and drove off. He sat back in his chair and got out his monogrammed handkerchief. A tiny bead of perspiration glistened on his bare forehead. He dabbed it carefully and then replaced the hanky in his breast pocket. The inspector hadn't twigged but then he didn't look like he was at the front of the queue when brains were doled out. To think that he and Saunders had been at Thomas's house that very Sunday afternoon he made a visit. Detective Inspector? He couldn't inspect his own navel, assuming he could detect it in the first place. Not that Biggs had done anything wrong that night, he had just been trying to preserve his reputation from some of the lies and insults that Alan Thomas had thrown in his direction, just before his untimely death.

As Walker drove out of the long arching driveway, he banged the dashboard. He had wasted a lot of time and got nowhere. It was always the same with dignitaries and businessmen; they never let you get the upper hand. A few months ago, he could have lived with that, but not now. Now his job was on the line, he was expected to deliver. It's me or them, he muttered to himself, me or them. He swung the car left and headed home defeated, taking the one route open to him.

The vehicle joined the main trunk road and picked up a head of speed. He kept pushing his car away from the countryside, towards town and his house. The spangled lights of his hometown winked below. Yes, home is what I need, home and some decent food. He tossed a ten pence coin onto the passenger seat. It landed heads. He'd lost. It sent him barrelling along the route he had just come, through the darkened countryside and winding lanes, in search of David Almond.

Chelmsford Constabulary had been using CCTV for two years. One of the reasons for installing it was to check on undesirables. There was always some fruitcake who wanted to attack a police officer outside a station or try to rescue his pals. It certainly wasn't for checking on the movements of a fellow police officer. Yet that was what Stephen Grayson was doing on a chilly Thursday night - trawling through hundreds of tapes. He didn't want to do it, he said it was pointless, but Walker had insisted. Why did he always end up getting all the shit jobs? Traffic duties, organising ID parades, notifying the victim's spouse. It always ended up in his in tray. Now, he had to check up on his closest work mate.

Each tape was labelled like it had been written by a four-year-old and a whole stack had been dumped into a large cardboard box marked 'tapes' It took him two hours of trial and error to find the one dated 16th October. He hit the remote and the tape wound on, through the twenty-four cycle, until he reached the afternoon. It felt like stepping back in time and then reliving it in slow motion. Suddenly, a light bulb of recognition popped across Stephen's livid face. He saw the man exit and pressed the timer. It read 15:02.25. He wound through the rest, seeing blurred images of people come and go about their daily machinations, like a silent movie, willing his comrade to reappear. All he wanted to see was his familiar body re-entering the station, carrying presents. On and on went the tape, distorting the late afternoon...until finally, Almond appeared. He hit the pause button. No presents were visible. Could be hidden under his coat? thought Grayson. He took a copy of the shot and saved it to disk. He still had to check the timer. His hand hovered over the button. *Press it, damnit.*

It flashed up: 16:15.31.

Grayson slumped back in his chair. Then he ejected the tape and stepped quietly out of the room.

No 14, Ryedale Avenue was no longer a place of working parents. For the first time ever, the house had become a refuge. David Almond had taken Casper, his dog, round to his parents and asked them to look after him for a few days. He told them he was going away for a holiday, to think things out. He had done nothing of the sort. Rather, he had settled into a routine that found him permanently inside the house.

The routine began every day at 6:30 a.m. precisely - a good time to begin observations of God's own world. At first, he had had to familiarise himself with the noises; the clatter of paper against tin, the clinking of a milk bottle and the huff of the boiler brewing up the water for a hot bath. Then he began to record each event as diligently as he could. The milkman arrived at around 7.a.m although sometimes his fizzing electric milk float was heard as early as 4 a.m. The postman, sometimes a postwoman - there was no continuity here - arrived at various times between 9.a.m and 10.15 a.m. Then there was a variety of people passing by his front window every day; mums taking their kids to school, people heading to town, shoppers, kids, old folks in their motorised vehicles and of course the constant procession of dog walkers, some of whom David knew personally. These he took particular care over, they had their own routines, their own agendas but he observed how all of them used the old trick of getting their dogs to deposit their pooh just outside the park so they that they wouldn't have to scoop it up.

Each one found an entry in his newly acquired, emerald green notebook entitled 'God's witness on Earth: Volume one'. He was delighted with the purchase, it was a significant improvement on his files because it was easier to carry and update. How he wished he had kept such a medium for recording everything about Susan and her affair with Alan Thomas! Every day, he was able to refer back to his earlier notes to compare times and events. Instantly, he could see that Mrs Foster, from No 23, walked her two German Alsatians early morning, noon and early evening at 6 p.m. and *always* used the unofficial dog toilet, come rain or shine. Mr Anderson always left at 6.45 a.m. sharp and baring disasters on the commuter trains, always returned at 6.30 p.m. with that characteristically haunted look (except on a Friday, when he returned at 6.10 p.m. with a more relaxed air).

Almond realised that could flick to anywhere in the book and make annotations, adjustments and dossiers, just to complete the picture (like adding that only one of Mrs Foster's dogs relieved himself at noon). He added other facts about the passers-by; their choice of clothes, peculiar habits (none of them seemed normal), their gait (never bolt upright; more shuffling, apologetic) and the prevailing weather at the time (overcast, cool, never sunny). God would have looked down fondly upon these human observations.

It had always been an ambition to use some kind of tonal description to give the event colour, make it come alive. But somehow, this ambitious new challenge proved beyond him. There was simply not enough space. He toyed with the idea of acquiring another notebook but when it came to going outside, he froze. Instead, he allowed the inconsistencies in his recording to take place, comforting himself in the knowledge that he still had more about his house and neighbours than any of the other residents.

For the most part, he stuck to what he knew and he knew that God would be happy with that. Time recording was the best single way of making some sense of it all. It was, for example, a given that, if anyone was late, they would be walking faster or shuffling more quickly. Conversely, anyone early would walk or shuffle with a more casual and relaxed air. The weather variations confused him at first because people wore what they needed to, rather than their individual choice, but since weather was also time-related all these other matters came back to time anyway.

As his documentation improved, he began recording the phone calls - how he would have loved to have had an answering machine but technology wasn't everything! Every cold call was logged and he grouped them according to their general subject matter: double glazing, kitchen units and stone cladding were lumped as home improvements; mortgages, insurance, pensions were described as financial plans; surveys, questionnaires and consumer research calls were simply described as marketing - anything to keep it simple. He found that most cold calls occurred between 5.30 and 7 o'clock in the evening but this was the busiest time for him when he had to cope with the last group of dog walkers before nightfall and people returning home from work. So he rarely gave the caller any time, just a quick, 'sorry' and he was off the phone and back to the window.

People knocking on his door also proved a distraction. He could see who it was by peeking through the side window so he usually ignored them, made a note and waited to see if the same person returned the following day. Meanwhile the milk bottles piled up and junk mail began to grow in the hallway.

His only emotional thoughts were about Cathy. She was still in the house and living her life, of sorts. He left her little notes around the house, just to let her know that was thinking of her. He tried to be upbeat: 'Hey, today is the first day of the rest of your life!' was one. 'Praise the Lord, for he is risen!' was another. Yet, day by day, he was jettisoning that and getting to grips with his new existence.

Gradually, he began to rebuild his life around himself. In the kitchen, he rearranged the condiments, put the entire cutlery into neat piles and pruned the fridge of out-dated products. Susan had loved humus, crispy bread, nuts, soft creamy cheeses and crunchy salads. He pulled these out and threw them into the waste bin along with the twenty-year-old fondue set and the rusting wok. He replaced these with sauces, chocolate, tubs of fruit flavoured ice cream and packets of crisps. The cupboards, shelves and fridge freezer slowly took on his own favourites or more accurately His tastes, and His own personality. Markers appeared, new brightly coloured labels were neatly attached to every type of product from freezer bags to washing powder, a different colour denoting the month he had acquired them. All the new items went to the back, old items to the front. In a couple of weeks, he figured, everything would be current. He would approve.

All this kept him busy but didn't prevent David Almond's nightmares getting worse. The previous night started badly, in discomfort, and finished badly, dripping in a pool of sweat but in-between - that was the worst part. That's when he saw his daughter slipping; helplessly and needlessly, down the slipway, muddied, furrowed with stones and sea kelp. He held out his hand but she just kept falling. On another occasion, they had been on a ferry. He had seen her walking across the deck, her thin, young arms outstretched to the wind and her hair flowing in the breeze. The next moment she had gone. He had rushed to the guardrail but nothing. He had thought he heard a vague cry. He had run around to the stern but all he had seen was the murky churn of fast running waters. A gull had risen on the air currents, its black eyes peering inquisitively and then it had turned away. No grip, a life slipping way beyond the present.

On another night, he had been sitting in the car on a slipway. He had leaned forward, pointing, pointlessly towards the grey, fermenting sea. Through the rain, he had seen storm-tossed fishing vessels stretched at their moorings, like dogs straining on a leash. And always next to him, his wife silent and still. The car had edged forward and she had turned to stare at him. Her mouth had opened but no words had come forth. The car had kept rolling. She was now sliding forward, those slender far-reaching legs opening so slightly, her soft, downy neck and shoulders, that low-cut blouse - she always wore blouses - and those cupola-styled breasts bobbing and heaving so gently. The car had gathered speed. He had seen alarm on her face. Then two, short, loud, destructive jolts of noise. He had turned to see her again. One half still recognisable, holding a fractured expression; grotesque, anguished, contorted with the horror. The other half dismembered, exposed bone, skin tissue hanging limply, the dried, blackened blood amidst the matted hair. He had looked ahead as the car had slid forward, into the sea. Then he had jumped out just before the car had sunk into the murky waters.

There were also daytime images. Sitting at the kitchen table, he found himself in a forest, falling into a very deep pond. The water was icy cold and blackened, discoloured by peaty soil. Submerged, he opened his eyes, unable to see beyond his hand, the world murky and ill defined. Somewhere above, the sound of distant voices, their words failing to penetrate. As he struggled to stay afloat, bubbles of despair broke the quivering surface.

Tears had long since dried up; the surface emotion had sunk deep below the skin. All heartache had passed. Now all he had left were his dulled emotions; immobilising, deadened nerve ends. He felt like the shell of a man he had once been; dusty, dry, almost gossamer thin. Every action, every deed, every thought now settled like a shroud over him. Why couldn't he feel his limbs, communicate with his daughter, pull himself together? God save me! Yet, he knew that everything was on hold. He had stopped existing for the time being and, like a cryogenetically-frozen body, he simply became inert, biding his time for something to come along that would jolt him and make him join society once more.

Then, suddenly, the writing stopped. One day David woke up, found the green notebook full and didn't feel able to go outside to buy a replacement. He couldn't face the cold, prying stares, the traffic noise, the dirty air and the sheer effort involved. He sat in the corner of his bedroom for some time mulling over the situation. There had to be an alternative. He went into the kitchen and practised on a kitchen towel. It didn't allow the pen to make a clear enough mark. He tried toilet paper too, with the same disastrous results.

By this time, he had missed the best part of two hours: five dog walkers, the postman, the milkman, one wrong number and several groups of schoolboys and girls, had come and gone. He began ripping some old books apart, taking the blank pages and placing them next to each other. Then he found that he didn't have anything to bind them together. He tried frantically to scribble some notes across his hand but his pen ran dry. Finally, he went back to bed, shivering, exhausted. As he gazed up at the ceiling from beneath the bedclothes he realised things were going badly out of control. He began to toss and turn, feeling hemmed in by the weight of the bedclothes and the low ceiling. He felt hot and breathless and, for the first time in his life, he felt scared. Somehow, he had to escape, but how and where to? After an hour of torment, he clambered out of bed, threw on some clothes and stuttered downstairs.

At half past nine, Walker pulled into the housing estate and stationed his car twenty yards from David Almond's house. He grabbed his jacket and wrapped it tightly around him. He had a newspaper, some snacks, and his pocket harmonica - he was expecting a long vigil. It was bitterly cold and Walker figured he'd give it a few hours and then shuffle off home to bed. At one thirty, Almond appeared, looked around, almost furtively, hurried to the gate and with his collar hunched up, climbed into his car. Walker flicked the ignition and pulled out behind him.

Soon they were both heading on the main carriageway out of town, past the Army and Navy roundabout and moving in an easterly direction. The road was almost deserted and Walker stayed well back, content to follow the glowing red lights of Almond's Peugeot. The vehicle moved erratically, sometimes veering wildly across lanes. He was concerned that an over-zealous traffic cop would pull him over so he put out a general alert to leave well alone. Along the A12, towards Clacton and Ipswich, he drove. He moved into the nearside lane and, without signalling, joined the B1015.

Hang on, muttered Walker, as it dawned on him. David Almond was going back to the scene of the crime.

As soon as he guessed Almond's intentions, he let him go and tore up the road until he came to the next turn off. Then he took the alternative route. By driving faster, albeit over a longer distance, he was able to arrive first, park the car off the main road and duck down behind some nearby shrubbery. There followed an embarrassing five minute wait with Walker, squatting uncomfortably behind a hawthorn bush, beginning to doubt his hunch and wondering what the hell he was doing out here in the middle of the night. Then he heard the distant drone of a vehicle and white light splashing across the park. He ducked down and saw the car stop and then…nothing. Almond just sat there, motionless, staring out across the sea.

The night was still, the wind had died away and a thin sliver of moon, like a slice of melon, appeared over his left shoulder. The silence was broken by the click of the driver's door. Almond stepped out and went towards the slipway. Almond stopped, his face mostly in shadow but betraying a mixture of bemusement and curiosity. 'What the?' mumbled Walker, the words hanging on his lips. Some thorns had already attached themselves to Walker's light jacket. Then he cocked his head and listened, the intense way a blackbird listened for movement of earthworms. He heard footsteps crunch on the gravel, and a low groan and he watched as his former colleague got onto his knees and began crawling around on all fours. Then he got up and returned to his car. Walker prepared to leave but Almond wasn't finished. He returned to the same spot and got down on his knees again, a torch shining into the night.

That's when Walker realised that his former colleague was going crazy.

David Almond didn't go out again. He stayed in the sanctuary of his house, curled up in a ball, chewing his knuckles. Directly beneath him, in the lounge, he could hear the muffled noise of a TV. It was showing a mid-afternoon game show. Contestants were asked to guess each other's professions. Each time they got it right the crowd would whoop and applaud and holler and he could hear Cathy shout out: 'Right on! Whoa! Get in there!' Whenever the contestant got it wrong, the audience would groan but Cathy would shout and heckle the hapless contestant: 'Get out of it! Loser! Wanker!!'

At last, David went downstairs. He walked through the lounge, went past Cathy without saying a word, and headed straight into the back garden. He grabbed some firewood, matches and petrol and in fifteen minutes, a fire was raging. Without hesitating, he strode back through the French doors, past Cathy and up the stairs. He plonked himself on the bed and punched out the number on the bedroom phone.

'Jack Richards.'

'It's me, David.'

'Oh, David. Get back okay, the other night?'

'Sure.'

'Technically David, it was breaking and entering,' warned Jack Richards.

'Technically, Jack, this man Thomas killed my wife and ruined my life,' stressed Almond.

'I know. That's why I went along with it. You're my long-term friend and buddy, I always loved Susan. She helped me a lot.' Richards said assuredly. 'That's why I did it. Did you get anything useful?'

'Letters, lots of letters, disgusting filth and photos - the ones I found stashed under his bed. I wanted to burn the whole house down, Jack, there and then. I would have done it too, if someone else hadn't been there.' His voice began breaking up. 'I would never hurt anyone. You know that don't you?'

'Yes, I do. Now, take it easy.'

'So I brought them all home and went outside, made a big bonfire in the back garden and burnt them. Burned them to hell. It was beautiful. The orange flames rose into the sky and all the letters and handwriting disintegrated. There's nothing left now. Just some grey ashes that I doused and then put in the bin. I've destroyed it all. I'm happy now. I know he's rotting in hell.'

'I'm pleased, David. Maybe now you can sleep.'

'I don't know about that. I'm too excited. I've exorcised the devil.'

'You just try and get some rest and I'll be in touch.' Jack said quietly and put the phone down.

David rested his head on the pillow. Downstairs, Cathy was still praising and abusing contestants in equal measure. The sounds began to drift away and, as he turned his head to the window, he saw the last few dying wisps of bonfire smoke float upwards. Then he fell asleep and didn't move for five hours.

'So, he went back to Mersey Island?' Grayson said, with complete bewilderment.

'Correct.'

'Motive?'

Walker could think of a hundred and one reasons why Almond would go back (and being an inquisitive cop was just another) but even he couldn't work out why, at two in the morning, Almond had laid out, spread-eagled across the causeway, mouth clogged with grit, his eyes rolling upwards.

'The guy's a fruitcake,' Walker said finally, 'we can take that as read but was this morbid or what?'

'Not necessarily.'

'Okay, smarty pants, you tell me what your buddy's up to?'

'He was getting in touch with the spirits.'

Walker guffawed, a cruel, spiteful laugh.

'Sounds like he was already in touch with the spirits,' Walker said.

'All I'm saying,' Grayson said, struggling to get the right words across, 'is that David Almond was probably going though some kind of cleansing, expelling the demons.' He said the last bit as quickly and as finally as he could in a vain attempt to avoid the cutting riposte.

'By rolling around on the ground?'

'Sure, maybe he'd been on the sauce but this was way beyond that. This was, this was...' He hesitated to use the word but found no substitutes, '...this was an exorcism.'

'Exorcism, my arse!' Walker snapped. 'This is a guy who's got the wind up. Going out, half pissed at two in the morning, to go and visit the sight of his wife's death. I tell you,' Walker continued, jabbing his finger, like a poisoned pen, 'your work colleague is up to something. How does this sound? He's lying in bed, bottle by his bedside, racked with guilt. Then he suddenly remembers. She had something with her, something that could incriminate him, something that could reveal the truth about our Mr Almond. So what does he do? He throws on some clothes, takes his car and goes off in search of this piece of incriminating evidence. He knows police procedures, he knows how slapdash they are and it might still be there.'

'It's possible,' Grayson admitted. 'It's *likely* but it isn't conclusive.'

Walker was up on his feet at this point, pacing the room, scratching his chin of non-existent stubble.

'Don't be so pompous, you little upstart! No, it isn't conclusive. Conclusions are what judges come too,' Walker lectured, still blindly convinced in his theory. 'Nothing we work on is conclusive. We work on clues, motives, evidence. But if I was to say one conclusive thing right now, I'd say that our once eminent detective inspector's reputation stinks.'

Grayson hesitated. 'I don't think we should be talking like this.'

'Oh?'

Grayson sat up and looked straight at Walker who was staring back at him, doubly so.

'Look Grayson, David Almond needs our help. This isn't about the investigation. Jeez, I've solved enough cases in my time not to worry about this one. No, it's about a friend, someone whom we both respect. I'm not asking you to do anything wrong. Christ, we're supposed to be part of a team.'

Grayson narrowed his eyes. 'So this is about David?'

'Of course! And think of Cathy,' Walker said.

'Cathy?'

'Sure. Look, let's not beat about the bush. Cathy is in that house with David. He's not functioning properly. She could be in danger. We have to find out.'

Grayson rubbed his eyes wearily and looked back at the man opposite him, who was unflinching. 'Okay, what's the plan?'

'From now on, I want you working only for me. Nothing we say or do goes outside. Got it?'

'Got it.'

'And you can start off by doing me a favour.'

'No problemo.'

'Good lad,' gasped a relieved Walker. 'Get close to David Almond, real close, so close you can smell him. I want to know if this smell is raw sweat or the stench of guilt.'

CHAPTER EIGHT

Friday, 1st November.

For three long days, the curtains remained closed. Phone calls bleated, unanswered; letters lay on the doormat, unopened; text messages sat on mobiles, unread. In David Almond's head, it was lists of events, chronicles and annotations of people's lives that mattered. In his notebook, he began cross-referencing feverishly all the incidents and events, in the hope that an overall picture would emerge. As the lines weaved and came back on themselves with dizzying frequency, he searched frantically for the meaning of it all. It must mean something, he thought, it must tell me what I need to know.

But, as he grappled for some sense of perspective, he lost sight of his intentions. What was it exactly he wanted, what was it he was looking for amongst the constant perambulations of people's behaviour? Somehow, everything had meshed into one giant intricate, continuum of time and place. Everything was interwoven like a spider's web; people, places, time and space, all connected and yet so complicated and intricate that they could not be viewed in singularity, in groups or even as a whole. To David Almond, the outside world had become tangled, dense and too complex to comprehend.

He decided to abandon his routine. He stopped waking up at his regular time and no longer set a specific time for retiring. Throughout the day, he no longer slavishly followed his own, self-imposed rules. His work had failed to produce results, only confusion. Gradually, David Almond withdrew into his own world; a world of despondency and cynicism, but a safer one. Here they were no demands, no lies, and no disappointments. The day blended into one long period of wakefulness, punctuated only by periods when he dozed fitfully. Soon the only thing he heard was the faint murmur through the thin walls of next door's TV and the occasional single-engined plane buzzing erratically overhead.

Monday, 4th November.

On a crisp, autumnal morning, Stephen Grayson headed for the library in a rush. He was under strict instructions from Walker: don't let David Almond out of your sight. He couldn't possibly do that unless he had everything to hand. He strode in through the gardens, past the water fountain and herb garden and up the steps leading into the picturesque Victorian building. Spying on an old friend was the lowest form of activity, he needed as much positive reinforcement as he could get. As he walked through the door, up to the counter, he recognised her immediately.

'Clara? Clara James?'

The girl behind the library desk looked up.

'What are you doing here?' he asked his old friend from college.

She looked surprised and then charmingly embarrassed. 'Oh, just filling in.'

'Yeah, right.'

'No, it's true! I'm waiting on a couple of interviews. In the city. Quite high-powered, actually. Look at you! Quite the establishment,' she said.

Stephen looked down at his uniform. He hadn't had time to change. 'Didn't I ever mention it, Clara? Bit of a family tradition.'

'No, you didn't, I thought you wanted to change the world?'

'Ah, that was three years ago. Now I'm trying to protect it.'

'So, Stephen Grayson, what can I do for you?'

'Books.'

'Fine, so you've come to the right place.'

'Lot's of books.' He gave her a quick overview of his present situation.

'Now if I remember you liked books with large print and lots of pictures. The kiddies section is over there.'

'Ha! Ha!'

'Spy novels?' she suggested.

'Why not.'

'Bit of surveillance, cloak and dagger?'

'Fine.'

'Maybe some local interest, gossip and intrigue?'

'Okay.'

She disappeared for a couple of minutes and returned with an armful of books. 'There,' she said, plonking them on the desk, 'that should help you to while away the hours while you snoop on innocent people.'

'Ta very much.' He crammed them in his bag and shook her hand.

'Goodbye PC Grayson. Happy stakeout.'

'Goodbye Clara James. Happy stamping.'

Somehow, in the confusion of tickets, books and others in the queue, he neglected to ask her out.

Grayson had Almond's address but he had forgotten where it was. All these new housing estates had confusingly quaint names: Elizabeth Fitzroy Homes, Belair Estate, The Hamlet, Castle Mead, Ryedale Avenue. They suggested rural havens of peace and tranquillity. For some reason they liked to put flags outside these estates, as if some kind of celebration was in order. *They should be at half mast*, thought Grayson gloomily, in respect for another part of greenbelt Essex callously submerged under concrete.

Finally, he arrived at the establishment occupied by David Almond. It existed under the epithet 'Chancellor Park' and had grandly called itself 'a landmark in exciting new housing'. There was nothing remotely exciting about the flat, bulldozed stretches of ground, awaiting buildings. In fact, the only register of excitement was Grayson's raised blood pressure as he acknowledged the fact that hundreds of acres of prime farmland had been turned into a citadel of cement.

He remembered the Victorian house that the Almonds' had lived in at the time of the Great Storm. It had overlooked a picturesque park and some of the large lime trees had broken and sent their branches crashing into their front garden. He had been a kid back then and thought the Great Storm was the most exciting thing that could have happened, a rare expression of nature in the raw. Fourteen years later, the Almond's had moved onto this modern estate, a cul de sac with driveways and newly planted shrubs in tiny gardens and doorbell chimes.

For the next two days, Grayson took occupation in a show home opposite. With his fresh face glued to the window, like a nosey schoolboy, Almond couldn't even fart without Grayson knowing about it. He set himself up for a stakeout just like he'd seen in the movies. Unfortunately, this real one didn't feature anything remotely cinemagraphic; it was just a middle-aged man going about his business. Grayson's limited experience of surveillance had taught him one thing; not a lot happened, so he consoled himself with Cold War thrillers, books on the history of the KGB and CIA and even a couple of books on the pictorial history of Mersey Island.

Grayson noticed that the upstairs room facing towards the road, of No 14 Ryedale Avenue, always had its curtains drawn and there was a light on continually. From his brief visit to drop off Cathy, he imagined it was the main bedroom. It appeared as if it was being kept in a state of suspended animation; preserved, as it had been the moment Almond came back the first time from Mersey Island. That wasn't entirely out of sorts, surmised Grayson, many people coped with loss by preserving objects like a shrine to the dead.

However, he couldn't relate to it. When his mother had died, his father had continued to sleep in the master bedroom and the only shrine was a small section of the back garden made into a memorial garden. He had often gone in and seen his father gazing abstractedly at old wedding photos but just as quickly he would put them away and get on with the tasks in hand. His dad was like that; secretive and shy about his feelings but in his own way, dignified and noble. He couldn't help wondering what Cathy thought of living in a preserved house; untainted, unblemished, a precise imprint of the very last moment her mother was there.

Each morning the milkman delivered a solitary pint and each morning a hand would appear around the door, pick up the bottle, and replace it with an empty. In this way, Grayson knew that a life of sorts was ticking over within the Almond household. He noticed a few cars come and go, mainly residents or tradesmen. Sometimes a learner driver arrived and did a painfully slow reverse turn that ended with the car mounting the curb, crab fashion. Just don't let them loose on the road, he cursed inwardly. A silver Mondeo appeared twice. It stayed for a nearly an hour and then drove off. The postman did his daily round, never delivering anything to the Almond - they were now *persona non gratis*.

After two days and nights of sitting in the room on a cardboard box slurping Pot Noodles and gulping mugs of tea, Stephen Grayson realised what was wrong with the estate: it had no soul. There were no kids playing in the streets and there was no heartbeat of a community. Daylight brought a rash of residents out, as they piled into their people carriers, in a flurry and drove out of the close on their way to work or to dump their kids off in a nursery. They didn't return until the evening. No one came to visit; there were no conversations over the garden wall, no one tending their prize Chrysanthemums and no sign of elderly folks, people that always gave a residential estate a sense of time and place.

Grayson knew that property developers like Biggs didn't give a flying fuck about the atmosphere but what about the residents? Did they ever concern themselves with what had gone before or were they so work-obsessed and blinkered in their ideas, as they drove their Volvo estates into the cul de sac, past the dovecotes and up the path to their red-bricked façade, that they thought it was normal? Did they, he wondered, ever stop to think that their squat house stood where curlew had once bred, where walkers had breathed fresh air and where kids had prodded sticks into pools in search of frog spawn? Never in a zillion years, he concluded, and maybe, they were actually happy now that their surrounds were uniformly arranged with swathes of tarmac, rows of breezeblocks and clumps of stunted shrubbery.

Grayson tried to calm down. Hyperventilating, in a tiny room with no windows open, wasn't good for him. He kept returning to the book on Mersey Island. It was actually more interesting than the so-called thrillers. There was something about an island, thought Grayson, that made it evocative. Was it the sepia-tinged photos of the men who wore hats, moustaches and sported some kind of smoking device? Or was it the women, with their woollen shawls, heavy boots and arms folded, emphasising the breadth of their shoulders? In most of the shots, the islanders stood to attention, with an unmistakable air of pride and quiet determination. Yet, what made it so memorable, was the way these unsmiling, expressionless characters merged seamlessly into the background of fields, villages, the local stores and the sea. These people and their landscape were as one.

Grayson played out that age-old conundrum; does man maketh the environment or the environment maketh the man? Nature versus nurture. And, like age-old philosophers, he didn't get anywhere. All he did know was that Mersey Island was frequently battered by winds, tides and storms and yet ultimately it was the people that mattered. Of course, at that time, they had little choice. They couldn't go off somewhere warm and pleasant like the Algarve, they had to survive and the only way to do that was to embrace the environment, rather than battle against it.

Self-preservation concentrated the mind wonderfully back then...except for the man pictured in the nineteen-forties driving an Austin Morris. He had attempted to cross The Stood at high tide. Built originally during Roman times, The Strood was the one connecting slither of contact with the mainland. The waves had lapped over the wheel arches. The route ahead had become impassable. Yes, it did look vaguely heroic but it looked even more comical; a new technology fighting in vain against the age-old elements.

Somehow, this naivety endeared these folks to Grayson. He even thought, that if he had been alive at that time and lived on the island, he would have had a go across The Strood, come hell or high water. One thing was certain: his life then would have been a bloody sight more interesting than sitting around on a cardboard box spying on a friend, who was doing absolutely nothing.

David Almond now ceased all forms of communication. He severed a lifetime of links and connections in order to clear his mind. He was getting all the clutter away. He began to stop eating, not just cutting back on the frivolous items of consumption like crisps and chocolate but outright fasting; first meat, then eggs and then bread. Finally, he stopped drinking.

Somehow, this was all coming naturally, part of an evolutionary step that reinforced his belief that to see the next part of one's existence one had to end the first part. It was a part that included his childhood (an errant but essentially honest youth), adolescence (fleeting passions amongst a sea of uncertainty and teenage angst), and finally adulthood (love, marriage and a steady job). Remove that and from now on, all sensations could come from within; from inside the familiar rooms and from inside his head. Everything was expunged, except for his faith which remained steadfast throughout.

For two days, he searched within, going deep into himself, hoping to spot something and pull it triumphantly above the surface like some deep-sea diver. He turned his mind over and over, pretending that his skin had internalised and that all his organs and veins had become fully exposed. He wanted the bare bones of his sinful body to come to the surface, so that he could see and feel the very evil pump and pulse of his living body. Yet nothing came. Nothing exploded as he thought it would, nothing presented itself and said: 'here I am! This is me! Beelzebub!'

He became very mournful. One night he lay awake feeling the tears lying just behind his staring eyes, pricking his skin. His arms ached, his neck stiffened and his whole body felt sore and jaded. It was telling him, that beyond his faith, the sins of his life could give forth no more.

The next morning he woke, completely oblivious of time. It was dark outside; it could have been night, early dawn or even late dusk. It just didn't matter. The side of the bed where Susan slept had been covered up with cardboard boxes. He opened the bedroom door. A thin slither of light shone underneath the door, across the landing. Cathy was in her room. He crept slowly downstairs, barely making a noise on the creaking stairs. A thin slither of light shone underneath the door, Cathy was in her room. The TV was still on, its ghostly glare flickering light into the lounge. He switched it off and went into the kitchen. All the food was labelled nicely and stacked up neatly. It hadn't been touched for three days. Cathy hadn't been in the kitchen for days.

The set of carving knives were illuminated by a splash of moonlight, cascading in through the conservatory. Almond took one of the knives in his right hand and held it to the light. It twinkled like a jewel, like a portal to another world. He turned it towards himself. The face of the blade slid slowly across his face. It felt cool and smooth. He turned it inward, feeling the edge against his skin, as sharp as glass.

His hands began to tremble, and his eyes turned wild with anticipation. Today was the day.

He cut himself some bread. Then he stuffed it greedily in his mouth and put his head under the kitchen tap to swallow.

He had many things to do and he was keen to ensure he overlooked nothing. There was a screwdriver lying on the window sill in the conservatory. He picked it up and stepped back into the lounge. His house was now part of him and he had it mapped internally in his head. He began scouring the territory, pacing up and down, examining all the possibilities. There had to be one object, above all others that made absolute sense and it had to be within the four walls.

He disappeared into the cupboard under the stairs and found what he was looking for. It was a black fuse box attached to the wall. He examined it briefly, the fuse and wire were in reasonably good condition, good enough to do what they had to. He returned to the lounge and began inspecting all the electrical fittings and appliances: Video, FM tuner, Multi-Tape, DVD player, radio, dimmer switches, arc lights, reading lamps, all great inventions of the twentieth century, all potential solutions, all channelling into the great elemental force of electricity.

Grayson thought about many things as he sat there for hours on end, only thirty yards from David Almond. One of his thoughts was about the first two months of the football season. He couldn't work out why his team had suddenly forgotten how to defend. They had the same defence, they were playing in a lower division and yet they kept giving away silly goals at set-pieces. Sloppy defending? Lack of concentration? Bad luck? The football season, he decided, was like a journey; with a well-defined beginning, middle and end. Throughout the journey, there would be obstacles, successes and failures and at the final whistle of the final game it would be possible to reflect and look forward to the next journey.

Not at all like this case, he reflected, or many others for that matter. None of them had been straightforward; none of them had been particularly successful, as victims and criminals alike had led the police a merry dance, and none of them had been solved. His detection rate hovered perilously below the critical thirty per cent mark. Now, the chief suspect was sitting opposite in the warmth of his own home, watching TV and listening to the radio while this investigator froze his butt off, sitting at on a cardboard box, stuffing himself with carbohydrates.

Sometimes, he thought about Cathy. He wondered what she was thinking. Had she liked the jewellery and what exactly was she doing in the house? What did young girls do, anyway? They never seemed interested in sport or bird watching. Where were her friends?

He also thought about God and David Almond. David had always been a Christian, though he never talked about it but Cathy had said he had become very devout. That signified a major change of mindset. An epiphany or just plain guilt?

He thought about how his hair never quite went the way he wanted it. He thought about how he was going to pay the mortgage, whether he would be up for promotion, why his car was making clanking noises and what he couldn't do for a big, fat, juicy steak

Most of the time, though, he thought about women: all types, all sizes, all educational backgrounds, all ages, all situations, everywhere.

At this time, it came down to one particular incident; at the local supermarket, a check-out girl, someone who served him behind the till. Her name was Betsy. Very literary, he thought. The events leading up were hazy; he thought he had prepared a shopping list but it could have been one of those impromptu visits where he lingered and dawdled and ended up buying nothing. What was certain was that he was unprepared. Not because this was the first time he had considered chatting up a check-out girl. In fact, he had tried it stacks of times, even though it was always fraught with danger (without the benefit of seeing her legs, it was impossible to know if he was chatting up a midget or a six-footer). It wasn't even his technique; carefully calibrated to take in hair, eye contact, mouth, speech and air of availability. No, on this particular occasion, it was the fact that there was none of this logical joined-up thinking and the reason for that had stared him in the face.

It was all because of her prodigiously, gigantic breasts. He could see they were enormous, because he triangulated the precise size based on estimated mass, weight and the bulge in her blouse. They were bigger than any he had ever seen, except in magazines. As he helped the articles of food on their way, her breasts spilled across the conveyor belt and very nearly touched his hands. Rice Krispies, packets of pasta, tins of fruit and bottled beer passed by in a blur of insignificance. His eyes became magnetised to her chest and followed the gentle motion and rhythmic sway of her tethered breasts as if his life depended on it. Food stacked up, on the other side, unbagged.

For some reason he felt incredibly hot. His mouth gaped open, his hands grew sweaty and his throat became parched but he couldn't stop gazing at the massive mounds of her chest. Was it, he wondered, a genetic defect, some secret hormonal ingredient in the milk or simply a freak of nature? Something (or someone) had made this part of her body so oversized and magnificent while leaving everything else relatively normal and standard-sized. It was unreal, like one of those plastic assembly kits where you painstakingly put all the parts together until a globule of glue unexpectedly forms and distorts everything.

There should have been a sign, he thought, above the counter, telling him and others to expect the unexpected. Yet all there was, was this harmless, innocent female and a plastic badge pinned to her lapel telling him that the burgeoning left hemisphere was called 'Betsy'.

'Five pounds thirteen,' she said, coolly. *Was this how much they weighed?*

Stephen Grayson tried to play it straight down the line. He would ignore them, concentrate on the transaction and just behave normally, like any sensible adult. Then she would think: yes, he's a sensible young man, I'd like to go out with him.

Yet somehow, as he stood there, trying to prise his eyes away from her chest, the numbers went off the radar. His sweaty hands began to flap inside his wallet like a fish in a net and a fifty-pound note fluttered onto the counter, in front of her. She swatted it and held it up.

'Fifty pounds.' She said, formally. She was definitely not talking about weight any more.

'Right.'

Just keep it nice and steady, he thought. Don't do anything stupid. Nothing to alert her attention. Just collect the change, put it in your pocket…and go.

She clicked the till. It sprung open, coming together exactly where he had triangulated her nipples to be.

How many times in a day did that little collision occur?

It was an Industrial Injury Claim waiting to happen.

He would offer her all the support she needed.

He tried to keep his slobbering mouth clamped shut. She pulled out some notes and coins and flicked off the receipt. The till slammed shut, giving much needed relief to her frontage. She eased forward and handed the whole little package to his waiting hand. He was nearly home and dry. *Take the money, that's it. Just take it.* She hesitated. *Cummon, just a couple more inches.* Then, in a moment where time froze and his life force drained away from him like sand, she retracted her hand. It actually disappeared from the counter, leaving his right paw, quivering like a poorly set jelly.

'Oops,' she said, 'I've got it wrong.'

'Oh? Don't bother.'

'No, I have.'

'Sure it's right.'

'No, no, it isn't.'

'Must be. Let it go.'

'I can't,' she said, grabbing his hand.

'It's gone through. See?' she said insistently. Then she thrust the receipt towards him, 'Here, want to look at my boob?'

Stephen wrenched his hand from hers, grabbed his groceries and left the girl with the receipt in mid-air, as he charged for the door. He never went back again. Not even where the severed head of a store detective was discovered one morning in the deep freezer, his mouth stuffed with olives. From then on investigating drug deals, bank heists, car chases and common assault were mere bagatelles compared to the experience at the supermarket.

David Almond looked at the clock. It was ten past four in the afternoon. He shook his head. He had been downstairs, attending to things for *nine* hours. He couldn't account for his time at all; everything he was doing was going very slowly while time was racing like a ghost. He thought he must be getting out of whack with his three dimensional world. Maybe he was already somewhere else? He was tired, and had a gnawing hunger and thirst yet these things would have to wait. In the corner, peeking out of the murky gloom sat the TV. It was the one appliance that summed up the outside world; its futility and all its obscene insincerity. He found himself examining the back of the TV. It looked as good as anything. He jerked the plug out of the wall socket and the TV light dimmed to nothing. He carefully laid the cable on the lounge carpet.

He went off to find a smaller screwdriver. In the cupboard under the stairs he flicked the light switch. The bulb pinged into failure. Typical, he thought, how lights always failed in darkness, so that you had to grapple around in darkness risking life and limb to get the thing working again. After several dispiriting minutes, flapping and groping in Stygian gloom, he opened the toolbox. It creaked and a puff of dust engulfed his nostrils. The toolbox was a living testament to some of his greatest DIY disasters, a time when had bothered, albeit in vain. Now it could prove to be his most reliable ally.

He took the box into the lounge and set to work. The screwdriver stayed surprisingly steady in one hand and he began to dismantle the socket. At one point, tiny silvery screws flew off and disappeared into a recess of carpet but somehow that always happened. Anyway, he didn't think he'd be needing them again. He tugged gently and the wires came away easily from their housing. He held them aloft; red and black exposed, sticking out like a forked tongue.

It seemed absurd, he thought, how difficult life was and yet how easy the solution could be. He knew God would approve. He stepped out to the bathroom and doused a flannel and then walked to the front door, locked it and threw the deadbolt. He came back and splayed his legs on the lounge carpet. He wanted to be comfortable as possible.

He decided to take one last look around. He felt he deserved one final reflection on days gone by. Many of them happy ones, like the first time they'd decorated this room. Susan had decided to copy an idea in House and Gardens. They spent three weeks over summer getting all the right accoutrements and arranging people to do it. Then she changed her mind. The room was the wrong shape, the ceiling too low and the light came from the wrong place. The futility of it all. Now, the room was a ragbag mixture of sixties kitsch, fifties austerity and nineties technology. Only a few days ago, Susan and Cathy had sat on the very sofa, enjoying the photo snaps, chatting about their plans. Susan had seemed relaxed, almost happy but who knew what she was really thinking. She was probably planning her departure at that very time. Nothing was as it seemed. He lay back and made himself comfortable. The least he could do was appear to be in comfort when friends came calling.

He studied his watch once more. Seconds flicking past, the final few moments. Ironically, for the very first time in his life, he felt in absolute control. I am master of my own destiny, he thought as the seconds went by more quickly than he had ever experienced. Maybe life does actually speed up as one meets one's maker, he concluded, a sprint to the finishing line. How long should he give himself? Five minutes, ten minutes, maybe even half an hour? How long did he deserve? He could now play God, at his most vengeful or in his most infinite mercy. Ultimately, he would decide,

The second hand continued rotating on its clockwise axis. Now it had a power of its own - it was counting down his life. He watched it jerk from one position to another, notching up another marker of time. It would have been so much better to be smooth, untroubled but this fractured motion summed it all up. His life had been a messy and stuttering effort all round.

Deep in his mind, he began to experience an intense emotion. All the objects around him were existing now, at this moment. They would continue afterwards, as if nothing had happened. At least everything in the room was tidy, ordered, prepared. All the objects were in their correct places, ready to carry on their function. That would be his legacy. Only the TV was in a state of disrepair, fair enough, he surmised, he didn't think that the first thing someone would do when they saw him was switch on the TV.

He strained his eyes and ears. He heard erratic, wavering noises and he realised they were coming from within. His thoughts had become swollen, his eyes had become sore and now he began sobbing uncontrollably. There was madness everywhere, he concluded; madness and sadness, it tainted us all, never far away, always waiting to take over. Like some leitmotif, it kept recurring; more pain, more misery, more heartache. That is what life was really all about.

In the deep and distant background a car horn sounded. Someone, somewhere was frustrated, tooting their horn to vent their frustration. What a pathetically futile effort, he thought. *Toot! Toot!*

He would walk through the electrical corridor with his head held high. There was no shame, no disgrace, and no mortal sin to recant. When he arrived, he would calmly announce himself, state his mode of death and then explain that it was best for everyone; for Susan his wife, for Cathy, friends like Jack young Stephen Grayson, his parents and for himself.

His eyes lowered to the palm of his hand, lying next to the wires. He counted down the last few moments, the final chapter, the last page, the final entry in his notebook of life. His job was only half-complete. Now for the remaining part. The wires stood out like multi-coloured tendrils; twisting, alive, reaching out to touch him. It seemed curious, he thought, how such an all-powerful force could lurk so quietly within this feeble cable. He wondered how it would feel to have it closer, lying in his hand. He picked it up and laid it carefully across the folds of his left palm until it sat snugly. It felt incredibly light, almost featherlike and barely perceptible in its load. Yet it had gravity, it had presence and in truth, it was just waiting, like a magic lamp, for him to bring it to life.

He was breathing heavily now, his hands hot and clammy, yet he was shivering with dread, he wanted it to be quick and neat, nothing messy. At last, it was time to put his trust in God. 'Yea, though I walk through the valley of the shadow of death, I will fear no evil...' The words of the 23rd Psalm echoed around the room, like an incantation, '...For thou art with me, thy rod and thy staff they comfort.'

Now he felt calmer, subdued, prepared for the final journey. He pressed the wet flannel into his mouth until it went fully against his gums. Then he placed the wires more fully into the centre of his palm and slowly wrapped his sweaty fingers around them. He closed his eyes and, like the blink of a camera's aperture, everything was plunged into darkness. Finally, with a great surge of effort, he clenched his fingers around the palm of his hand.

Then he squeezed hard.

From that moment the world outside ceased to exist. Just let it be clean and efficient, he thought.

The pain was nothing as he'd imagined. Somehow, he expected excruciating torment, a normal pain, at least normal in the sense of being crushed, stabbed, burnt or beaten up. Once as a child, he had caught his hand in barbed wire and, as he tried to escape, it ripped his flesh clean away. He'd cried so loudly that day that all the neighbours came out to see what all the fuss was about. He had run up to his mother in his shorts and showed her the dripping blood. But this was not that kind of searing pain. It was more of a force; controlling him, taking over and directing him to another place. It only took a nano-second for the force to surge through every extremity of nerve and limb. It flowed with such jolting intensity and power that it slammed him against the wall. Then it stayed, for several seconds, it seemed, as the convulsions raged, coming swift and hard, each individual tsunami rattling against his skull and teeth. His heart pounded until he thought it would explode and then, just as suddenly, everything went dark and his world collapsed inside of him. All sensations ceased.

CHAPTER NINE

A Technicolor whirr of zooming rockets, splintering sparks and booming explosions battered Ryedale Avenue, that night. It was Guy Fawkes Night and the night sky crackled and fizzed above the houses and gardens, waking dogs and scaring cats but No 14 remained unmoved. Somehow the residents of No 14 were living in a different dimension. The only reassurance Grayson received were the regular text messaged he got from Cathy. It was her form of communication and he found her far more willing to text message than she had been to talk. He pretended he was in bars, pubs, going to see films and flirting with women. Never once did he admit that he was watching from the house opposite.

She sent him messages at all times in the day, even in the early hours when Grayson was slumped on some cushions, fast asleep. She told him about the crummy TV she was watching, she told him about her favourite foods and drinks, about pop groups and some of the nicknames for her classmates. The only thing she refused to speak about was her father. Then, on the night of the fireworks, the messages stopped.

Stephen Grayson began to get very nervous.

He had kept punching out messages to Cathy to no avail. It felt like a one-way conversation to someone who was deaf and dumb. He was getting ready to call in reinforcements. They could storm the place, get Cathy out and haul David Almond off to the funny farm. He would give it until daybreak.

Wednesday, 6th November.

Daybreak came and Almond woke, his mouth parched, his head pounding with the vision and eyes smarting from lack of sleep. He cast a bleary eye at the clock. It blinked 7:50 a.m. The last time he'd looked it was 3:15 a.m. He reached for the tranquillisers and fumbled for a cigarette. A policeman of twenty years. Alert, conscientious, thorough, in control of his faculties - now reduced to a mental cripple. Cathy had already called him and then disappeared. He didn't care where. He turned over and went back to sleep. The start of another day. Then the doorbell rang.

Twelve hours earlier, he had hauled himself up from the lounge, staggered up the stairs and collapsed on the bed. Tapping his head repeatedly, to make sure it was still there, some thoughts slowly disentangled themselves from his cluttered mind. The voltage hadn't been high enough, he should have worked it out beforehand. Bad planning. What was Ohms law all about? Something about amps and resistance? His body had had too many ohms. How many ohms, 400, 600? Either that or there weren't enough amps. Whatever, the result was too few volts piling into his body. How many? 2,000? 1,000? - probably only a quarter of that. In the UK, over fifty people a year managed to electrocute themselves in the home, how come *he* couldn't? The bath would have been better, he concluded. A bath and a good old-fashioned electric bar heater to remove all those pesky ohms. Damn the electrician.

Grayson was dozing drowsily on a cushion when his mobile suddenly sprang into life. He flipped it open, tapped the keys and up popped a message.

'HAD A HICCUP. ALL OK. XX'

That was it. Tantalisingly short but proof enough that life, of a fashion, was continuing in the house opposite. It wasn't entirely reassuring, hiccups (or whatever euphemism she chose to use) not being exactly conducive to relaxation, but he let it go. He brewed up a cup of tea and helped himself to a bowl of cereals. He began sloshing the milk around and then covered it all with lashings of sugar.

Suddenly, a sight made him choke on his Coco Pops.

At 8 a.m. precisely, a 4x4 Landrover pulled up outside the house. A short balding man stepped out, shuffled up the driveway and pressed the doorbell. Grayson grabbed his binoculars and pushed them against his eyes. The man stamped his feet, trying to keep warm. Then he turned to face his onlooker.

Grayson dived for cover, waited a few seconds and slowly rose off his haunches. Then, he peered slowly out of the window. The door opened and the man went inside. Grayson recognised him immediately, same build, same height, same ungainly gait. Ten minutes later, the man exited, climbed into his vehicle and drove off. Grayson punched the air and rang his superior.

'You're kidding!' Walker shouted, through his mobile phone.

'Yep. I'm sure, sir. Matches the photo and description on file.'

'So what did Joe Biggs do?'

'He went inside, stayed for ten minutes, left by the front door and drove off. I've got the registration number if you want to check.'

'Don't think it's necessary but it fits. Grayson, I do believe our chickens are finally coming home to roost.'

'Going to arrest him?'

'What, Biggs? On what charges? He'll have us for harassment. No, let's get David Almond in, once more, for old time's sake. Though this time, no tea and biscuits, and bonhomie. Finish your breakfast, leave the house as discretely as possible and drive around the block a couple of times. Then bang the car door, walk up the driveway and haul his backside in for questioning.'

He entered the sparse, sterile room in a tweed jacket, green baggy cardigan and crumpled trousers. A tiny window offered scant daylight. For a second, he instinctively went for the interviewer's chair. Then he made a rueful smile and walked around the other side of the table. He decided that he wouldn't sit at all. They could keep him there all they liked and use every interrogation trick in the book but they would not get him to sit.

Officer Stephen Grayson flicked the button and spoke into the recorded. 'Interview with David Almond, Monday, 6th November, 10.30 a.m. Present with me is Detective Inspector Walker.' Almond backed away, until he was pressed against the wall, his arms running across the surface, like feelers. Now he was steady.

'Mr Almond,' Walker began, 'could you please explain your whereabouts on 16th October between the hours of fourteen-hundred hours and eighteen-hundred hours.'

'I was working…here.'

'Did you go out?'

'Um. Yes, I might have gone out. It was dear Cathy's birthday.'

'Look, Mr Almond. How about we sit down?'

'No way. I might be feeling weak but I'm not going to accept favours from you lot.'

'Cummon, pal, Walker said. 'It will make it easier for both of us. Hmm?'

'Let's hear what you've got to say.' Almond insisted.

'Okay, play it your way. How long were you out of the office for?'

'I don't know. A few minutes, might have been longer.'

'PC Grayson says he left you around two-fifteen. The next time he saw you it was five to six.'

Almond shot the young police officer an accusing look. Grayson nervously looked away, then began blowing his nose.

'We were working in separate rooms,' Almond said. 'You know how it works.'

'You say you were gone a few minutes. PC Grayson has checked. CCTV logs your time away at one hour and a quarter. Bit of a discrepancy?'

'This is ridiculous, I can't remember. Wait a minute, you were there, and you said you'd cover for me.'

'To go shopping, that's right,' Walker said.

'Maybe you don't know what it's like shopping for a loved one,' Almond said mournfully. 'You have to make it count, because it's these little things in life that makes everything worthwhile.'

'Did you go to any particular shop?'

'Hold on, I think I went to several shops. It was raining. I got wet.'

'Got a receipt. Might have the time on it.'

'I probably threw it away.'

Walker sighed. 'Never was that hot on paperwork, eh, Mr Almond?'

'Now look!'

Grayson began to blow his nose again and then went into a fit of coughing and sneezing. 'Sorry, sir. I've got to step outside.' He clicked the recorded off and rushed to the door, coughing as he went. Walker waited a couple of minutes and then Officer Parker came in and clicked the button. 'Interview resumes with Officer Parker, replacing Officer Grayson.'

'PC Grayson says that when you were driving out to the murder scene you knew the name of one of the roads, Bowers Lane, even though there was no sign,' continued Walker. 'How do you explain that?'

Almond raised his eyebrows. 'I've, I've been there before. I like to escape sometimes.'

'It wasn't that you'd been along that road just an hour before?'

'No, not a chance.'

'Police records show that you booked out a Smith and Wesson .38 on 11th October, five days before the murder. Where is it?'

David Almond shifted uncomfortably. 'It's in my house. I keep it as protection. I'm nervous.'

'A big policeman like yourself.'

'It's not a question of size.'

'Now, why did you really take it out?' Walker asked.

'I told you, protection.'

'From whom?'

Almond hesitated. 'I don't know.'

'You don't know. On 30th October, at around 2 a.m. you were spotted on Mersey Island, visiting the scene of the crime. What were you doing?'

Almond shrugged his shoulders and tried to laugh. He hadn't smiled in days. It came out as a grimace 'Once a police officer, always a police officer. I was feeling lost. I just wanted to see if anyone else had visited the scene. I needed to get my head round it.'

'Head round what, Mr Almond?'

'Every night since Susan was killed, I've been having nightmares. I wake up in the middle of the night in a sweat, I must keep Cathy awake, so I just thought that if I tried to confront it again…'

'This morning a man named Joe Biggs came to your house and you invited him in. What did he want?'

'It was business.'

'What kind of business?'

'Business business.'

'What kind of business, business?'

'None of your business, business.'

'Mr Almond, this isn't helping. What kind of business?'

Almond breathed in a lungful of air. He was finding it terribly claustrophobic.

'Joe Biggs is a property developer. You probably know that.'

'Yes.'

'He came to me a year ago with a proposition.'

'Go on.'

'He offered to put me and my family in one of his new homes, free of charge. He would pay for all the ground rent and it would be registered in my name. I would be able to do what I liked with it provided I lived in it for the next five years. Susan and I were struggling financially. We had sold our previous house. Susan had just started work and my pay wasn't great, as you know. I wanted to give Cathy the best education so we accepted. Look, do you think I could have some air?'

'So what did Mr Biggs get out of it?'

'Nothing,' Almond sighed, 'except he had a policeman living in one of his properties, on hand to deal with anything. He was worried about vandalism and graffiti and he thought that if a copper was living there, it would help him to sell the other houses.'

'So you became a security guard?'

'Of a fashion.'

'Did you ever declare this financial interest with CS Jones?'

'No I didn't.' Almond loosened his tie and undid his top shirt button. 'Any police matters related to the new estate, I did in my own time. I never mixed the two.'

'Were you aware that Mr Biggs was involved in a property development on Mersey Island?'

'No, not at that stage.'

'Did you know that Mr Biggs was a major client of Ridgely, Turner and Fowler, your wife's company.'

'No, I didn't. My wife would never discuss her business associates with me.'

'Did you know that Mr Biggs is a suspect in the killing of your wife?'

'No, of course not.'

'Did your wife know that Mr Biggs provided you with a house?'

'Yes, she did. I couldn't have kept it from her. Her firm helped with the conveyancing.'

'Don't you think your wife had a conflict of interest?'

'All right. Enough! For pity's sake, can't you let up? I can't stand it anymore!'

Parker flicked the switch and the interview was halted.

Outside in the corridor, Grayson was leaning against the wall and breathing heavily. It was nothing to do with nasal obstructions, purely his deep sense of unease. He had faked the sneezing fit simply to excuse himself from the agony of seeing his work colleague under the pump. It had been even worse, through the one way mirror, voyeurism of the worst sort.

David Almond had taught him everything he knew and here he was repaying the favour by an act of pure treachery. What had happened to the policeman's code? What had happened to loyalty and kinsmanship? He had supplied all the minutia of their time together in an attempt to be honest and sincere. Yet where had it got him? He had had to watch in horror as it had built up into an unassailable case against his colleague. He didn't know what was worse, his own actions or seeing a man he respected suffering so. And what of Cathy? She would never talk to him, or trust him again or call him uncle. In one act, he had destroyed two people's lives and lost their friendship.

It was at this moment, that he truly began to question his position in the Force. Was anything worth this sacrifice? Was the quest for the truth so unimpeachable that it could be allowed to shatter people's lives? Wasn't there ever a situation where common sense, diplomacy and tact should prevail? More pertinently, how could he continue acting like judge and jury when he knew that his own actions were flawed?

In the last few years, David Almond had saved his butt on numerous occasions, like the time he had flipped over a police car after a few Christmas beers. 'Policing is a learning experience,' Almond had said to him. 'Learning about the job, learning about people and learning about life. Without learning,' he insisted, 'you'll never make a decent copper.' After that, Grayson swore he would never drink again while on duty.

Stephen Grayson walked back into the interview room and saw Almond sitting there with his head in his hands. Grayson motioned Officer Parker to leave the room.

Her cornflower-blue eyes went towards his. 'You okay, Stevie Wonder?' she said, as she got up to go.

'I suppose so.'

'Want to talk about it?'

'No.'

Grayson sat down next to John Walker. The door closed. There was an unbearable silence, a tension that cut through the room. Nobody wanted to talk. Nobody trusted each other. Three strangers looked into space and wondered what to do. Eventually it was DI Walker that broke the fragile silence. 'Okay, we're not charging you…yet Mr Almond. You can go. PC Grayson, get his coat and get him into his car.'

Grayson helped him on with his coat. 'Sorry, David.'

'Sorry? Good God, Stephen, get a grip! You're just doing your job.'

Grayson looked crestfallen, but he was naïve. David Almond may have seemed like a broken man but as he walked out of the police station and towards his car, he felt anything but. Out from these charred, embittered ruins had come fresh thoughts. Crazy yet uplifting talk. His whole body was speaking to him and telling him that it wanted to live. His arms and legs felt strong and full of energy. His finger, face and toes all tingled and twitched, part of himself once more. He was no longer the central figure in a post mortem; a ropey electrician had saved him. Even the interview, conducted like hundreds before, had been full of meaningless observations, innuendo, and little to incriminate him. He had almost enjoyed the parry and thrust once he knew they had nothing.

He put his car into gear and cruised into the busy high street. This was not humiliation, it was salvation, a watershed. He was being recognised again, coming back into the folds of a community. At this moment, a milestone was achieved and a millstone removed. He would forget everything that had happened and move on.

He could do it, he thought, all it would take would be one concentrated effort, no regrets, no self pity. The car nosed through a busy shopping area; parents holding hands with children, traders plying their wares, schoolchildren skipping out from primary school. Life was still out there and so was he. It was time to reclaim it while he could, time to get back to the essentials, time to join the rest of humanity. From now on, his life would be about opportunities, it would offer him chances, things he had always wanted to do.

As soon as he got home, he rushed into the kitchen. A surge of a newfound strength had hardened his resolve. He shouted out to Cathy. He wanted to take her in his arms and kiss her but she was not there. He ran up the stairs. Yes, it was possible. *Anything* was possible. He picked up his faithful pen and scribbled frantically across the page Alive! Alive! The words jumped off the page. He sat back and sighed thankfully and a tiny tear formed in the corner of his eyes. The words formally announced the fact that David Almond was officially back into the land of the living.

PC Grayson walked thankfully into La Pourbelle. It was Wednesday evening and he needed some respite after a gruelling day at work. He was shown to the table where his name was clearly marked on a card on the starchy white tablecloth. The word PC was omitted. He didn't mind that; he preferred to be treated as normal.

As if his life could be. No one here suspected that he spent sixty-hour working weeks dealing with criminals and victims, the two most polarised sections of a community. No one knew that he was up to his neck in bloodied corpses, violent psychopaths and kids spaced out on crack while they sat demurely at their tables discussing money, sport, soap TV and complaining about the cost of everything. His eyes scanned across the room. They all looked horribly normal in their smart clothes, making convivial conversation, cracking lame jokes and flirting shamelessly with their dining partners. This was a place to be seen.

Grayson had learnt one thing from DI Almond. It was impossible to switch off completely. Work always interfered with leisure. You could never relax. Simple stuff like the sights, sounds and smells of a busy place filled his mind with troubling thoughts. Was the killer in this very room; were they talking about the very case, did that body language cover up a shooter and were they confirming each other's alibis? Not everyone looked like conspirators or perpetrators- it was nothing obsessively irritating like that - no, it was just that the skinny kid sitting over in the corner with his hand taking out his wallet had a face with guilt written all over it. It kind of made it difficult to concentrate.

The waiter produced a large, leather bound menu and invoked a gentle cough. He'd probably been standing there some time. Grayson took the menu with both hands and began unfolding it, like a priceless, ancient book. Even the lettering was in an antiquated style, so laden with gothic style characters that he could hardly make out the text. Then he realised that it was in French. English translations were coyly written underneath in parenthesis. For the peasants, he assumed, people like himself, who hadn't quite grasped Gallic despite the fact that the verbs had been ceaselessly pounded into him at school. Sometimes things just wouldn't stick if you wanted them to.

He leaned over to his left where a middle-aged man was eyeing the menu. His look of dispassionate interest, suggested he knew the place and the cuisine.

'Excuse me sir. I wondered if you've been here before?'

'Yes, many times.'

'Anything you recommend?'

'Oh, the duck's very good and so is the veal. Are you a meat eater?'

'Yes, I am.' Grayson said.

'Well, how about the steak? It comes highly recommended from the *maitre de*.'

The waiter cruised into position.

'Are we ready to order, sir?'

'Steak au poivre. New potatoes and peas.' Grayson said.

'And how would you like your steak cooked?'

'Well done.'

'Thank you, sir.'

Grayson knew the joke was there for the taking: 'Well done'. 'Thank you'. Yes, it had a ring of staginess about it, but then didn't all the classics of the restaurant joke genre: flies in soup, making the pork chops lean and 'how did you find your meat, sir?' He wondered if waiters were trained deliberately to accede to a playful customer; feeding the lines, allowing the customer to indulge in harmless vicarious pleasure at the restaurant's expense. Probably not.

Those joke's would have been icebreakers, provided they were delivered spot on and she was in the right mood. Assuming that he had a female companion, that is. Jokes weren't easy to deliver but they were a form of seduction. What woman hadn't said to him, 'I like a man with a sense of humour'. A smile, a snigger, even a broad grin could lift her whole countenance and lighten proceedings. However, anything rude, crude or tasteless was equally likely to darken those very assignations. Maybe he should just leave the funnies to others, more adept, not that he knew anyone in the Force.

Betsy, Clara, Flavia, Davinia or Sara? He couldn't decide. Like a chocoholic devouring both levels in a chocolate box, he wanted them all. Yet, if push came to shove, for one night only, in la la land, with a following wind, all things considered and bearing in mind that they would both be tipsy and bordering on the euphoric, then it had to be Sara. No one else, possibly in the universe, certainly not in Upper East Chelmsford, could have given as much fun in one night as Sara. She would sit opposite him, sweep back that massive bow-wave of blond locks, laugh infectiously at one of his jokes, flash those formidable milky-white teeth, and tell him how much she fancied him. They would drive off to an expensive hotel, book the honeymoon suite and spend a riotous night of unbridled passion on an enormous water bed until they awoke three days late, exhausted, sore and deliriously happy. Sara would have registered big time on anyone's Richter scale. *In his dreams.*

God, he was getting emotional. Was his life really so flimsy? Yes, he had phone numbers for all of them, but no, he hadn't dated any of them. In fact, he had only exchanged glances or the most perfunctory of daily conversation, just enough to get their names and numbers - like some nerdy trainspotter. It wasn't that he couldn't, it wasn't that he didn't want to, it was just that he felt that he needed to wait…just a few more weeks, until his choice was clear. It was all part of a plan.

The problem was that they were all extremely attractive, friendly, single and apparently available. Yet making that initial step was crucial. Get it wrong and it would set him back months.

Experience had taught him that women were always attracted to the shy, retiring types so the longer he waited the more likely he was to succeed. 'Yeah, right,' David Almond had said when he first heard the World According to Grayson, two weeks before the killings.

'I don't want to appear desperate,' Grayson had stressed. 'I try to keep away from them as much as possible. Make them pine for me.'

David Almond had found it hilarious: 'Faint hearts never won fair maidens, Stephen. I met my wife at a party, we started talking, I asked her out. We both discovered we were Christians. We fell in love. That was it. End of story.'

Only it wasn't.

Of course, there was always Officer Amy Parker…

The person who actually appeared, arrived wearing a long brown trench coat was Sergeant Alec Grayson. He had the same eyes and mouth as his son but there the resemblance finished. Alec Grayson was four inches shorter, thirty pounds heavier and smoked. He was also totally bald, a result of a bank robbery where he was hit in the arm and all his hair fell out. He never smiled and any joke would have sounded like a foreign language. Consequently, his office nickname was Smiler.

'Bloody awful weather,' he said, removing his coat and handing it to the waiter. Underneath, he revealed a grey suit with collar and tie, one he rarely wore these days. 'Sorry I'm late, Stephen,'

'No problemo.'

'Have you ordered?'

'Gone for the steak.'

'Excellent choice. Scotch beef, Aberdeen Angus. Finest fillets. I'll go for the same.'

'Dad, I'm not really used to places like this.'

'Nonsense! This is the best place to talk,' he continued, easing himself into a chair, the waiters here are very discrete, so go ahead.'

'Don't you want to eat first?'

'No pussy-footing. It's always best to get these things out in the open. Your mother and I never hedged an issue in our lives; it was straight out, blam! and let's see where we go.'

Stephen breathed in deeply. 'It's about John Walker.'

Alec pursed his lips. 'What's he done now?'

'It's the way he operates, dad. He's all over the place, messy. He doesn't write reports. He doesn't file anything and he behaves as if he knows everything. He's a bully. He's got this really annoying habit of treating me like a kid, ordering me around but I'm part of a team and we should be partners.'

Alec Grayson buttered himself a roll. 'I hear you, son,' he replied, popping a piece of bread into his mouth. 'It wasn't that long ago that I used to criticise my superiors. You've got to understand,' he continued, 'that DI Walker is one of the old school. He never went to University, he probably never even studied. He's no fool but he uses something he calls instinct.'

Grayson made a little laugh.

'He likes to think it puts him in control but it doesn't,' added his father. 'He's botched up so many jobs, I'm surprised he's still here. I shouldn't be saying this but the Super is not pleased, I can tell you. It's only the cost of paying him off that keeps him in a job. Look son, Walker is on a very thin tightrope right now, but this case is important. There's a lot of media interest. I don't think everything has come out yet. There could be some history here, something about the past being revisited. Walker is in the firing line but he has the experience to crack this case.'

'He's been going after David Almond.'

'So I've heard. I can't say I'm wild about it myself but he's doing his job. Look, what I suggest you do is hold fire, keep a few notes of what goes on and when, just in case. Don't question him too much, make it look as if you agree with him. The inquest is only a few days away and the case will be closed. Then you can move on.'

The steaks arrived and both men grabbed their knives like cudgels and began to attack their food with gusto. For several minutes there was silence apart from murmurs of appreciation and slurps of red wine. Stephen Grayson sometimes found it weird having his dad working in the same building but then he was the only reason he got the job.

'So, dad. You don't think I should go and see Jones and tell him?'

'No, I'd leave it for now, son. You don't want to get a reputation as a troublemaker. Maybe Steve Almond will come back.'

'I don't think so. He's in a bad way and so is Cathy.'

His father cut off a large piece of reddened meat and deposited it into his mouth. 'You see how lucky you are? You've got a good job, excellent prospects and you're learning all the time. So just take it easy.'

'No problemo.'

'One more word of advice.'

'What's that?'

'Stop saying no problemo…it infuriates the hell out of people.'

'Really?'

'Yes.'

'What everyone?'

'Everyone. Damn annoying.'

'Message understood.'

Alec Grayson sighed.

'Just say, okay, okay?'

'O-kay.'

The tones of *Mission Impossible* sounded through his jacket pocket at ten thirty-three. Stephen Grayson was told to proceed immediately to the house. The owner had claimed he had heard an intruder. With his food scarcely digested and half a bottle of robust red swilling around, Grayson screamed out of the restaurant driveway and drove like a demon. He arrived at the house not ten minutes later. He slammed the door knocker and then pressed the doorbell.

A dapper man with a face so cadaverous he couldn't have seen daylight since the 60's, opened the door. Another man, more animated, appeared behind him. Grayson recognised him instantly as the man who had visited David Almond. Grayson was frogmarched through the hallway to the drawing room where the French doors were swinging open crazily in the breeze. Artificial light spilled out onto the rear lawns. 'That's where they've gone!' he shouted, tugging at Grayson's sleeve. 'Didn't think I'd be alert. Took fright, the bastards!'

Grayson rushed out into the darkness and the cold. There were no footprints or signs of a break in, simply the wind rustling through the poplars. Grayson strode back in, beckoned the man to sit and flicked open his notebook.

'Won't be coming back, sir. Now, could I have your name, please?'

'Joe Biggs.'

'Any idea who *they* might have been, Mr Biggs?'

It was late but Joe Biggs wasn't tired. He began pacing up and down the room with feverish intensity.

'They? Could have been just one of them. Let me see now,' he said, , raising his hand theatrically in the air. 'How about David Almond? One of your lot. He decides that I am responsible for his wife's death and comes around to seek revenge. Not too fanciful, I think? Or maybe one of the relatives - police families all stick together don't they? Could be any Almond really, or an in-law, they like piling in whenever there's a feud. Here's another name in the frame: John Walker. Your boss, the man heading up the investigation. He was around earlier, asking questions, maybe on a recce, casing the joint? He decides he wants a better look - but can't be bothered to get a search warrant. Any of this ring true? Or how about relatives of the deceased Alan Thomas? Their precious, high-flying barrister, who like Icarus, plunges to Earth. He's chief suspect in a double killing so you can imagine how keen they are to get him off the hook. Not very pleasant for the dears, much better to blame someone slightly unconventional, like me. Hmm? Then there's the press; always snooping round for stories and filth. They've had me in their sights ever since I started business. Of course it's envy, but it doesn't stop them harassing me, printing lies about my sexual orientation, going through my dustbins. Or what about those rustic local stalwarts living on Mersey Island? Talk about sensory deprivation! People like Joe Hart and Alison Holmes who are desperate to escape their squalid lives and put their careers and self-advancement above integrity. They'd love to have a pop at me and get me put away once and for good. Now who have I left out? Well there's hundreds of suppliers – whingeing human wreckage, losers, the lot of them. Then of course, the bleating customers, who take everything I offer and then refuse to pay until the debt-collectors turn up on their doorsteps at 7 a.m. How about ex partners? Those fleeting amours that left the Biggs gravy train too early to get their rewards? Or Gabrielle Simons? Now there's a combustible character. She treats everyone with contempt and would love to put one over me. All to do with my lowly background, you see? How about Saunders, my butler? Maybe he did it, for the money of course.'

Grayson had started to fill out his notebook but had given up. Anyway, it was pathetically inadequate in the world of 21st century technology.

'You obviously have some ideas,' Grayson said, as the rant gradually subsided.

'Late evenings, best time of the day,' Biggs said, tapping the side of his head with his index finger. 'Grey matter needs the cool air to invigorate itself. Well known fact.'

Maybe Biggs had opened the doors himself, dozed off and then forgotten he'd done it. As Grayson wrote in the final full stop, he looked up and saw hundreds of glassy eyes staring back at him.

'Wow! Quite a collection, sir. Lapwings, quails, greenshanks, oyster-catchers, curlews…'

'Don't know. Don't care. I mean, that's not the issue, is it?'

'So, have you noticed anything missing, sir?'

'No, no,' he snapped irritably.

Grayson's eyes lit up on a wading bird with coppery plumage 'How about this Black-tailed Godwit, think he's lost his mate?'

'I don't know. Look, numbskull, don't you see? They're not interested in all this ornithological mumbo jumbo. Someone is out to get *me*.'

'Why would that be, sir?'

'They want to put the frighteners on me. Understand? I want a 24-hour guard.'

'We can't do that, sir.'

'Why the hell not?'

'We don't have the resources but I'll report it as breaking and entering and we will get someone to take prints and we'll take it from there.'

'Pah! Complete cop out! Bloody typical! Always messing around with the detail when the picture is staring you in the face. Do you know what the difference is between the private and the public sector?'

'I think you're going to tell me, sir.'

'The difference, PC Officer Grayson, is that the private sector spend all their time looking at how to do things, while the public sector spend all their time looking at how not to do things.'

'That's you're opinion, sir. Maybe you can use the private sector to employ a security guard. CCTV wouldn't go amiss, either.'

'God, you're impertinent! I tell you, I'm going to have words with your chief. Oh yes, I know him. We'll soon see if I get a guard or not.'

'Please yourself.'

Grayson let it go. There was no point telling Biggs how pathetic, misguided or utterly pompous he was. He made his way out of the drawing room. A stuffed badger stared out at him. 'Keep your nose clean,' Grayson said, as he tapped him playfully on his shiny black nose.

DI John Walker heard about the Biggs break-in from a breathless Grayson. He told him to calm down and do nothing. He couldn't put a guard around his house if he wanted to. He was sitting in his kitchen, unshaven, feeling sorry for himself. He had a headache and his neck muscles were too tight so that he couldn't move properly. Bloody useless, he thought. Anyway, at least Grayson was dancing to his tune. He was the young gun, full of ideas and convinced he could crack it. As long as he followed specific instructions, Walker would still be able to claim that he had solved the killings.

Walker unplugged the landline phone and switched off his mobile. He then poured himself a coffee, extra strong, no sugar. He really didn't want to speak to anyone, particularly not the Chief Superintendent. At least at home, he wouldn't have to put up with Jones waving the rule book, like some old testament scribe, his large fleshy fingers stabbing at the particular chapter and verse.

In all the years he had known him, CS Jones had never listened to a word of explanation from him. It was as if Jones took a sadistic pleasure in dressing people down, particular people like him who had become part of the furniture. Maybe that's what power did to people. Well, if Jones had something to say, he could damn well come and see him personally. He had more important things to do.

The contents of Alan Thomas's drawer needed sorting. He brought all the papers into the kitchen and laid them in front of him, making a neat line. He arranged the contents in piles; categorising them and then sorting by date wherever possible. He was surprised how much he had collected in a few desperate seconds of frantic hand waving, but then he was an expert.

He kept the business dealings apart from the personal details and then sub divided routine stuff like letters and correspondence, photos and dog-eared news-clippings from detailed documents like diaries and notebooks. Finally, he began to work through them, methodically absorbing all the relevant information and throwing away the junk.

It was tiring work, sifting through stolen goods. Very soon, he felt like his throat had been cut – breakfast time. He stepped outside and went into his carport, his secret kingdom. Whirring water tanks were piled up high, full of rocks, seaweed and seawater. Each tank had a thermostat and a pump to keep the water swirling like the tide, so that all the creatures moved as if held in the sway of a tidal estuary. He carefully examined each tank, checking for water quality, chemical imbalances and plant life. He was their gatekeeper, the man in charge of their lives, or more pertinently, their imminent deaths.

Shellfish had intrigued John Walker ever since his father had taken him cockling when he was five years old. They had waded out on the ebb tide, plunged their hands into the soft mud, and pulled out the little treasures beneath. Walker suddenly realised that shellfish lived in a dark, secret and mysterious world; unfathomable, unseen, almost existing in another dimension. To his child like sensations, they were aliens with their weird shapes and myriad colours.

He imagined that they were highly developed organisms, deliberately tiny and apparently defenceless to confuse their prey. They lived quietly in the most inhospitable of environments, eking out a life on a seabed in total darkness and mind-numbing cold. While fearsome tides buffeted coastlines, destroying human habitat in minutes, they clung tenaciously to rocks and crevices, waiting. Then, one day, they would rise up, leave their seabed and take over. It was only a matter of time.

Man had tried to destroy their habitats. Fisherman used nets, trawls, cages, shovels, anything to wreck their habitats indiscriminately. Yet, even as they scooped up the masters of the sunken world and hoisted them unceremoniously into the human oxygen-filled world of air and light, these shellfish survived. Only the pearl divers, with their ability to plunge almost forty metres and make a hundred dives a day, were allies of the shellfish. They would help the shellfish take over and become masters of the world.

He pulled up his sleeve and placed his hand into the cool water. He picked twenty of the largest green Maldon mussels and took them carefully indoors. He placed them under a cold tap. They didn't like unsalted water, it was another human environment, but it was the quickest way of sorting out the good from the bad. If only police detection were that easy, he thought, as he went about discarding those that refused to close. He teased away the beard, the calcified grit and crusty appendages until the carapaces lay, glistening clean. Then he lined them out in a neat line on a towel, like bodies in a mortuary.

Alan Thomas's journal turned out to be nothing of the sort - it was more of an appointment diary. Meetings, discussions, briefings, more meetings. No doubt, all these entries would be crosschecked to the firm's records and found to be *bona fide*. Five in one day, sometimes as many as seven. What on earth did lawyers get out of having so many meetings? Grayson and he got together everyday but never anything so formal as a meeting, usually a chat by the coffee machine or a brief update in the car park. There were minutes, meetings, agendas, action points. How one's life changed when all your time was chargeable to a client? Walker began speculating on how much it was possible for a lawyer to earn, not withstanding sleep, meals and other forced distractions. One hundred, two hundred, two hundred and fifty pounds an hour? It was obscene.

His hunger began to gnaw more heavily. He pan-fried some chopped garlic, sweated some onions in a pan, added a dash of chilli, a dollop of cream and a slug of white wine. Then the moment of truth: the moment he became chief arbiter, supreme judge and executioner, all in one. He lifted the shellfish high above the stove and plunged them into the boiling, fizzing waters. Books told him that they had tiny nerves but he didn't care, aliens didn't feel pain. As they writhed and trembled in the bubbling cauldron, they were no longer creatures but food. He placed the lid firmly on the saucepan and went back to work.

There were photos of loved-ones, close relatives, three curly-haired nieces and two god-children, all obligingly named and dated on the back. In the space of five minutes, Walker had a pretty good idea of what made Alan Thomas tick. Thomas was solid, disciplined, dependable with a strong work ethic and a keen sense of time and place, preserving the past in photographs and words. He liked, or at least he used to like, order, routine, and a formal structure to his life.

There was nothing to suggest why he would contemplate a suicide pact - only a cosmic shift in his life could explain such a premeditated act of violence. However, it had to be here somewhere, thought Walker, hidden away in all these papers. Otherwise, why would he keep all this stuff locked away in the first place?

Maybe he had deliberately placed all this memorabilia in the drawer as a symbolic act, a severing of a life past and done with. But if he *had* been planning to end it all and wanted it hidden then why only secure it with a flimsy lock? Why not completely destroy it, throw it away, incinerate it or, like an honest to goodness lawyer, shred it?

Then something clicked into gear. Maybe Susan Almond had discovered something here, maybe Thomas found out…perhaps. Or, perhaps someone else had been around to Thomas's house, sneaked in and taken everything on Susan Almond? That Sunday afternoon, when he saw two men leaving. They must have taken everything. They must have wanted to hide the secret of Susan Almond and Alan Thomas.

Walker returned to the hob. The steam from the saucepan had misted up the window. It was necessary to have intense heat because it provided the key. It unlocked the secret world of the mollusc.

Mysteries always disturbed him. External appearances were there for a reason; to confuse, to protect, to hide the truth. To reveal the solution and get back in control, it was sometimes necessary to be brutal.

He lifted the lid and a cloud of steam enveloped him. He peered into the mist. The concentrated heat had prised open the unprepossessing shells of scarred tissue. They now revealed the glories of the unsullied creature within. Pulsing like beads of light, the small orange and white treasures lay before him.

In a flash, he knew precisely what he had to do.

He gave the clattering shells a quick turn, the onions and bubbling cream foaming over the wooden spoon. Then he threw away the unopened mussels and poured the remainder into a bowl. At last, he sat down, surrounded his meal like a wagon train. The aroma was intoxicating; sweet, juicy and tangy with the sea. He plucked the first pulpy mussel from its shell and prepared to place it slowly into his mouth. He had cooked them to perfection. Then the door bell chimed.

Damn!

Walker walked along the hallway. He could see Jones's bulbous face pushed hard against the frosted glass. He hadn't wasted much time, Walker thought.

'John, are you in there?' came an angry sound. Walker swept back into the kitchen and crammed all the stolen papers and photos into a cupboard.

'Coming!'

'John!'

Soon their bony faces were squaring up to one another, head to head, eyeball to eyeball like a couple of prize-fighters.

'Sir?'

'John, you look surprised.'

'Oh, just didn't expect you. I didn't know you knew where I lived.'

'Of course I do, Walker. I know everything about fellow officers.'

'Best come in, sir.'

'Ta.'

Jones went striding into the kitchen.

'Yea Gods, mussels for breakfast!'

'Full of nutrition,' Walker countered.

'Best sit down and continue with your food. I won't be long.'

'Thank you. So what brings you here?' Walker asked. 'Drink?'

'Drink? Are you dumb or what?'

'Just asking.'

'Christ man, you think this is a social call?'

Walker slumped on his kitchen stool. A couple of photos of Thomas with his relatives lay face up on the kitchen table. He waited for the worst. Several minutes later, the fiercest part of Jones's electric storm had blown over. A-Z Securities had logged an intruder at 15, Melstone Court on Sunday 27th October, at 16:33 precisely. Residence of one Alan Thomas, deceased. The intruder was described as white male, 5'11" dark hair, wearing jeans, walking boots and a long grey overcoat. Jones glanced into the hallway to see a long grey overcoat hanging from the door and a pair of muddied walking boots lying on the kitchen floor. 'John, as of now, you're off the case.'

'You can't do this,' Walker demanded.'

'Yes I can. There's no appeal on this one. You're grounded,' Jones said flatly. 'God, it's bad enough trying to nail down criminals without finding my own team copying them. Hell's bells, what were you thinking, man? Thought some SAS tactics would come in use? Surely, you've been round long enough to know these activities are unacceptable? Well, from now on it's the boy scouts for you, sitting behind a desk shifting paper like there was no tomorrow and toggle or no toggle it's dyb,dyb,dyb. The next time I see you in the office, I want you tied to a bloody desk. Now I'll let you get back to that stuff you call food.'

Walker said nothing and did nothing. The mussels had gone stone cold and Jones was already past him, storming out the door.

PART TWO

'Poverty and oysters always seem to go together'

Pickwick Papers

CHAPTER TEN

Friday, 8th November.

Essex is much maligned, considered by many to be a flat, boring, concrete sprawl, with few natural features to commend it; an urban footnote with the capital to the West. I believe that to be grossly unfair. One side is indeed a giant commuter belt of tarmac and terraced housing but the other three sides are water. To the south, lies the Thames, the great artery from the nation's heart, connecting capital to coast. Sixty miles to the north, lies the Stour, a sleepy, winding river, connecting pastoral Suffolk to the flatlands of North Essex and to the east, the North Sea; gateway to mainland Europe, pounding the coast along the length of the county. These natural boundaries provide a great, bustling trading route of freighters and tankers, a picturesque landscape brushed by weeping willows and flecked by swans and a dramatic coastline where the rusty brown sea gnaws away at the land like a giant rodent. Hardly boring.

The North Sea feeds the Crouch, the Ter, the Brain, the Pant, the Roach, the Can, the Chelmer, the Colne and the Blackwater - a scurrying network of rivers, that course over boulder clay and spread out like a nest of vipers. It fuels their passage as they scour through salt marsh and mudflats and slice across agricultural fields and meadows. These in turn, nurture the backwaters; a mish-mash of creeks and brooks and swirling mud tides that crosshatch the arterial rivers and scurry into every corner of the county.

Twenty-two identifiable rivers delineate and define Essex but it is the backwaters that have had the greatest historical impact: Paglesham, Benfleet, Shelford, Holehaven and many, many others. These, seemingly inconsequential, waterways studded their imprint on the historical background of the county, like embroidery. Essex men knew every creek, every turn, every thread and texture of river and stream. Stowboaters, codbangers, salavagers and oystermen understood the tides, the currents and the swells and they knew how to exploit them to the full.

In the Eighteenth century, Essex became rich in the flow of illicit rum, port, gin and brandy, with local officials often the recipients, sending their booty to gin houses all over Britain. In its heyday, over a quarter of Britain's illicit spirits found their way in through the South East salt marshes. The creeks provided the routes for illegal cargoes of French blond lace, flowered silks, leather gloves, waistcoats brocaded with gold and silk from Chantilly and Antwerp and for outgoing goods like wool, corn and coal. Smugglers used their own specialised vessels, like bumpkins and smacks, to navigate the shallow, isolated channels and keep their business away from the prying gazes of the Customs men. In fact, many smugglers used the oyster fleets as decoys or actually masqueraded as fishermen, to avoid capture. Parish registers are full of smugglers whose occupation is euphemistically termed 'former oyster merchant.' This deception is only part of the story; many of the most notorious smugglers were Custom's officials themselves. Criminals and corrupt public officers, it seems, have been part of Essex for as long as rivers flowed and laws existed.

Water links the people to the sea, sea to land, villages to towns and towns to cities. Locals exploited these natural resources to the full by building wooden structures. On each and every river lies a hotchpotch of jetties, water mills, locks, rusting sluice gates, breakwaters, dikes and some of the finest buildings in the county. Places like Stisted Hall, built in Regency times with its imposing Doric columns overlooking the Blackwater; Great Codham Hall, with its dovecote; the weather-boarded Great Bardfield Mill, sadly bereft of its water wheel; Great Sampford, home of Dick Turpin, lying on the river Pant; Tudor-timbered Panfield Hall nestling on the river Pant and Barns Mill, a three storey brick and timbered building astride the canal linking the Chelmer and the Blackwater. Today, these structures are as much a characteristic of the 'featureless' county as the rivers themselves.

Alison Holmes, daughter of Councillor Holmes and close acquaintance of Joe Hart had drawn up this comprehensive list, accompanied by photos and historic profiles of all the major buildings and points of historical interest. Churches didn't matter - they had their zealous own band of supporters. Not even a rapacious developer like Joe Biggs would contemplate building on hallowed ground. He was more devious, more a backdoor man, creeping around the backwaters and dried-up ditches of Essex, finding idyllic spots and then buying up surreptitiously the freehold. She had crossed swords with him on many occasions and now they were once again on collision course with the development on Mersey Island.

'So how *do* you stop him?' she asked desperately as she took another gulp from her glass. Joe Hart shrugged his shoulders.

'Your dad's a councillor; he's on the planning committee, for Pete's sake!'

'I know Joe, but he's in the minority. From what I can extract, most of the council are sympathetic to Joe Biggs.'

'Oh and why's that?'

'You know I can't tell you that, Joe. Anyway, there's a meeting this afternoon. That's all I can say.'

They looked up. No one in the Fisherman's Arms that lunchtime was watching them, apart from one man. The regulars were drinking at the bar, telling jokes, smoking, joshing with the barmaid and keeping one eye on the muted TV. 'Okay, so let me guess,' Hart replied, fully knowing the answer. 'Mr Biggs has a degree of influence. Apart from promising to build local amenities and raising the quality of life, he takes some of the councillors to one side. He talks about that nice development at Castle Mead or Belair Estates. Maybe they could take a trip up there, in a chauffeur-driven limo and have a look at one of the show houses?'

'I'm saying nothing.'

'I could do checks on some of them but I think you need to take responsibility. I can only rake muck for so long before I become accused of harassment and that's me off the paper.'

'You're right of course, we don't want that,' said Alison flatly. 'We've already outed him and that backfired. I know some people who couldn't stand the odious man now feel sympathetic.'

'That's the thing with papers,' Hart explained, 'you can only push so much before you have to produce the evidence.'

When Joe Hart first joined the *Essex Times*, he was a sports correspondent. It had seemed like the ideal job; sit in a nice warm commentary box with a mug of tea and eat complimentary cakes while watching local football and cricket. Then a quick post-match interview with managers and players and some insipid answers and then off home with nothing to do for the next couple of days. He didn't pick the fixtures, it wasn't his fault players needed recovery time, but it left him with a lot of spare time on his hands.

He began taking an interest in the past players and their backgrounds. Soon he was visiting their places of birth, their schools and homes and speaking with relatives and school friends. He figured that a sportsman's success often came down to his close relatives and the school environment. Schools like Felstead produced Essex cricketers and schools like Barking Comprehensive produced footballers, not just county players but internationals.

Yet in the last five years, things had changed. Sport had gone through tough times. Labour considered it too competitive, too rough, too much like real life, maybe. There were too many losers and not enough winners. Then he watched in horror, as schools began selling off their playing fields to meet rising costs, first the athletics track, then the pitches and finally the whole playing fields. Developers like Joe Biggs moved in and transformed prime athletics tracks, muddy football pitches and oval cricket grounds into residential housing estates. Alison Holmes was right, Biggs had no loyalty, no sense of the big picture, no notion of history and pedigree, he simply came in and concreted it over.

'We haven't got a shred on him now,' Hart said. 'He's been skinned clean like a weasel.'

Holmes narrowed her eyes. 'Don't worry. I might have something for you after the meeting. Don't worry, you will be the first to know. You're not getting cold feet, are you?'

'No it's just that-'

'What about a demo?' she suggested.

'On the island? With the islanders? Have you seen them?'

Alison Hart nodded. Sometimes you could sense the mood and mien of the people, even just by looking at them. Romans, Vikings, Civil War, German bombs, nothing had shook them from their torpor.

'Well what happened with the biological survey on Mersey Island?' Hart enquired.

'Nothing,' said a peeved Alison. 'They came in for two weeks with their jam jars and microscopes and all they found were a few unusual bugs and some tasty eel grass that the Brent Geese eat. No rare orchids, no unusual rodents. Basically, it's just clumps of grass and mud.'

'Brent Geese are good.'

'Were.' Corrected Alison. 'They're found everywhere now and they can quite happily move up the coast if they want to. Norfolk's crying out to get some Brents so they can develop their bird watching industry further and say how some of their migrants fly in from Siberia.'

Joe Hart looked at the young woman. She could have been attractive but she allowed her hair to be unkempt, she didn't bother with make-up and she dressed as scruffily as he had in his student days. She was younger, wilder and, with a rich father, she could do what she damn well wanted. Unlike him.

When he had first met her, he hadn't reckoned on this. He thought it would be a partnership. Now, he shuddered sometimes with the things she said.

'So what are you suggesting?' he asked at last. He looked for a straight answer but saw instead that twisted smile flash across her face.

'Something dramatic,' she said coldly. 'Something so dramatic that he will not bother us or anyone else again.'

His face froze. Suddenly he saw someone much more deadly than he could have imagined. 'Jeez, you're fucking crazy!' Then she burst out into laugher. 'No, not that silly. At least not yet, hah! No, we need to frighten him, make him run like a scalded cat, put him on the back foot so that he can't think straight.'

Joe Hart put his pen and paper away. 'Your mixed metaphors do you proud,' he said, artfully trying to lighten the mood. Anyway, his views had changed with the receipt of the letter. It had come through the post that morning, a gold envelope, recorded delivery. When he opened it, it had changed everything.

The words were couched in phraseology, but if he interpreted it correctly, Biggs was willing to buy himself out of a hole. 'Sport in the county will enjoy a renaissance...competing at last with its more illustrious neighbours'. And, if this fairy godfather was to believed, 'Mersey development would be excellent for the community, with extensive new media facilities'. Finally and crucially, he said that 'all key personnel associated with the development would receive 100 per cent leverage on their mortgages.' In other words, a stroke of the magic wand would see his financial problems disappearing in a puff of smoke.

Yet how to tell Alison Holmes? She would laugh in his face, rip up the letter and call him a traitor. Best to keep things quiet for a few days, in the hope that everything would resolve itself.

He watched as Alison's face broke into smiles and giggles.

'Another drink?' She asked. 'I think we should be celebrating.' She was actually enjoying all this, he realised, she was getting a buzz out of trying to destroy someone, whatever the consequences.

Just then, a young man came up and took the spare stool. He slid it under his bony frame and looked at the couple.

'Sorry, that seat is taken,' Hart said.

'Not anymore. Joe Hart, isn't it?'

'Yes, who are you?'

'My name's Grayson, PC Grayson. And who might this lady be?'

'My name's Alison Holmes,' she replied hastily as she gathered up the papers and photos and crammed them into her satchel. They joined a hair comb, a box of codeine, a tin of pepper spray, jelly beans, a bar of dark chocolate, tissues, a purse with credit cards and a photo of her parents and niece, a fully written-up diary, a digital camera, an iPod, a tin of moisturising cream, binoculars, a handbook of radical feminist poems, fifteen pages of her first novel, a half an ounce of Moroccan red cannabis and one thousand pounds in cash.

'Dad a councillor?'

'That's right,' she confirmed, once the bag had been manoeuvred successfully under her legs.

'Glad I managed to catch up with you. I understand you're both involved in local community issues?'

'Maybe.'

'Bit like the police really.' Grayson said.

'Nothing like the police, really,' Holmes said, icily. 'And by the way, we were having a private conversation here, do you mind?'

Grayson blinked and continued. 'I'm making enquiries about the death of Alan Thomas and Susan Almond. Were you acquainted with the deceased?'

Both shook their heads.

'You are both active members of Mersey Island Conservation Society. Where were you on the night they died?'

'Is this an interview?' Holmes asked.

'No, all off the record.'

'Working.' Holmes said.

'Working.' Hart repeated.

'Both working.' Grayson noted. 'Glad to hear you're such industrious types. Did you see anything or have you heard anything?' There was more collective shaking of heads and an unfriendly pout from Holmes.

'Nothing,' Holmes said, eventually. 'Obviously I think that Biggs is involved. Money is always at the root of these problems.'

'Quite. You either have too little or too much,' Grayson said. 'What about you, Mr Hart? Money hard to come by? Bet you could do with a few quid.'

'I get by.'

'You've been active in your newspaper column. The politics of envy.'

'Didn't know you guys could read.' Holmes said.

'You'd be surprised what we can do. So Mr Hart, what's your latest view on the victims and how they met their demise?'

'My job is to report the facts,' Hart said defensively, 'and give the public what they want but, apart from what I've written, I know absolutely nothing.'

'Hmm. An intrepid report such as yourself?'

'Well maybe PC Grayson can help fill in the blanks?'

'Like how?' Grayson asked.

'Well, my readers are wondering why Inspector Almond isn't on the case?'

'He's on compassionate leave.'

'So, why don't the police seem to know if anyone else was involved?'

'Who said we didn't?' Grayson asked.

'Are you saying you do?

'No,' Grayson replied, playing with a straight bat that would have impressed someone like Hart.

'My readers think that maybe the police are covering things up,' suggested Hart, 'trying to make it seem like no one else was involved.'

'That's crap,' Grayson snapped.

'Can I quote you on that?'

'No.'

'So PC Grayson, tell me, off the record, is Inspector Almond a suspect?'

'Have a nice day,' Grayson snarled as he got up. He leapt from his chair and stormed out of the pub, leaving the locals to the sickly, cloying smell of stale tobacco and alcohol that lingered like after-dinner indigestion.

Walker passed up the opportunity to visit Hart and Holmes. He stayed put in the office, as per instructions. The sun was angling into the office, spilling across the desks. He had other things on his mind, well not things but CS Jones. Jones had flexed his muscles, like some circus showman. Only he should have done it years ago, when everyone was at it. Walker had never been taken off a case in his life - until now – and his investigation lay in ruins. All the evidence, paperwork, theorising and painstaking legwork, most of it inadmissible, had been blown away by this single, misguided and vindictive act.

CS Jones didn't care about justice, he didn't care about tried and trusted traditional policing techniques and he certainly didn't care about Walker. What he did care about was his public image, statistics, equal opportunities, working with the community and most of all, his own damned pension.

Walker kicked his chair so hard it crashed into the wall. He grabbed the files on Alan Jones and Susan Almond and threw them in the wastepaper bin. He took a lighter and set the papers alight. A plume of black smoke rose gently up like a funeral pyre. Flames began to lick the sides of the basket. Suddenly the smoke detector began bleeping like a reversing vehicle. Within ten minutes, John Walker had been ejected from the building.

As he was frogmarched into the car park, he was consigned ruefully to his fate. There had been a grinding inevitability to it all. It had been like this for ages; fighting a lone corner while everyone else piled in. No one could help him now. He had no allies, no allegiances and no one to call. Only his long term buddy, David Almond, could have helped him and he was one step away from the funny farm.

Walker picked up his jacket and threw it on the back seat. Then he climbed into his car and roared off. He was a man on death row; surveying all the debris of his career, his ambitions, and his existence. He jumped a set of lights and headed in an easterly direction. He leaned back and dragged the jacket onto the front seat. His diary fell out. It wasn't a very comprehensive diary, just a few names and the odd contact number. He pulled into a lay-by on the busy A127, as the traffic howled past.

He began shuffling through the pages, looking under every conceivable heading. Eventually, he found it, right at the very back, where he did all his doodles. The phone number was partially obscured by squiggles and thought bubbles. He switched on his phone. After several abortive attempts, something crackled at the other end.

'She's not here.'

Walker recognised the voice immediately. It was Simons's secretary, Ms Adams, - the one who liked a good weep.

'Any idea where she might be?'

'Who's speaking please?'

'DI Walker, Essex CID.'

There was silence. Walker could visualise her chewing her nails.

'Could be anywhere,' came the abrupt reply, 'she's doing the Essex Way.'

Essex Way? What was that? Some kind of dance or new lifestyle or maybe a sexual position? Perhaps, pumping away in the back of a Ford Escort, surrounded by white handbags? Then he thought of Gabrielle Simons and dismissed it immediately.

'It's a walk,' sighed the woman as condescendingly as any lawyer's secretary could.

'Right.'

Like the Lambeth walk, he wondered.

'Epping to Harwich.'

'Ah, okay, so did she leave a forwarding address?'

'No.'

'Do you have her mobile number?'

'No.'

'When did she leave?'

'Yesterday.'

Walker put the phone back in his pocket. Suddenly there was a slither of hope, the thinnest vestige of an opportunity. It lay with the one person he had never considered: Gabrielle Simons. She stood at the crossroads of his future. As coroner, she had the power to decide on the facts surrounding the case, and she had the power to bring him back in full glaze of the public eye. In fact, she was the only one who could save him.

Twenty-five miles away, the figure of a woman was walking along the grassy track. She wore gleaming white Nike trainers and an electric-blue tracksuit. It was so nice to be outside! Everything was perfect. The wind had dissipated to a faint breeze and the gentle sun was destined to be shining down on her and her path ahead for the whole day. There was not a single cloud to blemish it, nothing that could damage her prospects. She felt utterly relaxed at last.

It was her first proper break for over a year. She was timing her progress on an hourly basis, using her multi-featured digital watch. Each hour, a couple of minutes quicker and reaching her target without the bleeper going off. She was getting the hang of this! She found herself sucking in lungfuls of the clean air as she turned into a field, that opened up a magnificent view across the river valley.

At least, there were no more problems at work. Susan Almond, that conniving bitch was no longer around. She had taken too many liberties, ever since she had insinuated herself into the practice on a Back-to-Work scheme for full-time mothers. Well, she wouldn't be coming back to work now! Everyone could get on with *their* work.

Susan Almond hadn't flirted with all the men, just those that had trousers. Elderly partners, office juniors, admin staff and Alan, her fellow scribe, the most eligible for the lot. Keeping her sexual activities going on a diet of pills and alcohol and disrupting the whole office atmosphere was never going to be sustainable.

It might have been defensible if her work had been up to scratch. Yet the crafty cow had proved herself incapable of dealing with routine deadlines, client fulfilment and technical matters. Joe Biggs, their largest and most profitable client had complained but of course, she couldn't be sacked, so she had flounced around the office, gossiping and moaning while everyone else did all the work. Being paid to do nothing all day while distracting others with sexual overtures didn't seem right. A fair day's pay for a fair day's work, that was her motto, even for solicitors.

Anyway, the coroner's inquest started in four days time and that would be a straightforward decision. All of the evidence was already to hand and she already formed her opinion. A few days, of sitting in a stuffy courtroom, listening to various experts drone on and then she could collect her cheque and return to her place of work. Then she could deal with a much more soluble problem, how to replace an incompetent junior partner with one of the firm's many high-flyers.

Walker got back home and stepped into the lounge. He went straight to one of the reference books he kept amongst his books on shellfish. He had heard that the Internet could do this for him or those Sat Navs but flicking pages was a whole lot easier. The book confirmed the Essex Way to be 81 miles long, heading out in a north-easterly direction towards the North Sea and Harwich - if that's the direction she took. She could just have easily have gone in the opposite direction, south-easterly. Yet that was against the prevailing wind though and all the incoming weather. Would she really want to walk eighty-one miles into wind, rain and sleet? Would she really want to walk that distance anyway? What on earth would possess someone to do that? Was she looking for something, trying to run away or more accurately walk away from something…, or both? What the hell was the point of walking anyway, when you had a car?

He ran his finger along the route, picking out some improbable place names: Margaret Roding, Willingale, Good Easter. The question was how far would Gabrielle go in one day? Eight miles, ten, fifteen, twenty? Good Easter was seventeen miles. She seemed a fit sort of person; energetic, peppy, gleaming with health. He could see how those strong thighs and calf muscles could carry her long distances. Maybe twenty miles, Pleshey, where there was one of the finest Norman earthworks in England? Five hours continuous walking, four miles an hour. Yep, that worked. Gabrielle could do that and more, and she'd still have the energy to issue two writs, file six law suits and launch an injunction on some hapless soul.

He put in a call to speak to PC Grayson. He could give a hand here. There was no reply until Walker sent a text with URGENT all over it and the young officer got back to him.

'Sir.'

'Why didn't you return my messages?

'I thought after the incident with the waste basket-'

'It was an accident,' Walker interrupted. 'Damn thing caught fire. Trust Jones to lose it. Anyway, what have you been up to?'

'Been having a word with Joe Hart and Alison Holmes.'

'Oh, yes?'

'They were in the Fisherman's Arms. Not literally, of course.'

'No. What were they up to?'

'Nothing.'

'Wouldn't surprise me to find their fingers in a few juicy pies,' Walker said.

'I don't know sir.' Grayson hesitated. 'Anyway, need to get back.'

'Wait a minute.'

'I understand you're off the case.'

At this time in the day, Walker operated on zero tolerance.

'Whaatt?'

'I've been told that you're not exactly the flavour of the month. You're desk-bound. Now with this incident with the waste basket-'

'Forget about the waste basket. Who told you this?'

Grayson stayed silent. 'I understand that we have to wait for the inquest before we do anything else,' he said at last.

'It's balls!' Walker shouted down the phone. 'Biggest crock of shit I've heard in ages. I was never flavour of the month. Okay, look, I don't need to know who told you this. Whatever happened between CS Jones and me is off the record. We continue as before, understand?'

'No.'

'Look,' Walker began, more quietly, 'okay maybe we don't hit it off but I respect you. That's why you should trust me. Look, I know the facts behind this case better than anyone and I can read David Almond like a book.'

'True.'

'So, will you help?' Walker asked.

'Help?'

'Yes.'

Then Grayson heard a word he had never heard before from Detective Inspector Walker:

'Please'

Grayson was taken aback. Walker must be desperate. He lowered the phone. He hadn't been told officially that Walker was off the case, nor had he been reprimanded. He could plead ignorance if he had to. Besides, he was as determined as Walker to crack this case. He put the phone back up against his face.

'Stephen (another word he hadn't heard Walker use), this is important. We're that close. Look, if we crack it, you'll be the guy that gets all the credit. You'll be the blue-eyed boy.'

'I already am.'

'Yes, but for how long? How could you live with yourself if you gave up the chance to find out what really happened?'

'Look, I thought you said you wanted to help David?'

'I do, by finding out the truth.'

Everything Walker said made sense. Grayson would get the credit. For the first time he would be seen as a proper police officer. He wouldn't have to rely on family favours anymore, which meant that he would no longer have to bow and scrape, and seem grateful to everyone. He began puffing himself up a little bit. Maybe, it was time he made decisions for himself.

'I don't know. What if DS Jones found out?'

'He won't. Don't worry about that. I'll take the hit. You just follow my orders, okay?'

'What do you want me to do?'

'Get hold of Gabrielle Simons's secretary. I want to find out where Simons is.'

'The coroner?'

'Yes Grayson, the coroner.'

'The one you called the most fearsome, cold and utterly charmless woman you had ever met?'

'Grayson?'

'Yes?'

'Get on with it.'

Walker ran through all the paperwork over the phone. It was about time Grayson earned his corn - talking to nail chewing secretaries was more his line of work, anyway.

'Yes?' Tessa Adams answered when the phone bleeped.

'Excuse me, madam,' began Grayson, cautiously. 'My name's Stephen Grayson. I'm a police officer. I work for DI Walker. We're trying to locate Gabrielle Simons. I've got some place names and I just wondered if Gabrielle Simons might have mentioned them to you?'

'Go on.' Her tone was lighter than before.

Grayson read off a few names and each time she answered in the negative. He was making little progress. It was five minutes to three on a Friday afternoon, nearly the weekend. The sun had given up for the day and a fine drizzle was starting to show on the windows outside…time for some harmless frivolity.

'Shallow Bowels.'

'I beg your pardon?'

'Shallow Bowels.'

'I really don't know what you're talking about.'

'Ah, sorry,' Grayson said, 'it's my handwriting. Shellow Bowells.'

'Oh, Shellow Bowells,' she responded uncertainly, '…yes.'

'Yes?'

'No. I mean no, I'm sure I would have remembered that name.'

What a trooper thought Grayson. He wanted to ask her out just on the basis of their conversation but he'd been caught out like that before. Two years ago, he'd ended up in the clutches of a married woman, who went for men in uniform in a big way. He hadn't had the heart to tell her he was a plain-clothes policeman so he had borrowed a uniform from one of the constables. She was married to a fireman, was having it off with an ambulance paramedic and only needed a policeman to complete the 999 set. He presumed that when the emergency call came, it freed her up to go off gallivanting with someone else.

'Any idea what she might be wearing? It's important we find her.'

'Oh you'll find her.'

'Why's that?'

'She's wearing a bright blue shell suit.'

'Okay, look, I might need some more information. Could I have your name please?'

There was another testing pause before the woman finally replied: 'It's Adams.'

'First name?'

'Tessa.'

'Is that Mrs Tessa Adams?'

'No…it's Ms.'

'Thank you.'

The earpiece purred and Grayson smiled to himself. *Murse* or *Mizz* was always better than Miss. Even with its now widespread acceptance, it still told him more than the male equivalent. Some women used it to cover up, disguise the fact that they weren't married. To Grayson's unfailing optimism, it showed either an air of feisty defiance or a touching glimpse of vulnerability. Either way it was better than Mrs. That was always a non-starter. Of course it could have been a ruse, when all along there was a Mr Adams, like the Grizzly one, eight feet tall and hairy down to his toes just waiting to rip his head off but as he tapped in a message to Walker's phone, he brushed away this trifling doubt: Ms Adams was just as unattached as he was.

Walker read the details from his phone. He scrolled through until he had her photo, the one he'd taken at her office. Not flattering but accurate. He drove the twenty or so miles until he reached the edge of London and headed for the Underground station. The ticket inspector, shook his head. Apart from the thousand or so commuters that passed by the gate every day, no, he hadn't see her, not even if she wore an electric-blue shell suit. Walker tried going down a narrow path, the official start of the walk. All birdsong was sucked out by the undertow of low traffic noise. All around were disused warehouses and decaying industrial estates and rusting cars. Not an auspicious start for a so-called countryside walk, he thought. Maybe she started further down the route.

Walker then drove eastwards, towards the greenery, along the designated route. He began asking in the local pubs, village stores and churches. No one had seen her, hardly anyone did the Essex Way and they were sure they would have noticed her if she'd walked into their village wearing trainers and a blue shell suit. They suggested the next village, and in each successive village, they replied the same. Blue tracksuited walkers were thin on the ground.

She couldn't have remained inconspicuous, he thought, not with all these nosy villagers peering out from every window at her garish attire. He checked all the accommodation routes along the way, another dead end. Maybe, she was just going to turn up, unannounced, and ask for a room. Not very forward thinking, he thought, not for a hotshot legal executive. Maybe she hadn't gone on the walk at all, maybe she had gone someone classier, more appropriate. The British Virgin Islands sprang to mind.

The route left the villages and headed across open fields. He abandoned the car and strapped on his walking boots. He would have to continue reluctantly on foot. He followed the sign into a field of barley. Above, the sky was a mixture of white puffy clouds parting to reveal a pale blue sky, a 'Simpson's' sky he figured. At last, he was in the countryside. Dusk was an hour away, still good enough for spotting hikers. He heard a rustle and dived into a bush. A twig snapped. He kept still. Then another noise. Suddenly a pair of finches darted off and made an undulating flight path across the meadow. Then a cock pheasant spotted him and scuttled across a ploughed field like a Road Runner. Walker got up and looked around. He was playing his own version of a wild goose chase.

The path curved upwards to the top of a hill. Behind him, the village fell away. On the rise, he caught the freshness of air coming to meet him. It was a west wind - he was going the wrong way. *Damn!* He stomped back down the slope, across the deserted road and up the other side. He was soon in a woodland area. The sign showed a landscape full of the yellows of delicate primroses, daffodils and star-clustered marsh marigolds. The reality was a forest floor dead or dying and covered in strength-sapping mud. Soon his boots were covered in cloying mud as he slipped and stumbled along the route.

He peered at his watch: four-forty. A brief glow from a golden shaft of light, cascading through the trees, illuminated his way. The track ahead was even more muddy and soon he fell and barked his shin on a tree stump. Ramblers must be bloody mad, he cursed, as he made his way awkwardly over a turnstile and into the next field. This time the path took him to higher, drier ground and the track, running alongside hawthorn hedgerow was easier going.

He knelt down and peered into the muddy tracks. Sure there were footprints, but there were also dog paw imprints and hoof marks and piles of rabbit droppings. Some of the footprints may have been hers but there was no way of telling how long they had been there. Where was a Native American, when you really needed him?

The more he continued the more he felt he was chasing a ghost, a shadow, or perhaps something even more elusive…like an illusion. In the end, he gave up and headed back to the car.

He was filthy dirty and stunk of animal poo but as he slammed the car door shut there was only one place to go, Pleshey. The road was narrow and winding but that didn't prevent him overtaking on straights, bends, climbs and through tiny village high streets. As he raced through the deepening gloom, he could see his chance fading by the minute. He had to get to her.

He finally turned into the small village, past the post office and war memorial and into a deserted high street. What made her take off like that? Was this a way for a high-powered executive to relax, chill out and recharge the corporate batteries? Or was it simply a way of actually getting away from everything, pure naked escapism? Was she running away, had the finger of suspicion actually got to her?

She was distant, remote, like an asteroid, orbiting far away from him. Every answered she gave, was finally measured, like a chemist's medication. Maybe, it wasn't an escape at all, maybe it was work. Not so much a therapeutic exercise but another path that might lead her to establish just who killed Susan Almond?

He pulled his car towards the kerb. The sun fell behind a bank of cloud for the last time. The village became shrouded in a pervasive gloom. There was cathedral silence all around. He waited. No one walked in the dark, unless they were crazy. She had to come here, it was the only suitable stopping place for ten miles. A chill settled upon him. It didn't worry him. Cold, boredom, confusion, revulsion, tiredness and an overwhelming feeling of helplessness, they were all elements of the same equation. As the village clock sounded five, slow and sonorous like a death knell, he knew that solving it was the only thing he could do.

***

She stopped at the kissing gate, looked around her and then eased her way through it. Ahead of her lay a gravel path, which led, towards the large house. She continued briskly until the house was clearly in sight. The rear entrance was exposed to the setting sun and shimmered with a golden opalescence. She pulled the camera from her bag and left the path to get a closer view. Soon she had disappeared from sight behind the barn and out houses.

However, she had already been spotted.

In the distance, a man was sitting in his Landrover. He had his binoculars thrust eagerly to his eyes. He had been out earlier dealing with a storm that had damaged his prize tree. From the day when the Hurricane struck this tree had become the largest chestnut tree in Britain. Now one of the largest lower branches had fractured so that it was keeling over. It would need urgent treatment before it became diseased. He looked up and pounded the driving wheel in frustration, more expense.

On the horizon, he spotted the deer, only a hundred yards away. They chewed and twitched their noses while their tails wagged constantly, completely oblivious of the threat. Food on the hoof was up for grabs, but he was too busy. To make matters worse some idiot walker had left the official path and had started walking across his land. The person was trespassing; bloody walkers!

He knew it was a mistake when he had acceded to the wish of the Council to allow the route to pass by the grounds of his house. He had done it out of a grudging desire to appease the locals and curry favour with his new projects. He wanted to be seen as an astute businessman rather than some demonized property speculator. He didn't take boundaries and property rights too seriously but this was crazy. This person could have been any nutcase marauding on his land. He turned the vehicle around and drove his Landrover at full speed towards the hapless walker.

Walker heard a booming noise like a heavy load being dropped from a great height. He knew exactly what it was. He bolted from his car and dashed up the pathway. It was almost dark but he found his legs took him along the route with uncanny accuracy. Around a gently sloping bend, he raced alongside a brook and into a dip, before climbing once more onto a ridge. He dashed the last few yards and appeared at the scene only to see a Landrover disappear up the hill and into the distance. He rushed up to the woman and helped her on her feet.

'Thank you,' she said, as she took his arm and began brushing herself down. Then her face turned from alarm to anger as she recognised her rescuer through mud and grime. 'God, it's you! What are you doing here?'

'I needed to speak to you. What happened here?'

'I heard a noise, like a gun going off, tripped and you came along,' she said, through clenched teeth. 'But where the hell did you come from? She paused and her eyes narrowed. 'Were you following me?'

Walker beckoned her over to a wooden bench. 'Here sit down. Let me explain.'

'I should damn well think so.'

Walker squatted, leaned back, caught his breath and spoke as clearly and steadily as he could.

'I needed to speak to you. I rang your office; spoke to your secretary, Ms Adams, is it? She gave me some vague directions.'

'So you turn up like Sir Galahad, on a mission to rescue the damsel in distress. I tell you, inspector, I don't need any of this. I told the office specifically, that I was not to be disturbed. Get it? *Not* disturbed.' With that, she turned abruptly and stormed off.

'Hey, wait a minute! We need to talk! Think we can catch up before the inquest?'

'Not a chance,' she snapped and her figure trailed into the distance towards the village.

'That's what you get for saving someone's life!' he shouted out to her but she was already out of earshot.

Walker walked up to the fence and peered through the railings. The shot had sent the deer scattering across the hill and left an eerie silence. Simons had headed off and short of pinning her to the ground, forcing her to listen and telling her exactly what he knew, he had to let her go. Besides, hell would freeze over before she changed her views.

He stumbled back to his car and suddenly felt incredibly tired. The exertions had got to him and his heart was pounding like a steam hammer but as he had come out all this way, he wasn't going back now. He went back into police mode. A gun had been fired. An innocent member of the public could have been killed. He was there to protect and serve. For Inspector John Walker, the only place to head was the stately mansion shimmering in the distance.

As he turned the car around, it dawned on him. The grounds to the house were in Pleshey but the main frontage was in another village, a village he had visited recently. As his car pointed up the driveway and swept past the clipped yew hedges he realised that he knew exactly who would be answering the doorbell in a couple of minutes time.

'You again?' Mr Biggs spluttered as Saunders ushered in the police officer.

'Me again.'

'I would ask you to sit but I don't think you're staying.'

'Probably not. I'm not one to outstay my welcome.'

'Good.' Biggs poured himself a glass of decanted port and looked disdainfully at the scruffy copper. He took a generous swig. 'I'm surprised you dare show your face again,' he said, with a sly grin on his face. 'This time using the front door are we?'

Walker shook his head. 'Now we're being presumptuous.'

'Are we now? Look inspector, I know you think I'm one of these uncultured jonnie-come-latelys but I'm not stupid so please don't patronise me. I know all about you. I know your history, I know your police record and I know your methods. You weren't called PC Fixit for nothing.'

He was called Hoover, but Walker let it pass.

'Don't try to look all sore. I know about all those years ago when you teamed up with David Almond and got arrests up by fifty per cent. Only problem was the conviction rate didn't go up accordingly, did it? So next time you break into my house and try and find some evidence they'll be a nice little reception for you.'

'Like the shotgun you used today on an innocent hiker.'

'Touché. Nothing like a bit of parry and thrust.'

'What the hell were you playing at?' Walker demanded angrily.

'You might see it as a broadside, fired across the bows of someone who was about to trespass but the truth is somewhat more prosaic; I'm a poor shot. I was shooting deer, on my property.' He drained his glass and sat down. 'Perfectly legal.'

'So you didn't recognise the hiker as a former business associate?'

Biggs raised his eyebrows and lowered them just as quickly.

'Yunno,' continued Walker, 'I would have thought that you would have wanted to keep your nose clean right now, being a suspect in a murder case.' Biggs gave a cold, unflinching stare. 'Taking a pot shot at the coroner isn't going to advance your cause is it?' Walker baited, further.

'Rubbish, I've already said I was shooting deer. If you care to go into the kitchen you will see a haunch of venison, ready for skinning.'

'That won't be necessary. Maybe I can see the licence for your shotgun?'

'I inherited it from the previous owner. I'm sure I can find the papers if you give me time, but time isn't what you have is it, inspector?'

'Mr Biggs, for you I've got all the time in the world…if I want it. The truth, in my case, is that I really don't want to waste my time sitting in this godforsaken room starring at a bunch of stuffed creatures and the biggest of the lot sitting in that chair.'

'Get out! Get out!!'

Walker had already propelled himself out of the hallway, through the door and down the steps to the gravel driveway, brushing past an astonished Saunders, leaving only his muddied footsteps trailing across the marble floor.

He seethed at the sheer arrogance of Biggs, but that wasn't enough to arrest him. It was Biggs's word against a discredited police officer. Yet more annoyingly, he was livid at himself for failing to get anything resolved. Two key witnesses. Two botched interviews. One wasted and utterly futile, mud-caked day. Surely, things couldn't get any worse.

He slammed the car into gear and headed off. One by one, his suspects were falling by the wayside, literally in Simons's case, with no one to replace them. He wondered if Biggs and Simons actually knew each other. Surely, they had met before? Were they actually going to meet up with each other when he came crashing in? In a lawyer's world, she wouldn't be allowed to have contact with him - client confidentiality and all that. But did that matter anymore? The gloves were off with no hold's-barred. Maybe, Simons had deliberately chosen the route to spy on Biggs, put the finger on him as revenge for the death of two of her valued staff members? Maybe this crazy mission was just starting to get a little weirder with Biggs and Simons cunningly devious and up to no good. If this was the case, they would have their work cut out because the stubborn Walker had just got more determined than ever.

CHAPTER ELEVEN

Saturday, 9th November.

The morning began seasonally cold. A messy drizzle spattered the bedroom window and a faint wail echoed around the house as the wind whipped up the fallen leaves and sent them spiralling into the air. Walker was having a lie-in. He made himself a cup of tea and toast with marmalade and took it back to bed with him. He had the radio, TV, a couple of books, newspaper and on the inside back page, the crossword. What else did he need?

His father always used to do the crossword. It was a Saturday morning ritual; mum and dad in their pyjamas sitting up in bed, glasses on, flicking the pages of the daily news. Mum making abstract comments and dad turning to the inside back page, licking the tip of his pencil, adjusting his glasses and plunging into the daily crossword as if he was embarking on a journey.

Walker sucked his pen and started on the crossword straight away. Get the anagrams done and the rest will follow. It was like crime solving, you had to get past all the large obstacles before everything became clearer. There was only one difference. A crossword was self-contained: it had rules, logic and it worked within well-defined parameters. With this case, there were no boundaries and the only cast-iron certainty was that in three days time the coroner would sit and decide his future.

His father could polish off the crossword in forty-five minutes. He would explain aloud each solution while youngster John snuggled between them and gazed up at them. 'That is an anagram. See?' he would say, jabbing his pencil at the paper. 'Here, the answer is contained within two words. Last three letters and first two. See? but it can be any combination. Always one in every crossword.' Occasionally the young boy would ask a question and his dad would rise to the challenge. 'AB stands of able-bodied, a sailor. Sometimes sailors are called Tars and you will see things like RN for Royal Navy. Lots of nautical terms in crosswords. The compiler expects an Englishman to know about our maritime past.'

'So if it was Switzerland, they'd be lots of clues about cuckoo clocks.' Young Walker had speculated.

'Yes, probably.'

'And chocolate and mountains.'

'Quite so. Getting to know one's environment is one of the tricks of the trade.'

John Walker never completed the crossword in forty-five minutes, not even with dictionaries and self-help books. He either found the initial obstacles too great and gave up or reached a mid-puzzle crisis where he found himself going round in circles and unable to break out of a certain way of thinking. He would put the crossword down, distract himself with other matters and then go back to it only to find that, after solving a couple more clues, he clammed up again.

If someone's life depended on it, he couldn't help thinking things would be different but he couldn't hide the fact that he simply wasn't up to it. It was just too daunting a challenge.

Fifteen down: Essex causeway found on door step.

He leapt out of bed and hit the button on his mobile for Stephen Grayson. Yes, it was a Saturday, but that meant nothing when the investigation had reached a critical stage. The automated message kicked in.

Ten miles away, Grayson was off to have his haircut. He was going to sit down in the chair and tell Flavia precisely what sort of hairstyle he wanted: 'shaped, off the ears, left side parting, no highlights'. Then he would ask her out. Just like that. He mouthed the words: 'Flavia, steady with the razor, will you go out with me? And please make sure it's straight at the back'. It sounded fine.

This onrush of urgency had been coming ever since his restaurant meal with his dad. Playing hard to get was fine but what if tomorrow he was gunned down? What if the killer found out where he lived and decided that he wouldn't ever see Flavia again - or have another haircut, for that matter?

He arrived at the hairdressers at nine o'clock precisely. He stood in the cold, blowing on his hands, while all the other shops opened. He shuffled from one leg to the next, feeling his cold feet in more ways than one. Eventually, a man came by, nodded and unbolted the entrance.

'In you go, young man.'

'Is Flavia coming in?' Grayson asked.

'She'll be in later,' the man said, eyeing him from head to foot before waving him into the chair. 'Hmm, we're going to have our work cut out here, aren't we?'

Grayson slid into the barber's chair and his heart sunk.

'She normally cuts my hair.'

'Look, ducky,' he said, impatiently 'I've been cutting guy's hair for ten years. It really needs shaping and some conditioner to revitalise those tired follicles. First we have to remove all that nasty bum fluff.'

His hand flicked Grayson's neck and the razor began its nasally whine. Then Grayson's phone chirruped.

'You saved my frigging life,' Grayson confessed, thirty minutes later as the car rattled along. 'Some ginger was about to cut my barnet.'

'One isn't homophobic, is one?' Walker asked, hands clenched to the wheel.

'No, one isn't. It's just one prefers Flavia.'

'Ah Flavia! And does she reciprocate one's amorous advances?'

'She does not,' Grayson said curtly, picking up the newspaper and glancing at the crossword.

The car picked up speed and so did Grayson's brain.

'Any joy with Gabrielle Simons?'

'I tracked her down but she refused to speak.'

'Typical. Got one of your clues,' Grayson said smugly.

'Don't give me that?'

'I have.'

'Which one?'

'Fifteen down: Essex Causeway found on door step.'

'Go on.'

'The Strood.'

'Sounds good,' Walker replied, 'because that's precisely where we're heading.'

The Strood was a narrow causeway linking the mainland to the island. It was the only means of getting across to the island yet locals blamed The Strood for all the ills of society. It brought all the noise and dirt across from the mainland, as well as hoards of visitors. In fact, the locals would have been far happier with just their spirits; like the ghost in the Chapel, or the legions of Romans, that stalked the mudflats.

As the squad car raced towards the causeway, the horizon opened up to reveal a puzzle of marshes and creeks under a brooding sky. Beneath the bridge, muddy waters funnelled up from the River Colne and barrelled through the narrow Pyefleet channel making the island complete again. 'Is the tide coming in or going out?' Grayson wondered.

'Search me.'

The movements of water were endlessly deceptive; creeks could be emptying up to half an hour after the tide had turned and some filled in more quickly than others did. Grayson watched the waters billow and deflate with woozy ambiguity until he gave up.

'Anyway,' he said eventually, once they had crossed, 'guess what I was reading, the other day?'

'*Madame Bovary*?'

'No.'

'*Anna Karenin*?'

'No. Look, it was a book on Mersey Island. There were lots of photos of fishermen and farmers. It all seemed very long ago.'

'Probably was.'

'It said that, in the past, folks that used to spend too much time on the marshes often ended up with ague and rheumatism.'

'Not surprised.'

'Which resulted in a smaller physique and stunted development.'

'Well that explains Baines,' Walker sighed.

'It might also explain why we haven't had a response, sir. Not one of the leaflets or signs we put up in the village has had any effect. It's like the people don't want to know about the outside world.'

Walker angrily wound down the window, feeling the force of the breeze on his face. He wanted to shout out at everyone and get them to wake up. Yet all he saw were redshanks, swooping across the mudflats, dipping in the creeks and disappearing from sight. The creeks were full of worms and shrimps, borne by the incoming tide. As the car raced past, the birds flew off in all directions, emitting their shrill cry.

Within ten minutes, Grayson and Walker had navigated their way through the washed out browns and greens of scrub. They were standing outside Shed No 3, Chalmers Seafoods. A flock of gulls wheeled above, eyeing the crates of seafood covetously.

'Peckish?' Walker asked.

'It's only ten o'clock.'

'Perfect time for brunch, then.' Walker replied.

They headed inside, crunching across the wooden floorboards. Grayson walked up to the serving hatch while Walker found a wobbly table overlooking the gently sloping beach.

'Mrs Chalmers.'

'Oh, it's you again.'

'One plate of oysters for my colleague and I'll have a plate of chips.'

'What's wrong with the oysters?' she demanded to know.

'Absolutely nothing,' Grayson replied diplomatically, 'I just wanted to try your local spuds.'

'You couldn't have come at a worse time,' she said, plonking the plates of food on the counter. 'The festival's tomorrow so don't get in the way. We're very busy. Pepper and vinegar are on the table. Slice of lemon is extra. Ketchup's 5p.'

'And two teas, white and sweet.'

The tea was sloshed into cups and sugar was administered and merged with a quick rattle.

'Thanks. Is Jim Chalmers around?' Grayson asked.

'Pookie?' the woman said.

'Yes, Pookie.'

'He's out the back,' she said, tossing her head.' Busy. You want to speak to him?'

'Please.'

She gave him another daggers-drawn look.

'It's important.' Grayson insisted.

'I'll get him to come around.'

Stephen carried over the bowl of shellfish. Walker inhaled deeply: 'Ah! The scent of the sea!' Then his smile evaporated as he saw the chips. 'I see you're pushing the culinary barriers once more.'

'What?'

'Somewhat less indigenous?'

Grayson found a chair less rickety than the others and drew it underneath him. 'Oh yeah. Dead good there are, cooked in lard. Don't like all that sunflower stuff.' He took one long, soggy chip and waved it limply in front of Walker's face. 'Want one?'

Walker winced and tried to clear his mind. 'Did you know Grayson, that this used to be a smugglers haven round here?' he asked.

Grayson's mouth was crammed with chips. All he could do was shake his head.

'People made fortunes, all the rage a few years...Ah! Mr Chalmers?' Walker asked.

A large, bearded man had appeared, filling the doorway. He came through wearing a thick beige woollen sweater and size ten Wellington boots. On top of his head sat a mass of tousled hair. The only thing missing from his nautical appearance was a pipe but he had substituted it with a roll-up that flapped from his mouth like a wet kipper.

'Yep. Told you wanted to see me?'

'I'm Detective Inspector Walker, this is PC Grayson. Sit yourself down. We've been trying to get hold of you.'

'It's a Saturday morning.' Chalmers complained.

'We don't really work normal hours,' Grayson said, 'bit like you.'

'Yeah, well I've got lots to do before the festival,' Chalmers stressed. 'Look, this really isn't a good time.'

'Shame,' Walker observed, 'seeing as we've made ourselves at home.'

'Hope this is going to be quick.'

'Depends how quickly we get the truth,' Walker replied, popping a large, fleshy oyster into a gaping mouth.

'You've been elusive, Mr Chalmers.' Grayson said.

'I'm sorry. I got the message from my cousin but I've been up in Harwich getting me boat fixed. The winch snapped in a storm. Can't do nothing without it. I'm taking the old gal out for the first time in weeks today. I hope she behaves herself, with the festival an' all. Wouldn't do to break down with the Mayor on board, now would it?'

'I must compliment you on these oysters.' Walker said, as he helped himself to another.

Chalmers face softened. 'Thanks.'

'Prize winners?'

'Well, don't know about that, but they're looking good this year.'

'I've sure they are,' Walker said, soothingly. 'I've tasted oysters from all over but I would happily tell the judges that these are the finest around.'

'Well, that's nice to hear. Some folks just don't know what they're missing.'

'Absolutely,' Walker said, as Grayson buried his face in another handful of chips. 'Anyway, I've just been telling my colleague, about how everyone used to smuggle round these parts.'

Chalmers pulled up a chair. 'That be true, Long time ago, mind. It was, how shall I say, the local industry. Mind if I have a snout?'

Walker waved him on and slurped another oyster down.

Chalmers snapped the lighter and fire flashed out. He drew on his tab as if it were his last cigarette. With a great exhalation, he blew the first batch of grey smoke right across to the other side of the hut. 'Keeps it off the food,' he said. 'Don't want Heath and Safety getting their flame-retardant knickers in a twist,' he added through a fug of smoke.

'Quite so.'

'Course, hundred and fifty years ago, whole families was at it: kids, grandparents, brothers and sisters. These secluded creeks, see? It was dead easy to land a boat full of contraband. Customs cutters couldn't get through - too narrow and too shallow. So they tried to get informers but none of the locals were having it, even when they bribed them. So, they decided to employ people from North of the Border.'

'Scotland?' Grayson asked.

'No laddie, Suffolk and Norfolk. They towed in watch vessels to house all the spies from across the border. Darwin's ship the *Beagle*. She was No 7. Like a floating hotel she was. Course, soon as the smugglers heard about the *Beagle*, they was furious. Rumour has it, they tried to set light to it. In the end, the smugglers simply moved further up the coast. They always stayed one step ahead. Until of course, it became a hanging offence - that changed everything. Push comes to shove, people prefer their own necks to an extra few coppers. Isn't that right, Inspector Walker?'

Walker nodded.

'So what happened to the *Beagle*?' Grayson asked, as he mopped up a dollop of ketchup with a greasy chip.

'It was abandoned. All the people from Suffolk were packed off back home. She was sold. Slowly she got trapped in the mudflats and sank into the mud without trace.'

'So where is it?'

Chalmers shrugged his broad shoulders. 'Good question. Records show somewhere round Paglesham, I think, on the Roach. Some archaeologists have used aerial photography to try and find her precise location and they have carbon-dated timbers in houses and old sheds to the time of the *Beagle*.'

Grayson looked up to the timbered ceiling. 'Any chance these rafters have come from the *Beagle*?'

'Wouldn't be surprised. They're certainly old enough to have come from the old girl. Course, when she went down, everyone piled in and grabbed what they could.'

'Not like today, of course,' Walker said, 'everyone round here being fine, upstanding, law-abiding citizens.'

'Yeah, right,' Chalmers said.

'So, Mr Chalmers. Oyster fishing: profitable business is it?'

'Enough to earn a crust.'

'Land must be worth a few bob.'

'Maybe.'

Walker continued: 'Men like Joe Biggs would like to buy it up, willing to pay a lot for it.'

'Yep, so I've heard.'

'What, few hundred thousand, million?'

'No way.' Chalmers stated. 'We don't own the shoreline, the beach, the park or the water, inspector. Just two boats and a leaky shed. No, I know where you're coming from but we wouldn't sell.'

'So tell me about the afternoon of the sixteenth of October? Two bodies were found in a Peugeot at Graydon's Creek.'

'Heard about that,' Chalmers said. 'Alice told me. Terrible business. I hear old Bainsey has been helping you out?'

Walker rolled his eyes. 'Of a fashion.'

'He likes to be noticed, but he's harmless.'

'Is he?' Walker questioned.

'Tends to exaggerate, does Bainsey. Once told me he'd seen the Queen digging for lugworms. I told him the only Queen round here, is Joe Carter at the Fisherman's Arms. Call's himself Josephine, he does.'

'Likes dressing up, does this Joe?' Grayson asked.

'I should cocoa. Every Saturday. Anyway, gives us a bit of laugh.''

'Can you recall seeing anything, anything at all?' Grayson asked.

'It was a Tuesday, yeah?'

Walker nodded.

'Didn't go out fishing. Never take a day off normally but me missus was poorly.'

'So you saw nothing?'

'Hold on. Let me see. Judith, that's me wife, she got up in the early afternoon and was hungry so I went to the shops to get some soup.'

'What time was this?

'It must have been around three. I was in a rush because it was raining real hard.'

'Did you see anything?'

'Come to think if it, I did see something. Well, normally I walk along the road but because I was in a hurry I cut across the sea wall.'

'Why not drive?' Grayson asked.

'Don't have a car. No point on an island.'

'Sorry,' Walker said, scooping up the last of the oysters and dropping it ceremoniously into his expectant mouth, 'please continue.'

'Anyway, I took the seawall route. I wanted to check the weather for the next day and as I was walking along a couple came towards me. Then they turned back and headed towards the slipway. That's when I turned off towards the local store.'

'How were they acting?'

'Acting?'

'Anything unusual.'

'Didn't really notice,' Chalmers said and sniffed. 'Normal, I suppose, walking one foot in front of the other. They weren't walkers.'

'How do you know?'

'He was wearing a smart pair of dark trousers and a jacket and she had on long trousers and a jacket too. They must have been getting wet.'

'Height?'

'He was quite a bit taller, six foot, I guess. At first I thought, strange seeing a couple of business people on a walk in foul weather. Then I realised that they might be here because of the planned development. Lots of business folks are coming out sniffing round here these days, so I didn't think about it again.'

'Was there a vehicle there?'

'Yeah, black.'

'Was it a Peugeot?'

'Dunno. Not an expert on cars. Visibility wasn't so good. Chucking it down, it was.'

'Anything else you can say about the couple?' Grayson asked. 'It's vital.'

The fisherman began shaking his head. 'No, they just turned. Then they headed back.'

'What made them turn?'

Chalmers shrugged his shoulders. 'Dunno, probably got bored, ran out of time, maybe they'd seen what they wanted to see. Maybe it was too cold and too wet for them. Wait a minute, I think there were two cars.'

Walker leaned forward. 'Two cars?'

'Yeah, I'm sure of it now because I remember seeing the headlights shining. It was just parked there as the couple were making their way back.'

'Mr Chalmers.' Grayson asked. 'Can you describe the car?'

'Sorry, the lights were bright, must have been on full beam. I had to cover my eyes and then I headed off. There was one thing.'

'Oh'

'There was an illuminated sign on top.'

The lines on Walker's face hardened a little.

'A taxi?' Walker suggested.

'Possibly.'

Suddenly, in just a few seconds, the investigation had shifted perceptibly.

'You sure on this?' Walker repeated.

'Yep, definitely two.'

Walker glanced at Grayson. He had actually stopped eating and was scratching his head. Not just one, but two cars, or vehicles, maybe a taxi. It meant going through all the local cabbies and finding out their movements, but Grayson could do that. At least it might stop him thinking about women.

'Did you hear or see anything after that?' Walker asked.

'No.'

'What about on the way back?'

'Hmm. No, walking the opposite direction, see? It was still raining. I was in a rush to get back. Sorry.'

Grayson paid the bill and headed out the door. 'So what do you think, sir?'

'I think we have a sighting of a vehicle, colour indeterminate, model unknown and no registration number.'

'What sort of a name is Pookie?' Grayson asked.

'It's a nickname,' Walker explained. 'All oystermen have nicknames.'

'Do you think Pookie's telling the truth, or is a porkie?'

'Very droll, Grayson,' Walker said, 'it's not much to go on, is it? Anyway, if he *was* the last person to see the dead couple you need to check it out. Go and see his wife and drop in at the local. It's Saturday, might as well have one on me.'

'Thank you, sir but I don't drink on duty.'

Walker glanced at his young charge. When he was his age, he could drink all day and still drive home. Not like kids today. Walker looked up at the breezy skies. Clouds tumbled across the sky like boulders down a mountainside. 'Looks like a squall's coming in, Grayson.'

'No problemo.'

'Well, I'm heading back home. See you later.' Walker began tramping across the scrub, towards the car.

'Oh, how am I going to get back, sir?' Grayson shouted.

'Get a taxi! I'm sure Chalmers knows of one. Oh, while you're at it, make some enquiries with the taxi folk!'

Walker climbed in and drove off, ignoring his young charge. Grayson was now on his own.

Grayson hunched up his coat and set off. At least, someone had seen something, or at least had *said* they had seen something. Not the same thing at all. Chalmers might not have been the most reliable witness in the world but Grayson had a gut feeling that he was telling the truth. Why would he lie, unless he was the one going round killing off people with a revolver?

Grayson clambered up to the seawall to get a better view. All he could hear was the wind whistling across the mudflats. It would be easy, he realised, to come down to the slipway in a car, take them out and then reverse, remembering to cover up the tyre marks - one bucket of salty seawater should do it and water wasn't exactly in short supply round these parts.

In fact, it was just how he had imagined it from day one: someone else involved, a proper killer, tooled-up, appearing on the scene unnoticed. The killer spots the couple along the seawall. He dons a pair of gloves and then he takes the revolver, wipes off the fingerprints and places it carefully in his coat. Then he sits and waits. Once they are in the car, which is crucial, the killer goes over to the driver's side, carrying the fake smile of an assassin. The killer gets the driver to wind down the window, just to make sure the identity is clear. He orders them at gunpoint to drive to the slipway. Then blam! blam! From then on, it's all about deception; open the door, swipe the victims thumbprints on the gun, throw the gun on the floor, close the driver's window, cover up the tracks and head off: one assassination successfully completed. All very plausible - yet all very conjectural. It wasn't Walker's view but since when did he ever agree with his superior?

Grayson made the short trek along the seawall. He was brooding about Flavia. How could he make sure she cut his hair? It was too risky, with gay boy hanging around. He could end up having the shortest hair ever, and the most expensive, and still not ask her out. Complicated, chaotic and chancy - just like this case.

A slither of sunlight swished across the grey water like a flashing blade and was gone. Grayson gazed heavenwards. The sky had turned murky and angry. Across the metallic grey water, a film of inky, black cloud was bubbling up like a cauldron. He stepped up the pace, breaking into a run.

In a few minutes, a curtain of rain came sleeting in, borne by a fierce Easterly. It lashed into Grayson with a fearful force. He stepped up the pace. He had no raincoat and no hat. Soon he was streaking along the shoreline like a devil possessed.

He arrived at the doorstep of the Fisherman's Arms wet through. His hair was plastered to his face and water dripped off his nose. He pushed open the stiff door. A pall of smoke greeted him. Inside, a few locals were perched on bar stools, hunched over their pints of local bitter, cigarettes trailing into ashtrays. This time there was no sign of Holmes and Hart. Grayson made a pronounced cough and attracted the attention of the barmaid.

'Yes, dear,' said a middle-aged woman, sporting a cigarette through red lipstick. 'What can I get you? Raincoat?'

'Pint of diet coke and just a few minutes of your time, please.'

'Oh, well that's my luck in for today,' she chuckled and it set off a round of sniggers.

She pulled the pump and the fizzy drink spilled forth.

'There you go, Two pounds, sir.'

Grayson paid and took a sip of his drink. He leant against the bar. He sensed the eyes everywhere, stabbing him in the back like a stranger in a Western saloon. The air was so thick with smoke he found it difficult to breath. He took his ID from his soaked jacket and thrust it in front to the bar staff. 'Police. Don't we know about the smoking ban?'

'Ban. Oh, you mean mainland Britain?' teased the barmaid. 'Sorry officer. We're a bit slow on the uptake round here.'

Grayson resisted the temptation to state the obvious and gently reminded her that they were breaking the law. He knew the moment he left they would light up again but at least he had done his job.

'The real reason I'm here,' he continued and this time he raised his voice, 'is because I wondered if you could give me some information. It's concerning a police investigation.' He turned to address the drinkers who all looked away or buried their heads in their glasses. 'Did any of you see Jim Chalmers in here on the sixteenth October around five pm?'

Silence.

'Please. It's important.'

'The night of the killing?' asked one of the drinkers eventually.

'That's it.' Grayson said.

More Silence.

'Pookie?' Grayson asked.

'Ah, Pookie!' Someone exclaimed. 'Yep, he's in here most nights, isn't he, Joan?'

Joan the barmaid nodded. 'Yes, but I wasn't in that night, so I can't say. What about you, Joe?'

A woman in a dress walked across, her heels clacking on the floorboards. She shook her blond hair and touched her eyebrows.

'Sorry, love,' she said with an earthy rasp. 'I had a prior engagement that night.' Then she smiled, one of those hideous made up smiles that only transvestites could muster. Grayson tried to avoid it like a bullet. 'Anyway don't worry officer, I'll be available tomorrow at the festival. À toute a l'heure, mon cherie.'

The locals howled with delight while Grayson's face went ghostly white, Propositioned by two gays in one day was beyond the pale.

'I saw him!' shouted a man sitting in the far corner.

Grayson turned to see an extremely elderly man holding onto a stick. He began moving his gums until his teeth rattled. Oh no, thought, Grayson, not another Bainsey.

'You saw him. In here, sixteenth?'

'Yep.'

'How do you remember that?'

'Easy. He always comes in here just before the oyster festival.'

'He tries to get some poor sods to help him with his boat,' added another.

'Course, no one's interested,' the old man continued, 'that old tub's got more holes in it than my socks. So anyway, he walks in, wet through, cos it was chucking it down like today. Tells me his wife is poorly and how he's got some soup for the missus. Has a beer, then he heads off.'

Grayson checked out the times with the locals and they backed up Chalmers story.

It was still feasible that Pookie or Chalmers, or whatever the hell his name was, could have done it, in the time it took to get to the slipway and back. Dropping into a pub would have been a perfect alibi; but yet again, fishermen and guns just didn't seem to go together.

He gazed around at all the locals. They eyed him with collective suspicion, waiting for him to go. No doubt, they had important business to deal with, like smoking themselves to death.

'Thanks,' he said at last. 'By the way, anyone know where I can get a taxi round here?' More routine shaking of heads. Grayson quickly drained his coke and left.

The rain had eased as he stepped out into the clean air. He spent a dispiriting ten minutes trying to find a taxi on the island but his phone reception kept breaking up. The more he walked the more frustrated he got. Eventually a tractor came thundering along. Yes, he was going off the island, take a bit of time but climb aboard! Grayson hauled himself up and sat on the wobbly plastic seat as the vehicle ground its way tortuously back along The Strood, trailing an enormous line of impatient drivers.

'Serve the buggers right!' shouted the farmer. 'I've got my work to do.'

Walker was finally released from the painfully, uncomfortable cab at a bus stop. Two hours later, he eventually got a bus back to town.

It had given him time to think. 'That's it!' he exclaimed, as he spotted the comfort of his own car, nestled in the driveway. 'Enough is enough! I've had my fill of people playing games, chasing false leads and being a glorified skivvy. I've done John Walker a favour but come Monday morning, I will be telling him that that is it! I can't afford to cross CS Jones any longer. Dad was right: John

Walker's a dead man walking. He ignored his little pun. I'm going to shop him once and for all!

Unfortunately, none of these words were audible as Grayson sank into his car and headed back to the hairdressers. It was still early afternoon and his mind had moved onto other matters. He parked on a double yellow and waited. Then he spotted Flavia in the window. She was busy cutting some guy's hair, gently caressing it into shape, like a sculptress. She wore tight light blue trousers and a white t shirt. Knockout! He could see her faint, enigmatic smile; the one, he thought, she reserved for him. The shop was packed with young guys, slouching in their chairs, all sneaking a glance at her as she flowed around the room, hairdryer in one hand, comb in the other, queen of all she surveyed.

At the other side of the shop stood Mr Teasy Weasy, preening and crimping, putting a great bow wave into a young man's hair. He gave a little, limp wave as he spotted the police officer and his mouth made a small 'o'. Grayson waited a few seconds. Then he crunched the car in reverse, went up a side street and careered back the way he came, heading for home.

Twenty miles away, in a much grander area of Essex, Saturday began more sedately. Saunders woke at 7.30 a.m. prompt. He shaved using his faithful cutthroat razor and dressed circumspectly into his dark, newly pressed trousers and white shirt. He adjusted his tie and slipped on his matching single-breasted jacket. Weekends made no difference to him, it was a normal working day. He made his silent way from the East Wing down to the kitchen. Ten servants used to work downstairs. Now there was only one. Saunders prepared a pot of piping herbal tea and buttered two slices of golden toast with Tiptree conserve. He picked up *The Times*, placed it on the Georgian silver tea tray and walked up the flight of stairs. He cruised across the landing and down the corridor. Mr Biggs always slept in the West Wing, overlooking the grounds and his favourite chestnut tree.

Saunders knocked gently on the bedroom door. Normally he heard a grunt or a groan depending on his master's night's sleep. Sometimes an expletive if his master had been 'on the lash' as he called it. This time he heard nothing. He coughed. No reply. He tapped a little harder. 'Sir. Are we awake, sir?' Slowly, he pushed the door open. The bed lay unused, the green silk pyjamas lying on the chair untouched.

Saunders went downstairs and walked across to the study. Sometimes, if sir had been working hard or drunk, he would fall asleep in his chair. That was the most likely explanation. The room was dark and gloomy. Saunders fumbled his way to the window and flung open the sash curtains. The morning light flashed across the room like a searchlight. He made a little gasp and stepped back. The model of Mersey Island had been smashed to pieces. The table was broken and figurines and matchstick houses lay strewn across the floor. He bent down to pick them up. As he peered across the floor, his eyes locked onto another man's. He recoiled in horror. There, lying twisted and surrounded by a halo of blood, was the small, motionless body of a man.

CHAPTER TWELVE

Walker pointed his car back towards familiar territory. Some Country and Western music twanged away in the background, something about country roads taking him home. Saturday's should have been about crosswords, tidying up his garden and tending to his aquaria but all he could think about was Gabrielle Simons, peering down her long, aquiline nose like he was something the cat brought in. She might at least have shown a modicum of civility. There was no way of stopping her now. Like some last ditch gambler, he had had his chance, staked it all on one number and lost.

Walker finally slumped through his front door at twelve-fifteen. He felt bloated from an overdose of oysters. Was it possible to have too much of a good thing? He loosened his trousers, plonked himself on the couch and slept for over two hours.

When he awoke, he was still living the nightmare. The inquest took place on Monday. Simons would preside like a preening peacock (electric blue was her colour), hearing only what she wanted to hear. Then she would clear her throat, flutter her fingernails and make her portentous judgement. Within a couple of days the case would be closed - and probably his career too.

After three and a half weeks, he hadn't got any closer to the truth. A miss was, as Jones constantly reminded him, as good as a mile. All he had was a witness who said they saw a car. Big deal. No one would believe a third hand involved, least of all Jones and Simons. Only Grayson's tin pot theories suggested otherwise and he wasn't exactly up for any Sleuth of the Year Awards.

When he switched his mobile back on, a stream of text messages poured into his inbox. He activated them one by one. They were all from Grayson and couched in the strangled, esoteric parlance of text messaging. Why the heck couldn't he just speak English? Chalmers movements had been confirmed. That was all he needed to know. He breathed in deeply and set to work.

It wasn't a case of starting all over again, but it wasn't far off. He took a comforting sheet of A4 paper and a large ballpoint pen. Maybe things weren't quite so sketchy after all. Casually, he wrote a columnar list of a few people: Alan Thomas, Joe Biggs and David Almond. He headed these up as his alpha suspects. Then, he wrote down another heading: beta suspects, and underneath wrote Gabrielle Simons, Mr Baines, Jim (Pookie) Chalmers, Joe Hart, and here he surprised himself, Cathy Almond. Putting a fifteen-year-old girl in the frame seemed ludicrous like putting an answer in a crossword clue when you knew it wasn't right. It just screwed everything up. Yet she could have got the gun from her father, she could have discovered her mother was having an affair and decided to kill her mother's lover only for it to go disastrously wrong. Of course, she couldn't have followed them out to Mersey Island, unless she got a taxicab and there wasn't a sign of a taxicab was there?

How long would it take? Two minutes. Climb back in the backseat of the cab and coolly drive off. Yes, she would have to have bunked off school, but wasn't that what all kids did and wasn't it was she was doing right now? Of course, schoolgirls didn't walk out of school with their father's gun, take a cab to their mother's office, trail them to Mersey Island and end up with two dead bodies on their hands. Did they?

He was getting twisted up again, those little flights of fantasy that warped reality and made his head hurt. He put an arrow next to Gabrielle Simons and drew it pointing towards the 'alpha' column. Then he crossed it out again. He lay still for a moment, wondering if somewhere, someone was sitting in a chair playing back the moment they killed two people, feeling again the vibration as the revolver discharged itself into the victims' heads?

Walker glanced across to his answer phone. The green light was flashing. That was strange, no one ever rang him, apart from Grayson and only because he had asked him to. He punched the button. He heard the familiar faint hiss, two beeps and then a garbled, rather strained voice, came into earshot.

'Oh, er, Jones here. Thought you'd be in. I know it's Saturday morning. Something's come up. Think you should get down to Joe Biggs's house immediately. We can discuss the situation on Monday. Suggest you do whatever's necessary. Normally I wouldn't be contactable for the remainder of the weekend but if you're absolutely desperate, you can call me on my mobile. It's five, four, three, seven, seven…no *three, four*, three, seven, seven, six, two, one…no *two*. Oh fuck it!' There was a click, two more beeps and then the tape whizzed back.

Walker didn't have time to think about it. He reversed out his drive and sped up the road. It was a grey, drizzly day and the afternoon forecast was for more rain, how much more could there be? Thirty minutes later, for the third time in less than ten days, he found himself back at the house.

He was first on the scene. The front door was open. He called out. No reply. He stalked across the marbled floor, his shoes echoing across the hallway. He found the study without problem, his own personal radar working overtime. He spotted the revolver, he saw the body, short, dumpy legs twisted like a doll, and he joined them together, A gun shot wound to the head - always the head; forehead, temple, lower jaw, mouth - but always the head. He saw the broken model and the open curtains and an empty bottle of Cockburns port. No sign of a struggle. A newspaper lay face down. As he turned, he saw an ashen-faced Saunders, sitting in the corner like a gnome, hunched up, eyes closed tight.

'Mr Saunders? Mr Saunders?' Walker shouted out, trying to get the man to come to. 'Are you okay? Look, it's the police. Let me help you to the kitchen,' he said, grabbing hold of the frail man and pacing him slowly past the skirting board and the mahogany table now specked with blood. 'We'll get someone over to take care of you, make sure you're okay,' Walker finally deposited the man down on a kitchen stool. 'Did you hear or see anything?' The man sullenly shook his head forlornly.

Walker made some calls and went back into the study. The killer strikes again, was his first thought. Like one of those TV police dramas, where a body turns up just at the commercial break, to keep everyone from switching over. Then he noticed that there were no signs of anything missing, just a S&W and the bloodstained body of Biggs indicating a criminal act. The model of the island had snapped off but that appeared to be petty spite, not full-blooded anger. He picked up the paper. It was yesterday's evening newspaper, the *Essex Times*. He turned it over. Front page:

Mersey Island Saved! Victory for the conservationists!

At three-thirty this afternoon, it was announced that all approved planning applications received by Mersey Island Council in the last nine months will be revoked. In an unprecedented step, Councillor Holmes said it had been decided to compulsorily purchase all new developments. This would be with immediate effect and for a nominal sum. Such acquired land would revert to agricultural use or land defences to act as a natural barrier against rising tide levels. As a result, it would create one of the largest areas of wetlands on the East Coast and be a haven for wildlife. Councillor Holmes was quoted as saying: 'This action has been taken in view of changing environmental conditions and in the light of the appalling tragedy involving two solicitors working for Ridgely, Turner and Fowler'. The move is expected to result in losses of millions of pounds for rich property speculators like Joe Biggs and his controversial coastal development.

Joe Hart

Walker put the paper down. His eyes ran across the desk and along the floor until they observed the bloodied corpse. Were his ears burning? The man's face was frozen in a fearful rictus with bared teeth like one of the exhibits around the drawing room. He had obviously read the article. A silver-coloured gun lay by his side.

Everything screamed out suicide and, in this one act alone, the truth had slotted dramatically into place to complete the picture. It was Biggs that eliminated Thomas and Susan Almond. They refused to go along with his plans for the island and when they failed him as a client, he took revenge. He knew where they worked and one late afternoon, he followed them to the island, on a pretext of meeting them to discuss the building proposal. They walked along the seawall expecting to see him. He arrived, pulled the car next to theirs, lured them back into the car and murdered them in cold blood. He had no alibi that day, so he knew there would be suspicion.

It became a mission of his to do anything to avoid discovery. He turned his attention to Gabrielle Simons. She was an ally of Thomas and Susan Almond. She would have been an important witness. When Biggs heard that she going to be the coroner, he got desperate. He rang her up and asked her to visit him, giving directions to the rear of his house. Then he sat in his Landrover and waited. When she arrived eventually, she had to work out a way in. It gave him a grandstand opportunity. He trained his rifle and pulled the trigger. He missed. With that, all attempts to claim innocence had gone. From then on, he got desperate.

He visited David Almond, on the pretext of local security. In fact, it was to see if the police were getting closer to the truth. He discovered it would only be a matter of time. Finally, when he read the local evening paper, his world fell apart. All his physical and mental toils had been in vain. He would never be able to hold his head up in the area again. His empire would collapse and he would be banished like an outcast. There was no one to help him, no one to console his bitter disappointment and more to the point, no one to blame. He and he alone had created this unholy mess. With one final act, after drinking a bottle of port, the killing and the heartache stopped. Joe Biggs took his own life with his own gun. Now it was good riddance.

PC Grayson came stomping into the room just as Walker was preparing to go.

'Some Saturday. Missing the footie commentaries, stuffed up with Flavia, piss awful weather, bloody terrible journey back from Mersey Island…oh, wow, that is messy,' he said. 'He's not going anywhere is he?' he added. Then he unveiled a large Styrofoam cup of coffee from inside his coat, as they did on the streets of New York. Grayson slurped noisily on its contents. 'Anyway, here's one guy who didn't kill Susan Almond.' Grayson said.

'Oh, so that's what you think?' Walker replied sarcastically. 'Shall we all go home now?'

'So, what's your view, sir?'

Walker pointed to the local paper. Grayson stepped across to examine and began mumbling to himself. Then he began reciting the text: 'Mersey Island saved. Victory for the conservationists.' He went silent, got lost in the detail and then made a little whistle. 'So, he'd just lost a fortune?'

'Correct.'

'And he decides to top himself?'

'Maybe.'

'Written by Joe Hart, I see,' Grayson said. 'Our little hack has been busy.'

'Quite.'

'Any sign of a forced entry?'

'No.'

'Saunders see anything?'

'No.'

Grayson put the paper down and skirted around the body. 'One bullet through the left cheekbone from point blank range. Blood is dry. Must have been died last night, or early hours of morning. Hey, looks like another Smith and Wesson .38!' he exclaimed. 'That's weird.'

'Probably part of a job lot,' Walker said.

Grayson finished his Espresso and scrunched up the cup noisily. Walker headed out to the gunroom and came back. 'Biggs had one revolver and some shooting rifles, none of them licensed. Get ballistics to confirm the murder weapon is the .38 and we can all go home.'

'Or maybe,' Grayson suggested, 'he did kill Susan Almond and knew we were on to him and decided to take the easy way out?'

'Yep.' Walker said. 'So how about you don't touch a thing and make sure that forensics run their eye properly over this whole place.'

'Alternatively, this could be another killing faked to be like a suicide?'

'Uh-huh.'

'With the phantom killer still out there!' Grayson said dramatically.

'Could be,' Walker said, putting on his coat and preparing to leave.

Grayson crammed the jagged edges of the broken cup in to his pocket. 'Then there's the inheritance. Losing millions must have pissed someone off. Mind you, bet's he's still got a few quid stashed away. This house should be worth a few bob.'

'Loads of possibilities, Grayson.'

'Could be that some long lost relative has arrived on the scene. Someone from Australia?'

'Yep.'

'Wagga Wagga probably.'

'Definitely. So, get your thinking cap on while you wait for Mark Johnson to arrive. Tell him everything. Anyway, I'm wasting my time here; we've got a busy day tomorrow, early start.'

Grayson sat down in the chair once occupied by the property magnate. Yesterday, Biggs had been master of all he surveyed; now he was staring at the carpet with a broken skull. The chair was a black leather chair and it had a tilt, swivel and a footrest that appeared at the push of a button. It was a great chair.

Grayson pressed the control and with a whirr, it began to ascend. Ideal, he concluded if you wanted to intimidate your business associate sitting on the other side of the desk. He got one foot higher and then lowered himself back. He wasn't going to intimidate anyone now.

Walker was right, the thought that someone would walk in and calmly shoot Biggs in the face was ridiculous - at least, it was until he actually thought about it. Security was non-existent - Grayson had proved that himself by finding the main door open and strolling through the rooms undetected. The circumstances of death were worryingly familiar. Could it be the killer had struck again, this time because the victim knew too much?

Yet there was the newspaper article, hot off Joe Hart's press, enough, thought Grayson to tip Biggs finally over the edge. Yet how hot was it? Had it been delivered, did Biggs go out and get it or had the killer brought it along just to muddy the waters?

Grayson found Saunders in the kitchen, unmoved from where Walker had left him. Every inch of manservant grace had deserted him; he sat forlornly on a stool, his head slumped into his shoulders, looking every inch the pitiful wreck.

'Did Mr Biggs have the local paper delivered?' Grayson asked, with no warning.

Saunders looked up, his eyes hollow, lowered them again and slowly he shook his head.

'Did he go out and get the paper?'

Again, another shake, this time more pronounced as if he were losing the plot.

Grayson edged closer, towering over the seated man. Was this the killer? This pathetic, craven wretch, he was peering down at? Had the butler, in one final act, taken his official duties to an extreme? He'd gone to Mersey Island on his day off, removed the two lawyers and after a domestic tiff with the master, plugged him. Saunders was practised in firearms *and* he had the means and the opportunity to take a pop at Gabrielle Simons. Motive: a release from the daily drudgery and servility and a nice fat inheritance from the will. And, when all was said and done, wasn't it always the butler who did it?

Grayson moved away. The man was still sitting, bony-thin like a sparrow. He hadn't moved, yet he was breathing. Was he really capable of killing three people and taking a shot at another? Did he think he could get away with it? Maybe, it was the other way round, Grayson posed, Joe Biggs had actually asked Saunders to do it. Who better to ask, when you wish your life to be terminated, than your faithful manservant?

God! His head was swimming. Grayson went back into the study and sat in the great chair. He hoped it was a thinking chair. Was there any link between Saunders and Alan Thomas and Susan Almond or was it all through Biggs? Most of all, did any evidence categorically point to someone else being involved in their deaths? No, nothing except the vehicle with an illuminated roof sign. It wasn't enough. He had a noise outside and he saw Mark Johnson's car pull up. Soon, everything would be documented, labelled and bagged. Everything except the truth. That remained as murky as the muddy waters that swirled around the Mersey creeks.

Back in Ryedale Avenue, David Almond reacted to news of Biggs's death with a simple shrug. People died: fact. Alan Thomas, Joe Biggs, his beautiful wife, all dead, no longer part of this Earth but part of God's celestial kingdom or damned in the fires of Satan. It had happened. That was all there was to it. God had willed it.

In his own secular way, Joe Biggs had probably wanted to go anyway, once he knew his fortune was lost. He had no one else in his life, clearly he wasn't happy and would never be, and he lacked spiritual guidance. It was a sensible option. In the great scheme of things, even if it hadn't been suicide, the fact that someone else ended his miserable life, was probably justified.

He had seen many suicides and attempted suicides. In his line of work, it didn't do to get too involved. It wasn't possible to rationalise it in human terms, and it was too late to explain to them the sanctity of life, the fact that technically it was illegal. Somehow, you just accepted the victim's decision and went to notify their next of kin.

He couldn't even rationalise his own attempt. A misguided, foolish act or some predestined path chosen for him? In many, so-called uncivilised, countries there were executioners who made this process easier. After all, it wasn't easy to attempt to kill yourself, you had to summon up great reserves of moral courage, or cowardice - he couldn't work out which - and then carefully carry out the act with the minimum of fuss and the maximum of effectiveness. A Smith and Wesson .38 could make a big mess in the wrong hands - much better to use an expert.

At least Joe Biggs's death had relieved David Almond of his obligations. He was no longer anyone's gatekeeper. He didn't have to worry about security duties or yobbish behaviour in the estate. This actually cheered David Almond up. It was the first sign that something could happen to make things easier. Now, instead of maintaining a nightly vigil through his curtains with a camera, binoculars and a notepad, he could open up the curtains and let God's light flood in. There was a world outside, beyond the estate.

The house was no longer his one and only true friend, it had become a prison. Whereas, before, it kept everything out, now it kept everything in. He no longer wanted shelter and safety; he no longer wished to gaze at the dark world of his tortured soul. Now he wanted to look forward and outwards, paying homage to a bright and gleaming future where everything was fresh and vibrant.

He raced into the garden, casting his eye over every blade of grass and through the fruit trees, touching twig and branch and the few remaining shrivelled apples. He would start to eat properly again; lots of fresh fruit and brassicas like sprouts and broccoli that Susan planted in her plot. She had called them cerebral food. They would revitalise him and bring colour back to his cheeks and blood coursing into his brain.

He ran around the garden shouting to himself and, when he became exhausted, he went into the kitchen and switched on the radio. The glories of Bach's cantatas came flooding out. From now on, he would listen to Radio 3 and Radio 4, in his car, when he was making a continental breakfast and when he was quietly meditating on the joy of being alive.

He found it hard to contain himself. Monday, (yes Monday, there was no point in delaying), he would go to the library. He hastily prepared a list of interesting books to read. No novels, no thrillers, no biographies. He wanted books on hobbies: woodwork, pottery, photographer, stamp collecting (not sure where to start, probably Commonwealth issues), ornithology (so much on his doorstep, avocets and egrets were two of his favourites - white wading birds were so elegant), sailing (he'd always wanted to get on a sailing barge and tootle up the coast, like a salty dog), fishing (he would hit the brackish backwaters of

Maldon and learn from the experts how to catch dabs and juicy lemon sole) antiques, wine tasting, yoga, karate and brass rubbings. Oh, the list was endless!

There were so many things he could do, and so little time to do it! It was vital, now he was back on his feet again, to make up for lost time. He was starting out all over again, on a new journey, and not just of the mind. He had to get out but where should he go? He had never made decision like this before; Sarah had always done that, always a routine and someone to discuss it. Now, he could head in any direction, he could run or walk, he could take lots with him or nothing at all. He could wear what he liked. He could talk to people en route or he could remain silent. The route could be long or short, hazardous or difficult, arduous or easy-paced. He could explore every nook and cranny, even pothole, every crag and crevice or he could simply go forward ignoring all the distractions and complications, putting one foot resolutely in front of the other while his head remained poised. He was now focussed unambiguously on the Christian road ahead.

His head was swimming with pure delight. Everything had resolved itself! Cathy would find herself too, it was inevitable. She would take each step in her stride, just like her father. She would journey part of the way with him, enjoying the sights and sounds and smells, revelling in the glories of the outside world. She would tell him stories of how people lived their lives centuries ago, how they survived hardships, famine and plague. She loved history. She would be his new friend.

She was good at reading and even better at storytelling. Even as a young girl she loved to tell stories, enriched with that impudent smile and those honeyed tones. He could visualise the two of them sitting under an apple tree, after a hard day's walking, crunching on a windfall while she sat cross-legged and regaled him with stories of the past. Then, as the day slowly ended and a great moon arose, they would find a hostel and go to sleep exhausted and fulfilled.

David Almond heard the clatter at the door. Cathy had arrived back home. He rushed out into the hallway to greet her but she brushed past him, not even looking up at him. She dived into the kitchen, raided the fridge and then disappeared upstairs. He never followed her, her room was her kingdom, it had always been her room from the first day he had painted it pink and yellow. It had been her room the moment his wife and he had laid her in the cot for the first time and watched her large brown eyes gaze at the starry lights on the ceiling.

He returned to the kitchen and made himself a coffee. He couldn't ignore the fact that danger still stalked his life. It was still out there, waiting, toying with his fragile emotions. It could come crashing into his life at any time but now he was determined to fight it. He wouldn't give up on his resolve and knew that, with God's help, he could find salvation.

His first excursion would be a short trip to Mersey Island. Tomorrow. Sunday. He knew the lie of the land. He could take the coast road, past the houseboats - a pleasing mixture of old steam vessels, holed-out barges and converted sailing yachts - through St Peters Meadow, towards the small Anglican church. He would enter by the side door, through the vestry and into the nave. He would kneel in the front row and pray for forgiveness, for all the wrongs he had committed and all the times he had sinned. Then he would get off his knees and praise the Lord for his newfound freedom. He would bless the heavens and the Earth and all the people and he would walk out into the sunlit day, a new man. Then, taking great gulps of clean air, he would walk briskly along the beach towards the big marquee. There, he would rejoin the swirling mass of humanity and participate in the celebrations for the annual oyster festival.

Gabrielle Simons had not completed her walk, the Essex Way, nor would she ever do so. Ending up in some godforsaken seaman's pub in Harwich wasn't her idea of a triumph. Instead, she had grabbed the nearest taxi back home. The notion of putting one foot resolutely in front of another and just enjoying the moment had proved to be utterly vainglorious. It hadn't been relaxing at all, she concluded, as she sat on the couch, twiddling her toes in a bowl of warm, soapy water. All she had got were scratches, blisters and sore feet from useless shoes. Oh, and interference from some policeman called 'Walker'. Some irony that! No one could have looked less suitable for trekking.

To make matters worse, someone had taken a shot at her.

If anything, the walk had focussed her mind more clearly on the problems. Big problems. The practice was haemorrhaging cash without its two leading lights. They hadn't considered that when their embarked on their ill-fated lovers tryst. It had all been a bit of fun but she hadn't seen it like that and neither had Biggs. Clients were literally walking out the door and not coming back.

Yet this was nothing, to the next few minutes, when she answered a late Saturday night call from CS Jones.

'Sorry to catch you so late,' said an apologetic Jones. 'I tracked you down from your office phone message. It said in emergencies please ring…so I rang. It's about the inquest.'

'It's Saturday evening!'

'I know. The inquest is due in two days time.'

'Correct.'

'It's just there's, er, been a development.'

Simons was tempted to launch into an invective about police procedures and the incompetence of one officer in particular. She bit her tongue.

'Go ahead.'

'Today, we found the body of Joe Biggs at his house. He'd been shot. I'd rather you kept it under your hat, but we're not ruling out anything at the moment.'

'Oh, that's terribly news.' There was a major pause. 'God, where will it all end?'

Jones thought he could hear a slight sobbing and a sniffle.

'Are you okay?'

'Yes.'

A second pause. This one more opaque. It was quite possibly Simon's thought patterns, whirring, like wind turbines.

'It's a terrible shock,' Simons, blurted. 'Oh, that does complicate things, I have to say. He was one of our best clients and a friend.'

'But he'd finished with your firm?' Jones said.

'Indeed, but nevertheless…'

'I have to ask you, Ms Simons, what do you think about the inquest?'

'Alan Thomas and Susan Almond?'

'Correct.'

'Naturally it's very soon to make a decision, but…why, do you think they are connected?'

'This is completely off the record,' Jones said, 'but preliminary investigations reveal evidence linking Biggs to the murders of Susan Almond and Thomas.'

'Oh, now that really does put everything in a new light.'

'Quite so.'

'So, Chief Superintendent Jones, we can't have it can we? The coroner's inquest must be cancelled. Yes, forthwith. Monday, first thing I'll make the appropriate phone call. Thanks for keeping me informed.'

The line clicked and Gabrielle Simons sat back. She dabbed away a lone tear. Then she reached for the chocolates and popped one in her mouth. God, *quelle surprise*!

Three days ago, her firm had been looking down the gun barrels of a multi-million pound writ. Being sued for gross negligence was just about as bad as it could get for lawyers. Biggs could have taken them all down with one hand behind his back. Suddenly, Joe Biggs had ended up in the firing line, quite literally. How was that for role reversal!

It was like a gift from a seismologist! Everything shifting, like tectonic plates until eventually a new fault line appears, things or people disappear down the crack and a new state of equilibrium is reached.

That Saturday night as she walked across to her drinks cabinet and uncorked a fruity Chardonnay, the world seemed a far, far better place. Even her sore feet felt better. She filled the glass to the brim and drank it, thankfully.

However, just as Gabrielle Simons finished her drink and placed it on the cabinet, a rare smile etched on her face, what she didn't realise was that she had opened up unwittingly another Pandora's box. Fifteen miles away, the cancelled inquest had giving a crucial lifeline to DI Walker. He was back in business and threatening to get to the bottom of this case, no matter what.

CHAPTER THIRTEEN

Sunday, a.m. 10th November.

An early morning sun streaked low across the muddied sandbanks from the direction of Brightlingsea. It ambushed the two men in the car, giving them the very briefest of ethereal glows. The rain had thankfully departed. The forecast was for a fine day with a light southerly breeze. It was a Sunday, he was working, but DI Walker was feeling decidedly chipper.

The case had been reopened and he had complete authorisation from CS Jones to crack it, once and for all. The fact that his arch nemesis, Gabrielle Simons had at last backed off and cancelled the inquest only lifted his spirits further. The case against Joe Biggs was also stacking up nicely, even though rigor mortis had not yet set in. It could take a few days but there would be no one to interfere. It was suicide.

It gave him a welcome break. What better way to celebrate this, he thought, than by attending the annual Mersey Oyster Festival and sampling some of its produce?

His assistant quickly brought him back to reality.

'What do you think came first, sir?' Stephen Grayson asked, as he fiddled with his ID badge. 'The shell or the oyster?'

'Whaatt?'

'In evolutionary terms, do you think the shell existed or the little fellow inside?'

'God, I don't know.'

'It's just that I can't imagine an oyster surviving without a shell and yet I can't see the point of having loads of shells just lying around if there aren't any oysters?'

Walker glared at his colleague. It wasn't even worth responding but he did.

'They evolved, Dumbo, that's all you need to know.'

'Yes but-'

'All you need to know,' Walker said more slowly and emphatically. 'So how about *you* evolving for once? Let's see if you can be useful today by making sure that the festival goes off without any mishaps?'

'No problemo.'

It was the biggest day of the year for Mersey Island and all the buntings, kiosks and sideshows were in place. Large flags fluttered along the beach proclaiming it the biggest oyster festival yet. An official was testing out the microphone and hailers while another briefed his staff on car park duties. After delays from the Mayor, it was finally decided to go ahead with the festival. Retailers, organisers and sponsors were all agreed; tourism couldn't be allowed to suffer. Locals should get out and enjoy themselves, they said, not remain under the pall of superstition. That much was agreed by everyone.

Walker and Grayson made their way, along with all the other revellers, through the car park into the country park, just a few hundreds yards from where the killings had taken place. A local radio station was blaring out in one of the tents.

"*More about the killings on Mersey Island. We have just received reports that the inquest into the deaths of Alan Thomas and Susan Almond has been cancelled. Gabrielle Simons the coroner, was not available for comment but one of her colleagues said that the police have reopened the case and are treating it as a murder enquiry. This dramatic development comes one day after the prominent local businessman Joe Biggs was found shot dead in his house. The Mersey Island Oyster Festival is taking place today despite misgivings from some local parishioners and officials. Over to our local correspondent on the scene, Joe Hart.*

'Thank you Katie. Yes, I'm here today to witness the thirtieth Oyster Festival. Amongst all the gaiety and celebration, there is considerable sorrow. The lives of two of our prominent business people cannot be brought back and many feel that the festival has just come too early this year. Will this be a public relations disaster? Many people I spoke to believe it would have been more respectful to have left it for a couple of weeks and say that due to commercial interests, their wishes have been ignored. Furthermore, there is increasing pressure on the local police to establish the facts concerning these killings and the man heading up the investigation has been criticised by many for failing to-
'"

'Get them to turn the bloody thing off!' Walker shouted.

Grayson entered the tent but before he could intervene, the news item had switched to sport.

Three hundred yards away, a fifteen-year-old girl was arriving in a taxi. Cathy had decided to come to the festival too. It would get her out of the house. She hadn't told her dad, it was none of his business. Anyway, she was getting sick of the sight of him; seeing him mope around, like a wounded animal. It was okay for a kid, that's what you were supposed to do, but to see your dad behave in such a pathetic way made her feel sick. He was supposed to be her father, why didn't he go out to work instead of creeping around the kitchen like a cripple? He started quoting the bible, that made her shout back. She told him he couldn't keep living in the dark ages.

In previous years, her mother had taken her. She had driven her there, held her hand and they had walked together across the beach and bought candyfloss in the marquee. She had always loved the festival; danced and laughed and got slightly tipsy. How she wished her mum was with her now.

As she climbed out of the taxi on her own, she paid with her dad's credit card. The festival site looked bigger and busier than she had remembered it. Now there were cars, coaches and vans jammed into the car park and queues everywhere. Yet there were hardly any young people at all, certainly none her age. At least, she thought, she wouldn't be spotted by any of her school friends, wandering around on her own, looking completely lost.

She made her way through the crowds into the main site. Most of the people were elderly, hobbling along the beachfront, along specially designed walkways, stooped, clutching their walking frames, muttering to themselves and dribbling like dogs. They must have arrived in one of the big coaches from the East End, she decided, a great herd of old people converging on the place like a plague of locusts. That wasn't nice but why should they still be alive when her mother wasn't?

She tried to get away and wanted somewhere that was playing some decent music and not the terrible trad-jazz served up by the jetty. A bunch of middle-aged losers were dancing - she thought it was called jiving - grabbing hold of each other and then flinging them around like it was a throwing competition. They really fancied themselves, she only wished they could see themselves in the mirror and realise how ridiculous they looked. Some of the crowd were clapping but others where whooping and hollering like a bunch of school kids. Ger-ross!

There was a small kiosk, past the burger van and before the face-painting stall. She hadn't seen it in previous years. A youngish woman smiled at her as she walked past. 'Hi, have you got a moment?' the woman asked. Yes, she had a moment. She had a whole lifetime.

'What are you selling here?'

'We are campaigning to stop coastal developments. We believe they are unsustainable. Do you want one of our leaflets?' Cathy put her hand out and received the piece of green paper. She read it quickly; it was concise, well written and very worrying. It talked about the loss of native mudflats and ecosystems, coastal erosion, global warming and rising sea levels, all of which she'd heard about at school. She wanted to find out more about the campaign, how she could help, but she didn't know what to say and there were others in the queue also taking an interest, so she walked away and dissolved into the crowd.

The only person who noticed her was an old man. He had a grizzled beard and a sore head. His early morning ruminations had been fearfully disturbed by the racket of sound systems, hailers and cries of people. He had stormed out of his hut and tried to quell the noise, to no effect. They all ignored him. It always happened at this time of year, people with no consideration for others, came bulldozing across the causeway, thinking how exciting it was to be on an island and somehow losing all notions of decorum and responsibility. Even the spirits of Roman soldiers had been driven out by the fearful din.

He watched the girl take out a hankie and dab her cheeks. Then she turned and he watched her as she headed back to the site, almost dragging her feet along. How utterly lost she looked! Unexpectedly, he felt a degree of kinship with this little girl. She too hated the festival. He began rubbing his knuckle with his spare hand. Then he moved towards her. He got closer. She spotted him out of the corner of her eye. Her pace quickened. Suddenly two burly men appeared. He scuttled back down the seawall, went back to his hut and slammed the door.

On the jetty lay three smacks, two bawleys and a bumpkin. It was all that remained of the one hundred and fifty smacks that used to trawl the local waters.

The three smacks were 18 tonners, fifty feet in length and used for dredging, oystering and trawling. They looked a magnificent sight, fully rigged, their decks scrubbed, the woodwork and brass work gleaming. The crew and dignitaries including the High Sheriff of Essex, were assembled, standing in line, in their full regalia, ready for sail.

It was the start of the Oyster Dredging Match. Each boat was built for speed and, with a mix of crew, locals and guests, would compete to see who could collect the most oysters in a single dredge. The route took them out into the Blackwater before beating southwards past Stone Point, into Pyefleet Channel where they would drop their wrought-iron dredges. There, they would reef the maroon mainsail and set a small jib set to reduce speed. Then they would trawl for one hour precisely. Afterwards, they would tack across the River Colne, around Rat Island before setting a broad reach for home using all three sails: mainsail, staysail and jib. The estimated time was four hours.

A large crowd had gathered and, as the boats prepared to cast off, the Mayor made a formal address: 'Residents and valued guests, we are here today to celebrate the harvest of *Crassostrea*, the humble oyster. Farmed here since Roman times, it is woven into the thread of all people here. It represents food, wealth and prosperity and provides employment for the people of this island. This year, it is particularly poignant, because just three weeks ago a tragic accident befell two of our much-loved and respected local citizens, Alan Thomas and Susan Almond. Their lives were tragically cut short and it is to their memories and their loved ones that we dedicate this race and this year's festival.'

The Mayor raised a glass and pledged allegiance to the Queen. 'We wish that you may all go in peace. Enjoy the day and God speed!' There was a ripple of applause and the ropes were unfurled. The painter was slung onboard and the final crewmen boarded. A klaxon sounded and the boats slowly eased away from the jetty.

The crowd waved and cheered as the boats headed for the channel. The larger smacks lead the procession with sails aloft. A keen cross-offshore breeze offered the perfect start. The crowd meanwhile, headed for the beach and all the offers on show. Only one person stayed on the jetty. Cathy stood silently, watching the boats become specks in the haze. She put her head in her hands, her shoulders began to heave and tears streamed down her cheeks.

A large group of stalls had opened for business selling seafood and hot snacks. The Chalmers' family were in the main marquee and all the family, except for Mr Chalmers and his son, who was helming for the Mayor's boat, were involved, including their youngest child. They had the largest stall, next to the entrance. There was a long queue and Walker and Grayson joined it and waited. More and more people were coming through the tent, inspecting all the marvellous produce, smelling the sweet aroma of the shellfish. Eventually the two policemen found themselves in front of the queue. 'Pretty good turnout,' said Walker to Alice who looked very prim with her hair up, a smart pair of jeans and a clean apron emblazoned with the logo of the festival.

'Can't complain, considering,' she said. 'What's it to be Inspector Walker?' He had never seen such a bewildering selection of oysters, their glaucous bodies glistening in their trays.

'We've got plump Pacific oysters, juicy Eastern oysters - *Crassostreas Vigrinica* - these are Olympia oysters, here are some from Galway (go down a treat with a pint of Guinness), then these ones are from across the water, Cancale, in France, local from Whitstable and some from Maldon. Then of course, we've got the best, our very own Mersey oysters caught yesterday.' Walker smacked his lips.

'Hurry up, I've got people waiting to be served.'

'I'll have some of those.'

'Just you go and sit down at that table and I'll get someone to bring them over.'

'Grayson,' said Walker irritably, 'why don't you appreciate the finer things in life? Oysters are the fruit of the sea; they are the essence of what an island race is all about.'

'More like garbage disposal units. All that filth and muck they sift through.'

'Poppycock! They're bivalves, that's what they do.'

'Yeah and flies spend all their time on shit but you wouldn't eat them.'

'You're a peasant, Grayson. An unreconstructed peasant!'

'Yeah, me and Jews and Muslims and even Seventh Day Adventists.'

'My, you have been doing your homework.'

The waitress brought over the plate and put it down in front of Walker. 'Now, why don't you just have one,' teased Walker, as he raised the plate in front of Grayson. 'Ugh, awful!' groaned Grayson, as he pulled away. Walker picked one up and drained it slowly into his mouth, feeling its plumpness as it made its way down his gullet. Then, he anointed the others with splashes of Tabasco sauce.

'Epicure would be green with envy!' he exclaimed.

'More like green with food poisoning,' Grayson replied, caustically.

Just then, a young man came and sat down beside him.

'Excuse me. Do you mind if I sit?'

Grayson recognised him instantly. 'Go ahead. It's Joe Hart, isn't it?'

'That's right. This must be Detective Inspector Walker?'

'Correct,' said Walker, annoyed that someone had interrupted his meal.

'See you're tucking into the local produce. I'm a big fan myself. Which ones did you go for?'

'Mersey, of course. What do you want?'

'Well, I just thought I'd introduce myself. Find out how the investigation is going. As you know we are covering the event and I wondered if you had anything to say?'

'No.'

'How do you feel about coming to this festival when there is a case to solve?'

'No comment.'

'Members of the public will be assuming that you must have solved it, being able to come out here and tuck into the local produce.'

'Will they?'

'Do you have any to say, inspector?'

'Actually,' said Walker, wiping his mouth, I'm glad you came.'

'Oh?'

'Yes, Walker said, 'because we definitely wanted to talk to you.' He leaned forward with his plate. 'Now how about a delicious oyster, hmm?'

Ten minutes later, DI Walker found the need to relieve himself. Grayson tagged along behind as they weaved their way through the crowds. People continued to pour into the main tent - rarely had the occasion been so well attended. They headed across the festival site, Grayson in tow, like a trailing dog, towards the portable loos designated 'Guys'. As they squeezed into the small cabin, the floor creaked. A small cloud of mosquitoes hovered close by, moving dizzily above the urinal as if intoxicated by the proximity of bodily fluids.

Walker shuffled into the cubicle and steadied himself.

'It's nice out,' Grayson said, looking at his superior just about to commence voiding his bladder.

'Whaatt?'

'Yeah, but put it away, a policeman's coming.' Grayson added and began to chuckle to himself. 'It's an old TV gag, sir. A man goes up to another man at the seaside and say's it's nice out. And the other guy says…well, you get the drift. Morecambe and Wise, circa 1970's.'

'Morecambe and Wise eh? Then you must be Morecambe.'

'That's good, sir. I always believe that moments of levity are essential in our line of work.'

'Oh, do you?'

'Yes.'

Stephen Grayson sidled next to DI Walker, moving into his urinal.

'Let's share,' Stephen said playfully, 'see if we can dissolve the tablet in one go.' He tugged at his flies and his hand went inside, groping in the groin area.

'You get ten points extra points if you can fire it out of the urinal.'

'Bugger off,' Walker shouted, barging him out of the way. 'For God's sake, Grayson can't you grow up?'

'Just a jape.'

Almond gave his young charge a baleful look. 'Look, you little prick.'

Walker knew immediately he'd picked the wrong phrase. Grayson burst out laughing.

'Ha! You've been looking! Sir, you've cracked a funny and you didn't know it. First time in living history. I do believe it's a major break through.'

Walker was furious and stumbled to find the right terms of abuse. They all seemed to be loaded with innuendo. In the end, he uttered a rather feeble, 'Grayson, just bloody behave,' and zipped up his flies

'Sorry, sir. Just feeling the festival spirit.'

'Oh really? Well feel it somewhere else. God knows how Almond coped with you.'

Walker stormed out of the loo into the gathering throng and strode past kiosks selling arts and crafts local to the islanders. There were carvings, crude paintings of the shoreline and someone had taken some of the driftwood, pasted it to onto a piece of hardboard, and was trying to sell it as art. All tat, concluded Walker as he made his way back angrily to the beach. Then Grayson caught up with him and tapped him on the shoulder. 'Sir?'

'What do you want now?' Walker snapped.

'See over there? That kiosk? There's a young woman with an assortment of pamphlets, stickers and badges on display.'

'What about it?'

'That's Alison Holmes'

Walker's eyes suddenly lit up. 'Is it now?'

'I'm certain.'

'Want to introduce me?'

'Go on.'

'Alison Holmes!' Grayson exclaimed, 'Small world. Now what brings you here?'

'You're a copper, go work it out,' she fired back, going back to tidying up the literature.

'It was a rhetorical question,' Walker replied. 'I'm DI Walker.'

'Are you?'

'Yes. I guess this campaign of yours never stops, even during festival time. Agitating, cajoling, foisting opinions on others.'

She stood there, slack-jawed, mouth gaping wide, the jaundiced expression of someone who wished she didn't have to listen to all this.

'You've got it in one, inspector.'

'Can't have people enjoying themselves, can we?' Walker suggested.

She stopped shuffling the pamphlets and looked up. 'Of course we can but some things are more important. Like people's livelihoods.'

'I thought you of all people would be celebrating?' Walker asked.

Her demeanour changed from sour to inquisitive. 'Celebrating?'

'Yes.'

'Oh. The council decision. It's great news, of course, but it won't stop someone like Biggs.'

'I think it will.'

'Think you're wrong, inspector. It would need an elephant gun to stop him.'

'Maybe, or maybe a revolver.' Grayson added.

'Doubt it. He's got the hide of a rhino.'

'So you haven't heard?' Walker said, enjoying the moment.

'Heard what?' she asked.

'Not been listening to local radio this morning?'

'Haven't had time, inspector.'

'Mr Biggs was found dead in his study yesterday morning.'

Alison Holmes went very pale for a few seconds, as if her spirit was visibly draining from her body.

'You're kidding?'

'No, we're not,' Walker said.

'Someone killed him?' Holmes asked.

'Suspicious circumstances,' Grayson replied.

She looked up at Walker and then at Grayson and got the same stony expression. Her face tensed.

'Now wait a minute-'

'No, *you* wait a minute,' interrupted Walker. 'We will be talking to you in due course but if you've got nothing to hide then you've got absolutely nothing to worry about. Now I suggest you just pack up your things and call off this nonsense. People have already died. Your friend Joe Hart is in the tent. Why not go and join him and plot your net victim? Come on, Grayson. We're going for a stroll.' They left an open-mouthed Alison Holmes, staring at them as they headed towards the beach to observe the sand castle competition.

'Looks like everyone's crawling out of the woodwork,' Walker said.

'It feels too much like work, sir. I'm going to play in the sand. See if I can pick a winner?'

He made his way down the slope onto the beach while Walker began heading back to the marquee. Suddenly there was a piercing shriek. A woman came rushing out of the main tent, screaming and asking for help.

Walker rushed up to her. 'Grayson, get up there quick!' Walker bellowed.

When Grayson arrived, hundreds of people were streaming out of the tent and medics were rushing in. Grayson pushed his way through and saw a young man, writhing on the ground, clutching his throat.

'Poisoning?' he asked one of the medics.

'Looks like it.'

'What, a dodgy oyster?'

The medic knelled down and began pumping the man's chest.

'Doubt it. Never seen a reaction like this. This isn't dodgy food. Someone's tried to poison him!'

Across the beach, up behind a sand dune, crouched a craven looking David Almond. He had earlier been down to the festival site but the noise and crowds had been too much. He had wandered aimlessly for an hour and had then fallen asleep beside an old rowing boat. Now he looked alarmed as he saw people stream away from the marquee and medics pile in. He thought he spotted Walker and Grayson amongst the crowd, remonstrating and getting people out as quickly as possible. It was like a crime scene. It *was* a crime scene.

He didn't want to have anything to do with it. It looked chaotic, like ants coming out of their nest after a disturbance. God's will. He panicked. He had to get away. He broke cover and ran up onto the main road and then around the back of the site until breathlessly he reached his car. He jerked the handbrake off, pushed the throttle down hard and accelerated up the road as fast as he could.

Meanwhile, the old man scratched his stubbly chin. He couldn't resist a little smile seeing all the folks running around like crazy. The other boats were starting to arrive back from the race but the jetty was deserted. Everyone had left the site and were heading back home. His smile turned into a grin as he watched the mayor step gingerly off the boat looking bemused. Where were all his people, where were the other dignitaries he had invited to greet the triumphant team? The Mayor shook himself down, straightened his regalia and marched away. As the old man peered into the distance, all he saw was a collection of police and ambulance vehicles assembled outside the main marquee.

Monday, 11th November

When Grayson and Walker met up by the coffee machine, Walker barely had time to punch in the right numbers before a furious Jones came barging along the corridor. He had transcended from Perfect Storm to Human Wrecking Ball.

He hauled Walker into his office and closed the door.

'Good God! What the hell's going on?' he shouted, pounding the desk.

'Someone was poisoned at the festival.'

'I know that. I've had the mayor on the phone and the commissioner. What I want to know is why you tried to poison a well-respected member of the press?'

'Whaatt??'

'You heard. Joe Hart. You offered him an oyster, next moment, he's choking to death.'

'Look sir,' Walker pleaded, 'It wasn't like that. Someone poisoned the oysters, well, one of them, but it wasn't me! For Pete's sake! Don't you see, the poisoner was trying to kill me! It was my plate, but I offered one to this man Hart and he took it.'

'So you like offering poisoned oysters to total strangers?'

'He came up to *me*. I was just sitting minding my own business.'

'Well, I've just heard from the hospital that's he's going to be okay,' Jones said, 'so you're very lucky. We could have had a terribly embarrassing incident on our hands. The mayor and the sheriff sail off in a smack on a quiet autumnal day and come back to see a scene of complete chaos. Yea Gods, Walker, can't you simply go to a festival without creating carnage?'

Walker was as outraged as Jones as he left the room. How could anyone do such a thing? To plant rat poison inside the beautiful shell of *Ostera Edulis* was bordering on the heretical. The culprit was not just utterly ruthless but lacking in any sense of decency. Slowly, he walked back to his office. Now he had yet another crime to solve: not involving firearms but oysters.

Walker's mind went spinning back to the tent: he was in the queue with Grayson. Finally he reached the front. He was asked what he wanted. He *chose*. He actually decided which oysters he would eat, he pointed to them. So they couldn't have been poisoned - *at that stage.* Alice picked out the oysters herself, six large, plump oysters and placed them on a plate. Local oysters, from Mersey - fresh as a daisy. Then she put the plate down, *behind* the counter.

Alice? A murderer. Surely not. Then she said: 'Just you go and sit down at that table and I'll get someone to bring them over.' So he did and someone did bring them over. But which someone? He didn't even notice. A waitress, he thought, but it could have been a waiter. There were so many people around, all he remembered was seeing an arm come out and the food come down in front of him. Not even sure if they wore a ring. No word, either. That was strange? Just serving it up like that. Didn't even ask if it was the right table. Surely, a normal waitress would do that.

Maybe someone else was hovering, just waiting for the opportunity. *Start thinking man!* It couldn't be Alice. She wouldn't have jeopardised the whole family business by putting poison in one of her own oysters. She would have been first suspect and why would she want to kill him anyway? No, it had to be someone else, someone incredibly devious, opportunistic, someone who had a grievance against him that could only be assuaged by cold-blooded revenge.

Then he wound forward to Joe Hart. He only ate one oyster, maybe he was unlucky or maybe he wasn't poisoned by it at all. Maybe he had been eating oysters all day and *it was one of the other ones that had been poisoned?* In which case, maybe the killer had been trying to murder Hart after all? Walker felt relieved and confused. Then there was the motive. Who would want to kill Joe Hart? His mind went back to Alice. *Poison one of the other oysters.* That would put the skids on other oyster farmers, competitors from Maldon or Kent. He knew that business wasn't great for the Chalmers but attempted murder to save the business…it was taking a big risk. Yet when wasn't attempted murder risky? - and of all the hundreds of criminals and murderers he'd come across, none of them ever actually wore a label around their necks marked 'killer'.

He repeated the question. Who would want to kill Joe Hart? Joe Biggs, he answered to himself, drawing a bubble out of the character's head and filling in the words. But Biggs wasn't going to harm anyone, not anymore. Forensics report had just come through. Walker read it through carefully. Biggs died from a single gunshot wound to the face. The weapon was a Smith and Wesson .38 revolver. Only one shot was fired, from a distance of no more than three feet. Fibres found on the sleeves of one of his jackets matched the upholstery from Thomas's car. There were also DNA traces of the two victims. *Bingo*. Also identified were tiny particles of gunshot that could only have come from a .38 bullet. Moreover, Biggs had no alibi at the time of killing of Susan Almond. He also had a motive, the means and the opportunity. Now the guy couldn't even plead his own fat innocence.

So Joe Biggs was the killer, Walker concluded, with a big underline of his pen. Yet it didn't explain Joe Hart. Maybe Joe Hart knew who killed Joe Biggs and had to be silenced? In which case someone tried to kill Hart, not for what he was but for what he knew? Whatever possibility welled up and threw itself into his suffering mind, he was certain of one thing; the three deaths and attempted murder of Joe Hart had to be connected. Moreover, if they were connected, then there was still the very real possibility that the killer was still out there. If he was, he wasn't going to stop now. He had tasted it, he had smelt it and he had felt it. Killing had got under his skin. And, once that killing instinct kicked, it was impossible to stop. It convinced DI Walker that the killer was going to strike again and soon.

Monday morning was typically busy: new recruits, officers returning from training courses, computers going down over the weekend and new theories to bash around. Walker couldn't wait; he had to get out of the office and quickly before Jones made any more career-threatening decisions. He climbed in his car and headed straight for the Island. He didn't even notice the bright, breezy day that spread above his car in the big Essex sky. He also ignored the waves lapping as he crossed the Stood. His destination was Chalmers Shed No 3 and he got there just in time. Alice Chambers was just packing up as his car pulled outside the sheds. She gave him a baleful look and rushed inside. Walker wasn't going to play hide 'n' seek with anyone.

'Mrs Chambers! Mrs Chambers! We need to talk about yesterday!'

Slowly one of the doors creaked open and a harassed looking Mrs Chalmers appeared, carrying a bag and locking up the gates.

'*You*,' she said, in a slow, deliberate manner, pointing as if he were the devil incarnate. 'I don't want to talk to *you*.'

Walker strode right up to her and didn't say a word. 'We're closed,' she insisted. 'Closed.'

He could see she was furious and emotional, barely simmering beneath the surface. He offered a large handkerchief and she grabbed it. 'Last thing I'll ever take from a copper,' she said. She blew her nose and wiped her cheeks. Then Walker put out a placatory hand and the two of them sat on the seawall.

'Yesterday was a disaster,' Mrs Chalmers said eventually, as if the enormity of it was just beginning to dawn on her. 'That's it, we're ruined. That will be the last oyster festival we have. Thirty years we've been running it. Half of our income comes from that one day alone. Now we won't be able to carry on. Three generations of us wiped out because of what happened.'

'I'm sorry,' Walker said. 'Really, I am,' but he didn't mean it half as much as the next part. 'Mrs Chalmers, we have a killer in our midst. He must be stopped. Joe Biggs was found dead and yesterday, Joe Hart was poisoned. Someone put Thallium in one of your oysters - rat poison. We have to find this killer before they strike again.'

She looked up, her eyes watery and red from lack of sleep. 'Of course. How is the young man?'

'He was lucky. He was treated quickly by the on site medics. There was enough to kill him within an hour if he hadn't been treated.'

'What do you want to know, inspector?'

'I want to run through the events yesterday to see if they trigger anything?'

'Okay.'

'So, the morning begins. The oysters are unpacked and placed on trays. Who did that?'

'I really don't know. Let me explain. Around nine o'clock we brief the volunteers.'

'Do you have a list?'

She shook her head. 'Inspector, this is a festival, it's supposed to be a happy, relaxed atmosphere. People turn up, all sorts: locals, strangers, travellers, friends of friends, specialists, they get allocated roles like setting up the stalls and helping out and off we go. We have been doing it that way as long as I can remember and we will continue like that until someone comes along and forces us to do otherwise.'

'Go on.'

'During the day people switch jobs, some go, others join. It's extremely fluid. People use something called common sense. At the end of the day, they all line up and get paid fifty pounds. Everyone gets the same. Cash in hand. No one signs a damn thing. Remember, this is an island. We do things differently. No, we don't have a list.'

'Fine. You recognised most people though.'

'Yes, most people, the pub regulars, but there were probably ten to fifteen newcomers.'

'Do you know who was working in the main marquee?'

'Not everyone. We had about ten waiters and waitresses. They also did the washing up.'

'Can you give me any names?' Walker asked.

Mrs Chalmers mentioned a few names that went straight into Walker's book. He rang them through to Grayson who feed them into the computer database.

'When I was being served, you said my name.' Walker observed.

'Did I? I suppose that's force of habit.'

'Do you think someone overheard?'

'It's quite possible.'

'A waiter or waitress?'

'Yes.' She paused momentarily until the penny dropped. 'So you think someone was trying to kill *you*?'

Walker nodded. 'Thallium is extremely soluble. It could have been placed in one of the oysters you put out for me and then brought to my table. Only one of them was poisoned, the one that was inadvertently eaten by Joe Hart.'

'God, it gets worse. To think I was probably talking to the killer and I didn't see a thing.'

'Did you notice anyone acting strangely, anything that might help?'

'Inspector, it was chaotic. As you know, we had long queues, we were working flat out, everyone was buzzing around. Sorry, I can see how frustrating it is for you, but it would have been very easy for someone to do it and then disappear. No one would have noticed. We were all so busy. There is one thing though?'

'Oh?'

'My son. Scratchie. He took a lot of photos. Maybe someone might show up.'

'That's possible. Can I get my colleague to contact your son?'

'Of course.'

Within an hour, Stephen Grayson had received all the photos from the festival taken by young 'Scratchie' Chalmers. He took the email attachments, saved them to his PC and then ran them through a large display unit. The colour was good, the resolution was excellent but the content was abysmal. Grayson realised that most of them featured the dredging race and the five boats. Scratchie had crewed for the bumpkin and many of the photos were of smiling sailors and views of the island creeks, tiny islands and channels around the River Blackwater.

It couldn't have been any of the crew members because they were all on the water when someone was doctoring Walker's oysters - assuming Walker was the target - so Grayson discounted them immediately. The remaining photos showed the boats lowering their dredgers, towed by bass rope warps from the smacks, and then hauling up the metal cage and emptying the catch into shallow baskets. There were good pickings and crews stood posing theatrically as they culled the oysters for size and threw back the smaller ones along with limpets, weed and other rubbish. There were a final few shots of the crew returning to the jetty, smiling and arms raised in triumphant manner. By that time, the festival had ended abruptly, so the final photos featured long distance shots of people trailing away and a couple of ambulances standing in the car park. He zoomed in to get more detail. The car park was largely empty and the cars were frustratingly below ground level to see number plates. All he could see were the backs of people's heads.

At least one issue had been resolved: the killer of Thomas and Almond couldn't possibly have arrived and departed by boat. Only small, light clinker-built boats could navigate their way through these shallow channels and it required expert knowledge of tides and currents. The photos showed that the skippers required at least two crewmembers to board and cast off. Only someone like Chalmers would have even contemplated such a thing and he would have needed at least two accomplices.

Walker received the news with the predictable air of someone who knew that things were destined to go against him, but still persisted. Hookey, Pookie and Scratchie? Three family members, all in on it? Maybe Alice as the Matriarch? Oystermen involved in murder? Smuggling maybe, but murder? It was the worst of worst case scenarios he could think of and one he kept denying. 'Go back through them again,' he told Grayson. 'And recheck the names of every worker given by Mrs Chalmers.'

For the third time, Grayson went back to the photos. One in particular drew his attention. Three men standing on board, in overalls and boots, holding an oyster shell in each hand, grinning wildly, undoubtedly enjoying the day and their companionship. The man in the middle was shorter and older than the other two but was clearly enjoying himself. He looked familiar. Not instantly recognisable but there were characteristics about his fluffy, white hair, scratchy beard and reddened face that Grayson had seen before. He texted the photo to Walker's mobile. Walker almost leapt out of his chair.

'Know who this is, Mrs Chalmers?' Walker asked waving the phone picture in her reddened face.

'Why, old Bainesy! Didn't know he was on one of the boats yesterday.'

Walker thought he heard a click, as if something physically snapped into place in his mind. Then he drew away from his thoughts and for the first time a piece of the picture was revealed. Bainesy the nicknamed, smiling, sailor man on board the smack, Baines the deluded tramp in his hovel and somehow - and still to this day he can't explain how he connected this part - Baines, the lawyer. That was the key. Somehow, he had trawled out this connection from the original name of the firm of lawyers. He had seen it in the correspondence section in the files he had stolen. It might have been inadmissible but it wasn't ignorable. There was an old letterhead. He wasn't sure he could find it, but from memory, the letter was at least ten years old. The letterhead simply read: Baines, Ridgely, Turner and Fowler. That meant three Baines, or was it two Baines, or were they in fact the same person?

It was still Monday morning, just, an excellent time to visit offices. Office workers hated Monday mornings too, they would say anything to get a nosy policeman off the premises. He jumped into his car and sped away from the coast. He took the trunk road back to Chelmsford, around the one-way system and into view came the grainy, yellow stone columns of Ridgely House.

For a fleeting moment, he wondered if Gabrielle Simons would see him. He pushed it to the back of his mind - she wouldn't have any choice. If she had thought that the last two meetings were bad, she had underestimated how completely unreasonable he could be. Five minutes later, he was striding past reception. The receptionist recognised him and dived for the phone. 'Leave it!' he shouted. 'Don't you dare,' he warned as he stormed along the corridor. A flurry of activity saw a procession of Hacks, Gonads, Serfs and Scribes emerge from offices and seminar rooms. They came up behind him like a procession, his very own welcoming committee. He swivelled round to confront them.

'None of you are going to interfere! This is a police matter, got that?'

They all stopped in their tracks and looked aghast. He rapped fiercely on her door.

'Enter.'

'Ms Simons. It's me again.' He barged in and closed the door. 'We need to talk.'

Simons was caught off guard. With all defences breached and a harassed looking police officer walking into her room as if it was his domain, she looked perplexed. For the first time ever, Walker thought, she actually looked scared.

'I suppose I should be grateful you didn't smash the door down. You'd better sit.'

'Ms Simons, I want to know who Baines was?'

Her eyebrows twitched. Then she closed her file, told reception not to interrupt and made a little cough. 'Martin Baines? You want to know all about Martin Baines?'

'Yes.'

'Firstly, I take a very dim view of you barging into my office. Secondly, my secretary says that you were rude to her and that is absolutely unforgivable and you will be reported. Thirdly-'

'Ms Simons,' Walker interrupted, 'let's stick to Martin Baines.'

'Very well.' She began as if reading from a book, very matter of fact, perfect diction in fact, just what was expected from a lawyer, cool under pressure. Once she had provided some colourful background about his privileged past she moved the story forward. 'One morning, I heard a noise in reception. I came out and saw Martin Baines wielding a revolver at one of the members of our practice. His eyes were wild and he started shouting and screaming that he was going to kill someone. The previous day, in a meeting, he had accused Alan Thomas of dragging the firm through the mire. He had also accused him of trying to get rid of him by employing women and getting them to take over. When he burst into reception, he had demanded to see both Thomas and Susan Almond. Security arrived just in time and slowly calmed him down.' She paused and swivelled in her executive chair. 'I think he must have had a fit, something like a brainstorm. It happens. Then he went very quiet, withdrawn and he began to apologise profusely. Eventually he was escorted out of the building. I never saw him again.'

'You didn't ring the police?'

'No.'

'Yea Gods!' Walker exploded, 'a man comes into the office with a firearm and threatens two of your staff who later turn out to be killed and you don't tell anyone?'

'I'm sorry. It was wrong. We all know that now but at the time it didn't seem like the right thing to do. It would have created terrible publicity and affected our client relationships. There's a lot of tension flying around here sometimes. It's the nature of our business. We all knew him well. He wouldn't hurt a fly. He looked quite pitiful when he walked out and as I say, we never heard from him again, except for a letter of resignation. After that, we had a long partners' meeting. It was decided to remove him discretely from the letterhead and say nothing more. That was seven years ago. Everything seemed to be settled. We were sure we had seen the last of him.'

'What did he do afterwards?'

'As I say, we lost contact. The last I heard, he had handed his house over to an agent and gone to live on Mersey Island. He bought up an old shack. A few weeks later, one of our junior partners had to get some papers signed so he went to see Baines. Baines told him that capitalism and expensive possessions weren't for him. He said he had given all his money away to charity. He didn't have any relatives from what I understand, apart from a sister. He said he had decided to have nothing more to do with the law. Every lawyer was a crook, he said, no one had scruples anymore, everyone was in it for the money. He ranted on about all the *nouveau riche* types but he still had this very sharp mind and went through the papers in great detail before he signed. People change,' she sighed and spun a slow, graceful arc in her chair.

'Do you think he was serious?' Walker asked.

'He said he was going to stop anyone building on the island. He said he would be like Canute, standing on the shore, holding back the waves of progress. Any new building, he said, would be over his dead body. Finally, he began a rant about Joe Biggs, who he discovered, had acquired his old house. It must have driven him crazy. The junior partner got out while he could. We could do nothing more. That's all there is. From then on, I understand that everyone dismissed him as mad.'

'But he wasn't and still isn't.'

'I don't know. Have you met him?'

Walker nodded. At the time, he had appeared delusional, remote and frankly pathetic. He had been dismissed as the local idiot but this new evidence put his behaviour in a new light. Walker had underestimated this man, had seen him simply as a pawn whereas his whole life he had been something akin to a king; controlling and manipulating, to support and enhance his powerful position. Suddenly Martin Baines had become the connecting rod, linking three unsolved crimes, the killings of Thomas and Almond, the shooting of Joe Biggs and the poisoning of Joe Hart.

Walker got Grayson on his mobile.

'Guess where we're going, Grayson?'

'Hmm, I wonder.'

'I'm heading there immediately. I'll see you in about twenty-five minutes.'

'No problemo.'

By mid afternoon, Walker and Grayson were back on the island. A small group of avocets waded cautiously through the brackish waters, dragging their bills through the ebbing tide. A snowy white egret stalked its prey with unwavering concentration. Neither police officer noticed, they were too busy clambering through sand dunes, across driftwood and saltings until they burst into the lair. Baines was squatting on a rough blanket, warming his hands around a mug of tea. He yelped in surprise and leapt to his feet.

'God, what is this?'

'We want a word with you, Martin Baines,' Grayson said sternly. 'We have reason to believe that you can help us with our enquiries concerning the killing of Susan Almond and Alan Thomas.'

'Get out of here! This is my house! Get out!' Baines picked up the steaming teapot and hurled it at the police officers. Grayson ducked but Walker wasn't so lucky and the scalding object hit him on the shoulder and emptied its contents over his coat. He raced up to the pathetic wretch and grabbed him around the throat, until he had him in lock.

'Don't mess up my coat, or I'll mess you up,' Walker shouted. 'Understand?'

Baines was wheezing and spluttering his way to the next breath and could only nod.

Walker released him and the old man collapsed in a crumpled heap.

'Now we're going to talk.'

Baines nursed his neck and slowly moved it from side to side to reassure himself that it was still working.

'Okay, okay. I'll speak,' he said slowly, his regional accent no longer apparent but replaced with an educated tongue. 'Just leave me be, alright? I'm an old gentleman.'

Grayson nodded.

'No bullshit, not this time,' glowered Walker, wiping his coat with his handkerchief. 'From the beginning.'

'No, no bullshit, as you put it. I just need to get myself comfortable. My legs are giving me gip.' He sprawled out his bony legs in front of him and eased a cushion under his rump. 'Well, I have to say things haven't turned out the way

I thought they would,' he said ruefully. 'It's all very unfortunate. My parents would be ashamed if they saw me now. They imagined me happily married, living in the mansion, prosperous, children and grandchildren filling the drawing room with laughter. Are you married, inspector?'

'No.'

'No, I thought as much. We're both lost souls, aren't we?'

Walker rolled his eyes. 'Let's stick to the facts, Baines. I hope this is going somewhere. You've wasted enough of our time.'

'Quite so, no I just think that being single makes life more difficult. You follow your own destiny, do you not? Mine has been downward and yet,' he said ruminatively, 'not altogether uninteresting. When you get to the top, you suddenly find yourself questioning everything. At least, I did. There was no one with their hand on the tiller, to rein me in and keep me going in the right direction. In those circumstances, you are just as likely to run aground as you are to drift endlessly for days. I was drifting, utterly disillusioned with my professional life.' He paused to rub the side of his neck with his hand. 'I used to sit in meetings for hours listening to these young lawyers pontificate and drone on about seizing the moment and breaking the mould and God if I hear that 'thinking outside the box' ever again I think I will murder someone - speaking metaphorically, of course. So, I left it all, I walked away from my valued clients, my briefs, my solid gold pencil case, my position as founding partner and my fifteen-bedroomed mansion. I left it just like that, as if I was dead.'

'But not before pointing a gun at some of your fellow employees.'

'True. I don't deny it. They deserved to see a bit of life, red in tooth and claw. All these young people are wrapped in cotton wool all their lives. They just expect benefits, favourable treatment - all it is, is me, me, me all the time. They don't know what danger and pain are all about,' the old man said insistently as he began running one knobbly hand over the bare knuckles of the other. 'They have to be woken up.'

For the first time, Walker began to see the truth. Baines was crazy: not in a jokey, madcap way but in a much more sinister way. He was cold-blooded, determined and utterly ruthless. He could even be the killer.

'You saw Alan Thomas and Susan Almond that day, didn't you?' suggested Grayson.

Baines nodded.

'You couldn't believe it,' Walker said. 'Seven years after you had threatened them they suddenly appeared on your doorstop, on your island. You recognised them instantly. You were going to ward them off but, no, you had a much more evil plan in store. You came back here, got out your gun and went over to them, said a few words, they must have been shocked, but they would barely have recognised you. Then you pulled out your revolver and shot them in cold blood.'

'No, no, I didn't do it. Honest, I didn't. Yes, I did intend to scare them off but I didn't kill them. Look, the truth is that I heard another car and I ran quickly away.'

'The other car you heard was Joe Biggs. He arrived in a taxi. He was on the island at the time looking at his development site. He had arranged to meet the two victims. He wanted to build on the island and that was unacceptable. He was also the man that actually took over your house. You couldn't bear that, having a common man like Biggs living in your ancestral home. You knew how to get in, you took your gun along and there you shot him.'

'No, I didn't.'

'Now you were on an orgy of killing but you wanted everyone away from the island,' Walker baited. 'You were losing control. You were hallucinating, imagining people that weren't there. You heard about the festival so you tried to poison someone at the festival to ruin it for everyone. You poured some rat poison into an oyster and then set off on your sailing trip. The perfect alibi. There was me thinking the poisoner was trying to kill one person in particular and had to be there but you didn't care did you, anyone would do, as long as the festival was stopped? You're an evil, nasty, warped, vindictive and vicious old man. PC Grayson…'

Grayson moved towards him. Baines shifted uneasily. Then a twisted smile flickered across his face. Walker noticed his eyes dart to one corner. A silvery object winked. 'Quick!' shouted Walker. 'Get it!' Grayson dived across the room, slid on a mat and went skidding into the corner where he grabbed the object, just as Baines outstretched hand clutched at thin air. 'Got it!' shouted Grayson. Then he jerked the handcuffs from his back pocket and clicked them around Baines's bony wrists.

The old man bared his teeth. 'I wasn't going to use it, you fools. I just wanted to hide it. I know what you think but it was given to me by an acquaintance. It gets very lonely out here at nights. I don't have a phone. I don't know anyone. If anything happened, the police would take ages to arrive. I needed to protect myself, out here. That's all it is.'

'Smith and Wesson .38, sir.' Grayson said.

'Right,' Walker said sternly, 'Martin Baines, we are arresting you in connection with the murders of Alan Thomas and Susan Almond. We are also arresting you in connection with the murder of Joseph Biggs and the attempted murder of Joe Hart. You have a right to a lawyer and the right to remain silent.'

Grayson began hauling the accused to his feet. 'You've got it wrong!' he said at last. 'I wouldn't hurt a flea, I'm innocent,' he moaned as tears began to well up. Very soon, police back up arrived in the form of Officer Parker. She hauled the man out of his hut and bundled him into the back of the squad car. In five minutes, the two cars were making their way back to Chelmsford.

CHAPTER FOURTEEN

Monday, p.m. 11th November.

Martin Baines sat in the sparse room waiting for the door to open. He had said nothing, he had done nothing, except make one phone call. The gloating Inspector Walker sat opposite him, his smug expression, one of the most unappetising sights he had seen in a long time. Having defended numerous clients in the past, he knew that such over confidence could only lead to one thing: disaster. No one, not even the greatest barrister at Lincoln's Inn, ever assumed anything. He always relied on the facts and how well he presented them. There was not such a thing as *prima facie* guilt; it was always down to the prosecutor, the disposition of the judge and the perceptions of the jury that were ultimately decisive. He knew one more thing: that as soon as the person walked through the door he would be off the hook.

The door finally opened. In walked Gabrielle Simons.

Walker wilted visibly. Grayson groaned with despair.

'Inspector, what in heaven's name is going on?' she said, barely controlling her voice.

Walker got up and held out his hand. It was left hanging in the air as Simons pulled up a chair. She sat down and looked at her client. She barely recognised him. Seven years had changed him into something more ape-like than human. His white hair had grown long, straggly and lank and plastered his face and shoulders. His face was also covered in facial growth, a beard and moustache that rambled up to his bony cheekbones and down to his scraggy throat. His clothes were more like a thin extra covering of extra skin, hanging onto bony extremities and filling in hollows.

'Martin Baines?' she said slowly, wondering if this thing in front of her could actually talk.

'The very same.'

Only his fruity, Home Counties accent assured her of his identity.

'God, I'm sorry, but you look awful?'

He nodded. 'I know, the years haven't been so good, but you look fine.'

'Thanks.'

'No, thank you for coming so soon. You could have left me to stew after how I behaved all those years ago.'

Simons turned to Walker. 'I need to speak to my client, alone.'

'Sure.'

Grayson and Walker went to the door. Simons got up and followed them.

When the door closed, Walker asked 'I thought you wanted to be alone with him?'

She put her thumb and forefinger to her nose. 'God, he absolutely stinks! It's the most awful rank stench I've ever smelt.'

Walker made a little smug smile. 'It's your client,' he said, as he walked away.

She didn't let it go. She went chasing after him down the corridor and grabbed hold of his arm.

'Hey buster! Don't get all clever with me. I could have your arse in stir if I wanted to,' she hissed. 'Making false arrests, fabricating evidence, perverting the course of justice, any of those would stick. I can still reconvene the coroner's meeting in less than forty-eight hours if I have to. Now get my client cleaned up, hose him down if necessary, get him some decent clothes, I'll foot the bill, find a razor and then ring me and we will start this again, this time without any tricks. Okay?'

Two hours later, Simons was back in the interview room, this time sitting suitably adjacent to a freshly scrubbed Baines. Baines wore socks without holes, shoes with laces, trousers that weren't impregnated with sweat, piss and shit and a shirt and tie the like of which he hadn't experienced for seven years. Even his Fu Manchu-style fingernails had been cut and the underlying grime removed. If he was guilty, thought Simons, at least he looked clean.

Simons read slowly the statement that her client had written and signed. She shook her head. She hadn't spent years training as a lawyer just to accept pieces of paper. 'This flimsy effort,' she sneered, waving it around like toilet paper, 'where is the evidence, inspector? Where are the witness statements, where is the forensic proof, where is the ballistics report? All you have is a signed confession. My client now tells me he wants to retract the statement. He says it was obtained under duress. He says he is suffering from fever and cannot always concentrate. He says he was refused food and drink. He says-.'

'Stop it!' shouted a weary Walker. 'Your client was refused cigarettes, because it's illegal to smoke. He was refused whisky, because we're not a distillery. He signed the statement of his own free will and he can't explain where he was at the time of the killings. His claim to be suffering from feverish malaria is somewhat disingenuous since malaria hasn't been found on these shores since 1953. We found a similar type of handgun to the one used in the first and second killing and he has no alibis. Your client is already one of the biggest liars I have ever met and still I don't believe a bloody word he says.'

Gabrielle Simons was lost for words.

Walker continued. 'Now, before you weigh in and start banging on about your client's rights, I'm going to have the truth out of Mr Baines today come hell or high water. He is a major suspect and if he can't give us the answers we need, then he is going to be locked up and refused bail until such time as he is taken to court. Do you understand?'

Simons saw an angry man and remained quiet for a few more seconds, in order to let his temper subside. Then she spoke softly. 'Okay, inspector. My client is ready. Let's start once more at the very beginning, this time let's take things a little more slowly, this rat-tat-tat doesn't do anyone any favours We'll go through everything relating to the crimes and at the end we will all be in a position to decide on a further course of action.'

That's what happened. It took three hours, it involved backtracking, sidetracking, repetition, crossings out and insertions but eventually, when evening had arrived, a statement was prepared and one that Martin Baines was ready to sign.

'He's innocent,' Simons said finally, at the end of a gruelling session.

'I know,' Walker said. 'I always had my doubts.'

'So you're back to square one, inspector.' said a satisfied Simons.

'Not really, just one fewer suspect to worry about and one step closer to finding the killer.' Walker replied.

Baines and Simons left the station together and headed for Simons's car. Inspector Walker collected up his papers and walked back down the corridor to give Chief Superintendent Jones the bad news.

Tuesday, 12th November.

Going back to a scene of crime was a fundamental for DI Walker. He had already been back three times and each time another piece of the jigsaw fitted into place. Normally, he would be at the fishmongers but this Tuesday was different. He was going to find the final pieces of the puzzle so that a complete picture could emerge. He was convinced it was hours, not days, it was incidents not events and it was fine-tuning not an overhaul. One small piece of evidence would be enough to flush the prey out of his hiding and into Walker's grateful arms. All he needed was the tiniest of breaks. What he got was PC Grayson at the wheel.

Grayson was driving but only in the loosest sense. When he commandeered a vehicle, everything was exaggerated. Usually, he leaned forward, his hands gripping like crazy, his eyes almost glued to the windscreen. Other times he sat back, head turning, one hand resting on the open window, the other on the wheel, making the slightest adjustments to minimise on effort. He was either some laid back dude in his pimpmobile or some hotshot rally driver making mincemeat of the field. He really was the worst driver on Earth.

'Yunno sir, I've lived in Essex all my life. My parents were from here and my grandparents too. That's three generations. It takes you through a century of times lived in Essex. I was born here, went to school just down that road there,' he said using his spare hand to point out the location, 'I attended college two miles along here and I've worked all over the county in the last couple of years.'

'Watch the road, Grayson,' Walker observed.

'It's taken me a long time to understand the people round here,' he muttered despairingly.

'You, me and the rest.'

'Look at it this way,' he continued, waving his hands about irresponsibly in the narrow confines of the Escort, 'you have the materialistic people in the south, you have country bumpkins in the north, you have hard-nosed city dwellers in the west and then you have the sea faring types in the east.'

'They're all stereotypes, Grayson.'

'Oh, are they?'

'Yes, they are. Essex Man, doesn't exist either,' Walker said. 'Nor, Essex girl, never did. It's all a myth.'

'I think you're wrong, sir. I think it's possible to identify where people come from.'

'So that's your great theory, is it?' Walker sneered. 'You think you can recognise where people come from in the county.'

'Yes,' confirmed Grayson, 'I can tell if someone is from Colchester or Dengie or Southend or Barking. It's easy.'

'By their accent?'

'No, their geographical footprint.'

'Their what?'

'Their geographical footprint. Each area has its own footprint.'

'Very useful for criminal profiling.'

The car veered perilously close to the kerb.

'I tell you,' Grayson continued, gesticulating wildly, It's all about breaking down all the component parts.'

'How about braking this car so that it stays on the road?' Walker warned.

Grayson ignored him. 'I think that once you understand the background, you can fit this case all together.'

'Maybe it doesn't fit,' Walker suggested. 'Maybe,' Walker paused to check how close the car was to the kerb, 'you should leave it to me.'

'Maybe.'

'Look, Grayson,' Walker said, 'Words of advice. Everyone, everywhere has the same fundamental urges.'

'Sure, but everyone *acts* differently. Even you sir, given the right circumstances.'

'Nah, not me.' Walker said dismissively

Grayson tightened his hands on the wheel and leaned forward in mock exaggeration. The car lurched forward. 'Yes, *exactly* you. You could be just a few seconds away from being a killer. I could attack you right now and stuck in this miserable vehicle you would lash out to defend yourself and strike a fatal blow. Question is would you use your fists, grab a blunt instrument like a torch or go for the glove compartment?'

Walker looked mildly surprised. His fingers fluttered momentarily across the dashboard.

'Hah! See, you are making a decision!' Grayson exclaimed.

'Yeah, I'm making a decision all right. I'm deciding that I've got a fuckwit in the car with me and I'm wondering whether to put the radio on or strangle him. Now pay attention to the road, otherwise we'll miss our turn-off.'

Grayson settled back and adopted a classical driving position.

'Better?'

'Okay,' Walker said. 'So, as a matter of interest, know-it-all, where are you from?'

'Upminster, sir. Tube station. End of the line.'

'That figures.'

'It's the suburbs, just lines of housing, really. Nothing ever happens, bit like my life. See, that's what I'm talking about. My home environment defines me.'

'Your home environment *defines* you,' Walker repeated slowly. 'Do you know how bloody stupid that sounds?'

'It means that my thought processes and consequent behaviour patterns are determined by my environment.'

'That sounds even worse. You should listen to yourself one day, Grayson. Is this what they taught you at college?'

'Studying sociology gave me an insight.'

Having a knife stuck to your throat, a shotgun pointed at your chest, or a broken glass waved in your face, that gave insight, Walker thought, having experienced all three in his career. Even having CS Jones sitting next to him for company would have been infinitely preferable to Grayson, but he didn't have to listen to this horseshit so he turned the radio up loud.

Grayson persisted.

'It's like the birds, they are all specifically adapted to feed or build their nests in their own way,' Grayson shouted, above the noise of some MOR music. 'Humans are the same. Let's just say, someone on Southend seafront wants to do someone in. They use a knife, don't they, a nice little sharp, pocketknife; one that gets hidden in the crowds. Stick it right in, pull it out, wipe the blood off and run like hell. Get it all the time don't we?'

Walker nodded. 'Yes, genius. I've read *Brighton Rock* too, but it's *fiction*.'

'Let's head off to Felstead. Nice cricket school there. Peaceful, rural, clean living. Yet sometimes a farmer's shotgun makes its mark on some hapless sod who wanders off whack.'

'Let me see, *Straw Dogs*?'

'Then we head off to the coast, Burnham, Maldon, even Harwich, we can smell the ozone, the land flattens, the sky opens up. Big burley fishermen, hauling in nets. Blistered fingers, bulging biceps. Notice how people up there end up there on the wrong side of strangulation?'

'All the time,' Walker mumbled, 'in your fevered imagination of books and films.'

'Sorry, sir. Couldn't hear you.'

'You've missed the bloody turning!! Is that loud enough?'

Grayson swivelled his head, spun the car in a full circle and headed back in the opposite direction, as if it were a standard driving move. 'Think we're back on track. Now, this bit you'll find interesting, sir. Can I turn the music down a bit?'

'Yeah Gods! Let's just get there,' Walker screamed.

Grayson tweaked the radio off. 'I've been doing a bit of research. 1899, the murder at Moat Farm in Essex involved a shotgun. One year later, at the fishing port of Great Yarmouth, a woman is strangled. After the Great War there was an upsurge in crimes involving firearms.'

'Your point?'

'A criminal uses whatever is most suitable, according to time and place.'

'So, Professor Grayson, following your line of thought: Smith and Wesson, a shooter. Has to be concealable, fear of being spotted, loads of people. Easy to purchase and to get rid off. We're talking East End, aren't we?'

'Exactly!' Grayson exclaimed. 'We're inhabiting the mind of the metropolitan, who wants to do it properly, just like the seasoned gangster who is born just down the road from him in a dingy terraced house on the Mile End Road but who now lives in a villa in Marbella.'

'And there was me, thinking that it was about clues, motives and opportunity,' Walker murmured. 'Well, Grayson, you really have earned yourself some merit points today. First thing tomorrow, we'll go and charge the Crays, on suspicion of every crime involving a revolver, but before then, let's see if my antediluvian methods past muster.'

Walker demanded to see the witnesses' statements once again. Anything to get Grayson to shut up. He rested them in front of him as Grayson weaved his way through the heavy traffic. When he suspected that the silence was about to be broken by another extract from The Criminal Mind by Stephen Grayson, he began reading them out. They all had a depressingly voyeuristic nature to them but it was worth it, just to keep Grayson quiet.

'Mrs Spencer knocked on my door and told me to come and have a look'; 'I was in the Fisherman's Arms when Ted came in and told me to put my beer down and come along'; 'I was in the supermarket when Nancy came up and said she had seen Mrs Dean and she had said there was a murder so we both went to investigate.' A whole village mobilised in minutes. 'It's like *Whisky Galore* without the fucking Whisky,' Walker cursed. 'A bunch of rubbernecks. Of course, none of the times of events actually match up, we have errors of addresses and some of these names we can't put a tracer on. Parker did a good job.'

'I think she was trying to do her best,' Grayson said lamely.

'What is it with you youngsters? Everything's a bloody game,' he grumbled.

'The rain was driving down and there was a howling gale. I'd like to see you do any better, sir.' Grayson murmured to himself.

'It's basic procedural work. You check and cross check.' Walker said grouchily. 'Did she follow up the statements later and validate them?'

'I'm sure she did,' Grayson said. At least she said she had.

'Like fuck.'

Grayson swerved into the opposite lane to avoid a regulation agricultural machinery that had the audacity to be on the same road. He also picked off, like bunny rabbits, the traditional slew of recreational drivers on their way to the coast. In no time, they were back in the car park. The weather turned. Clouds bubbled up, swept in by a strengthening breeze.

'Seems like only yesterday we were here,' Grayson said.

'It was.' Walker said as he finally climbed out of the car. He took off, tramping across scrub and uneven ground, back on familiar territory. As they approached the perimeter of land and stepped over samphire and coarse grass, the heavens opened; first, a steady drip, like a military drum beat, then a staccato rhythm and soon a torrent, like crashing timpani. Rain into water, rain upon land and rain falling into creeks and dried up riverbeds as the tide swept in, transforming solids to liquid. In minutes, the landscape had been transformed from the bare bones of shoreline, exposed beach and muddied creeks into a smooth, rounded coastline with the cracks papered in, like a plasterer's mortar. They raced back to the safely of the car.

'Jeez, was this forecast?' Grayson asked.

'Don't know, Walker replied gloomily as the rain pounded the roof of the car. I leave all that metrological stuff to you.'

'We happen to be in the driest part of the country.'

'That's reassuring.'

'Do you know if the tide was going in or out when we discovered the bodies?' Grayson asked.

Walker looked confused. 'Is this another one of your theories?'

'No, sir. It's just that I'm trying to think. We drove across the island, got a little lost and then arrived at Graydon's Creek. It was raining.'

'Sure. It was raining,' Walker confirmed. 'Everyone said that, everyone knows that. What are you getting at?'

'It was six thirty, six thirty-five, I guess.'

'I'm sure we can check,' Walker said, disinterestedly.

'Then we stepped out and approached the vehicle. It was lying on the slipway. Yes, I remember now, I slipped. I made a joke about that.'

'Not like you to make a joke,' Walker suggested. 'So the approach was slippery?'

'Yeah.'

'And there were a lot of seabirds around, waders.'

'So the tide was going out?'

'Must have been.'

'For how long?' Walker asked.

'Don't know. Not long, I suppose,' Grayson said. 'The water was still lapping around the front of the vehicle.'

'One, two hours?'

'Probably two. Thing is, it's what one of the witnesses said.'

'Which was?'

'One of the bystanders in her statement said she had come across the island at five, to visit one of the old churchyards.'

'Right.'

'In the rain?'

'People do go to cemeteries in the rain, Grayson.'

'I think I should check the tides, sir.'

'She came across the island. There is a bridge, Grayson. It's called The Strood. We just crossed it,' he said impatiently.

'I know sir, but I was reading this book and The Strood…'

'The bloody Strood,' Walker cursed. People said they wished it didn't exist, others wanted it blown up. These people had never been off the island, they suffered panic attacks whenever they thought they might have to leave. Somehow, he couldn't understand how an island population, when faced the constant threat of flooding, just like 80% of the world's population, still wanted nothing to do with their only escape route.

'Okay,' Walker said wearily, 'why don't you go off and see Chalmers. See if you can get this tide thing resolved.'

In a couple of minutes, the rain stopped and the sun broke through like a blister, making the tiny rills and mudflats sparkle. Grayson set out on the short walk to the sheds but it was hard going across shingle and into a driving wind. Oystercatchers scuttled across the beach, probing every crevice, pushing their beaks deep into the mud. It must give you a headache, thought Grayson, like pounding your head repeatedly against a wall. Not like this case, then. They took off, their piping cry echoing across the mudflats until they disappeared from sight.

Grayson pressed on, at least he had some time to think, without fear of criticism. His mind went back to the black 1940's Austin Morris struggling, the rickety chassis shaking like a jitterbug. The wheels were spinning, he imagined the driver pounding the oversized steering wheel, pumping the gas pedal, urging the vehicle on, just as he did. Yet, there was no contest, not when the water swelled up to the ramparts and then surged across the causeway.

Chalmers was repairing some nets when a breathless Stephen Grayson came up to him.

'Ah, the helper! Here, just give me a hand putting these baskets in, will you laddie?'

'No can do. Bit busy.'

'Are we now? And you think I'm not?'

'Of course, it's just that. Look, I wanted to ask you about the tides.'

'Ah, the tides!' said Chalmers with mock surprise. 'Still trying to solve the crime are we? Comes in, goes out regular as clockwork.'

'Yes, but there are variations.'

'Of course.'

'So was there anything unusual about the tide of the 16th October?'

'Well it was a spring tide.'

'In Autumn?'

Chalmers looked disdainfully at the young charge. 'Sounds like you need to go back to school.'

'With respect, sir. I don't, I just need to hear the facts about tides.'

'There are two extreme tides; neap and spring and they both occur twice a year, based on the position of the Moon in relation to the Earth and Sun. When the Moon and Sun are pulling in the same direction you get big variations tides…here, take this for a minute.'

Grayson took hold of a bucket while Chalmers tapped one of the oysters with his knife. It made a hollow sound.

'It's a clacker.' Chalmers confirmed, as he cracked it open. All it contained was a lump of wet sand. 'Don't take things at face value, laddie.'

He then proceeded to insert his oyster knife into another shell. He worked it around expertly until the top was levered off in a flourish. Then he did two more and positioned them on the ground. 'Earth, Moon and Sun,' he said, moving them around until Stephen got the hang of it. 'When they are aligned thus, you get extremes.'

Grayson nodded.

'You know some people used to think the Moon was made of cheese.' Chalmers said.

'Takes all sorts.'

Chalmers picked up the 'Moon' shell by the narrow end, supporting it underneath with his fingers. He held the wide part to his mouth and drank the oyster from its shell, 'Actually, laddie, it's made of oysters,' and he gave a throaty laugh. 'Ever eaten one?'

Grayson shook his head.

Chalmers pointed his hand towards the ground. 'Go on, life's too short.'

Stephen picked up the 'Earth' and looked at it warily.

'You've got the world at your fingertips.' Chalmers said.

'Sir, about the tides?'

'Four ounces, at least,' Chalmers confirmed. 'We still use imperial measures.'

Grayson nurtured it in his hand, suddenly noticing the coloured veins throughout, mauve, milky white, khaki. 'It's quite a thing.'

'The oyster is a thing of beauty. It's been revered down the ages. Go on, taste it.'

'Don't think I should. Not a great fan.'

Chalmers took it off Grayson. 'Well, at your age,' Chalmers, said casually, 'you probably don't need it anyway.'

'Need what?' Grayson asked.

'Oh, yunno, a little help with the ladies?'

'Huh?'

'Assistance?'

'Well, I don't know-.'

'It puts lead in your pencil, young laddie. More precisely, zinc.'

'Oh?'

'It's an aphrodisiac.' Chalmers confirmed at last. 'Casanova polished off a plateful every breakfast,' he added but Grayson had already snatched the shell from Chalmers and swallowed the Earth whole. Then he gulped the Sun for good measure, and two more, non-celestial bodies. He swallowed these whole too. In thirty seconds, he had wolfed down three oysters.

'How many do I need?' Grayson asked, stuffing another three in his mouth.

'Need? Just the one should do the job.'

'Oh.'

Even as the final plump creature slid down his gullet with a resounding plop, he felt full of foreboding. 'Not sure about this rich man's food,' he burped, 'more of a pie and beans man, myself.'

'Rich man's food, you call it?' Chalmers asked. 'Oysters were a staple diet round these parts for hundreds of years. Everyone ate them from the herdsman to the milkmaid. The only reason that they don't now is because someone, somewhere decided it should be a luxury item.' Chalmers lent forward. 'Between you and me laddie,' he whispered conspiratorially, 'it's a load of old cobblers, what they say. I've never found it helped with the ladies.'

'Thanks.'

'Give me Mussels any day- richer taste, much better for getting John Thomas to pull his weight.'

'I get your message,' Grayson said, wiping his mouth of the remnants of liquor. 'Mr Chalmers, do you think it was possible to drive across the Causeway at high tide?'

'The Strood at high tide? On the sixteenth?'

Grayson nodded.

'Not unless their car grew flippers,' Chalmers said.

'Right.'

'The tide would have been sloshing around the wheel arches. They couldn't have crossed for at least another hour either side.'

'So between four-fifteen and six-fifteen the bridge would have been impassable?'

'Correct.'

'Any other way onto the island?'

'Only that,' Chalmers said, pointing to the boat.

'Thanks, that's just what I needed to know. Thanks for the food. Excuse me. Well, must be heading back.'

Stephen rushed back to the car. He felt delighted. Here at last was a breakthrough, something to raise his spirits yet shot through his elation was a sense of unease. He felt it lingering on his tongue and each time he burped he tasted the sickly mix of seawater and salty mudflats in his mouth. When he got back, he found the car but no Walker. He took out his mobile and speed-dialled Walker. No reply. Oh well, Grayson thought, as his stomach rumbled, sit tight, he'll appear soon.

CHAPTER FIFTEEN

Walker had switched off his phone. He didn't want to be disturbed while he was in deep conversation with a key witness. He had strolled up the road. Wisps of smoke welled up like fumeroles from the chimneys of dimly lit cottages. He had stopped outside number fifteen. She was in. Formalities dealt with, he was ushered into the front room where he sat docilely next to a Grandfather clock that chimed eleven times. Enough to drive anyone batty, he thought. He was given a cup of tea, which he nursed on his lap, and a digestive to bite on while the television blinked its silent messages.

'Mrs Dean. I'd like you to think back. You were out walking your dog…'

Right on cue, a Labrador came up to Walker and began nuzzling his nose into Walker's crotch. 'Get away, Toby!' Mrs Dean said, taking him by the collar and yanking him from under the table.

'Thanks.'

'Bad boy!' she said, wagging her swollen finger. 'Not at the table. How many times have I told you?'

Toby sloped off to curl in front of the fireside. 'He's a good dog but he gets in the way sometimes. Doesn't help having rheumatism. Makes it difficult to take him walking and he needs his exercise otherwise his tum will get too large and we don't want that, do we Toby?'

Walker moved in his chair. Time was ticking away as he could see from the large clock. He wished he could put a filter on her or jump straight to the important bits.

'You said that you noticed the car at five thirty-five?'

'Oh, did I?'

'Yes.'

'Well, must have been. It was raining.'

'You said that a little while later a woman approached you. She let you use her phone.'

'Er, oh yes! Nice lady.'

'But you didn't hear or see anything, before, when you were out walking?' Walker asked.

'Didn't I? Well, it was windy. No, that's right.'

'No sounds of a gun being fired?'

'No.'

'Or a vehicle driving off?'

'No…mind you, Toby began to get excited but then he'll see things like rabbits and voles that I won't even notice.'

'Can you tell me which route you took?'

'Along the seawall, past the Fisherman's Arms and then straight along the path to the creek.'

'Heading on what direction?'

'South West, I suppose.'

'Thank you.'

'Do you still think it's murder, inspector?' she asked, her face full of lines like a roadmap. 'Be terrible if there's a murderer round these parts. Don't know what I would do.'

Walker closed his notepad and began to rise. 'I wouldn't worry, Mrs Dean. If it was murder, then the killer would be miles away by now. Anyway, thanks for the tea. We'll be in touch.'

Walker left by the same route, past the pub and then along a trail edged with hawthorn and scrub until he reached the muddied creek. A small egret wheeled off towards the old churchyard, its wings as light as a pillow. Walker turned his head towards the car park. It was only visible once he had crossed the path, almost at the end of the walk.

The wind was racing in from the sea, screaming like a banshee. He could barely hear his footsteps. Then the penny dropped. The wind would have taken any noises of guns or cars scattering away across the island, far out of earshot. Anyone out of vision could have approached the victims and then driven off. Mrs Dean had mentioned that Toby had become excited, if only he could talk, thought Walker. But it was enough; it convinced Walker that Mrs Dean had been telling the truth. That meant the killer was still out there.

Grayson climbed into the squad car and waited for Walker. Some of the papers were lying in the glove compartment so he picked them out and began to leaf through them. He was looking at the witness's statements and specifically for any mention of times. Mrs Dean's statement was brief but crucial; at least that's why Grayson thought Walker had gone to see her. That left the motley crew of onlookers. Nearly all of them arrived at the SOC between six and seven and they were all locals. Database searches had confirmed their addresses and no criminal backgrounds. That left one other. Her name was Mrs Stevens. She had specifically mentioned a time, much earlier than the others. She wasn't a local. Grayson read through it again and again.

'Name?'

'Mrs Stevens.'

'When did you get hear?'

'Dunno.'

'Approximatly.'

'Five o'clock, s'pose.'

Even without Officer Parker's typing mistakes it wasn't going to rival Livingstone and Stanley. Bits of Tippex were flaking off the paper. Typewriter? Didn't they have computers on ships? The time could have been typed wrongly too. He ignored the *s'pose*. It had been less a supposition, more a qualification of fact.

Five o'clock, she said. Mrs Stevens had not been traced since the incident. Grayson spoke to Officer Parker about her, four days ago. Over a glass of wine, she had confessed that the address might have been wrong too. A visit to the address had taken them both to a little old lady whose only mode of transport was a motorised buggy - not exactly conducive to travelling onto an island of marshy mudflats and killing people.

This anomaly hadn't been noticed by Walker, or at least hadn't been investigated. God knows, what went on in his mind, Grayson wondered. It was strange; Walker had gone obsessively after David Almond, Joe Biggs, Baines and even Alice Chalmers, yet this one had squeaked through. Was she just too insignificant? Had a potential killer evaded detection simply by falsifying a time, name and address? Was it that easy to outwit a senior detective?

Walker's ample frame came lumbering into view in the rear mirror just as Grayson pushed the statements back in the glove compartment. Walker got in the car, signalled for Grayson to pull out and didn't say a word. Grayson turned up the winding road, back towards Chelmsford. Eventually the silence began to gnaw at Grayson.

'How was Mrs Dean?' Grayson asked.

'Fine.'

'Any problems?'

'Nope.'

Walker kept peering out of his passenger's window, deep in thought.

So much for bloody teamwork, Grayson thought. As they crossed the roundabout, leading back to town, Grayson began a monologue to try to break the boredom.

'Today, I ran through some checks. I rang up Coastal Waters HQ. High tide for the Blackwater was 17:15, at a depth of 6.9 metres. That was precisely thirty minutes before the bodies were discovered. Then, I went along to see Chalmers. He confirmed that it was a spring tide and it would have been impossible to cross The Strood one hour either side. He'd only ever experienced spring tides like that thirty or so times in his life. He told me that each time locals had had to sit in their cars and twiddle their thumbs, until the waters receded. Then I tried to tally this information with the witness statements.'

Grayson glanced at Walker who was still looking sullenly out of the window.

'Sir?'

'Go on.'

'Get this: Mrs Stevens, one of the bystanders, said she arrived at the SOC at five. That means she would have had to come across the bridge at no later than quarter to five, but she couldn't have done.'

Grayson waited. At last, Walker's broad head slowly turned and looked directly at Grayson.

'Right,' Walker said, 'let's assume she lied. Why would she do that?'

'To confuse us?'

'So, by her saying she came over at five, she was trying to convince us that she couldn't have committed a murder.'

Grayson hesitated. 'Exactly.'

Walker looked away again. 'Maybe, she just got it wrong.'

'Wrong?' Grayson questioned. 'She couldn't have got across any later than four-fifteen. She said five. That's forty-five minutes out.'

'Spare me the maths lesson.'

'Sir, we know that Mrs Almond and Thomas left Ridgely's at two thirty-five. Thomas's car would have arrived at ten past three, at the earliest. Mrs Stevens must have arrived after that time.'

'Why not before? She said she went to a churchyard.'

'Because she was following them.'

'Any proof?'

'No, but you see, she was way out on her times,' Grayson said, exasperated. 'It wasn't just a few minutes wrong, she was nearly an hour wrong!'

'Calm down, Grayson. I can do the maths.'

'So the question is: why would she lie?'

'Because,' said Walker painfully slowly, 'people lie. I do. You do. Everyone does. It's called human nature. She was probably doing something she didn't want us to know about. Maybe her watch was fast. Maybe she was having it off with the local vicar, maybe she lost track of time.' Walker's stretched out his hand so that it covered up the dashboard. 'What's the time now, Grayson?'

'Pardon?'

'What's the friggin' time? It's a simple enough question, isn't it?'

'Oh. It's about ten past four.'

Walker's hand drew away from the LCD display. It showed five to four.

'Now let's get back.'

Grayson sat back and fumed. He looked at the road ahead. It was unbelievably busy; everyone in a rush, cutting each other up, no proper signals, no one sparing any courtesy to their fellow drivers. God, sometimes he hated Essex drivers! Sometimes he hated Essex! Up ahead, were several large trucks spewing out inky, black diesel. Every day, it got busier and busier. Every day, more traffic, more accidents, more aggravation. It wasn't just the roads, it was the streets, the towns, the villages. Where would it end? He ripped past the trucks and then blasted up the road exceeding the speed limit.

Walker raised a stubby finger and stabbed it at the Speedo.

Grayson slipped back into the nearside traffic and dropped his speed. Stop the world, he mumbled to himself. I want to get off. Finally, he spoke.

'Every time I come up with something, you always dismiss it out of hand. *Every* bloody time.'

Walker turned abruptly. He gave him a thunderous look.

'Like bloody school, it is,' Grayson continued.

'Don't you dare talk to me like that, you insolent pup!' Walker shouted, his face contorted with anger. 'You don't know the first thing about solving a crime! Just because you've been to bloody college and learnt some pointless bullshit about social profiling, you think you're bloody Maigret, yet all you do is mess around like an overgrown school kid. The only reason you got this job was that your father worked for us. He wouldn't recognise a clue if it jumped up and bit him on the arse! The reason why he lost his hair was because he got scared. He lost his bottle during a robbery. You're from the same mould. You can't even ask a girl out! So don't you dare start telling me about how we should go about solving a crime! Now, just shut up and drive us back the station.'

Grayson did precisely what he was told to do. It felt like the longest journey he had ever made.

Wednesday, 13th November

The press conference was called for eight o'clock sharp. The preposterously early start was all part of a cunning plan to discourage attendees: it didn't work. The massed ranks of the press corps filled the press lounge to the brim and more milled outside. Behind the front desk sat a grave looking Gabrielle Simons to the left and CS Jones to the right. They both sipped their glasses of mineral water nervously, while the crowd grew in front of them. Jones fiddled with his microphone, eventually tearing it off his jacket and calling for a standing one. He tapped it several times, blew into it and then looked towards the door. Five minutes passed.

At eight-o-seven, an harassed looking DI Walker entered the room. An array of cameras flashed, TV cameras whirred, and a sea of expectant faces watched him as he made his way quickly behind the desk, and sat between his colleagues. He was centre stage. Jones made a daggers drawn expression, unfolded a piece of paper then made a little cough. He proceeded to read out a pre-prepared statement of such acute banality that it had the awaiting press corps checking their recording equipment to ensure he had actually said something. It made *taking a lead in making Essex safer* seem like the Gettysburg Address. At the end of it, he mumbled: 'So, we will have five minutes for questions, and then we will wrap things up.' Immediately, a flurry of hands and waving papers and pens rose as one in the air. 'You!' shouted Jones to a scruffy looking journalist who was sitting in the middle row.

'You have three deaths and one attempted murder, all in the space of three weeks. Aren't you a little out of your depth and shouldn't you be calling in the Met?'

Jones crooked his little finger, the coded sign to indicate that he would answer.

'I have every faith in the personnel in our investigation.'

Another member of the press: 'Is it not true that you have already brought in several suspects for questioning, one an elderly gentleman and the other a respected police officer and had to release them? Do you actually know what you are doing?'

This time Jones's finger didn't move. Walker cleared his throat.

'The path to criminal detection never runs smoothly,' he said opaquely and a look of bemusement flickered across the audience. They all waited for him to amplify but he just sat there, the silence weighing heavily in the air. There followed several quick-fire questions to the coroner about the inquest that never was. Simons flat-batted them back to the questionnaire like a seasoned lawyer.

Then to the left, a woman came barging through the door. She was dressed in green combat trousers and a battered t shirt. A steward tried to stop her entering but she pushed her way through and squeezed herself into the first row. She waited for a couple more questions and then began waving her pen frantically. Walker recognised her as Alison Holmes. She must have got a press badge from Hart.

CS Jones took her question. 'Madam.'

She stood up. 'Thank you. I'm pleased to see that at least one police officer provides some civility. One of my trusted colleagues, Joe Hart, nearly died because someone poisoned him. So far, the police have refused to make any comment. Innocent members of the pubic that live on the island have been harassed and insulted by the police, yet still they refuse to confirm either way if he was the intended victim. The Mersey Island community is scared, people are losing faith in their police force, everyone is wondering where it will end. It is intolerable in this day and age-' Then the heckling started, at the back and then moving forward like a wave. Holmes caught the mood and waited until it had subsided. Finally, she directed her gaze towards DI Walker: 'Isn't it about time you got your act together and caught the killer before he kills more innocent people?'

Walker looked at Jones's finger. It wobbled and finally bent double.

'Joe Hart,' Jones replied 'was the innocent victim of a malevolent act by a ruthless individual desperate to do anything to avoid detection.' Everyone in the room groaned, how many times had they heard that excuse? 'However,' Jones persevered gamely, 'we believe that the person responsible will be arrested.'

'When?' came a collective cry.

'In the next twenty-four hours.'

There was a sharp intake of breath all round. Pens began scribbling, mobile phones went crazy and suddenly a sea of hands began waving in the air. Yet, Jones had already got up and left, leaving his astonished colleagues sitting on their chairs looking dumbfounded.

Ten minutes later, a furious DI Walker tracked Jones down to the men's room.

'Sir, what was that all about an arrest in the next twenty-four hours?'

Jones was in front of the mirror, straightening his spotted tie. 'Officer Grayson, didn't he tell you?'

'No, no, he didn't'

'He spoke to me last night. Did a bit of digging around.' Jones added, as he swished out his comb from his back pocket and drew it carefully over his grey hair. 'He's got a suspect. Better speak to him quickly if I were you.'

John Walker flew out of the toilet and rushed down the corridor. Grayson's desk was empty with no sign of occupation. Even his computer screen was blank. 'Anyone know where he is?' All the other police officers ignored him or shook their heads. He tried to ring him on his mobile. 'Come on, come on, you little bugger!' There was no reply, just a bland automated voice that could only speak at one speed. 'Leave a message. I'll get back. No problemo.' Walker left a message and then punched out some pithy text messages.

Stephen Grayson was in bed at this moment in time, or more accurately, leaning out of the bed into a slop bucket. He had been sick five times during the night and each time he had tasted that metallic rasp of dodgy seafood. His stomach had cramped up so much he thought it had caved in. Now, he was gushing more liquid than Iquacu Falls, each gush causing his stomach to tighten once more like a vice. Never again, he thought, never again. Next time, it's bangers and mash.

Eventually he tried to focus his bleary eyes on the blurred text. 'Ring me. Bloody Urgent. Walker.'

'What the?' He groaned and slowly typed replied 'Ill.' Then he pinged it into the ether off before collapsing back into his bed.

Walker was furious when he got the reply. 'Why that little shit,' he swore to himself. He wasn't going to waste any more time on 21st century communication protocols, he was going to give his young assistant a good old 20th century rollicking. He jumped into his car and gunned it to Grayson's flat. He pounded the thin front door. 'Grayson! Grayson!!.' Then he began shouting questions through the letterbox: 'I know you're there! What's all this about a suspect, huh? Twenty-four hours? Seen one too many cop shows. Who the hell are you now, Perry Bloody Mason?'

Stephen finally appeared as a crumpled heap in the hallway of his flat and opened the door feebly. Walker grabbed him by the lower legs, threw him over his back and then carried him to the car, like a rolled-up piece of carpet. Then he flopped him down in the passenger's seat. 'Now, talk!'

Ten miles away, a woman was making last minute preparations. She checked herself in the mirror, fiddled with her dyed blond hair and gave it one last look. She wasn't happy. Her eyes had lost all their sparkle that attracted so many men all those years ago. Her hair too had lost all its lustre, now a horrible tangle of loose ends. Her husband had always liked to run his fingers through it, fat chance now. She stared at her reflection, wondering where it had all gone. The image that stared back looked tired and nervous. She placed her hand slowly across her throat. It covered up the scraggy folds of skin that hung like a turkey gizzard. Everything was either collapsing, shrivelling or losing its natural colour - as if the very essence of a life force was draining away. Not now, she said to herself, not when I need strength. Just hold it together…a little while longer.

Oh, what did it matter? It would end soon, anyhow. Everything would resolve itself. It always had. Her life had been one long catalogue of events and turning points from the moment she was born on the Mile End Road on VE day to yesterday, when her eldest son was expelled from college. She squeezed her right hand hard. She felt the muscles grip as her knuckles went pearly white. Still some residual use there. The arthritis would take over eventually, but not just yet, not today.

She glanced at her watch. Just enough time. One last look at the photo of their wedding, the happy couple standing on the steps on the church, she clutching flowers, he with a broad grin. He had been a handsome sod. It was cold that day, but they hadn't noticed. Not even the old bill had spoilt their celebrations. *So long ago.* She grabbed her bag and went downstairs. 'Mum's going out for a little while. You'll be okay, James?'

'Sure, mum.'

Her son was lying sprawled on the coach watching TV. She bent down and tried to kiss him on the cheek and he backed off. 'Oh well, be like that,' she snapped. 'I'm off. Don't wait up' She went out of the front door, quickly gazed up at the cloudy sky and headed for the driveway. Then she fired up the car and drove off, leaving the estate while her son stared at the latest news reports.

'You eat one bloody oyster and you can't function?' sneered Walker. 'What is it with the younger generation, Grayson? At your age I could eat two Lobster Thermidors, one Dungeness crab, a plate of New Zealand green oysters and still be up for squid.'

Grayson's face was bleary eyed and had a tinge of bilious green. His arms hung limply by his side, his clothes barely on. He was in no state for anything. 'Please. Do not talk about seafood.'

Walker shoved a bottle of mineral water into Grayson's feeble hand. 'Here take this and drink it all.'

Grayson drank the contents in one go, made a burp, automatically lurched forward and then fell back.

Walker drove them out of his estate and onto the main road, through two sets of traffic lights. Once moving properly he wound down the window. 'Now breathe deeply.'

'I don't feel too good, sir.'

'You don't look too good either, but then you don't deserve to. Now tell me more about this suspect of yours?'

'Oh that,' Grayson mumbled.

'Yes, that.'

'Checked out the vehicle registration number, just on a hunch.'

'Huh.'

'I think I hit the jackpot.' Grayson muttered.

'Oh you do? So does CS Jones. So does the whole of the bloody media who are now baying like a bunch of bloodhounds. Seems I'm the only one who doesn't know anything about it.'

'Sorry, sir.' Grayson went on to explain the situation in words of one syllable.

'You've betrayed me, Grayson. You know that?'

'I'll try and make it up.'

'It's a mess,' Walker said, stepping on the accelerator, 'but we need to check it out.'

Walker flicked the switch and the siren began its wail.

'Dicky oyster or no dicky oyster,' Walker shouted, 'you'll be fine. Not sure I will though.'

But Grayson wasn't fine. As soon as Walker made a sharp right at a roundabout, in front of a looming 4x4, Stephen's stomach came up. A great whoosh of semi liquid atomised into a fine spray across the road.

'Serves you right, young man!' Walker exclaimed. 'Anyway, you'll be right as rain now. We could be seeing some action so I suggest you pull yourself together. Couple of hours you'll be gagging for another oyster.'

Stephen wiped the spittle from his mouth and sat back. 'No problemo', he mumbled to himself as the squad car gunned all the way along the dual carriageway, heading due north.

CHAPTER SIXTEEN

Wednesday, 13th November.

A few minutes later, a well -dressed woman was parking her silver Mondeo at the bottom of the road. She waited for the girl to leave and watched her as she padded up the road in beat-up jeans and trainers. Same age as my son, she thought. In another life…

She stepped out and walked along the pavement, looking at the new houses. Some were still unoccupied with sale notice boards impaled in lawns that hadn't been cut for ages. She could see how some people might find the estate a little dull. *Not for much longer.* Here it is, she said, Number 14. She walked up the pathway towards the door. She deliberately avoided looking in through the windows. It didn't do to be nosy. In her right hand, she clutched a shoulder bag, which she held tight. She took a long, deep breath and rang the doorbell.

After a couple of minutes, a man came to the door. 'Yes?'

'Mr Almond?'

'Correct.'

'I'm Dawn Probyn. Social services. Just popped round to see if there's anything I can do. Are you alone?'

'Yes.'

'May I come in?'

'I suppose so.'

Almond lead the woman through to the lounge. 'Take a seat.'

She began to unbutton her coat and he was about to ask her if she wanted a cup of tea when he froze. From out of her shoulder bag, she produced an item. Not dramatically, but casually as if she was producing a packet of cigarettes.

He found himself looking down the wrong end of a .38 revolver.

For a spilt second he froze. Tiny impulses ran through his nerves like a tingle, followed by an incredible surge of emotion until every muscle in his body tensed. In his *house*. In his *lounge*. It felt like he confronting death again, but not like the first time. This time it was more threatening, this time it out of his hands. The surprise jolted him so much so that he actually became paralysed on the spot. Then his mind flashed to Cathy. She had just gone out, a few minutes, she said. She had to stay away.

The woman stood still, unsmiling. Then, very deliberately and very slowly, she walked backwards, until she had her back to the wall. Then she waved the barrel towards the chair, just like her husband used to do.

'Gotcha! Now, sit.'

'What is this about?' Almond demanded, as he sat slowly.

She stretched out her arm. He noticed her wedding ring, a bracelet with bangles and the gun pointing directly into his face.

'Me husband died seven years ago. He was in the vehicle at Rettendon.'

'Who was that?'

'Jimmy Davidson.'

'Jimmy Davidson was your husband?'

'Yeah, fucking right, Mister Big Shot.'

'You're Elena Davidson?'

'Elena Edmonds, now. I reverted to my maiden name, didn't I?'

'Look, your husband was a hardened criminal-'

Suddenly a look of blazing rage flashed across her face. She lunged at him with the butt of the gun. It struck him on the side of the head. Almond felt the metal object crash against his skull. 'Don't you dare speak like that!' she screamed.

He slumped to one side and lost consciousness for a few seconds.

'Don't you bleedin' dare,' she repeated, more steadily. 'He was me husband, and now, Mister Big Shot, you're going to sit quietly, very quietly and bleedin' listen.'

When he shook himself back to his senses, his hand went up reactively to his face. He felt the warm viscous liquid as it streamed over his fingers. 'Can I?' he asked.

She nodded.

He pulled out a handkerchief from his pocket and carefully applied it to his head. He applied pressure, trying to stem the flow of blood that was seeping from the gash on his forehead. His head pounded like a steam hammer. He thought he was going to pass out again with the pain. A million thoughts rushed through his mind. None of them seemed helpful. The gun was real, but did it have blanks? She was dangerous and violent but was she a murderer? Was she overlooking something? Could he take her out? If so, how swiftly and how effectively? As quick and brutal as necessary, he decided.

She stepped back once more and coolly cocked the firing pin.

Click.

Now the bloodstained barrel was pointing directly at his head. He had much less time now, the distance was against him too, and the element of surprise. He also had his left hand occupied, holding the handkerchief to his wound. His chances were diminishing by the second. He wondered how Cathy would cope on her own? Fifteen years old. No friends. What kind of life was he giving to his only daughter? The woman narrowed her eyes. They stared icy cold, reptilian, devoid of mercy. She took a deep breath and the nozzle wavered for a second. Then it steadied.

'Seven years ago, like, Jimmy received a tip-off. One of his mates. Someone was going to do our house that night. Some geezers from the East End had moved down. Begun muscling in on Jimmy's business, like. They tried to put the frighteners on us. I phoned the rozzers and asked for protection. Jimmy went ballistic, he didn't want nuffink to do with the narks. I told him, I said 'anyfink that affects the house affects me and me family and I want protection'. Anyway, the rozzers didn't give a damn, did they? Seems that protecting criminals from other criminals is the last fing they bleedin' care about. So, one night it happened. Two masked men smashed their way into me house. Jimmy went mental, began shouting and threatening them with his gun. He chased them up the stairs and they ran into our young boy's bedroom. Jimmy was screaming at them. One of them charged him. Then the gun went off. The bullet went through a window. Anyway, Jimmy shot one of the men through the head and the other ran off. One month later, like, Jimmy got his revenge didn't he? Tracked him down and cut him up real good. Problem was, the gang rumbled and come back two days later and caught Jimmy at Rettendon. It was me that identified the body. Right bleedin' mess. Know who was at the scene?'

'I've never forgotten it.'

'You were, scumbag,' she hissed, 'Mister Big Shot,' she sneered, 'thought you were so bleedin' important, didn't cha? Scum, that's what you is.' Tears began to roll down her cheeks and her hands began shaking uncontrollably. Almond tensed, prepared to run at her but she sensed it immediately and tightened one hand on the shooter and wiped her eyes with the other. 'You probably thought that getting two criminals off your patch was the best fing that happened. Cos, it was you that got all the credit! Fancy Detective Inspector after that. All made up.'

'It wasn't like that.'

'Those times were the worst of me life. I vowed revenge.'

'I was going my job.'

'Shut up! There's more, scumbag and you're going to listen.'

Blood was dripping steadily through his hands onto the floor, making the carpet moist and turning it ruby red.

'Fifteen years ago, the Great Storm. Remember it?'

'Of course.'

'I bet you do. You were taking your darling wife to the hospital. Having a nice baby. All very nice. Happy bleedin' families.' Her voice was rising again 'Know where me oldest son was? Eh? Eh??'

'No.'

'Jawick Sands Holiday Camp. Yeah, workin' as a caretaker. But he weren't workin'. He was under a bleedin' caravan, trapped. No one answered the call. Ambulance, fire brigade, rozzers. Nuffink! Know how long it took him to die?'

Almond had his hand on his head, feeling the sticky wound as the bleeding began to stop.

'Look at me! Look at me!!! Do you know how long he was under that pile of wood, pushing down on his chest until it crushed his ribs. Go on Mister Big Shot, guess, guess!'

'I didn't know,' Almond said, barely audible.

'Of course you don't bleedin' know because you weren't on duty was you, you useless piece of shit! Two hours. Two bleedin' hours. Know the only fing that's kept me alive these last few years?'

Almond shook his head.

'Revenge. Oh, I've wanted to see you suffer. Long, hard and very, very slow. I wanted you to know what it was like to lose your loved ones, eh? What it was like to be alone? Utterly abandoned. Makes it a cold place, dunnit? I hope you're feeling it now.'

'Yes.'

'Louder, scumbag!'

'Yes.'

'Good, Good!'

Almond tried to compose himself. Keep talking, he thought. Keep talking.

'So you thought you'd complete the vendetta,' Almond said hesitantly. 'You knew what my wife looked like, you'd been stalking her. You decided to do it on the very anniversary of your son's death.'

'Me son's buried on the island. I went to visit 'is grave. I was in the car park, like, when I saw your car parked on the slipway. The rain was pouring down. I couldn't see a bleedin' fing but it looked like the same model and colour as yours. A man and a woman got out. From the back, he looked just like you; same build, tall, middle-aged, bigheaded, nasty looking, like. They kissed each other. Course, didn't know then that your little lady was playing away from home.'

Almond tensed and then let it go.

'I recognised her right away. They headed along the seawall.'

'And you had the gun sitting in the glove compartment.'

'Bit of security. Old family habits die hard, scumbag.'

'Suddenly, you saw the opportunity. You waited until they got back in their car and you walked slowly across the gravel.'

'Pretty much as you say, big shot.'

'Then you did the dirty deed.'

'It would have been so easy.'

'What?'

'Someone else obliged, didn't he? Did me a bleedin' favour. Saved me two bullets.'

Almond didn't believe her. He knew now she was cold and callous enough to kill. Her eyes were like cold steel.

'You opened the driver's door and shot my wife coldly in the head. You shot her first just to see how I would suffer. Then you realised it wasn't me but someone else, but it was too late. You had no choice; you had to shot him too. You heard someone coming. You didn't have much time. Then you got clever. You put the gun in the man's hand and tried to stage it like a suicide pact. You could have escaped, but Mrs Dean came along with her dog. You could have got away then, why didn't you?'

'If that's what you want to believe. Bit late now anyway, seeing as you'll be joining them soon but you're right; when I realised that the wrong man had been killed, I decided on the next best thing. I wanted to see your bleedin' face. I wanted to see how you reacted when you saw your wife had been shot. And did I! That moment when yer big flash car pulled up, siren wailing. You got out, so bloody sure of yourself, and strutted across the car park, Cock of the North.

It was cold and raining and you dismissed us all like dummies. We were like pieces of dirt on your shoe. No respect for others, Almond. No respect,' she spat. 'Yeah, I was in that crowd and if you had been a little more observant maybe, you would have recognised me. But, you were in your own little world, eh? Then you looked inside the car. It was priceless. That moment, when you bent over and peered inside and saw what you thought was a routine slaying. Then you suddenly realised it was your wife. I'll never forget it. You just walked away, unable to comprehend what had happened.

Did I feel sorry for you? No, that was the precise moment, I felt alive once more. You don't know how good that made me feel. At long last it was you who was suffering, not me…and that felt so, so bloody good.'

Her grip tightened. It was the first time he had been on the receiving end of such a torrent of hate since he had put away the Rettendon gang. Yet he didn't feel a trace of fear: At first, it had worried him but only for Cathy's sake, now he was calm. He wasn't remotely scared of dying. God was at his side.

He was watching so much loathing at the other end of the firearm; he was starting to believe it. Maybe his life wasn't worth saving, maybe he deserved it, and maybe she was right. His beloved wife was dead, his only daughter hated him and blamed him for everything and his career was in ruins. In front of him was another whose life had been destroyed. Would it, he asked himself, really matter if he were to go, wouldn't it actually help and bring an end to this whole, bloody mess?

'I suppose you killed Joe Biggs?' he asked, at last.

'Huh, that low-life. Twenty years ago, he kicked us out of our home in Angel Lane to turn it into rich man's area. We got nuffink. He thought he could mess about with cockneys, but he was bang out of order. Then I read about him in the papers and recognised him immediately. A few months ago, I would have happily got him out of the way but I says to meself, I says Elena, it's too easy, stick to Almond and Walker, they're the coppers that are to blame. They're the ones that really ruined me life and killed me family.'

'I suppose you had something to do with poisoning Joe Hart at the oyster festival?'

'Of course! All going swimmingly. Dead easy to get a job as a waitress at the festival. I knew my victim would be there. He can't resist seafood. Then I waited for Alice Chalmers to identify him. Course, I recognised him at once, coming up and asking for food, like Oliver, 'cept he had a fat, greasy face. It was easy, then. Nice bit of rat poison for a lowly rat, worked a treat.

'But you ended up getting some kid from the local paper. Poor lad.'

'I was after John Walker, scumbag. You remember, he was there at Rettendon, too. You were falling over each other like two peas in a pod that day. Both destined for the pot.'

She was grimacing, her rotten twisted teeth bared like a hyena as she prepared for the kill. He didn't think he had much time.

'Vengeance is mine,' she snarled. 'Not the Lord's but *mine*. Oh, I could have killed your precious daughter too, that would have made it evens,' she added, 'but then I fort, why should she suffer, why should she be the victim? No, after all, it was *you* that needed to feel real despair. I hope you're feeling it now DI Almond, because you ain't got much longer. Soon be over, luvvie. Oh, I know what your wondering Mister Big Shot, what are the odds, do I have the guts to pull the trigger, are you close enough to stop me, am I really serious? All those police training videos, are they going to help you now? Well, I can read that mind of yours like a bleedin' book. So, Mister Big Shot, want to take that risk…hmm?'

Almond looked up at her, her face was contorted with hate, her eyes ice-cold.

'I ask for forgiveness for your actions, 'Almond pleaded. 'Repent now, please, while you have the chance. If you don't, your soul will be tormented forever in the fires of damnation. Repent!'

She leaned against the wall, her legs slightly apart, half-shaking half stricken, a pitiful, twisted wreck of retribution.

Outside, two men were approaching the front door.

'Light on upstairs, car in driveway,' Walker said, as Grayson rapped the door. No reply.

Stephen called through the letter box. 'David, David, are you in there!' He could see the hallway was deserted but he thought he glimpsed a flicker of movement in the lounge. 'There's someone there,' he said to Walker who stepped back and charged the door. It buckled and the two of them charged once again, an almighty shove, and the door crashed open and the policemen surged through just as a gunshot was heard.

'Quick, the lounge!' Walker shouted, but as soon as he charged along the hallway there was a flash of light followed by the bang as another shot rang out. When he reached the room, there were two bodies, barely moving, lying on the floor.

'Jeez. Get the gun!' Walker screamed as both he and Grayson dived onto the floor. Grayson picked it up with one hand. Smoke still issued like a funeral pyre. The woman lay unmoving, face down on the carpet, her body overlapped by an ever-increasing crimson shadow. The man lay on his side and another red smudge extended out from his head. Walker crawled across the floor and touched him gently on the shoulder. 'David? David??' An eyelid flickered slightly and his limbs began to move. 'David?'

Then his lips trembled.

'Yes?' came the faintest murmur. 'Who's that?'

'John Walker, mate.'

'John, ah! Yunno, I think I'm okay, John. Thank God.'

In twenty minutes time, two paramedics had patched him up and he was sitting on the sofa with a shawl around him and a cup of tea in his hand.

'When I heard the door,' Almond said, gathering his thoughts at the same time as he spoke, 'I saw my chance. For a second, she looked away from me, that fleeting moment it was just enough. It was her or me, John,' he continued, shaking his head forlornly. 'I suddenly realised I didn't want to die. Simple as that. Cathy needs me. I realised that losing a wife makes your own life even more important. You have to stand up. I know now that there's so much to live for, so much more to see and feel…sorry, I'm feeling a bit emotional.'

'That's okay.'

'I went for the gun and tried to wrest it from her grip. She was fighting like a tigress, nails like claws. I nearly ripped her arm off. Still she wouldn't let go. Then the gun went off.'

'Do you know who she was?' Walker asked.

'Maiden name, Elena Edmonds, married name Mrs Jimmy Davidson.'

'Davidson? Hold on, the hood we found at Rettendon that day?'

'That's the one. She blamed me. For the last few months, she has been planning her revenge. She admitted she wanted to kill my wife just to hurt me. Can you imagine that? Thomas was an innocent victim. We've seen some bad things in our time but this was pure, cold-blooded revenge. She wanted to make me suffer. Nothing more, nothing less.'

'I'd forgotten completely.'

'She hadn't. She tried to poison you, too.'

'At the festival? Jeez. Anyway, you've got Grayson to thank. He put us on to her.'

David looked at Stephen Grayson.

'Well done, Stephen...and thanks.' The young officer looked enormously pleased with himself.

'David,' Walker continued, 'I've got to ask you this?'

'Go ahead.'

'Some months ago, you took a Smith and Wesson .38 out of stores. The murder weapon was a .38. Why did you take it out?'

'David looked up at Walker. He began shaking his head. 'No, no, you've got it wrong. I took it out as protection.'

'O-*kay.*'

'She'd been following me for months in her silver Mondeo. I ran the details through the vehicle licensing centre and came up with her name. It didn't ring any bells until I checked out the address and realised it was Davidson's place.'

'Right.'

'I needed the gun in case she did something,' Almond continued. I wanted to protect Susan and Cathy...' His speech began to falter. 'You've got to believe me!'

'You didn't use it to do away with your wife's lover?' Walker asked.

'No, of course not. God, do you think I am a madman? Killing my own wife!'

'So, um, where is it?'

'What? The gun?'

Walker nodded.

'Look, it's in the shed. Buried behind all the garden tools. Go on, check it out. It's there!'

John Walker disappeared and a couple of minutes later he came back holding the weapon in a handkerchief.

'Thank God,' sighed Walker. 'I'll take it back to the station.'

'So there were two .38s?' Grayson asked.

'Correct.' Almond replied. 'This one and the murder weapon.'

'Know how she could have got hold of a .38?' Stephen asked Almond.

'Yes, her husband must have kept them. The one I requisitioned from stores came from the Rangerover at Rettendon. She probably found another one in the house and used it to kill my wife.'

Walker picked up the gun lying on the floor, and compared them.

'And this one to try and kill you?'

'Correct.'

'Must have been a job lot,' Walker concluded. 'Well,' he sighed, 'that's all we can do for now. SOC and Forensics will be able to take it from here. Best to give them some space. Johnson's been a busy guy these last few weeks.' Walker made a motion towards the door and beckoned Grayson. Grayson headed off and brushed his hand with Almond in a low-key 'hang five'. Walker followed him. As he passed David Almond, he turned to look at him. A cruel and twisted smile played across his face. Then very slowly and very deliberately, he drew an imaginary line across his throat.

The door slammed shut and Almond sat still. Immediately, he forgot what he'd just seen. He began listening to the pound of his heart slowly recede. Thump.Thump..Thump…His fingers, white and ghostly, had stopped shaking and his feet were now properly anchored to his feet, no longer quivering like flippers. No one else was around and a strange, eerie quietness passed over him. Everything seemed to have gone from the house, drained away, like a dried-up river. All that remained was the body of Elena Edmonds, lying there, her life now over, her arms and legs twisted in one final deathly gesture. Forensics would soon be all over the place like a proverbial rash but for the meantime, peace…then something else caught his eye - glinting in the corner of the carpet; a tiny jewel-like object.

It must have fallen off in the struggle.

His eyes stared at the object, tiny yet…he bent down and picked it up. The teardrop shape settled snugly in the palm of his hand. The effervescent greens and iridescent mauves colours shimmered in the gloom. It was one of a pair of cufflinks. Yet, it was a very unusual cufflink, a rare type of *Mother-of-Pearl* cufflink. For a moment, he marvelled at the craftsmanship. So neat, so intricate. As he tilted it, it glistened fleetingly. Then something happened the cufflink stopped suddenly being just an eye-catching moment and became a catalyst. In that spilt second, it changed and so did he.

It made him come alive again. It awakened in him all the behaviours, mannerisms and thought processes he once had. Something clicked and a mini projector began whirring in his head, flickering images onto his retina. Walker leaving, the hand going up…that contorted mouth. All his work and experiences as a police officer came flooding back. Thoughts tumbled forward until one of them finally fell into place.

The cufflink was the clue.

Almond stumbled across to the chest of drawers and tugged feverishly until the drawer opened. Inside was the tiepin. It was the one he picked up that night on Mersey Island when he had rolled around in the grit. He had had it checked out, taken it to Mrs Chalmers. It came from the blue Arabian waters, extracted from the finest shells of oysters and abalones. He placed them side-by-side on the chest of drawers. Tiepin, cufflink. Cufflink, tiepin. Perfect match. Almond swallowed hard.

'It would have been so easy.'

Would have been. Why hadn't Elena Edmonds admitted her guilt? At such a climactic moment, with time running out, with everything laid bare, why had she lied?

'Someone else obliged, didn't he'

She was trying to pass the blame. '*Saved me two bullets.*' Another person, a man, with a gun? Someone capable of murder? Right to the last, she had refused to own up. For what reason?

There was only one reason.

His mind began to race once more but, before he could think, he was at the front window watching Walker and Grayson climb into the car. He swung open the front door just as their car was departing down the driveway. He banged on the passenger door and began gesturing manically. Grayson stared through the window and attempted a weak wave. Almond began yelling and screaming. Then Grayson understood and Walker too. The car burst into life. Grayson flung open the door and rolled out onto the driveway as the car screeched off into the road and careered around the bend.

'God! What's going on?'

'Quick, come with me!' Almond shouted, 'no time to explain.'

Almond zapped his Peugeot 307 and jumped in. Stephen ran around and piled into Almond's car just as it was pulling away from the kerbside.

'He did it. He did it!!' Almond bellowed.

'Whaatt??'

'He killed Susan. He left a tiepin at the scene of the crime. It matches perfectly with this,' continued an excited Almond thrusting the tiny cufflink into Grayson's view and then lurching the car out into the busy road. 'See? Mother of Pearl. Identical. Not a job lot. Hand-crafted.'

Grayson began shaking his head wondering if Almond's bang on the head hadn't affected him. 'Are you sure?'

'Positive. Dear God, I've been so stupid! Such a fool but it's true, Stephen. I can prove it, but right now we need to catch him.'

'There he is!' Grayson exclaimed, as he spotted the Escort in the distance overtaking like the wind.

'He's not getting away this time,' Almond snarled, but the Escort went further ahead until he was lost from view. Almond banged the dashboard and a piece of plastic flew off. 'Damn,' Almond cursed, but as the road straightened Grayson spotted a flash of white amidst the greys and silvers. 'There!' he cried as the Escort weaved out of the traffic and went charging along the bus lane. He was disappearing into the distance but the lights changed and the traffic froze.

The cars up front weren't moving but Grayson could see Walker sitting there, his head nodding slightly, plotting his next move.

'Sir, do you mind?' Grayson asked. He rushed out of the car, ran around the driver's side and swapped places just as the lights changed.

'I didn't get a chance to say, no!' Almond shouted, as he struggled to fit the passenger seat belt.

'Bit late now, sir. Just going to crank it up a bit. Give it some welly.'

Grayson slammed his foot down hard and the rear wheels spun crazily until the car rocketed forward. A stink of burning rubber rent the air. 'To think this got confused with a 308 Gti. It's a joke.'

'It's economical,' Almond insisted.

'I've seen more oomph in a butterfly,' Grayson bawled, above the roar of straining gears. 'Let's see if we can get this gelding off its arse!'

Almond sat back, not daring to say a word. He stared at the windscreen as cars fell away left and right. Grayson was all arms and legs, switching down every few seconds and then pumping the accelerator as if he was stamping his feet. 'That's it baby, come to Stephen!' Almond could see Grayson was gaining. Slowly it was coming down; five cars apart, four, three…Almond glanced at his driver who gave a boyish grin. 'Like old times, eh sir?' You, me, a crap car.'

'Cheeky blighter,' Walker thought and then he realised that Stephen Grayson wasn't nervous at all; he didn't have a shred of fear in his whole body.

'Not sure about the petrol situation, Stephen.'

Grayson glanced at the gauge.

'Oh man, don't you ever fill it?'

'Been meaning too. Just not the time.'

Grayson looked again and rapped it futilely. 'I think we're on borrowed time,' Grayson said, 'fifteen miles max. How about back up, sir?'

'Oh yeah.'

Almond leaned forward and punched the buttons on his mobile. He got through to Control and he began blaring frantically into the mouthpiece. They passed under a bridge.

'Damn,' Almond cursed, 'cut out.'

'Keep trying sir, you've got to tell them our precise location.'

Suddenly Walker threw a hard left, causing the two cars behind to break sharply. Grayson nearly toe-ended the car in front but avoided it, courtesy of Essex County Council's grass verges. He went bumping along until he wrenched the steeling wheel and joined the left turning. Now he found himself directly behind Walker. 'Yahoo!' Grayson screamed. 'He's going nowhere.'

'Remember, Stephen he's got a gun.'

Grayson's face froze. 'Shit, I forgot. Was it loaded?'

'Not mine. Not with Cathy in the house. But he's got the woman's as well.'

'Let's hope he gets them mixed up. Wheels against wheels, that's the way it should be.'

They had entered a straight piece of dual carriageway. Walker was around a hundred yards up the road but creeping further ahead as he bashed the squad car at eighty-miles an hour on a forty-mile limit. A speed camera flashed and then flashed again with Almond's car racing in its wake. Grayson kept gunning the car, throwing the rev counter needle crazy until he was right behind him, almost touching his rear bumper. The cars raced along, almost as one, for nearly thirty seconds, while other vehicles swerved, hooted and slammed on their brakes.

Then Walker's car took another left. Grayson jerked the wheel and went haring after him.

'He's heading for the A12!' Grayson shouted. 'Shit.'

The A12 was the fastest road in the county. It was also one of the slowest...and the most dangerous. It ran from London to the coast and oscillated from five lanes to two. It swerved and dipped through river valleys, industrial estates and housing complexes. Just when drivers expected acres of open clay fields of corn and rapeseed, along came a new town. During the summer, it was occupied by caravans, campers, coach parties, boy racers and Londonites desperate to get the hell out of the sweaty metropolis. The rest of the time, it was HGV's, snaking their way slowly in a north-easterly direction towards the container port of Felixstowe.

On the A12, everyone was in a rush, everyone had something urgent to deliver, everyone was more concerned with the destination than the journey and everyone ignored the rules. It was Essex's trunk-road version of Russian roulette.

As Walker's squad car and Almond's Peugeot careered around the intersection and then levelled onto the feeder lane, all they had done was introduce another dangerous, random variable to the chase.

Out of nowhere came a helicopter, hovering above them like a giant dragonfly. The dull thud of blades battered the air above Almond's car. As they both swung into the nearside lane of the A12, a dizzyingly number of vehicles lay in front. Walker hit his siren and screamed across the lanes. With lights on, cars dodged and panicked as he blasted a trail towards the horizon. The chopper was still above Almond, and as he craned his neck, he saw the fibreglass cockpit, like a bulbous insect head. He put his hand out and gesticulated wildly as the wind raced past. The noise abated as the great flying object wheeled away. Then it came back, clinging to the space above his car like a limpet. Almond made contact with Control again but still the chopper held its airspace.

'What's he doing now?' Grayson shouted.

'He's telling us to stop!' Almond replied. '*Us!*' and just at that instant, he knew why.

'He thinks *I'm* the criminal,' Almond roared. 'Walker must have got on the radio and told them that a criminal was pursing him. He must have convinced them that *I* was the killer. Oh, he's good.'

'That's crazy!' Grayson said. 'You've got to speak to the CS.'

'Maybe, but tell me,' Almond hollered, above the roar of wind and engine noise, 'who would you believe, a senior DI in charge of a murder investigation driving a squad car or some mentally-scarred ex-cop with some juvenile assistant by his side driving a beaten up Peugeot?' Then Almond's mobile went dead again.

'Blast!'

Grayson's grin disappeared in a flash. 'You're right, sir. Walker's got all the aces.'

'Not all,' Almond snapped. 'You're the best driver in the Force. How about you showed it?'

Grayson suddenly threw all his energies into the car. He punched the warning light sign, flipped to full beam and belted the Peugeot into the fast lane in hot pursuit. He ignored the chopper that now bellowed out instructions from a giant speaker. He wound up the window and took cars on the inside, the outside and in between. The needle rose; eighty, ninety, ninety-five. He kept the horn blaring as brake lights flashed, trucks swerved and huge loads toppled. Up ahead the squad car was creating equal mayhem, tailgating and switching lanes at random but Grayson was able to follow in his slipstream and didn't have to worry about getting vehicles to shift. They swerved into a long gradual bend barely reducing their speed as they flashed past a service station. Walker glanced at the fuel gauge. It was way past red, right up against the dial.

'We're running on empty, sir.'

Suddenly, the road ahead collapsed, from four lanes into two. The laws of physics demanded that the vehicles slowed but they screamed along for another mile, neither giving a quarter, cramped for space but barging their way through like school bullies. The sign said 'Dedham 2', which signified the border between Essex and Suffolk. It was known for the river Stour, rolling hills and Constable country. It wasn't known for two vehicles locked in a deadly pursuit, neither side giving quarter. Suddenly Walker careered across lanes and ploughed into the central reservation.

'What the?' Grayson gasped as his eyes blinked twice.

Walker's vehicle came to a slithering halt. For a split second, Grayson thought he had him but Walker spun the car sending a spurt of gravel showering across the road and into Grayson's windscreen. Then he stormed away, disappearing up the other way.

'Oh, he's good,' Grayson purred as he too tried to do a similar 360-degree manoeuvre in front of an army of approaching traffic. He wrenched the wheel and flung the vehicle onto the fast lane but didn't have enough horsepower to pull away. Cars concertinaed behind him and an enormous juggernaut reared up behind him like a mountain. 'Don't look in the rear mirror sir, it's a nightmare.'

They rattled on for another eight miles, the sweat pouring off Grayson. 'Can't hold it much longer sir, the engine's going to seize.' Sure enough, the temperature gauge was way past red, into unknown territory. Then it hit Almond. 'He's going back on the island! That's where he's going!' Sure enough, Walker scuttled down a minor turn off, through a couple of villages and hurtled along a narrow road as the island came into view. Then up ahead, the familiar sight of The Strood. Then Almond and Grayson saw what they didn't want to see; a phalanx of vehicles and flashing lights across the width of the causeway.

It was a roadblock.

The helicopter wheeled away like a bird. Grayson held his breath. Time froze. Almond braced himself. Walker's car kept accelerating, towards the obstruction.

'The road's flooded! He won't try it.' Grayson shouted.

'Don't be so sure.' Almond said. 'He's lost it completely.'

Walker's car clipped the barrier on the causeway and spun across the lanes. It keeled over to one side and then slithered sideways. It tipped over several times like a matchbox and finally piled over the edge, nose first until it teetered over the swirling creek.

Grayson jerked the handbrake and Steve Almond was slammed forward, his face inches from the glass until an airbag mushroomed into his face. Almond wrestled with the inflatable and then finally got out. He tumbled onto to the tarmac and rolled over. He got up and crouched low as he made his way, through broken glass and twisted metal, towards the edge of the causeway. Police officers and ambulance crew came rushing towards them and they converged on Walker's police car as it dangled precariously off the edge, the rear wheels spinning like a Ferris wheel. All the windscreens had been shredded into a criss-cross mosaic of fragment glass and dripping from the driver's window was a steady stream of blood. Then with a creak followed by an almighty whoosh, the vehicle plummeted into the muddy waters and went straight down. Thirty minutes later, a crane was lifting the car out of the waters, like a soggy old shoe, Walker's body still pinned in the driver's seat, with no signs of life.

CHAPTER SEVENTEEN

Friday, 15th November.

David Almond was sitting in his familiar chair waiting to be called in. He looked up to see Stephen Grayson come bounding in, as excited as a March hare.

'Hey, it's Robocop!' Grayson exclaimed. 'Mr Indestructible.' His boyish enthusiasm is irrepressible, thought Almond.

'You look insufferably smug this morning, young Stephen.'

'Yeah, every right to be. Everything's going brilliantly.'

'So I heard. They're going to make you up to sergeant. It's well deserved. Many congratulations.'

'Thanks.'

'It will be confusing with two Sergeant Grayson's.'

'Oh, dad's leaving but I've got my old mate back on board…you sir.'

'Oh, didn't you get on well with Walker?'

'Sir, I tried every thing to make myself annoying to him: lame jokes, Mickey taking, general incompetence.'

'Stephen?'

'Yes?'

'You didn't need to try.'

'Hah! Got me in one, sir but you can't make me depressed today.'

'Why's that?'

'Something happened yesterday, something big.'

'As if the previous day wasn't enough for you?'

'That was work, this was pleasure.'

'Oh?'

At that moment, a dazzlingly beautiful girl walked in, a riot of bare limbs and long hair. She bent over and planted a big wet kiss on the young officer's cheek.

'I'd like to introduce you to my girlfriend. Amy. This is DI Almond.'

'Hi.' she said holding out a hand like she was trying to get rid of it.

'Hello,' said Almond shaking it and trying to ignore the perfectly sculpted face and body, ending up looking somewhere around her navel.

'*You're* Officer Parker?' asked a wide-eyed Almond.

'Out of uniform,' she replied. As she sat down, her short skirt, six inches above the knee, shrivelled to a waist belt.

'I can see that.'

'Actually, I quit,' she continued, loosening her hair and letting it tumble free. 'This police work isn't my scene at all. I decided to leave it to Sergeant Stevie Wonder here to rid the world of organised crime.'

'Any plans?'

'I'm going to free ride for a few weeks, shot the breeze, live a little, see what comes up. So you were his boss?' she asked.

'Colleague. I tried to keep him in check, but most of the time he did what he liked.'

'Those days are coming to an end,' Amy said with a twinkle in her bright blue eyes.

'Glad to hear it,' Almond said.

'It's taken him six months to ask me out and now I'm getting my own back for being kept waiting.'

David glanced up to see Stephen's sheepish grin. 'Hey, I don't mind,' he said. 'I love being dominated.'

She'll make mincemeat of him, thought Almond. Then the phone rang. 'Excuse me, you kids,' said Almond. 'The Great White Chief calls.'

Almond got up, said his farewells and walked down the corridor. As he was about to knock on the door, a woman came out, closing the door behind her.

'Detective Inspector Almond?'

'Correct.'

She gave him a firm handshake. 'Gabrielle Simons. I've just seen CS Jones. Don't think we've ever met. I knew your wife very well. Lovely woman. So sorry.'

'Thank you.'

'I understand that John Walker was behind all these terrible murders.'

'Yes.'

'Wretched man. Never liked him from the first moment I set eyes on him. Had grubby fingernails. Never like that in a man, shows a certain louchness, don't you think? Know what the worst thing was?'

'No.'

'He made it worse by wearing cufflinks. It just draws attention to your hands, don't you think?'

'Yes. Very much so.'

'So how are you bearing up?'

'Lots of small, rapid steps, one at a time,' Almond said gamely. 'Nothing too big. Occasionally take a few backward steps.'

'I understand, you poor man. We lost our biggest client but that's nothing compared to losing two of our best employees. Susan was a treasure. Irreplaceable. I feel so for your poor daughter, Cathy, isn't it?'

'Yes.'

'She must feel dreadful. I lost my partner three years ago. Everything becomes pointless but I have a young boy. He keeps me going.'

Almond nodded knowingly.

'Ah well, *nil desperandum*. Anyway, anytime you want a chat, here's my number. Give me a bell.' She peeled off a gold-plated business card, put it in his top pocket and patted it gently. 'There. No knowing when you might need a lawyer.' She took his hand and squeezed it. 'Take care.'

She was gone in a flash. He straightened his tie and knocked on the door. A booming voice echoed from the other side.

'David! It's good to see you again,' said a genuinely pleased looking CS Jones. (It was one of those momentous occasions when CS Jones was inviting a fellow police officer into his office, and not to fire him) 'You're looking great,' he added but he knew that his officer looked awful.

'Thank you sir.'

'Well enough to talk?'

'Sure.'

'Nasty cut on the head.'

'It stings a bit.'

'Excellent report,' Jones said fingering it slightly and then placing it on the desk. 'Lots of cogent facts and informed comment,' he continued, patting it gently like a dog. 'Obviously the old brain cells are unaffected. Still haven't finished reading it yet. Quite a tome.'

'Thank you.' He hasn't read a word, thought Almond, the lazy-

'So Elena Edmonds was innocent?'

'Well, she didn't kill Susan,' admitted Almond. 'She just said she did.'

'Out of revenge?'

'Yes, to make me suffer. Oh, she was going to and had a revolver all loaded and ready. She arrived at the island on the afternoon of the killing, to pay respects to her dead son. She saw the back of a man holding hands with my wife and thought it was me. When they returned from their walk, she was just about to get out when a police car suddenly arrived so she drove away from the scene and hid. She waited for some time and when the police car finally headed off, she went to investigate. She found the two dead bodies and realised that the dead man wasn't me after all. She was going to head off but when she got to The Strood she found it flooded so she turned back. She met Mrs Dean and got her to phone the police and ask for me. Then she waited until the police arrived, just so that she could see my reaction.'

'And Officer Parker took her vehicle number plate?'

'That was the key. Officer Grayson checked it out. It wasn't registered in the name of the witness, Stevens, so he delved a little deeper and discovered it was in the name of Elena Edmonds. When he added that to the wrong time in her statement, he knew he was on to something. He tried to warn me, but I didn't get his message. My phone wasn't working. At least, he got round to my house in the nick of time.'

'Awful. All this goes back a long way.'

'Correct,' Almond said. 'Over fifteen years ago. She blamed me for her son's death, on the day of the Great Storm. He died when a caravan collapsed on Jawick Sands. We didn't answer an emergency call in time.'

'But surely she couldn't...'

'Oh, she did. Then seven years ago, her husband died in the Rettendon killing.'

'You were first on the scene, weren't you?'

'Correct.'

'About a year ago, she began stalking me. It was all harmless stuff at first, the odd phone call or an anonymous letter. She took her time, prolonged the agony. I got scared. I moved house to try to make a clean start. I had these terrible nightmares and suspected that she was hanging around outside my house, looking at Cathy. That's why I got the gun. I needed protect myself and my family.'

'So she didn't kill Biggs either?'

'No, she might have wanted to because she had a score to settle with him but that was a long time ago. She had moved on to me.'

'What about Joe Hart?'

'Ah, now she *did* do that. She took a temporary job waitressing at the oyster festival. She knew I was going to be there so she took along some rat poison, stood behind the counter and waited. The problem was that I didn't show up in the marquee - not a big shellfish fan - but guess who did?'

'John Walker.'

'Exactly!' She recognised him. Suddenly that shooting in Rettendon came flooding back, once more. Here was the other policeman who was responsible for her husband's death. It was too good an opportunity to miss so she dropped the poison into one of his oysters. Only, as we know, poor Joe Hart took the fateful oyster.'

'Right,' Jones said, 'I'm getting the hang of this.'

'That's good.'

'Still not sure how you knew that Walker killed your wife?' Jones asked.

'We both worked with and knew John Walker - at least, we thought we did. As you know, we were partners for several years. He always cut corners. He could do that because he knew I would never squeal. We were a team. Now, I'm the first to admit I wasn't exactly gleaming snowy-white…you know how it was in those days, sir?'

Jones nodded.

'But he was seriously shop soiled. Anyway, once you split us up and put us into new teams he got twitchy.'

'Oh,' Jones said, 'so it was all *my* fault?'

'Not at all, sir, but his job was everything to him, fifteen years on the force - it was his life. He thought that he would be investigated, it would be the end of his career, he'd lose his pension and everything.'

'There's no doubt about that,' Jones confirmed. 'You were always the bright one, David. You spent all your time covering his backside. If he hadn't held you back all these years, it would be you sitting in my chair.'

'Thank you, sir.'

'So he flipped?'

'He must have felt like a cornered rat. He wasn't going to accept his fate so he fought back the only way he knew,' Almond said, drawing a deep breath. 'He decided that my wife would be an easy target. So he hatched this crazy scheme.'

'As any madman would,' Jones added.

'On the day of the killing, he intercepted a telephone message from my wife saying that she had to go to Mersey Island and would be late. It sounded too good to be true. He knew I had to go out so he came in and offered to cover for me.'

'Bang goes your alibi?'

'Then he checked that Grayson wouldn't be wanting him and headed off. He took the fire exit and picked up the squad car he had parked down the road.'

'So he wouldn't be spotted on our CCTV tapes.'

'Correct. Management letter point there.'

'Noted.'

'He headed out to the island. By the time he arrived, my wife was already there but she had someone else in the car.'

'Alan Thomas?'

'Right. Walker was planning to make it look like Susan killed herself but with two of them he had a problem. He spotted them walking along the seawall. They were there to see the effect of the high tides on the proposed development site. It would have made the whole scheme unfeasible. It was raining so hard they didn't have a chance to take any photos, so they turned back. Walker sat in his car and waited. The only way he could do it was to make it look like Thomas had killed Susan and then himself. So, when they got back to the car he approached them at gunpoint, and ordered them to drive onto the slipway. He had checked the tides and knew that the rising tide would wipe away all trace of his footprints. Then he shot them both and put their fingerprints on the gun. He probably had traces of blood on his shirt so he ripped off his shirt and tie and took them home to burn and changed into his spare clothes he had in the car. Then he deleted all the photos on their digital camera, just in case his car had been photographed, and threw it in the back seat.'

Time was of essence. He had to drive like a maniac to get back across The Strood, before it got flooded. He got back to the station, at four-thirty, came in through the fire exit and sat at his desk. The call didn't come through for another hour and a half. He had plenty of time to establish his own alibi with Grayson. Then he changed the time on his computer and created some documents so that they appeared to have been written at the time of the murder.'

'Another management point?' Jones suggested.

'No.'

'So what did Walker do next?'

'He didn't have to do anything. He knew he would be chosen to head up the criminal investigation. He was the only possible candidate. That was a masterstroke,' admitted Almond.

'Masterstroke? I was a bloody fool,' confessed Jones. 'He convinced me that he would do everything in his power to bring the truth to light. He told me he knew stuff that no one else did. He said he would help you to get back on your feet. I believed him.'

'And once he was put in charge of the case,' said Almond ruefully, 'no one would suspect the investigating officer.'

'From then on, he thought he was invulnerable.'

'Correct. It was right up his alley,' Almond said. 'He believed he could handle everything. At first, it was quite easy to make it look like no one else was involved. He broke into the lawyers offices and found some dodgy dealing relating to the Biggs case that implicated Thomas and my wife. He then put these papers into Thomas's briefcase found at the scene of the crime.'

'Doctoring scene of crime evidence would have been a doddle for a man like Walker,' Jones admitted.

'Another management point, I think sir. Then he discovered they had had a relationship. It would be hard to prove that lovers had killed one another so he broke into Thomas's house.'

'To destroy all the love letters sent by your wife?' Jones suggested.

'Yes, but I had already broken into Thomas's house and taken them. Then I burned them.'

'And Walker was spotted on CCTV.'

'That's when you took him off the case.' Almond added.

'Bit bloody late.' Jones admitted. 'Carry on.'

'Walker was close to putting a convincing story to the coroner when a witness came forward.'

'Jim Chalmers, a fisherman.'

'Chalmers said he had seen another car at the scene, around the time of the killing.'

'Walker's car.'

'At the time, Chalmers had only glimpsed the top of a vehicle. He thought it was a taxi.'

'Because of the illuminated plastic roof sign?'

'Correct, but it was a police squad car.'

'So Walker had to discredit the eyewitness's account or get some poor, innocent suspects lined up pretty damn quick.'

Almond nodded.

'Biggs, Baines, you.'

Almond nodded again. 'He had to make it look thorough, so he just kept lining up the suspects. Then, when their alibis came through, he just moved onto the next.'

'It nearly worked.'

Jones asked for a comfort break and rustled up some refreshments. Soon the two of them were sipping teas and biting into chocolate biscuits. 'Look at this,' said Jones, tapping his protruding stomach. 'Bloody disgrace for a CS. Need to work out. Always promising to do it. Anyway, back to the case. Please continue.'

Almond drank the tea and put the mug down.

'Baines was easy to set up but Biggs was more of a problem,' Almond confessed. 'He was like a loose cannon. Biggs had spoken to Gabrielle Simons and discovered that Walker had been to the lawyers' offices. Simons told Biggs that Walker had stolen some confidential files relating to his property deals, but couldn't prove it. Biggs was furious. Of course, he didn't know Walker's real motives. He thought Walker was trying to put the finger on him, for his dodgy deals.'

'So, Biggs went on the offensive.'

'Correct. Biggs began sniffing around. It didn't take long to discover that John Walker was rotten to the core. Biggs had influence and could dish out dirt like the best of them. More significantly, he was never going to follow the policeman's code. He had no qualms about going public. Walker had to act quickly.'

'So Walker tried to set Biggs up?' Jones suggested.

'He broke into his house, intending to make it look like Biggs was Susan's killer.'

'By planting the gun?'

'He left it lying around so that Saunders, his manservant, would spot it. Then he took some dust particles he had collected from the scene of the crime and sprinkled them over Biggs's jacket just to get the DNA boys excited.'

'So why did Walker decide to get rid of Biggs?'

'When the local newspaper broke the news of the refusal of planning permission, Walker knew that Biggs would be desperate. He would take everyone down with him. He couldn't afford the risk, so he acted.'

'By faking Biggs's suicide?'

'Yes. He took the newspaper along with him and returned to kill him with the gun he had planted. The manservant Saunders was convinced it was an act of suicide. It was easy for Walker to convince others that here a man acting full of remorse after murdering my wife. I hate to say it, sir, but throughout this whole nightmare, Walker was incredibly thorough.'

Jones paused to reflect on a life of sitting in his chair listening to fellow officers as cases unfurled. He'd been doing it for twenty-five years. No two cases were the same, no two murders were exact, no two motives were identical. Yet somehow, the capacity of humans to inflict pain on others never changed.

'He just couldn't stop himself,' Almond observed. 'Walker would have succeeded again if it hadn't been for the tiepin.'

'The tiepin!' Jones exclaimed. 'Never saw the benefits. Bloody stupid piece of apparel. Serves the bugger right!'

'He always wore it with a very exclusive pair of cufflinks, perfect match. Problem was he dropped it.'

'So how come our Scene of Crimes Officer, Mark Johnson, didn't spot it?'

'Tides,' Almond said.' When he tore off his shirt and tie what he didn't realise was that his tiepin had fallen off. If you recall on the day of the killing it was a spring tide. The Strood was flooded. The tiepin was washed away by the tide so Scene of Crimes would never have found it. Walker went back but couldn't find it. He sent Grayson back but he couldn't find it either. It was his one error.'

'But when you went back, on a low tide, it had been washed up again.'

'Correct.'

'Bloody lucky.'

'Not really, sir. I just used my local intelligence. I waited for the next spring tide. Everything you throw out there, is washed back eventually. It's the way the currents work around the island. Just ask the guys on the oyster smacks.'

'Okay, point taken,' admitted Jones. 'Get on with it.'

'Of course he could have dropped the tiepin at the scene at any time during the investigation but it was the guns that made me realise his guilt.'

Jones hesitated. 'So, er, how many Smith and Wesson .38's were there?'

'Haven't you been paying attention?' Almond asked.

'I got slightly confused,' Jones admitted.

'Five.'

'Five?'

'All five revolvers were a job lot from the Rettendon raid - Walker was at least telling the truth about that,' Almond said. 'All of them had the serial numbers scratched off. Baines got hold of the first one, seven years ago. He was defending some of the suspects after the Rettendon raid.'

'I remember that,' Jones interrupted. 'He defended some of Jimmy Davidson's acquaintances.'

'At the Old Bailey.'

'If I recall correctly,' Jones said, 'some of the bastards were let off.'

'Correct.'

'Even with Walker trying to stitch up the evidence.'

'I think we all had a go on that one,' confessed Almond with a wry grin.

'So Baines knew Davidson's wife?'

'Correct, sir. Back to the guns?'

'Sorry, please continue, David.'

'Jimmy Davidson's gang went to Baines's house and gave him the revolver. They said he could use it as protection, it was a gift for services rendered. He had never seen a gun before but it starting him thinking. What if he did take it? Maybe he could use it some day? Not to shoot anyone but just to brandish it, put the wind up some of the people in his firm who were giving him problems. So he took it. It was supposed to be a bit of a joke taking a gun into a firm of solicitors but it backfired.'

'Not literally.'

'No, sir.'

'We confiscated three of the other guns,' Jones recalled.

'Correct. Elena Edmonds hung onto the last one…just in case.'

'Like a gangster's moll, which she used to try and kill you?'

'That's it. The other three were as follows…do you want my pen?' Almond asked cheekily.

'Get on with it.'

'The first one I requisitioned from stores for my own personal safety.'

'Because you thought you were being followed?'

'Correct. Once Walker realised that I had removed a gun from stores, he knew he could take a similar one out. Big management letter point here, sir.'

'Go on,' Jones said testily.

'The register has to contain the unique serial number otherwise the guns can be switched.'

'You said they were scratched off?'

'They were. But no one thought to have them etched on again.'

'Yup,' Jones agreed. 'They should have been. It meant any one of the five could have killed your wife.'

'Correct. Then when it is taken out, it has to have the name of the actual recipient, not the officer in charge.'

'Like my name appearing on the register?'

'Exactly.'

'Bloody useless shower we've got down there.'

'So, Walker got another officer to sign for it and then used it to kill my wife. He then left it at the scene of the crime. He then got yet another officer to take out the final one and this time left it with Biggs. In this way, he connected

Biggs to the same type and model revolver used to kill my wife, making him another prime suspect.'

'Clever.'

'Then he made Grayson go through all the registers to make me a suspect.'

'Because there were no serial number checks.' Jones repeated.

'Correct,' Almond said. 'The only chance I had of proving my innocence was to produce the gun...'

Jones said nothing.

'...thereby proving that the one that killed my wife wasn't mine?'

'Look, David, you don't have to spell it out, okay.'

'Sorry,' Almond said.

Jones was now getting in his stride. 'So when Walker came round, apparently for a chat, Jones continued, 'and then to rescue you from Elena Edmonds, he had to get your gun.'

'Correct. I wasn't thinking straight. He asked me about it and offered to go and collect it from the shed and take it back to the station. I thought he was being a pal.'

'Of course, he was doing nothing of the sort.'

'No, he was going to destroy it and at the same time destroy my story.'

Jones finished his tea and bit on a biscuit which he then waved admonishingly in front of Almond. 'Ah, but you knew that someone was out to get you but you never told anyone?'

'I suspected it was Walker sir, but I had no proof. I also suspected Elena Edmonds. I was starting to get paranoid. I could have made some discrete disclosures but nobody would have believed me. I know it sounds crazy but it would have been too risky, with Cathy's life in danger. At one stage I thought there might be a conspiracy.'

'Wouldn't be the first time,' Jones said, *sotto voce*.

'Anyway, by now, I was thinking that everyone was involved. Then there was the night Walker saw me go out on Mersey Island. I was looking for clues at the scene but I suspected I was being watched so I began eating grit to make out I was mad. At least I found the tiepin.'

'Correct,' Jones said. 'You did bloody well. So did Grayson.'

'Just one point on that, sir.'

'Go on.'

'The lad's a good kid and all but…'

'Continue.' Jones said.

'Walker fooled him. Walker saw Mrs Edmonds's car on the day of the murder. He checked it out. He knew who she was and why she was trailing me. He deliberately left the evidence lying around for Grayson to discover so that it would appear as if he had discovered whom the killer was. So damn clever.'

'Oh.'

David Almond suddenly stopped talking. Everything was welling up inside. His head went down. He put his hand up to his forehead and then his shoulders began to heave. Jones tapped him gently in the shoulder.

'Look, it's over now, David.' Jones said at last.

Almond took a great gulp of air and raised his head. He rubbed his eyes of moisture. They were already red raw from countless sleepless nights. He was feeling incredibly tired and utterly drained.

'Yes, it's over.'

'From now on, you need to take it easy,' Jones said softly. 'Have a couple more weeks off and see how you feel. Take Cathy on a holiday. We need men like you in the Force. Whatever you do, don't let this get the better of you. Okay.'

Almond nodded. 'Do you know the worst thing about this whole sorry mess, sir?'

'No.'

'It's the fact that I worked with him for ten years and I never thought him capable of anything like that. I completely failed to judge him. Because of that, I lost my wife.'

Jones smiled ruefully. 'That's not true. For God's sake, don't take it personally.'

'No?'

'It's utterly tragic David, but Walker fooled everyone, you, me, all the police officers, the coroner. He was on the inside, looking out. He knew a criminal's mind and he knew a policeman's mind. He could manipulate them both. He was warped enough to think that he could use all that knowledge to get away with murder. I truly believe,' said Jones, even more quietly, 'that even if he hadn't killed Susan, Thomas and Biggs, he would have killed some other poor innocents.' He looked up at Almond. 'Listen, David, John Walker was a psychopath. Pure and simple.'

***

Now, I never look back to that day in October, 1987, the day of the Great Storm even though it was a day that transformed the landscape of Southern England. Millions of trees were destroyed and millions of pounds worth of damage was caused. For the first time in many people's lives, they began to see this benign part of the world as capable of great meteorological uncertainty. God's Earth.

No one took things for granted anymore; people took precautions against the weather and listened to weather forecasters, even though they had famously failed to spot the Hurricane. I look at it differently; it was the day my daughter was born. She is the most precious, the most treasured thing in my life and not a day goes by when I don't thank the Lord for his beneficence. Yet, if that day was indeed joyous, I also realise that it planted the seed of a cancerous growth that wormed its way insidiously inside my family's lives until it exploded out fifteen years later.

I don't know if my grief is any different or any worse than anyone else's. I know that the circumstances were as cruel as it was possible to be and that I never go a day when I don't relive that moment I peered inside the vehicle on Mersey Island. It still fills me with dread, if I have to look inside a car. The dear Lord took Susan and I rejoice in her afterlife. My only regret is that I didn't have more time with her on this Earth. Sometimes I wish and I pray that I will wake up and see my Susan smiling gently at me from her side of the bed, hair slightly ruffled, sleepiness in her eyes. Yet I know this can never be.

God has given me strength, I never knew I had. He has helped me to look forward and embrace the dawn of every new day. I regularly shed a tear and find everything unbearably difficult at times but these moments pass and I can move on. He has also left Susan within me, so that I can always call her when I need to. She is now closer to me than she has ever been. She will comfort me as I grow older, and hopefully wiser, and also be on hand to help Cathy.

Never before have I felt such belief in my faith and never before have I seen the evil so close at hand, that lurks just beneath the surface. Knowing both extremes makes me think that all humans are capable of both, yet we must strive to achieve one at the expense of the other. I don't hate John Walker or Elena Edmonds, I actually pity them because they allowed evil to fester in their hearts until eventually it killed them. I don't even despise Alan Thomas, even though he cuckolded my wife and put her life in jeopardy. It also pains me to think that he saw the last few precious moments of her life. I only hope that as she sat there in the car, she gave Cathy and me a passing thought. They are all gone now, their spirits are free and I must get on with those who are still alive.

I continually live with the knowledge that I could have acted better, that I could have improved people's lives more tellingly than I did, that sometimes I abused my privileged position and most of all that I could have done something to avoid the terrible chain of events. I regret all these things and repeatedly ask forgiveness for my sins.

However, I only have the benefit of hindsight and I can only be grateful to Him for sparing me. It was faulty wiring that saved me from going the same way as my darling wife. It might have been some dodgy electrician that installed the wall socket but it was He that gave me back my life and told me that I must go in peace and not be bitter with rage.

Joe Hart came around to see me last week. He wanted to speak to Cathy. We sat and talked about sport and things and I made a cup of tea. Then Cathy appeared and they began talking like long lost friends. He has now offered her a part time position in his local newspaper, in charge of the youth page. Alison Holmes also came round and told her that she wants Cathy on her team to help document some of the historical treasures around this county. Through carbon dating, they are convinced that Chalmer's Shed No 3, holds timbers originating from the keel of *HMS Beagle* which could prove invaluable. They are now certain that the ship lies deep in the mudflats just off Mersey Island and it needs people to get out there and begin prodding around and start excavating. Bit like police work really. If they can locate the boat in the mud, it will be one of the greatest scientific archaeological discoveries of the decade and the land will be saved from developers, forever.

I think Cathy's going to pull through. Last night she polished off an enormous steak and kidney pie with carrots, peas and leaks from the garden. She has started to go out and the phone doesn't stop ringing with admirers wishing to take her out. It makes me feel proud and God has proved to me that no matter how much pain and suffering you endure you can pull through, provided you have faith in yourself, those around you and belief in God Almighty. Oh, and the good fortune to employ a bad electrician.

THE END